SLASHER CRASHER

DAVID NORA

Black Rose Writing | Texas

ISBN: 978-1-68433-328-8
PUBLISHED BY BLACK ROSE WRITING
www.blackrosewriting.com

Printed in the United States of America
Suggested Retail Price (SRP) $21.95

Slasher Crasher is printed in Calluna

Dedicated to my father, David Sr., for bestowing upon me the greatest gift
of life—horror—and my mother, Marian, for providing infinite support to
a child who lives on dreams.
All the days, Joo.

And to my best friend and muse, Kathleen: nothing.

Don't do it, Eleanor told the little girl; insist on your cup of stars; once they have trapped you into being like everyone else you will never see your cup of stars again...

- Shirley Jackson
The Haunting of Hill House

Guys, I think I lost my vagina.

- Samantha
Lunch, Sophomore Year

SLASHER
CRASHER

I.

The Day He Just Wanted to Get the *Fuck* Home

1

Nick Roesch, 5:00 a.m.

It started like an '80s slasher film. Not John Carpenter's *Halloween*, the classic of suburban horror, but the countless, mostly Canadian copycats that emulated its simple-but-effective formula of the escaped mental patient who [choose one: had been burnt in a high school prank, buried in your run-of-the-mill mining accident, and/or mentally abused by Santa Claus] and picks off a sexy group of no-good teenagers on [a beloved American holiday].

In this crude rip-off, it was Halloween, and Nick Roesch, a massive, pineapple-shaped teen wearing an oversized gray sweater and blue scrubs, was running through the vast wooded area surrounding Summer Hill House, the psychiatric hospital in Hannibal, New York, where he'd spent the last five years. After a window dive from the hospital's second floor, he was following the early-morning light that trickled through the pines, hoping it would lead him to a house or road.

Eventually, Nick got lucky. After barreling through the maze of trees for nearly thirty minutes, the eighteen-year-old, pale-faced beast came upon a long stretch of road and stopped in the middle of it. *Gotta get home*, he thought, bending over and heaving a deep breath. *Need car.*

He stood up and scanned the road, waiting for the next vehicle. Again he was lucky; a moment later, as a red Volvo wagon popped out of the horizon, his strained breath eased into its normal inhale-wheeze-exhale rhythm. Spotting the dingy car racing toward him, he puffed out his chest like a superhero and walked directly toward it, initiating a horrific version of chicken. Unfortunately, the driver, a seventy-five-year-old man with the distant vision of a headless mole, couldn't see past his headlights and unwillingly entered the game.

About twenty yards away, the man finally noticed the towering figure in the road—"Bigfoot!" he screamed—and swerved out of the way. It was too late, though; he was going too fast to brake and slammed into the guardrail with a thunderous crack. The car lifted off the ground, spun around, and rolled forward, creating an explosion of smoke and dust. After a couple seconds, it stopped, the front end twisted into a modern art sculpture. Still, the left headlight remained intact, shining a yellow beam through the brisk autumn air, while the engine buzzed with a hint of life.

With a wicked grin, Nick turned around and marched toward the car. When he reached it, he opened the door and pulled out the white-haired driver with his large taloned paws. The elderly fellow, his face smeared with blood, was writhing in pain, mumbling, "No, please," but the giant didn't care. He dropped the old guy onto the road like a wad of bellybutton flint and climbed into the Volvo.

And then, finally, Nick's luck ran out. As he reached for the gear selector, his malicious smile disappeared. The car had a manual transmission!

He let out a growl then punched the busted dashboard with a hairy fist. How the *fuck* was he supposed to get home? He couldn't drive a car with a stick shift! Dr. Bonesteel had never taught him!

2

Betsy Coleman, 7:29 a.m.

Betsy lay on her white iron bed, her round angelic face fixed on the heart-shaped clock on her nightstand. "Okay," she said under her breath. "You can do this. Just stay calm and try not to s-s-s-stutter."

After moving onto her back, she kicked her mattress and exhaled a hard sigh. *Thirteen years of speech therapy and you still stutter. Might as well forget about the party and just...stop talking!* As a pink-colored rash crept up her neck, her large brown eyes peered through the dim room, attempting to tuck the teen angst into the pocket of her mind that stored overdramatic anger. "All right, calm down." She closed her eyes. "You're just nervous. You need to t-t-t-take a deep breath and f-f-f-focus on something in the room."

After a long steady breath, she opened her eyes and turned to the other half of her small bedroom. In the right corner stood a glass-top writing desk, the two compartments underneath filled with school papers and drawings saved from childhood. In the left stood a light-brown four-drawer dresser, only three of which worked. A wide smile stretched across Betsy's face as she stared at the wall behind these two items.

The dusty wall, like the other three, was painted plum blossom, which instantly had become her favorite color when she was perusing the paint samples at Kmart. She was ten years old when she had asked her parents if she could paint her room. Her father, John, the sheriff of Onondaga County, immediately said no, telling her they didn't have enough money. Betsy's mother, Patricia, Syracuse School District's Favorite Pre-K Teacher twelve years in a row, interjected and suggested it could be a Christmas present. After bickering with him back and forth for an eternity (which actually was three days), Patricia finally persuaded her husband into letting Betsy paint her room.

Still smiling, she took another long breath. *Don't worry. Daddy will let you go to the party. Just ask Mom one last time.* There was a hard knock on her bedroom door. "It's seven thirty," Betsy's father said in his gruff voice. "Time to get up."

Startled by the sudden noise, Betsy's body went century-old corpse. *Okay,* she thought with a quick breath. *You got this. Just stay calm and don't stutter.* A second knock came. "Betsy?"

"Yes, Daddy," she said with a sleepy but sweet pitch. "I'll be right down. I just need to say my p-p-p-prayers." Her face winced. *Damn it.*

"All right. Do you want me to make you some eggs or something?"

"No. It's okay. I'll just have *ssss*some c-c-c-cereal." Betsy threw her head back, mouthing, "Oh my God."

"Are you sure?"

"Mm-hmm."

"All right. I'll be in the kitchen."

"'K," Betsy replied, listening to his slow footsteps descend the stairs. She turned back to the wall, her plump lips pinched in disgust. *Great,* she mumbled; her stutter was out of control, and she hadn't even gotten out of bed. She definitely needed to talk to Mom.

Sitting up, she brushed the dirty-blond strands of hair away from her forehead, made the sign of the cross, then recited the Our Father. She inhaled deeply and continued. "Good morning, Mom. Happy Halloween." She gave a small smile. "Hope you're doing good today. I'm doing pretty good myself." The smile disappeared. "Well, not really. Ashley R-r-r-rathburn's party is t-t-t-tonight." She stopped for a breath. "I uh...know I keep asking, b-b-b-but I really want to go. Luke Gerasi said he would come, and I like him, and I think he l-l-l-likes me, so uh...*please*, if you can, make D-d-d-daddy let me g-g-g..." A frustrated shot of air expelled from her nose. It would be a horrible day if she couldn't control her stutter.

After a second of silence, she took another deep breath. "I promise...nothing will happen...between Luke and me. I swear on my life." She paused, turning to the nightstand. Next to the clock was a framed picture of her at age eight, along with her mother—a large woman with curly blond hair and the same brown eyes—standing in front of Niagara Falls with big touristy smiles. "Okay. Thanks, Mom. Love you." Betsy made the sign of the cross again then stood up and walked to her dresser.

It was Friday, which meant that she—a senior at Bishop Dullen, one of the three Catholic junior-senior high schools in Syracuse—could skip the khaki pants and green polo with the school's name embroidered on the chest (the standard Dullen uniform) and dress down. On most Fridays, she wore a pair of jeans and a basic cotton top from Old Navy or JCPenney, but not today. She had her best outfit (a pair of gray sateen pants and a blue-striped oxford from Abercrombie & Fitch her Aunt Carol had given her for Christmas) laid on top of the dresser.

Betsy's cheeks filled with excitement as she lifted the shirt by its sleeves. "Tonight's gonna be *so* amazing. Like a million times better than my birthday party." Suddenly the glee was sucked out of her face as if those last two words were emotion-extracting vacuums. "Shoot." She returned the shirt to the dresser then quickly made the sign of the cross once more. "Sorry, Mom. I almost f-f-f-forgot. K-k-k-k—" Pressing her lips together, she groaned. She followed it with a brisk inhalation then went on. "Kathleen...is coming back...to school today, so...if you could, please let me not run into her, okay?" She waited for a moment in silence. "Okay, thanks. Love you."

She made the sign of the cross one last time then headed to the bathroom to shower.

•   •   •   •   •

Sheriff Coleman, a broad-shouldered man, forty-two, with dark, angular features, sauntered into the small '90s-styled kitchen. Tightening his maroon robe over his plaid pajama bottoms, he stopped at the tile countertop and curled his thin lips into a sour pout at the Keurig machine. It had been four years since he'd had a good cup of coffee. Or a good drink. *Stop it,* he chided himself, biting his upper lip. *You shouldn't be thinking about that. Especially today.*

As he presided over nineteen towns, fifteen villages, and eleven "census-designated places" as county sheriff, his plate was always full. Today, however, would be particularly laborious. He had no doubt that a plethora of teenagers would be out on the road drinking or doing something equally stupid. And he had to make sure the dumb kids didn't kill each other or anyone else.

"Good morning, D-d-d-daddy."

Fear flashed through his bright-green eyes when he turned to his daughter, who was entering the dimly lit room. *Where's her uniform?* his fatherly instincts questioned, and *Why does she look like a college student?* "Good morning, honey," he said hesitantly. "Is it dress-down day?"

Betsy stopped and looked down at her clothes. "Yeah," she said, looking back up. "It's F-f-f-friday, but I think a lot of people are going to wear costumes."

Sheriff Coleman blew a mental sigh of relief. She was wearing a nun's habit compared to some of the outfits he'd seen girls her age wear. "You're probably right. You sleep okay?"

"Yup." Smiling, Betsy walked up to him, stood on her tiptoes, and kissed his cheek. "You?"

"Like a baby." Sheriff Coleman flashed her a grin back.

Betsy laughed lightly. "That's good. Could you hand me the c-c-c-c-cereal?"

"Of course." He handed the box of Apple Jacks on the counter to her.

"Thanks, Daddy."

"You're welcome." He turned to the Keurig again. As the hot, bitter-smelling coffee dripped into his mug, Betsy poured herself a bowl of cereal then grabbed a carton of milk from the fridge. Taking his cup of coffee, Sheriff Coleman let out a hearty laugh. "Just in time. Can I get the milk after you?"

"Of course." Still smiling, Betsy poured some milk into her bowl then handed him the carton.

"Thanks."

As Sheriff Coleman stirred his coffee, Betsy grabbed a spoon from the dish rack and sat down at the Formica table in the center of the kitchen. A thick air of silence passed between them as Sheriff Coleman blew on his coffee then took a quick sip. His lips squeezed in revolt. It wasn't horrible; it just wasn't his Patricia's coffee.

"Daddy?"

He turned to her, wiping the residual coffee from his salt-and-pepper mustache. "Yeah, honey?"

"Um"—Betsy stared at her cereal—"is it okay...if I g-g-g-go t-t-t-to Ashley R-r-r-rathburn's party tonight?" She looked up with an innocent expression. "P-p-p-please?"

Sheriff Coleman released a frustrated breath. *So that's why she's dressed up.* "No, Betsy."

"Why not?"

"Because..." He paused to think. There were several reasons why he didn't want his daughter to go out tonight, but he chose the most obvious answer. "Did you forget what happened at your birthday party? I caught people drinking."

"*Sssso.*" Betsy knitted her brow. "That was t-t-t-two weeks ago. And I wasn't drinking."

"But your friend was—"

Betsy's befuddled expression twisted into a web of furious lines. "Kathleen isn't my friend!" her raspy voice echoed through the kitchen.

Surprised, Sheriff Coleman took a step back. He couldn't remember the last time his daughter had talked back to him. He took a deep breath and shook his head. "Doesn't matter. If there was alcohol at your party, there's a good chance there'll be alcohol at this one, and I don't trust the kids who'll be there. All right?"

Betsy sucked her teeth. "This isn't fair!"

He slammed his cup of coffee on the table. "Young lady, I'm your father. You should know better not to talk to me like that. Now I—" Just then the phone in the living room rang, and he let out an irritated grunt. "Goddamn it, that's probably the station." He stalked off into the living room, a boxlike space with a modern country decor. "Hello?" he said, after picking up the phone.

"Hi, Sheriff." It was Bill Riley, a young sergeant who was working dispatch that morning. In his cheerful voice, he added, "And glory to God for another beautiful day. Am I right?"

Sheriff Coleman's lips stiffened as he repressed another grunt. "Yes, Bill. Is something wrong?"

Bill's voice deepened. "Well, I just got a call from a Dr. Bone...steak." He paused, chuckling. "Sorry. Dr. Bonesteel. A psychiatrist from Summer Hill."

Sheriff Coleman scrunched up his heavy brow and shot a confused glare at the fireplace across the room. "Summer Hill? That psychiatric hospital upstate?"

"Yes, Sheriff."

"All right. What does he want?"

"He says one of his patients escaped this morning—"

Sheriff Coleman's eyes grew wide. "*Escaped?*"

"Yes. About two hours ago. Dr. Bonesteel said the man's very dangerous, and he's most definitely on his way to Manlius."

"Manlius? Why?"

"I don't know. He hung up before I got a chance to ask him."

Sheriff Coleman opened his mouth to chew out the sergeant for his mistake, then stopped and sighed, realizing it was better to take immediate action. "All right, fine. I'll be down there as soon as possible. Wake up the emergency response team. I want a patrol car at every exit off 81 and four cars patrolling Manlius. Did you get a description of the patient?"

"Yes. The doctor said the man is six feet tall, about two-hundred-fifty pounds, and wearing a gray sweater and blue pants."

"Okay, good," Sheriff Coleman said, staring at the braided blue area rug at his feet. "Anything else?"

"Um, yes. He said the guy has a pale, emotionless face with eyes that look like black pits that...um...lead to the gates of hell."

Sheriff Coleman's head jolted up. "What?"

After Bill reiterated the description, the sheriff mimed an angry huff. *Is this a sick joke or has Bill lost his crazy Christian mind?*

"John?" Bill said.

"Yeah, I'm here," he replied. "Are you sure that's what...Dr....uh..."

"Bonesteel."

"Are you sure that's what Dr. Bonesteel said?"

"Yes. It's written on my notepad."

Sheriff Coleman's mustache flitted with doubt. "Okay. Well, then call the response team and...make sure you give them that description. Excluding the 'gates of hell' bit. Got it?"

"Yup," Bill said, then returned to his usual light-hearted tone. "Praise be to God."

Sheriff Coleman gritted his teeth. *Jesus Christ...* "Yes, praise be," he said and hung up. *Escaped patient*, he repeated in his head, giving the phone an odd look, then laughed through his nose. Some knucklehead was probably playing a Halloween prank. Still, it was better to be safe than sorry. He took a quick breath to refocus then turned to the kitchen. Betsy was still at the table, her head practically submerged in her Apple Jacks. "I gotta get dressed and go to work, Betsy. Can you take the bus?"

"Yeah," Betsy said with a slow nod, then stood up and headed to the living room.

"All right, good. I'll call you later. Love you, honey."

Speed walking past her father, Betsy grabbed her purple jacket and her book bag. She walked out of the house and slammed the door behind her.

"Betsy, for Christ's sake!" Sheriff Coleman moved toward the door then stopped himself from making an eight-in-the morning, dramatic street scene and threw up his fist, preparing to punch the suede couch by his side. "Goddamn it," he muttered, lowering his hand. After taking a round of slow, soothing breaths, he raised his head toward the ceiling. "I'm sorry, Patricia. I know you probably would've let her go, but I had to say no. She'll be safe tonight, okay?" He gave a reassuring nod and started for the bathroom.

3

Kathleen Strife, 7:30 a.m.

Kathleen was on the edge of death. Her pasty, bloated body lay across two mattresses stacked on top of each other, while her hefty arms pressed against her legs like two planks of lumber. Her face was buried in a hodgepodge of various-colored sheets. Any indication of life—be it rapid eye movement or breathing—was obstructed by her tangled mess of greasy black hair. And then, suddenly, there was a spark of life.

A quick but loud fart came from Kathleen's ass. "Shit!" she shouted as a sharp pain stabbed the top of her right ass cheek. She remained face down, waiting for the pain to dissipate, but it remained a throbbing "Fuck you" sting. She let out an exasperated sigh. "Goddamn it!"

After rolling out of bed, she dragged herself to her half bathroom and stopped in front of the cracked mirror. She pulled down her black sweatpants and saw exactly what she had feared: the cyst on her ass—a dime-size sac of puss that had formed the day after she was suspended from school—was as big as a half dollar. "Fuck it," she said, pulling up her pants. "They can suspend me for another two weeks. I'm not going back."

Facing the mirror, she froze upon seeing her reflection. Looking back was a full-figured eighteen-year-old girl with an oval face consisting of two portly cheeks, enormous dark-brown eyes, and thick black eyebrows that read: *Don't fuck with me.* Kathleen wanted to see a strong, beautiful woman, but she knew that the rest of the world had a different view of her: a big, fat bitch.

And then, like twisted clockwork, her stomach screamed, *Feed me, you obese cunt!* Kathleen snorted then turned away and headed to the kitchen. Built in the early twentieth century, the spacious room had a Victorian-style design, furnished with a checkerboard floor and large oak cabinets painted baby blue. Long ago, these furnishings had been busted, chipped, scratched, torn, and coated with a layer of nicotine and dollar-store olive oil. Opening the refrigerator, Kathleen gave a hard laugh as she took in the artifacts: two forty-ounce cans of Natural Ice, a handful of ketchup packets, and a box of baking soda that looked like it fed the evil Mohawk spirits that inhabited the house. She closed the door then checked the cabinets, which were barren too. "Of course there's no food. Who the fuck eats around here except me?"

She turned around and stepped into the living room. Again, its lavish architecture had been stripped away and replaced with a meth lab decor, complete with a beige carpet covered with dark stains and various garbage, and a matching leather couch and recliner that looked like they'd had a knife fight over who was going to handle the drug money. Kathleen's father, Robert "Bobby" Strife, a heavyset man in his late fifties who had kept his tan from his Texan childhood, lay in the middle of this disgusting scene, passed out on the recliner with a line of beer cans at his feet. "You're really working for that disability check, aren't you, Pops?" Kathleen grumbled.

Staring at her father, she pressed her lips together and made a quick "hmm" sound. *At least he's here*, she thought, imagining that her mother, Bridget, was at her eighty-six-year-old boyfriend's house, jerking him off for his Xanax.

She checked the time on the cable box. "All right, I guess I'll go to school. This place is too fucking depressing." She headed to the full bathroom near the kitchen, took a shower, then returned to her bedroom. There, she changed into purple pajama bottoms, a black hoodie, and a HIM T-shirt; grabbed her car keys; and continued to her white '94 Ford Tempo outside.

Stopping at the car door, she turned to the house, took a mental picture of its rotted exterior, then looked down the street at the dilapidated conditions of the other homes. The paint on those houses had peeled off and lay on their lawns as leathery sheets; windows were cracked or covered with plywood or trash bags; and graffiti was scattered around the block, noting where "d$" had "smoked bluntz" and/or "snuffed bitches."

House repair was a bottom priority for the people of Southside, one of the most dangerous neighborhoods in Syracuse. Shootings, robberies, gang fights—it was a miserable place to live, and unfortunately only a few ever left. The lack of opportunities and extreme poverty kept a tight grasp on the residents of Southside, and Kathleen imagined she wouldn't be an exception.

This is the rest of your fucked-up life, she thought, looking at her house once more. *Get used to it.* With a short exhalation, she pulled her shirt over her exposed belly then opened the car door. As soon as she sat down, another sharp pain shot up her ass cheek. "Fuck!" she shouted, then slapped the steering wheel. "I'm stealing some fucking food whether that Lunch Nazi likes it or not!" Grunting, she shoved the key into the ignition and turned it. The engine cranked, but the car didn't start. Rolling her eyes, she turned the key back and tried once more. It failed again.

"C'mon, you stupid piece of crap," she said, trying to start it for the third time. As the engine cranked, she punched the side of the steering wheel, and like a Criss Angel magic trick, it fired up. She expelled a loud, diabolical laugh. "There you go, you motherfucker!"

Pulling out of the driveway, she turned on the radio and cranked up Nirvana's "Smells Like Teen Spirit." She then sped off, screaming, "I feel stupid and contagious" as loud as she could.

4

On the north side of Syracuse was a quant, blue-collar suburb called Mattydale. At the end of the main road, beside the neighborhood's community center/secret sex ring, stood a two-story white-and-pink house, with the front half of the roof covered in a black tarp to protect the hole created by this past summer's freak windstorm. On the second floor, in the first of the two bedrooms, David woke up to a light knock on his door. "Good morning, poojoo," his mom's velvety voice sang from the hallway. "Happy Halloween."

Yawning, he rubbed his eyes then stretched his thin, hairy arms. "Happy Halloween," he said with a small laugh, then turned on his side. "I'll be…" He stopped, noticing the large erection pushing against his Scooby-Doo pajama pants. He clenched his teeth. "I'll…um…be right there."

"Okay, baby," Mrs. Ecklund said. "Want some breakfast?"

"Uh, yeah, sure," David answered, trying to constrain his erection with the strap of his tighty whities. "Just some eggs and toast, okay?"

"Scrambled or sunny-side up?"

He rolled his eyes as his erection slipped out. "Scrambled, please."

"Okay. Anything for my baby boy."

David pretended to laugh. "Thanks, Mom."

"No problem. See you in a minute."

"You too." He remained in his blue futon bed, waiting for her to walk away. Hearing her start down the hall, he rolled onto his back and let out an uneasy breath through his nose as he tucked his erection into the leg band of his underwear. *Geez Louise. Why on earth do I keep having the same dream about* Mike Barrett? *And why the fuck do I always get a boner from it?*

His bow-shaped lips slithered into a grimace. It was probably best to not think about it, he imagined, then threw the Teenage Mutant Ninja Turtles bedsheet off his legs, stood up, and pushed his bed into its futon position.

With a second yawn, he headed to the closet across from him and opened it, revealing five large plastic storage bins. He grabbed the top bin—labeled "Action Figures"—placed it behind him, and removed the lid of the second box. Inside was a trove of Halloween costumes and accessories, including the masks of slasher icons and their corresponding weapons—except Chuckie. He had wanted nothing to do with that devil doll ever since he was five years old and had sneaked a peek of his father watching *Child's Play.* The question "Why is that doll killing that poor voodoo man?" had haunted him the rest of his childhood.

A jack-o'-lantern smile spread across his face as he pulled out a blond bob wig and a fake cell phone. He placed the wig over his head, raised the phone to his ear and, in his best Casey Becker voice, said, "Why do you want to know my name?"

His smile faded away as he turned to the mirror that hung from his door and saw a lanky teen who looked like he was doing drag for the first time. "Wow," he said, taking off the wig. "The apes are definitely going to call you gay if you go to school like that." After returning the bins and shutting the closet door, he chuckled. "David, they'd call you gay even if you were knee-deep in pussy." He made a gagging sound. "Oh, man, you really shouldn't think about the p-word when you're about to have scrambled eggs."

From the tan hamper in the opposite corner, he grabbed a pair of jeans, then continued to the two plastic dressers next to it: the right dresser was clothes, the second DVDs. From the clothes dresser, he fished out a red sweater, socks, underwear, and his gray jacket, then headed for the bathroom.

"Your father's in there."

David stopped in the hallway and turned to the cookie-cutter kitchen, with its basic brown cabinets and Americana everything else. A thin woman with mousy blond hair and a red cotton robe wrapped around her stood at the kitchen stove, scrambling eggs. "Oh, sorry, Mom," he said.

"It's okay. You can check out your Halloween treats in the living room." She pointed over his shoulder with a wooden spatula.

David looked behind him and searched the L-shaped room, designed almost exclusively by the Nate Berkus aisle at Target. "*Mom!*" On the flannel espresso sofa lay a collection of gifts, including three large bags of candy (Whoppers, Skittles, and Caramel Creams, his favorite) and a straight-to-Netflix DVD. He clicked his teeth as he turned back to her. "You didn't have to do that."

"Yes, I did," Mrs. Ecklund said with a proud smile. "I know how much my poo loves Halloween."

David held his next words at the tip of his tongue. He wanted to tell her he wasn't a little kid anymore, but worried that would hurt her feelings, he feigned a quick laugh. "Yeah, I do." He looked at her, searching for something to say, then sighed. "I hope Kathleen—"

"*Emily*," Mrs. Ecklund shouted, turning to the door near the stove. "You gotta get up, or you'll be late for school!"

David looked down at the recently vacuumed turquoise carpet and rolled his eyes. Why was she trying to wake up his big sister? Wasn't raising the dead easier?

"What were you saying, baby?" Mrs. Ecklund asked, returning to the eggs.

David looked up, brushing the strands of his shaggy brown hair from his forehead. "I was just saying I hope Kathleen comes to school today. If she does, can she come over and watch horror movies with me?"

"Of course. You know she's welcome here anytime." Mrs. Ecklund spooned the eggs onto a paper plate and put it on the table. A ceramic pig swaddled in the American flag lay in the center. "Do you want some orange juice?"

"Yes, please." As his mother headed to the refrigerator, David looked down again, processing the thoughts that were creeping into his mind. "It's so weird, don't you think?"

Mrs. Ecklund bent down, searching through the stacks of leftover casserole and three army-size jars of Miracle Whip. "What is?"

"Well, I've been Kathleen's and Betsy's friend since the eighth grade, but they've been best friends since kindergarten, I think."

"Yeah?" Holding a five-gallon jug of Sunny D, Mrs. Ecklund headed to the cabinets. "Why's that weird?"

"They're complete opposites. Betsy's this sweet, quiet girl and Kathleen's...not." David laughed. "I mean, it's pretty amazing they stayed friends all this time, but then this one little incident happens, and their whole friendship is in jeopardy. Yeah, Kathleen was drinking at Betsy's birthday party, and yeah, Betsy's father shouldn't have called the school and gotten Kathleen suspended, but it's done with. Why can't they just apologize to each other so things can go back to normal?"

Mrs. Ecklund placed the glass of juice on the table. "I'm sorry, sweetie. So things still aren't good with the three of you?"

"Not really," David answered, watching his mom return the "in case of nuclear war" container of Sunny D to the refrigerator. "Kathleen hasn't answered her phone since she was suspended, so I have no idea what's going on with her, and Betsy's pretty much been avoiding me." He paused, his button-nose crumpling with uncertainty. "And I don't know if it's because of the party or if she just wants to spend time with her new boyfriend."

"Hmm." Mrs. Ecklund was back at the stove, starting another batch of scrambled eggs. "Well, maybe they called each other and made up."

David snorted. "*Umm*, I don't know about that. I have a good feeling they're probably still angry with each other so"—he clenched his teeth—"who knows what's going to happen with *us*?" He made air quotes. "I still like Betsy, but Kathleen's probably going to want me to side with her and...I probably will since we like more of the same stuff, you know."

"I know," Mrs. Ecklund said, nodding with a long exhalation. "These things happen, though. People who've known each other for years, even decades, can have a falling out. Sometimes it's because of one little incident, or it's been building up for a long time. And depending on who those people are and what they want, they could make up with a single apology or never speak to each other again. Just remember: whatever happens, you keep being your wonderful, amazing self. All right?"

David attempted a smile despite his low self-esteem. "I'll try. Hey, can I bring some of that candy to school?"

"Of course, my little poo-loo," she replied, then placed the new batch of eggs on another paper plate. "By the way, did you start your college essay for Fordham yet?"

He mentally groaned. *Behind that sweet exterior is a raging helicopter mom.* "Not yet."

"Well, you'd better get on it. The deadline's coming up fast."

Rather than argue, he forced his cheeks into a second smile. "I know. I'll start working on it this weekend."

"Good." Carrying the plate of eggs, Mrs. Ecklund walked over to his sister's bedroom door and gave it two hard knocks. "C'mon, Em! You gotta get up. Your food's ready."

David laughed again. *The dead want human brains, Mom. Not chicken fetuses.*

"Come *on*. I'm not kidding. You're gonna—"

"All right," came a low, uncivil voice from behind the door. "I fucking heard you." The discolored slab of wood opened, and a two-hundred-and-forty-pound woman, wearing nothing but pink briefs and an XXXL shirt with Tweety flipping the bird, stood between the fluorescent glow of the kitchen and the infinite darkness concealing the contents of her room.

"Real nice." Mrs. Ecklund offered the scrambled eggs to Emily. "Here. Do you want some juice?"

"Sure." She tied her stringy, bleached blonde hair into a ponytail with the purple scrunchie from her wrist then took the eggs.

"Did you study for your contouring exam last night?" Mrs. Ecklund asked on her second trip to the refrigerator. A blunt 'No' was her daughter's response. "Oh, well. You'll still do fine."

David did a double take as she retrieved the chemically altered orange juice and continued to the cabinets. *Are you kidding me*, he wanted to burst out. *Why aren't you up her ass for not studying?* He looked over at his sister, who was picking at the plate of eggs with her chubby fingers. *Just because she's a bitch and I'm not I'm the one who—*

Suddenly Emily looked up with a runny glob of eggs in her mouth, and a death threat injected into her bulbous eyes. "What the *fuck* are you looking at?"

"Emily!" As the magnum of orange juice slipped from Ms. Ecklund's hands and hit the kitchen counter, David jumped back then turned and took a step toward the living room. His instinct was to hide in the wicker trunk used as rat poop storage, but then he froze as the bathroom door opened, and Mr. Ecklund, a tall potbellied man with a black crew cut, emerged.

"Oh, hi, Dad."

Mr. Ecklund stopped and replied with a quick "Hi."

"Happy Halloween," David said with an anxious grin. Just then he heard his sister's bedroom door close.

David's dad stood squarely in front of him and nodded, his long, pallid face trained to block any emotion trying to escape. "Happy Halloween."

Fucking robot, David thought, then looked down at the white button-down shirt and black slacks his father was wearing that morning (and what felt like every morning for the past ten years) and projected a telepathic sigh. *God. What if I told you I was gay right now? Would you simply nod, or would your straight-man circuits explode?*

"Have a good day, David."

"Yup, you too." David immediately turned his body against the wall and slid past his father, hoping he wouldn't catch his chronic dullness. After heading into the bathroom, he locked the door then stopped, seeing his reflection in the mirror. "Yeah right," he murmured to the scrawny pipsqueak staring back at him. "As if you're brave enough to tell anyone you're gay."

5

Betsy, 8:00 a.m.

Eight miles west of Syracuse was Fairmount, a suburban community that had been a sprawling dairy farm in the late nineteenth century. Little of the farm had survived, except a pair of landmarked farmhouses and the land itself, a two-hundred-acre tract consisting of flat, flower-rich meadows and thick elm forests. Preparing for winter, the forest was stippled with bright oranges and yellows, making it look like a van Gogh painting on one of his happy, non-cutting-ear-off days.

Living on the east perimeter of this forest, Betsy passed the time waiting for her bus by staring at the colorful landscape, wondering what she would do after high school. Would she stay in New York for college or would she travel to a different state? What would she study? Did she even want to go to college?

This morning, however, those questions lay dormant in her mind. Instead, her head was an iron cage filled with a pack of furious thoughts trying to snap off the bars. *I hate him so much,* her inner voice screamed. *He knows I don't drink, so why's he being such a jerk? Is he really so mad about the party that he'll never let me have fun again?*

A hoarse laugh erupted from the back of her throat. "Does he ever let you have fun?" she asked, then immediately answered, "No. You're the only one in school who has a curfew. And you're probably the only teenager in this neighborhood—no, the entire city—who doesn't drive or have a cell phone. *And* he embarrassed the living crap out of you at your birthday party." Squeezing the straps of her book bag, she let out a high-pitched squeal. "God, why did Mom have to die? It should've been *him!*"

Suddenly a strong breeze blew past her, knocking off her balance. "Okay, that's it," Betsy said with an exaggerated huff of frustration. "The stupid bus is late, and it's freaking cold. I'm walking." Zipping up her coat, she stormed off toward the bike trail at the end of the street. Even though the trail was a five-minute walk to school, her father had forbidden to use it. Not only because there was a supposed drifter, Bike Trail Bob, living in the adjacent woods (waiting to "take her innocence"), but also because it lay along Route 5, a narrow backwoods road notorious for car crashes by high-speed travelers trying to get to New York City without having to see Syracuse.

Betsy started down the trail's winding dirt path, a dark stretch of woods on her right side and the tight road on her left. Stuffing her hands into her coat pockets, she kept her eyes on the leaf-covered track, her thoughts far from the fearful visions that usually haunted the minds of those who walked alone in the woods. "Why the hell was Kathleen drinking at my party?" she barked at the path. "She knew Daddy was going to be there. So it's like she either didn't care or she wanted to get me in trouble." Confusion extinguished the hatred emitting from her eyes. "Why would she want to get *me* in trouble? I didn't do anything to her."

As Betsy rounded the first bend of the trail, her face was still until a sudden thought provoked her soft features. "Wait, was she mad because—"

She stopped and turned toward the harsh sound of car tires squealing against the road. Her long eyebrows shot up in alarm; a red car with its front bumper bashed into an unrecognizable swirl was coming down the street as though an armless raccoon was behind the steering wheel. First, it moved for a second. Then it stopped. Then it moved again and stopped a second time. It kept starting and stopping until it finally stopped for good. And then, with the ravenous howl that was the complete opposite of an armless raccoon, a large beady-eyed boy wearing a gray sweater and blue pants burst out of the driver's side and punched what was left of the front end.

Betsy gasped. *He's crazy!*

As the burly guy whipped his head in her direction, Betsy's eyes went wide with fear. *Shit*, she thought, then turned and quickly walked away. She hurried up the trail for half a minute, and then, wondering whether the strange man had returned to his car, she reached the second bend and peeked over her shoulder. *Oh, crap*, she thought, as the sight of the crazy man walking toward her shook her spine with an icy shiver. *He's following me!*

Betsy turned around and continued up the dirt path, picking up her speed. Again, after a few feet, she took another cautious/curious glance over her shoulder. The huge man was still behind her—this time running in her direction with his meaty paws spread out to grab her.

Firing out a piercing scream, she bolted toward the other end of the trail with a speed she hadn't produced since her elementary-school days of girls-versus-dumb-boys races. Less than a minute into this instinctive dash, her lungs stung with an uncomfortable chill, and the muscles in her legs felt as though they were strangling the bones inside. However, the thought of death swiping for her heels forced her to keep running as fast as she could until she reached the small grassy clearing that led into the school parking lot. Gasping for air, she stopped and turned to look behind—

A driver in a rusted-out white car slammed the brakes, stopping a couple of inches from Betsy. Her entire body froze—except for her heart. The frightened, little muscle felt as though it had leapt into her throat.

Honk! Betsy's large eyes glared at the unknown driver behind the tinted windows. Why were they honking at her? Weren't they going to step out and see if she was okay?

Honk! Honk! Honk! Shaking out of her disbelief, she moved aside and watched the spoiled lemon wedge of a car speed by, its doors rattling from the music blasting inside. As the car continued into the parking lot, Betsy noticed the huge dent at the back and recognized it instantly (How could she not? She was in the backseat the night it had happened.) She gave a short, raspy sigh that prickled her chest. "*Kathleen!*"

And then, remembering the beastly psycho who was chasing her, she turned around. The man was gone.

•　　•　　•　　•　　•

So you wanna play—

"Nope," Kathleen said, and switched to the next station.

Because I'm—

Next station.

Let it—

"Where the fuck is the good music?" She switched stations as she turned down the road to school. And then, like a gift from Satan's rock minions, a gravelly voice screamed, "All aboard" from the radio then followed it with a diabolical laugh.

"Fuck, yeah!" Kathleen liked Ozzy Osbourne, but she *loved* "Crazy Train." So much so that she planned on playing it at her wedding and/or funeral—whichever came first. After bobbing her head to the guitar intro, she shouted the first word of the song: "Crazy!" She lifted her hands off the steering for a moment and sang the rest of the first verse.

Trailing off at the bridge of the song, she glanced toward the long stretch of woods to her right, then drummed along with the melody. As she pulled into the school parking lot, she turned back to the steering wheel, singing the chorus. "I'm going off the rails—"

A scared, frumpy-looking white girl— "Lena Dunham!" Kathleen exclaimed—was right there, in the middle of the entrance! Immediately she hit the brakes.

Screeeeech! As the car came to a jarring halt, she was thrown forward then backward, her head crashing against the hard headrest. "Fuck!" she screamed, as she closed her eyes and let the whiplash rattle her nerves. She scowled, opening her eyes to the one person she would have gladly run over in exchange for flying through the windshield. "Goddamn it, Betsy. Of all the days the brakes actually work." Clenching her teeth, she pounded the horn.

Betsy stood still, staring at the car as though it were made out of twelve-inch black dildos.

"*Move*, you fucking horse!" Kathleen blasted the horn repeatedly until finally, Betsy moved to the side. "Idiot!" she yelled, then pressed on the gas and sped into the parking lot. She parked at the other end of the lot and lit a Marlboro Red.

While "Crazy Train" pumped out of the radio, she cackled at Betsy, who was pitifully trudging up the school's stone steps. "Chill the fuck out, bitch," she said, then took a long drag off her cigarette. "You're still alive."

As Betsy disappeared inside the building, Kathleen's enormous eyes narrowed, shooting invisible bolts of hatred. "Go ahead, you dumb twat. Just wait until I see you in school."

6

The Sheriff, 8:30 a.m.

Sheriff Coleman parked his black Ford Escape (SHERIFF emblazoned on the side in yellow) in front of the Onondaga County Sheriff's Office. Stretching across two blocks in the heart of downtown Syracuse, it looked like the average office building with its simple concrete exterior. If a small, rectangular sign hadn't hung over the glass door, announcing the name of the office, they probably would've received more people—other than the occasional senior citizen who thought it was the Department of Motor Vehicles.

It wasn't the DMV, though. Inside, there was a floor of holding cells that housed a revolving collection of drunk drivers, transsexual prostitutes, and Catholic priests, as well as three other floors, each an intricate maze of offices dedicated to law enforcement. Most days the building was like an ant colony, a nonstop fury of activity that didn't bother Sheriff Coleman in the least. "Busy" meant the nineteen towns, fifteen villages, and eleven "census-designated places" of Onondaga County were safe from the motorcycle scum and street gangs trying to muscle their control into his territory.

After a deep breath, he delivered the same prayer he said every morning before he started the day. "God grant me the serenity to accept the things I cannot change, the courage to the things I can, and the wisdom to know the difference." He then added, "And please, let this morning's call be just a stupid prank." He grabbed his sheriff's hat from the passenger seat, placed it on the top of his head (completing his all-black uniform), then got out of his car, and headed to the entrance.

As he walked into the colorless, dentist-office-like lobby, he locked eyes with a stocky bald man—whom he guessed was about sixty—sitting on a wooden bench by the wall. The older man, wearing a brown trench coat and a checkered gray suit underneath, sprang up from the bench and, in a squawky voice, said, "The Devil is coming to your town, Sheriff."

Fuck. Sheriff Coleman turned to the front desk, which Sergeant Bill stood behind, looking back with his bearish face and small eyes stuck in a brainless stare. With a sigh, the sheriff turned to the short, agitated man. "All right, you must be—"

"Dr. Alfred Bonesteel," the man said, gazing at the sheriff with piercing blue eyes. "Did you hear what I said, Sheriff? A creature of pure evil is at the footsteps of this town, waiting to take its innocence—"

"Okay, Dr. Bonesteel." Sheriff Coleman raised his hands in surrender as he looked around the empty room, relieved this man didn't have an audience of early drifters for his satanic pep talk. "Why don't we go into my office and you can tell me what happened?"

"All right, Sheriff. But Nick Roesch is out there, ready to kill."

"Nick Roesch? Is that the name of the escaped patient?"

The doctor nodded again. "Yes. Nick Roesch. *That* is the name of the Devil."

Is this guy for real? "Um, all right." Sheriff Coleman turned to the front desk. "Sergeant Bill, did you get the spelling of the patient's name?"

"Yes, I did, Sheriff." A toothy smile replaced the sergeant's dopey stare.

"Good," Sheriff Coleman replied, then turned back to the doctor. "My office is over there, last room on the right." He gestured to a long fluorescent hallway. "Go in and take a seat. I'll be with you in a second."

"Thank you, Sheriff." Dr. Bonesteel carved a haunting smile with his shriveled lips, then started for the hallway.

"You're welcome." Sheriff Coleman glanced behind him with a heavy look, wondering whether this so-called "doctor" was telling the truth. *Maybe he's the escaped patient.* He shook his head. It didn't matter; he had to follow protocol. "Look up this Nick Roesch on the computer and see what's there," he told Bill. "Did you call the extra patrols to Manlius yet?"

Sergeant Bill nodded. "I divvied up locations. They're on their way now for security detail."

"Good. I want the morning patrols on their usual assignments too. Tell them to call in anything unusual." He paused. "And get me the number for the county station near Summer Hill. I want to talk to the sheriff over there and see what they're doing."

"Yes, Sheriff."

"Okay." Sheriff Coleman started for his office. "I'm going to talk to—"

"Wait, John. I have a question."

He stopped. "What is it?"

"Well..." A red, penis-shaped blotch appeared on the sergeant's forehead. "I was wondering if you'd like to come to the St. John's Annual Men's Winter Retreat next month." From an invisible pocket, he produced a pamphlet with a mountainous landscape superimposed with a crucifix. "Snowshoeing!" and "Scripture Discussions!" appeared in big bubble letters at the bottom. "It's usually for VIP members of the church, but I spoke with Father Dan, and he said you're more than welcome to come."

As he looked down at the pamphlet, Sheriff Coleman's face tightened into a hard glare. Was Bill really trying to promote his weekend powwow for Bible thumpers while a supposed madman was on the loose?

"Since you've been busy with work and all, I know you haven't been able to come to Sunday Mass...for the last six months, so I thought this would be a good way to get you back into the club, sort of speak." A friendly laugh escaped through Bill's nose. "And my friend Hank can't make it, so you know, since I've...helped you out with everything, this'll be an easy way to return the favor." Another laugh. "What do you say?"

I say you can shove your favor up your ass. Suddenly, Sheriff Coleman's stomach sank into his legs, as if his conscious had pulled an inner "Don't be an asshole" lever. *Shit, John,* his conscious argued. *He saved your life. The least you can do is spend a lousy couple of days with him.* "Um, sure," he said, looking up. "I'll go. I uh...have to see if my parents can watch Betsy, though."

"Oh, yeah, no problem." As he folded his hands in prayer, Sergeant Bill's face lit up like a fleshy saint's candle. "Wow. Thank you. Thank you *so* much, Sheriff. Praise be."

"Uh, yeah." Sheriff Coleman tipped his hat, then headed to the hallway without looking back. He walked to the frosted door marked, SHERIFF, and continued into an office that looked like a room for a man concerned more about his work than its decor. There was a black U-shaped desk, a black mesh chair for him, two plastic folding chairs for visitors, and a wooden bookcase stacked with police manuals—handed down by the previous sheriff as door stoppers. Taking a seat across from Dr. Bonesteel, he rummaged through the piles of papers and folders on his desk for a pencil and legal notepad. "All right, Doctor," he said, turning to the first blank page. "Can you tell me what happened?"

"Certainly," Dr. Bonesteel said. "I've been Nick Roesch's court-ordered juvenile psychiatrist for the last five years, so as usual, I was driving up to Summer Hill for our twice-weekly six a.m. sessions. I was in Nedrow when the hospital director called to tell me Nick had escaped. Apparently, he stabbed an orderly in the eye with his long nails, jumped out of a two-story window, and then, completely unharmed, ran off into the woods."

Sheriff Coleman chewed his lip. *Fantastic. The escaped lunatic is superhuman.* "Any witnesses?"

"Yes. Jackie Nebolt, a nurse at the hospital."

Sheriff Coleman wrote her name on his notepad. "All right, Summer Hill is about two hours from here. He must be somewhere near there still."

Dr. Bonesteel shook his head. "Not if he got hold of a car."

"He knows how to drive?"

"Well, yes," Dr. Bonesteel said, tucking his chin into his saggy neck in regret. "Nick's a teenager—eighteen to be exact—and I've tried to normalize him as best as I could. I threw him birthday parties and celebrated the holidays with him, and then, when he was a little older, I taught him how to drive with a pair of orderlies. Just an automatic, though. Not a stick shift." Immediately he stopped and looked at Sheriff Coleman with a fearful stare. "Let's pray to God he doesn't come across a car with an automatic transmission."

Sheriff Coleman's face froze into a quizzical squint, his mind trying to put together the pieces of this odd-shaped puzzle. *So I'm dealing with an escaped superhuman who doesn't know how to drive a stick? How the hell is this not a prank?* "Okay. So let's say Nick Roesch does get a hold of a car...with an automatic transmission. Why would he come here?"

"Because," Dr. Bonesteel said, his eyes growing even wider with horror, "he's coming back to kill the babysitter!"

"Huh?"

"Jamie Strode."

"Jamie Strode. How do you spell that?"

Dr. Bonesteel spelled out the girl's name, then continued. "Would you like to hear the story?"

"Yes," Sheriff Coleman answered as he drew an arrow from the girl's name on his notepad and wrote, "Call parents?"

Dr. Bonesteel straightened up like a wizard telling his apprentice a tale of dark alchemy. "Nick Roesch wasn't a normal child. Born into a wealthy family who owned a line of printing presses, he wasn't like his two older brothers. They played sports, had a large circle of friends, went to dances and parties—like typical American teenagers. Nick, however, didn't speak until he was six years old, and when he did, it was usually the same couple of phrases. He also kept to himself, hiding himself in his room, reading comic books. His parents thought he was severely autistic, but since they were worried that having a child with a disability would give them a bad reputation in town, they didn't seek out any therapeutic support. Nick refused to go to school anyway, so they kept him at home and left him to his own devices.

"Things were pretty quiet until five years ago today. Nick was thirteen years old when his parents went to a dinner party and left him with his babysitter, Jamie. About an hour later, her boyfriend, Steve, came over to study with her, and then, out of nowhere, Nick stabbed the boyfriend to death with a piece of broken glass. The courts determined he was criminally insane and sent him to Summer Hill. You didn't hear about it?"

Sheriff Coleman nodded slowly. "I remember seeing something about that on the news now," he replied, "but my wife—she uh...passed away about six years ago, so I took some time off the force to deal with that."

"Oh," Dr. Bonesteel said with a flash of surprise. He frowned. "I'm sorry to hear that."

"Thank you. So are you certain he's coming back for Ms. Strode?"

Dr. Bonesteel's eyes nearly popped out of their sockets. "Yes, I'm certain! I spent five years watching that wicked thing stare out the window with a blank expression and then"—his voice grew louder while his wild eyes stayed fixed on the sheriff—"just like that, tear into a wild tantrum, piercing his nails into his skin so hard that he drew blood and screaming he'd return to Manlius one day. For revenge, I can assure you!"

"Okay, okay," Sheriff Coleman said, raising his hands again. "I'm sorry, Doctor. I just...wanted to make sure. Typically, escaped criminals don't return to the scene of the crime. But I'm quickly realizing this isn't a typical case." He looked down at his notepad. "I'll have Sergeant Bill look up Ms. Strode. If she's still in town, we'll give her a call and ask her to come to the station—"

"No!" Dr. Bonesteel shouted. "That's not enough! Nick Roesch is an emotionless monster. He hurt a handful of people when he escaped the hospital and won't think twice about hurting or even killing anyone he comes across. Think of all the children who will be trick-or-treating tonight. We have to go to the girl's house so I can...I can..." He choked out a frustrated breath. "Look, I'm the only one who has a chance at stopping Nick. We have to get to Jamie Strode ASAP and end this madness!"

Sheriff Coleman flicked a worried glance at the doctor. *If this man's actually telling the truth...* "Okay," he said. "We can go to Ms. Strode's house, but I'll still ask Sergeant Bill to try to contact her or her parents. There's a possibility that they might have moved." He paused, almost sinking into the deluge of thoughts sweeping through his mind, then went on. "In the meantime, I've ordered a team of officers to patrol Manlius. I'll have my other officers keep a close eye on all the schools too. All right, Dr. Bonesteel?"

The doctor's stocky body relaxed a bit. "Yes, Sheriff. That seems appropriate. Thank you."

"No problem," Sheriff Coleman said, standing up with his notepad. "We'll get going in a few seconds, but first I need to make some phone calls. Would you like anything—a cup of coffee or some water—while you wait?"

Dr. Bonesteel stared at the white wall in front of him, his eyes glazed over like two crystal balls attempting to look into the future. "No, I just want to send the Devil back to hell."

"Oh, *okay*," Sheriff Coleman said, then headed for the door. He stopped, reaching for the knob, then turned back to Dr. Bonesteel, whose stony gaze was still fixed on the wall as though he were drawing up a game plan to defeat Satan. *Crap. This isn't a joke, is it?*

7

Nick, 8:15 a.m.

From the shadowy arch of the wooded path, Nick watched the curvy blond girl stand in front of the beat-up white car like a wooden doll. *Run her over. Run her over. Run her over,* he mentally repeated, then gave an uneasy jiggle of his concrete head. *No, you gotta go home. Find a better car.* He then turned and walked away from the school parking lot, following the street up a gentle hill until he reached a row of brick houses nestled in a mass of large maples, most of them stripped of their leaves.

The neighborhood was like a forgotten graveyard; the land, covered with a blanket of dead leaves, lay quietly underneath the houses, aligned like a chain of mossy tombstones, each a different size and shape. There were no signs of life in this damp bone yard, not the sound of a baby crying or the sight of a street sweeper or even a couple of cars parked along the long, crooked road. Nick continued to the end of the block, then turned the corner. He smiled instantly, spotting a beige Astro van parked in the driveway three doors down. It was the same model—excluding the color— that Dr. Bonesteel had taught him to drive. The only problem: where were the keys?

Sneering, he walked over and peered into the driver-side window. *No keys.* He looked up at the green ranch-style house behind the car and watched the front windows until a short redheaded woman walked across, talking on a cell phone. His small, hungry eyes started planning the hunt. The keys were in the house, he assumed, but how would he get them? Could he slip in and find them on a kitchen countertop, or would he have to kill the woman?

If he had to kill her, he didn't care. Like the old man that morning, the woman was an object to him, like an inflatable pool tube, and there was nothing in him—no right and left shoulder angels—to stop him from popping one more tube for the opportunity to get back home. He started for the house, then halted his emotionless march when he heard a car coming from the other end of the street. *Suck big lizard balls,* he screamed in his head as he turned and saw a police cruiser heading in his direction. He raced straight for the opposite street corner, hurried through the lifeless street of houses, and continued down the hill to the school parking lot.

He slithered through the rows of parked cars then stopped between a red Jeep and a white pickup truck. Kneeling behind the front wheels of the truck, he watched the top of the hill, waiting for the cop car to drive by. A couple of seconds later, the police cruiser appeared, but instead of passing by, it turned down the hill, entered the parking lot, and parked on the opposite side of the white truck.

With the sex grunt of a female crocodile, Nick swiveled his head, looking for an escape route. There was the school, a one-story brick building, the front made almost entirely of windows, and an empty football field on the right-hand side. Squeezing his oily hands into fists, he chewed on his bottom lip until his vampire-like teeth punctured the wet skin. *No home, no home,* a mental alarm frantically rang. He couldn't make a run for it without being seen, and he couldn't attack the cops either. There were at least two of them in the vehicle, and they probably both had guns.

He was completely fucked. Again.

8

Betsy, 8:20 a.m.

Breathing panicked breaths, Betsy hobbled down the school's main hallway, the cogs in her mind spinning rapidly as she tried to rationalize the wild woods chase/near roadkill incident she'd miraculously survived. *It's okay*, she told herself. *That guy was probably some crazy weirdo trying to scare you, and Kathleen—well, she was just being Kathleen.* She took a long breath in and exhaled. *Don't worry. You're safe. The guy's gone, and you won't have to see Kathleen until...third period.*

"Damn it," she muttered as she approached the senior wing. About ten feet away, David stood at his locker, loading his backpack with books. Betsy watched him for a moment, hoping he'd quickly finish with his backpack, but no, as usual, he was packing the compartments as if he were still a neurotic freshman with the nightmarish thought that he'd be a second late for class. *Just go over there*, she ordered herself after a couple seconds. *You need your math book and the bell's about to ring.* She paused, still watching him. *And it's not like you're mad at him. He didn't do anything wrong.* Her round face sank into saggy despair. *Yeah, but he's probably going to tell Kathleen and—*

"Hey, Betty Boo," David said in his womanly lisp. "How are you doing?"

Betsy looked down, pretending she wasn't standing there watching him like the Christian youth group—The God Squad—that visited Dullen every year to pray away "teenage indecency." "I'm g-g-g-good," she answered, looking up. "Sorry. I thought I dropped s-s-s-s-something." She ignored the confused glance from Jim Pastore, an onion-soup-smelling junior who once told her he had a "major boner for her," and headed to the locker next to David's. "How are you?"

"I'm all right," he said, then fashioned his lips into an overly excited smile. "Happy Halloween!"

Betsy feigned a smile back. "Yeah," she replied, opening her locker. "Happy Halloween."

"Are you doing anything to celebrate?"

Betsy shook her head as she stuffed her coat and book bag into her locker. "No. I'm um...kind of grounded."

David gasped. "What? Why?"

Betsy clenched her teeth, trying to maintain her mock smile. *Damn it. Why did you have to say you're grounded?* She looked at David for a moment, trying to concoct a lie. As the seconds ticked by, she worried she looked like someone who had a strange fetish for staring blankly. Finally she said, "Because of what happened at my birthday p-p-p-party."

David huffed loud enough for everyone in the hallway to hear. "Oh, my God. I am *sooo* sorry, Betsy. I had no idea Kathleen was going to bring booze to your party. Actually, as soon as I found out, I was going to tell you, but then I saw you with Luke"—he laughed nervously—"so I uh...didn't say anything because I didn't want to bother you two."

"It's okay," Betsy said, blushing, then quickly changed the topic. "So what are you d-d-d-doing tonight?"

"Oh, I don't know. I was going to ask Kathleen to come over and watch horror movies"—David rolled his eyes—"but who knows if she'll even be at school today."

Betsy pursed her lips. "She's here."

"She is?"

"Yeah, I saw her in the parking lot."

"Oh, good," David said with a smile that cut through his messy hair and connected at the back. "Now I know she's alive. Thanks!" There was an awkward break in the conversation, heightened by the excitement coming from their classmates, and then he laughed. "Heavens to *Betsy*. I don't know why I just thought of this, but do you remember when Kathleen and I came over to your house last year and watched *The Shining*?"

Betsy let out a quiet chuckle. "Yeah, I was pretty scared."

"I know! But then the movie kept freezing whenever someone was screaming, so Kathleen called it *The Sharting*!"

Betsy snorted. "Yeah, I..." A thought popped into her head. "Actually there was this man—" Feeling a tap on her shoulder, she turned around and saw Luke Gerasi standing in front of her. With his tan, well-built body and unblemished baby face, a stranger might've thought he dressed up as a supporting character from *High School Musical*. It wasn't a costume, though. It was the real him, a quasi-movie star wearing a pair of Lucky jeans and a yellow-and-black-striped polo.

"Hey, Bets." Out of habit, he licked his soft, pink lips. "How's it going?"

"Oh, hi. I'm g-g-g-good." She looked away, getting a glance of David, who'd hidden behind his locker door. She turned back to Luke. "How are you?"

"I'm all right. Excited about tonight. Can you come to Ashley's party?"

Betsy looked down and frowned. "No."

"Shit. Why not?"

She passed a low sigh through her dry lips, then looked up at Luke. "Because I'm g-g-g-g-grounded."

"What?" Luke's stunning amber eyes darkened. "Why?"

"My f-f-f-father won't let me g-g-g-go..." She stopped and took a slow breath in, then exhaled. "Because of what happened at my party."

"Really?"

"Yeah."

"Fuck," Luke said, slapping the locker next to Betsy's with the side of his hand. "So you can't go just because of what that fat bitch did?"

Betsy's eyes widened. "Oh—"

A high, musical laugh emitted from behind David's locker door. Luke glanced over, his usually smooth face contorted into an ugly mask of hate. "What are you laughing at, fag?"

No, Betsy thought, turning to David, her features scrunched with worry. He was silent as he gazed into the infinite blackness of his locker.

"Hey," Luke said, raising his erotic voice to a threatening rasp. "I asked you a question, *fag*."

"*Ohhhh*," someone nearby hummed. "There's going to be a fight." Betsy turned to Ed Woodfork and Kevin Wicks, who stood across from them, simpering like a pair of no-brain jackals, then turned back to David. He continued to stare at the black void, then closed his locker, grabbed his bagful of outdated midseventies textbooks, and walked away as fast as his scrawny legs could take him.

"Yeah, that's right," Luke shouted. "Walk away, fudge packer!" Laughing a brutish cackle, he turned to Betsy. "Can you believe that?"

A lump of thick vile churned in Betsy's stomach as she watched David race to his homeroom. *Oh, my God, you should've said something. Right?*

"Betsy?"

Feeling Luke's strong hand brush her arm, she snapped out of her concerned daze and turned to the breathtakingly handsome boy. "Oh, yeah..."

"So you really can't come to Ashley's party?"

Betsy slowly shook her head, still wondering whether she should've told Luke to stop being mean to David. "No."

"All right." Luke paused, then said, "What about Mike Barrett's party? At least his house isn't in the middle of the woods."

Betsy laughed lightly. "I c-c-c-can't. Sorry."

Luke shrugged. "It's okay. I guess I'll go to Mike's by myself." He gifted her with a hypnotizing all-white smile. "Maybe I can stop by your house before I go."

Her face flushing, Betsy looked down at the gray vinyl floor. "Oh, um, yeah. Maybe."

"Is your dad gonna be home?"

She looked up, shaking her head. "He won't be home until t-t-t-ten."

"Really?" Luke's eyes filled with excitement and mischief. "Then I should definitely come over."

Betsy looked down again and laughed, her cherry cheeks turning to rotten grapes. *Yeah, right. There's no way—*

Taking a step forward, Luke placed a firm hand on hers. "Maybe we can finish what we started at your party."

Betsy's entire suit of flesh ignited into a bon fire of white-hot embarrassment. *Shit*, she thought, panic filling her mind. Did anyone hear him? What would they say if they did? What should *she* say? And then, by good fortune, the morning bell rang. Betsy's head sprang up. "Sorry. I got to g-g-g-go to homeroom."

Grimacing, Luke relaxed his eyes. "Okay. Do you wanna sit together in study hall?"

Betsy nodded. "Sure. S-s-s-see you later." She grabbed her pre-calculus book then closed her locker. "Bye."

"Bye."

She flashed a friendly smile, then rushed to her homeroom faster than David had. The class—about a third full—looked like the backlot of a 1950s movie studio. She took in the cast of characters, both in and out of costume: Harley Quinn was laughing with Batman and a hot dog; Darth Vader was battling Zombie Jason in a lightsaber/machete showdown; and Jessica Viola, the school's token goth, wearing the black corset dress and knee-high boots she wore every dress-down day, was giving the evil eye to two varsity cheerleaders who had dressed up as Party City's watered-down versions of goth chicks.

Like Mr. Underwood, a frumpy, bald man who served double duty as her homeroom and Participation in Government teacher, Betsy ignored this chaotic pageant and went straight to her desk. While her so embarrassing she could die-interaction with Luke replayed in her head, her tongue went back and forth, furiously licking the top and bottom rows of her teeth—a nervous tic to fill in the gaps when she wasn't stuttering. *Nobody heard*, she told herself. *Everyone was busy talking to each other or whatever, so just forget it even happened.* Her teeth seized her tongue as her mouth flattened into a miserable flap. *I can't believe he was such an asshole to David. He's usually so sweet. He was really nice at my birthday party.*

Her body stiffened, the truth creeping up behind her and casting a shadow over her colorless skin. Yes, he had been kind and friendly and fun to talk to at her party and the two weeks since then, but the truth was, before that, he was just the popular lacrosse player Kathleen and David had ridiculed from time to time. Throughout their six years of junior and senior high school, they'd had a handful of classes together and not once did they say hi or even exchange an accidental bump. In fact, the only reason she had invited him to her party was because Kathleen had asked her.

So why, all of a sudden, was he being so sweet to her? Betsy stared out into space, pondering this until suspicion slithered from underneath her and took over truth's tight grasp. *Maybe he was being nice so he could—*

"Hey, girl!" Alice Harmon, a curvy Chinese-American girl, wearing a skintight white dress and a chunky black belt, jumped in front of Betsy. "Happy Halloween." She smiled, showing two rows of perfect teeth.

"Hey," Betsy said. She attempted a smile as truth and suspicion retreated to opposite corners of her mind. "Happy Hallow—"

Alice didn't waste any time, cutting off Betsy's last syllable with, "Do you like my costume?" She turned to the side, revealing a pink body pillow tapped along the length of her back.

A swipe of confusion broke Betsy's smile. "Uh, yeah. Are you a sleeping bag?"

"Get the *F* out, Girl Scout." A machine-gun-like laugh shot out of Alice's mouth. "I'm a piece of sushi!"

"Oh," Betsy replied through a soft laugh. "That's really cute."

"Thanks." Alice took a seat next to Betsy. "You're looking super cute yourself. Are you going on a date with your *new* man?"

Betsy's eyes bulged. "What?"

"C'mon," Alice said, waving a hand at Betsy. "You don't have to be so secretive. You've been spending an *awful* lot of time with Luke since your party. So are you guys official lovers or what?"

Betsy bowed her head, diverting the angry glint in her eyes. *For crying out loud, does the whole school know?* "No," she said, regaining her composure then looking back at Alice. "We're just f-f-f-friends."

"Really?"

"Yeah."

Alice pouted, pushing a long croak through her plump lips. "That's too bad. I think you guys would make such an *adorable* couple."

Betsy gave another light laugh. "No," she said, but her subconscious squealed in sweet virgin delight.

"You totally would. You'd have some tough competition, though. Especially from Kathleen." Alice fired off a second loud laugh.

Suddenly the truth leapt out of Betsy's mind and stabbed her in her chest. "What?"

"Kathleen has a crush on Luke."

"She does?"

"Yeah, she told me like a week before your party. That's why she asked you to invite him, right?"

Betsy was about to say "No," but stopped herself, remembering the day it had happened. They were walking to lunch when Kathleen had asked her. Thinking it was a joke, Betsy had laughed. Immediately Kathleen's face— saturated with a rare happiness—drained of color and emotion, leaving a static void staring back at Betsy. A silent tension wedged itself between the two girls and started to separate them until Betsy, worried Kathleen would gouge out her eyes, said she would invite Luke. *No*, she thought, waking herself out of the memory. *She can't like Luke. She's too...too... It's just too crazy.* "She was only joking."

Alice raised an eyebrow. "She was?"

"Yeah," Betsy quickly replied, feeling like she had to defend herself. "Her and D-d-d-david call him names all the time, and-and-and I don't think he would go out with s-s-s-s-someone like her." She stopped, catching a surprised look in Alice's eyes. "I mean, she wouldn't go out with him."

"You think?"

"Yeah, he's not really her type. She likes guys who are—" She stopped again, looking at Alice, who was staring back with two freakishly white eyes, patiently waiting for the next words. Betsy had them, hovering at the edge of her tongue, but she was afraid they'd ruin yet another friendship.

"Betsy Coleman," Ms. Cheryl, the school secretary, said over the loudspeaker, "you're needed in the main office. Betsy Coleman, you're needed in the main office."

A rush of relief washed over her. "Oh, s-s-s-sorry," Betsy said, launching herself out of the desk. "I gotta go."

"Okay, TTYL, girlfriend." Alice's cheeks puffed up into two olive-colored bulbs as she made another all-tooth smile.

"Yup." Betsy waved back, then raced out of the room, grateful to escape the hole she was digging herself into.

9

Kathleen, 8:30 a.m.

Kathleen stubbed out her cigarette on the pavement, walked into school, and continued to homeroom without a visit to her locker. *What a bunch of douche bags*, she mumbled as she stopped in the doorway of the classroom; there were only two other students who weren't dressed as a sexy morning-after pill or a suppressed homosexual superhero—Boguslaw, the mute exchange student from Slovenia, and David, who was sitting at his desk in the opposite corner with his head down.

I gotta tell him about Betsy, she thought with a wicked smile, then started for the other side of the room.

"You're late, Ms. Strife."

Kathleen stopped and turned to Mrs. Kierney, a short, raisin-skinned woman whom she had nicknamed "Math Troll." "Sorry. I had lady problems."

"You had lady problems last week," Mrs. Kierney said, suspicion in her glassy eyes.

Kathleen shrugged. "I'm a lady with a lot of problems."

Mrs. Kierney's withered face constricted into a cold warning. "I'm marking you down as tardy," she said. "One more time and you'll get detention."

"Okay," Kathleen replied, then turned and continued to the back of the room. Scowling, she whispered, "And I'll burn the bridge you live under, Math Troll." She took a seat next to David, the devilish cheer returning to her heavy cheeks, and said, "Hey, I almost killed Betsy a few minutes ago."

"Oh, good," David replied, fiddling with his long, bony fingers. "*Almost.*"

Kathleen raised one of her bushy eyebrows. "What's wrong with you?"

David inhaled the overdramatic breath of a nineteenth-century Bowery fairy. "Oh, nothing really. Luke called me a fag in front of the entire student body, *so*...there's that."

"What?" Kathleen asked, her eyes blazing. "When?"

"Like five minutes ago. When I was talking to Betsy in the hallway."

Kathleen's heated stare hardened into a villainous glower. "You were talking to Betsy?"

David scoffed. "Uh, *yeah?*"

"How nice," Kathleen said, turning toward the grimy windows on her left. "I'm glad you guys are best friends now."

"My God, Kathleen." David laughed briskly. "We're not best friends. I asked her what she was doing for Halloween. That's it, all right?"

"Mm-hmm," she said, then turned back to him. "So why did Luke call you a fag?"

"*Well,*" David groaned, "like I was saying, Betsy and I were talking at our lockers when Luke walked up and asked if she was going to Ashley's party."

Kathleen's searing gaze went still, like a rattlesnake watching its soon-to-be lizard dinner.

"But she said she couldn't because she's grounded for what happened at her birthday party," David went on, "so Luke got mad and called you a fat bitch. I laughed because I was like, 'Are you serious? I'm standing right here.' So he heard me laughing, and that's when he called me a fag, and, um, I think a fudge packer." He nodded. "Yeah, he called me a fudge packer too." He paused for another sarcastic laugh. "The worst part, though, is that Betsy just stood there like nothing was happening. Can you believe that?" He looked at Kathleen for a response.

Kathleen stared forward, venom bubbling in the yellow-tinted whites of her eyes. *That fucking cunt. She knew I liked him.*

David nudged her. "Kathleen? Hello?"

"How long have they been going out?"

"I don't know if they're actually going out, but they've been pretty close for the last two weeks." He chuckled then leaned in like a Southern belle with good gossip and whispered, "If you ask me, I think she might've given him a blow job at her party."

"How do you know that?"

"I saw them go into her room, and then, when her dad came down and yelled at you for drinking, I saw Luke playing with his jeans like he was trying to hide an erection... Oh! And by the way, I'm still waiting for you to tell me why you decided to drink nearly a whole pint of Jack Daniels at the party. *Hello?* You knew Betsy's dad was going to be there, didn't you?"

Kathleen scanned the childish innocence of his face, deciding if she should tell the truth, then turned away, scratching an itch on her left breast.

Nah. He'd probably just laugh at you. "Sorry," she said, turning back to him. "You should've called me when I was under house arrest."

David expelled a hard gasp. "Are you serious? I called you like a hundred times. What the hell were you doing for two whole weeks?"

Kathleen grinned. "Well, I got another cyst."

"Oh, no," David said, laughing. "The return of the cyst." His hazel eyes radiated a wicked excitement. "Hey! We should write a horror movie about that."

"Ha! We should. It'll be about a girl who gets a cyst on her ass that's possessed by a demon."

"Yes! And it'll kill people by shooting puss into their faces—"

"Betsy Coleman," the school secretary said coldly over the loudspeaker, "you're needed in the main office. Betsy Coleman, you're needed in the main office."

Kathleen snorted. "Speaking of evil puss coming out of my ass."

David tossed his head back and laughed. "Oh, my God. Does that mean your ass is possessed by a demon named Betsy?"

"Yup. And I need a lesbian nun to exorcize it. Do you think Sister Babcock can help me with that?"

"I don't know," David said, laughing again. "I've got religion first period, so I'll try to ask her. Hey, I know we've talked about this before, but seriously, don't you think it's weird that her last name's Babcock, but she's a lesbian? Well, *possible* lesbian."

"Yeah. Her name should be Sister Babcunt."

Just then, the bell for first-period rang. "All right," David said, standing up with a smile that struggled to hold his lanky cheeks. "On that note, I have to go to religion."

Kathleen let out a quick, baby raspberry fart. "And I have to go to the bathroom!" A riotous laugh followed her wide-eyed look of surprise.

"*Kathleen.*" David looked around, worried someone had heard her until he caught the overpowering smell of shit-flavored Cheetos. "Oh, gross." He grimaced, pressing his nose down with the back of his hand. "That shot out the bowels of hell."

Kathleen snickered. "It definitely came from bowels."

"Uh-huh." David pretended to gag, then started for the door. "See you in study hall. Or should I say, 'Smell you'?"

"Bet on smell."

"All right, I will. Bye." As David walked away, Kathleen stayed at her desk, studying him. *He's so cute, and he doesn't even know it,* she thought as he left the room, his tight butt cheeks swaying side to side like a British rock star. *If only he wasn't gay...*

"Oh my God," Kelly Oropallo (Dumb Bitch in Princess Costume 1) said to Christine Martin (Dumb Bitch in Princess Costume 2) the next row over. "It smells like *shit* in here!"

Kathleen's eyebrows whooped out an "Excuse me, bitch." She then turned to Kelly and dryly said, "Are you sure you ain't smelling Christine's twat?" As the two razor-thin girls stood still, their mouths hanging open as though they were preparing for tonight's festivities, Kathleen stood up and headed for the door with her trademark "Fuck you" confidence.

10

David, 8:40 a.m.

David sat down in religion class and opened his backpack on his desk. As he took out his textbook and notebook, his bag of Caramel Creams, which he'd forgotten to put in his locker, fell to the floor. *Geezy La Wheezy*, he mentally grumbled, bending down and reaching for the bag of candy. Suddenly a white sausage-like hand cut through his vision and grabbed the prized snacks. Looking up, David watched Mike Barrett (aka Satan, disguised as a two-hundred-pound linebacker) make a sadistic Ted Bundy-smile with his chunky lips then take the seat behind him.

David sighed. *This* is *religion class. Right, Jesus?* He turned to Mike. "Sorry. That's mine."

"So?" Mike said, ogling David's fragile body. "It's mine now."

For a second, David went cross-eyed, trying to find the logic in Mike's dumb-jock reasoning. "But my mom gave it to me."

Mike let out a deep, gorilla-like laugh. "Your *mommy* gave it to you?"

David's cheeks went bright red. *Did I say "mom" or "mommy"? Ugh, who cares? It's mine, dickweasel,* he told himself then said, "C'mon. Can you please give it back?"

Mike laughed again. "No."

David shrugged, attempting his best tough, straight guy-attitude. "Fine. I'll just tell the teacher." He raised his hand.

"Yes," Sister Babcock, a middle-aged woman with a sturdy build beneath her Hillary Clinton pantsuit, along with the quintessential lesbian mullet, said from the podium.

"Mike took my bag of candy."

A round of laughter erupted from the class. *Damn it*, he thought, blushing for the second time. Why were they laughing? Did they think he was funny? Or was it because he sounded...gay?

Sister Babcock grunted like a construction worker. "Mike," she said, "please give David his candy."

David smiled. *How do you like them—* Feeling the bag of candy hit him in the shoulder, he turned around. "I'm going to kick your ass after school, fag," Mike muttered with a prisoner-on-death row stare.

David's smile vanished. *All right,* he thought, taking the bag and turning back around. *Two fags, a fudge packer, and a death threat in less than an hour. This is going to be an awesome Halloween.*

"Okay, everyone," Sister Babcock announced. "Turn to page forty-two in your textbooks."

After David opened his book to page forty-two, Sister Babcock read the first paragraph aloud. "In today's times, it's typical for adolescents to be anxious..."

Does Mike seriously want to fight me? David wondered while Sister Babcock's Boston cadence droned on. *Or was it just an empty threat?* Thinking, he glanced out the window and let out a silent breath of frustration. *How the hell do straight guys work?*

"What the hell?" he mouthed as he spotted a whale of a man crouched behind a white truck in the parking lot. *Why's that large beast man sitting there? And why are the cops here?*

Spotting the police cruiser parked across from the hefty stranger, he was about to raise his hand but stopped himself. The quiet, queer kid didn't need any more attention, and besides, there had to be a reasonable explanation. Maybe the guy was homeless...and was hiding from the cops because they wanted to take him back to the shelter.

David pouted. *Ohhh, that poor homeless man. You should get him a cup of cocoa.*

11

Nick, 9:20 a.m.

"Fucking Christ on Grandma sucking his big sweaty balls," Nick whispered with a death glare at the red Jeep he'd been staring at for the last hour. *I want home. Now!* He gave a powerful kick to the Jeep's front tire then got up to his feet in one swift motion. As he crouched behind the hood of the truck he'd been leaning against, watching the two cops talk to each other in their cruiser, a low grumble escaped his lips. He needed an escape plan, or he'd drive himself to suicide.

After a minute of brainstorming, he came up with two options: he could take the chance and crawl until he got to the woods on the other end of the field, hoping he wouldn't be seen, or he could kill the two cops. If he slithered on his stomach, he could sneak over to the driver's side, smash the window, and pull out the first cop. He'd break his neck then move on to the second cop. He'd have to be fast, though. If the second cop pulled out his gun, he'd have to use the first cop as a shield while he made his way to the second cop and broke his neck.

Or maybe he could grab the first cop's gun and shoot the second cop.

Fuck, fuck, fuck, fuck, he thought, gazing at the two, dusty sacks of potatoes sitting in the cop car. *I hate this parking lot. I gotta go home.*

Nick looked around for something to smash the window, but there was nothing but a mess of cigarette butts and an empty bag of Funyuns. And then, hearing a second car in the distance, he looked up and dug his eagle-like talons into his sweaty palms as he spotted another cruiser driving down the hill. *No*, he warned as his emotionless eyes came back to life. *Don't turn—*

The cruiser turned into the parking lot then stopped next to the first cop car. The passenger-side window lowered, revealing two more pouches of potatoes—one with a thick black mustache and the other bald from head to chin. "Hey," the passenger of the second car said as the driver of the other car rolled down his window. "Looks like you guys are just fuckin' around."

The two cops in the first cruiser laughed. "Fuck off," one of them said.

"No," the passenger replied. "We wanna see if we can join you."

As the four cops laughed, Nick balled his veiny hands in rage and imagined running out of his hiding spot and bashing their fat heads into cop-brain putty. *Stupid retard*, he scolded himself, remaining by the side of the truck. *You can't take on four cops.* He then turned around and took his anger out on the rearview mirror of the Jeep, smashing it with his glazed ham of a hand.

"Hey, did you hear something?" one of the cops asked.

"Yeah, I think Rick's telling us he had a big breakfast. My God, what does your wife feed you?"

The four cops laughed again as Nick sank to the pavement, returning to his spot. He would have to keep waiting.

12

Sheriff Coleman, woe written on the deep lines across his forehead, stood at the front desk with the phone pressed against his ear. *Wow*, he thought, staring at a mug shot of Nick Roesch, a curly-haired Dennis the Menace. *How can he be evil? He looks like a scrawny kid.* A bitter laugh bounced off his skull. *He is, John. He was only thirteen when he killed—*he flipped through the police report in his hand—*Steven Brian Kanavy, age seventeen.* "God, I don't want to live on this planet anymore," he said under his breath.

"Good morning," an older woman said over the phone. "Bishop Dullen, main office."

"Good morning. This is John Coleman, Betsy Coleman's father. Could you please call Betsy to the office? I would like to speak with her."

"Of course, Sheriff Coleman. Is everything okay?"

"Yes, everything's fine. I just forgot to tell her something this morning."

"Okay. I'll page her right now."

"Thank you, ma'am."

"No problem. Just a moment."

While Sheriff Coleman was on hold, he said hello to two pink-cheeked officers coming off the graveyard shift, then looked again at the mug shot in his hand. "Did you get a hold of Jamie Strode?" he asked, turning toward Sergeant Bill.

"No. Dr. Bonesteel said he tried the parents' home number, but no one picked up. He didn't have any other numbers, so I've got Richard checking the databases. I also tried web resources like Facebook, but again, no luck."

Sheriff Coleman mumbled a miserable "All right," then added, "Keep trying, Bill. She's gotta be out there somewhere."

"Yes, Sheriff," Sergeant Bill said, nodding. He turned to the computer on his desk, a statue of Jesus holding two thumbs up on the tower.

As the sheriff turned to the mug shot once more, Betsy came on the line. "Hello?" she said with a quiet, irritated tone.

Sheriff Coleman frowned. *She's still angry, isn't she?* "It's your father, Betsy. I need you to do something."

"What?"

"Go straight to Grandma and Grandpa's house after school and stay with them until I get home, okay?" He waited for a response but received only the soft buzzing of the electricity passing through the two phones. "Betsy?"

"Why do I need to go to Grandma and Grandpa's?" she huffed.

"Because I asked you to," Sheriff Coleman said sharply. "I already called them, so they'll be expecting you. All right?"

Again, no response.

"For crying out loud," he said after a heavy breath. "I don't have time for this. Tell me you're going to your grandparents' after school."

Silence. Sheriff Coleman crumpled the mug shot of Nick Roesch and barked, "Damn it, Betsy. Answer me!"

"Fine. I'll go," Betsy said, on the shaky verge of tears. "I guess I won't have a life as long as I'm living with *you!*" Before Sheriff Coleman could open his mouth to reply, she slammed the phone down on the receiver.

As he held the phone to his ear, a wave of shock prickled his arms. *What on earth? She's never been like this before.*

"Sheriff?" Dr. Bonesteel said from behind him.

Startled, the sheriff let go of the phone, then immediately retrieved it with a clumsy hot-potato shuffle. "Yes?" he said, finding the troll-like doctor standing an arm's length away.

"Is everything all right?"

Sheriff Coleman took a quick breath, reeling himself back into the stern demeanor of county sheriff. "Everything's fine," he replied, returning the phone to the receiver. "Ready to go?"

Dr. Bonesteel nodded.

"My car's out front. It's the Ford Escape with sheriff on the side. I'll be there in a second."

"Okay," Dr. Bonesteel said, his right eye swelling to a big blue ball of crazy, then shuffled to the front door. As he left the building, Sheriff Coleman turned back to the front desk.

"I'm heading out to Manlius with Dr. Bonesteel," he told Sergeant Bill. "Radio me if you get in touch with Jamie or the patrols pick up anything suspicious, and tell Tom he's in charge of the fort. Got it?"

"Got it."

"Good." With the bent mug shot in his hand, he headed outside. After opening the passenger-side door for the doctor, he got in on the other side, dropping the picture onto the police laptop and reaching into his pocket for his keys.

"Oh, I almost forgot. I have a recent photo of Nick." Dr. Bonesteel reached into the left pocket of his trench coat. "No, that's not it." As he dug his hand into the other pocket, a low squeak ejected from his lips. "That's *definitely* not it. Where'd I put that dang picture? Ah, here it is!" he said, his hand diving into the inside flap of his coat. He pulled out a weathered Polaroid and handed it to the sheriff.

"Oh, wow," he said, dropping his somber gaze on the faded photo. Nick Roesch, who was about a hundred pounds heavier than the kid in the mug shot, was sitting on a hospital bed in a black hoodie and blue scrubs, staring at a paper plate with a piece of ice cream cake. Focusing on Nick's sunken black eyes centered in his pasty moon-pie face, Sheriff Coleman thought Dr. Bonesteel was right about his description—almost. Those dark eyes, gaping at the plate as though there were nothing on it, were soulless pits—not leading to hell but a real world of horrific ideas.

Bottom line: Nick Roesch wasn't a lanky teen anymore but a large lump of a man who had killed and could kill again. And he was on the loose.

"That was taken a year ago, on his seventeenth birthday," Dr. Bonesteel stated. "He's a bit bigger now."

Sheriff Coleman let out a quick murmur of curiosity as he held his gaze on the picture. *Yup*, he thought with a mental nod. *You were a hundred percent right for sending Betsy to Mom and Dad's house. If this lunatic is on his way, at least she'll be safe.* He placed the picture on top of the mug shot, then glanced at his watch. "We should be in Manlius in about forty-five minutes."

"Okay," Dr. Bonesteel replied, directing his fiery right eye—which had inflated to a beach ball that was unable to hold any more air—on the calm morning. "Remember, though: the Devil could destroy the world in forty-five minutes."

"Oh, um..." Sheriff Coleman's face slumped into a gob of bewilderment; he had no idea how to respond to the doctor's statement but opened his mouth out of habit and answered anyway. "Hope the roads are clear."

The droopy ends of Dr. Bonesteel's mouth responded with a twitch. *You're an idiot*, Sheriff Coleman reprimanded himself with a mental groan, then reached for the steering wheel and started the car.

13

As Betsy slammed the phone down, Ms. Cheryl's banana-shaped head popped up from her soiled copy of *Fifty Shades of Grey* hidden behind her appointment book. "Oh, my," she said, then squeezed her shriveled lips into a purplish sphincter. "Is everything all right, sweetie?"

"Yes," Betsy said, bowing her head so the old woman wouldn't see the tears collecting in the corner of her eyes. "Sorry. I gotta get back t-t-t-to class." She spun around and raced out of the office, heading for her first-period class. *No,* she commanded, stopping in front of the senior wing. *You can't go to class. Everyone's going to look at you.* Her wide shoulders sank into a miserable slouch as she scowled at the thought of walking into her pre-calculus class, seeing the "What's wrong with her" glances from her classmates, then hearing the badly masked snickers and whispers that would follow. *You need to go to the bathroom and cool down your face.*

With a low "Yes," Betsy turned around and started for the girls' bathroom in the opposite wing. As she picked up her urgent pace, a new line of thoughts occupied her mind: *Why do I have to go to Grandma and Grandpa's house? They're always mean to me, and it smells so disgusting, and it's full of creepy Jesus stuff.*

"I hate them! And I hate Daddy," she cried out, as she stormed into the bathroom and stopped at the first sink. She turned on the cold water, grabbed a handful of paper towels, and placed them under the water. Pressing the wet towels against her right cheek, she looked up at the bathroom mirror and exhaled a frazzled breath at her reflection. "I'm not going to their house," she said, then moved the towels to her left cheek. "I don't care—"

An elephant sneeze of a fart blasted from the stall behind Betsy, immediately followed by a hard, jester laugh.

Recognizing that hideous cackle, Betsy felt her heart catapult to her head, screaming, *Go!* She turned off the water, threw the paper towels into the trash, and hurried for the exit.

"Whoa, whoa, whoa," Kathleen said, stepping out of the stall. "I didn't know my shit smelled *that* bad."

Betsy's nose flinched in disgust as she continued to the door.

"I heard you gave Luke a blow job at your party," Kathleen said with exaggerated sweetness. "Tell me: is it hard giving a blow job with a stutter? Or does it make it easier?"

Betsy stopped, gritting her teeth until a small spark sprouted between them. *No,* the growing wrath in her tightened muscles declared; she'd been grounded, chased by a crazy man, almost run over by a car, and now Kathleen was harassing her in the school bathroom. She wasn't running away. Enough was enough!

•　　•　　•　　•　　•

Kathleen sat on the toilet, her husky arms crossed in resentment. *So...what? Betsy and Luke are a couple now?* She gave a short, sarcastic laugh. *No fucking way. Luke would never go out with someone like her. She's too—*

Just then the bathroom door swung open with a metallic boom, followed by the heavy footsteps of someone running to the sink. Caught by surprise, she skidded against the toilet seat, thrusting her cyst against the cold porcelain. A shot of pain rocketed through her large ass and along her spine. Biting down on her tongue, she waited for the pain to subside then leaned forward and peered through the space between the stall door. It was Betsy!

Well, goodness me. This is the perfect moment to punch that cunt in the face, and here I am taking a dump. Without warning, a thunderous fart shot out of her bowels. *Fuck it,* she thought with a mighty laugh.

After pulling up her pajama bottoms, Kathleen stood up and stepped out of the stall. "Whoa, whoa, whoa," she said, as Betsy barreled for the door, "I didn't know my shit smelled *that* bad."

Receiving no response, Kathleen rolled her eyes. *What the fuck do I have to do to get a reaction out of this little Christian bitch?* "I heard you gave Luke a blow job at your party," she improvised. "Tell me: is it hard giving a blow job with a stutter? Or does it make it easier?"

Betsy froze, her hand reaching for the door handle. *There we go*, Kathleen thought, her thick arms shaking like a demonic butter sculpture coming to life. *Now we can talk.*

"What d-d-d-did you s-s-s-say?" Betsy asked, narrowing her eyes as she turned around.

Kathleen smirked. She didn't mind repeating herself; it was a pretty good line for something she'd made up on the spot. She responded with a slow, mother-speaking-to-her-deaf-child articulation, "I said I heard you gave Luke a blow job at your party. So please, tell me, is it hard giving a blowjob with a stutter? Or easier?"

Betsy's taut eyes melted into two brown puddles, disbelief rising to the surface. "Why are you doing this?"

Kathleen kept smiling, knowing she was testing the limits of Daddy's little cocksucker. "What exactly am I doing?"

"You're m-m-m-making up nasty lies about me."

Kathleen took a step forward. "What nasty lies?"

"You j-j-j-just said I g-g-g-gave L-l-l-l-l-l-l—" Betsy huffed. "I didn't...give Luke...*a blow job*!"

Kathleen pressed her lips into an innocent heart shape and batted her eyelashes. "Well, I don't know if that's true," she said in a soft but provoking tone. "I was downstairs getting drunk. Remember?"

Betsy scoffed as tears glistened in her eyes. "Why are you being s-s-s-so mean?"

Kathleen let out a sharp laugh. "Are you retarded or something? You told your dad I was drinking at your party. Why? You could've came downstairs and told me to stop, *but no*, you didn't." She took another step toward Betsy. "You told him for some reason, and he went batshit crazy. He called the principal and got me suspended for two weeks and kicked off the basketball team, which means I probably won't be able to go to college because I can't get a sports scholarship." She took another slow, threatening step. "So why the *fuck* did you tell on me, huh? Was it because you're a psycho bitch who secretly hates me or because your dad caught you giving Luke a blow job, so you made me your scapegoat?" She stopped in front of Betsy with an "I want an answer right now" smirk. "Which one is it?"

Betsy's eyes bubbled in hesitation while her lips performed its klutzy dance of nerves. Suddenly she bowed her head and filled the musty bathroom with a loud, guilty sob.

Kathleen's eyes widened. *Oh, my God. It's true!* She laughed in shock. "I can't believe it! You gave Luke a blow job, you fucking slut!"

Betsy's face snapped up. "I didn't give him a blow job!"

Kathleen stretched her lips into a monstrous smile. She had turned the backstabbing bitch into a pathetic, blubbering mess, but was she done? Nope, she wanted to totally annihilate the hypocritical cunt. "Yes, you did," she said, taking a final step, so she was eye to eye with her former best friend. "You're a slut. I know it; all your friends know it; and so does your mother."

"*You fucking bitch*!" Betsy shouted, then raised her hand and slapped Kathleen across the face.

Kathleen stepped back, screaming in shock. She'd always considered herself a tough chick—she had played three years of high school basketball, where the toughest lesbians had smacked and elbowed and kicked every part of her body—but Betsy's slap was more painful than the time she accidentally had fallen on her plastic alligator in second grade, bursting her hymen.

Covering her face with her hands, she heard Betsy run out of the bathroom. "Yeah," she yelled, "you'd better fucking run!" Turning to the mirror, she found a red handprint the size of a silverback gorilla's across her right cheek. "Oh, fuck no!" she screamed. "I'm getting that little slut back!"

14

The Sheriff, 9:10 a.m.

After a silent forty-five-minute car ride to Manlius, Sheriff Coleman turned onto Jamie Strode's street and slowly drove up the wide unsoiled road, a pair of adult fern trees standing on the edge of each house's perfectly mowed yard. Sheriff Coleman laughed, imagining the town's bluebloods telling the Syracuse bumpkins who passed by, "Here's a glance at our beige castles. Now go back to your one-story shacks!"

Continuing up the flawless street to a small hill, he noticed the growing number of trees—more ferns, but cherries and maples as well. *Shit*, he thought, watching this vibrant barricade rise before him. *This must be for the really rich assholes.* He squinted, trying to read the addresses, but could barely make out the houses' front doors through the thick shrubbery. "I can't see anything," he said, turning to Dr. Bonesteel. "Do you know...which house it is?"

His voice faltered as he looked at Dr. Bonesteel staring out the window, both his eyes bugging out like Minnie Mouse finding Mickey in a three-way with Donald Duck and Goofy. *Good Lord. What the hell is wrong now?* "Dr. Bonesteel?"

The doctor whipped his head, directing his crazy cartoon eyes at the sheriff. "Yes?"

Sheriff Coleman pitched his bottom lip forward. "Uh, are you all right?"

"No," Dr. Bonesteel said, slowly shaking his head. "The Devil's here. I can feel it." He slowly turned back to the window.

Sheriff Coleman's lips retreated. He should've expected an answer like that. "*All right*," he said, turning back to the road. "I'm having a hard time reading the addresses. Do you know which house it is?"

"It's right there." Dr. Bonesteel pointed with his disjointed pointer finger.

The sheriff followed the doctor's crooked aim to a row of cherry trees casting their gnarled shadows onto the road. Then, passing the row of trees, he spotted the dark entrance of a stone driveway and stopped the car at the side of the road. Squinting through the narrow pathway, he made out the dim outline of two bow windows.

Shit, he thought; the other houses were hiding from the road, but this one was hiding from the world. He turned to Dr. Bonesteel, a kink of apprehension in his brow. "This is the house, Doctor?"

Dr. Bonesteel nodded.

"All right," Sheriff Coleman replied. "I'll pull up in a moment. I want to call into the station first."

"Mm-hmm," Dr. Bonesteel said with another cautious nod as he gazed down the driveway.

Sheriff Coleman picked up the hand microphone from the car radio. "Sergeant Bill, do you copy?"

"Yes," Sergeant Bill answered in his chirpy "Our God is an Awesome God" tone. "Loud and clear."

"Did you get a hold of Ms. Strode?"

"No, Sheriff. We found nothing in the databases, so I called the Manlius Police Department. They said they'd check their computers. I also suggested they cold-call the neighbors."

"Sounds good. What about Nick Roesch? Any leads yet?"

"No. No leads from any of our officers. No reports of suspicious activity in town either."

"All right. Keep the patrol going. The doctor and I are going to check out Ms. Strode's home."

"Yes, Sheriff. Ten-four."

"Over and out."

"Over and out." Sergeant Bill quickly added, "And thank you again for coming with me to the retreat. It's going to be a heck of a lot of fun."

"Yeah, you're welcome," Sheriff Coleman said automatically, then set the hand microphone down. He turned to Dr. Bonesteel, who was shooting the house an evil eye. "Are you ready?"

"Yes," Dr. Bonesteel said quietly.

"Okay." The sheriff backed up then pulled into the driveway. As they drove farther up, a dense forest of cherry and maple trees engulfing them in a patchwork of light and darkness, the house slowly revealed itself; first the two bow windows seen from the road appeared, followed by the hunter-green front door. Sheriff Coleman was impressed; the yellow colonial-style edifice was simple for its massive size (three floors, four picture windows arranged in three rows across its square shape), a perfect example of old money elegance, except for the horrific murder that had occurred inside.

Sheriff Coleman reached the end of the driveway. *Here it is. Hidden in these woods like a terrible secret.* He gave a cynical laugh in his head. *For crying out loud, John. You're starting to sound like the doctor. It's just a damn house.*

He parked perpendicular to the grandiose front door and shut off the engine. "I'm going to check if anyone's home, Doctor. Do you want to come with me or stay here?"

"I'd like to come with you."

"Okay, let's go." Sheriff Coleman stepped out of the car, headed to the house, and knocked on the door. "Onondaga Sheriff's Department. Open up." There was no answer. He tried a second time. Again, nothing. He then turned to Dr. Bonesteel, who stood next to him, easing his hand into his coat pocket as he eyed the house with a heated distrust. "Guess no one's home."

The doctor removed his hand like a child caught reaching for a jar of forbidden cookies. "I'm not so sure about that," he said, then turned away and started for the corner of the house.

"Hey, where are you going, Doctor?"

"I'm just going to…" His birdlike voice drifted off as he turned the corner and disappeared.

15

A shaking mess of tears, Betsy bolted out of the bathroom and headed directly to the only place she knew she could be alone: the chapel. Having served as a liturgy leader since freshman year, she raced to the center of the cross-shaped school, certain that none of the student body would be there on Halloween—unless the rumor was true that Jessica Viola was a practicing Satanist.

"Oh," she said, bursting through the double doors of the small, circular room then stopping at the edge of the red velvet carpet that covered the floor. "I'm s-s-s-sorry, S-s-s-sister Margaret. I didn't know you were in here."

Sister Margaret—a short woman, around sixty years old and wearing the black veil of her habit over her thin gray hair—turned to Betsy from the first pew. Two rows of wooden pews were positioned in front of a simple brown table with a white tablecloth draped over the top. "That's okay, dear," the nun said with a warm smile. "I wanted to say the Rosary before I left for the day...and to make sure Jessica Viola didn't sneak in. Is everything all right?"

"Yes," Betsy answered. She lowered her head and tucked her hair over her ears, trying to settle the typhoon of emotions rushing through her face.

A low "hmm" came from Sister Margaret. "Are you doing something for Father Dan?"

"Um, no," Betsy said, looking up. She couldn't lie to Sister Margaret. Especially not in front of God. "I wanted to uh...make a confession."

"Oh, okay." Sister Margaret stood up, revealing a white turtleneck and a long black shirt covering her ridiculously large breasts. She made a slow shuffle over to Betsy. "Where's your next class?"

"I have s-s-s-study hall," Betsy replied. "In the cafeteria."

"Okay," the nun said with another smile. "I'll tell Mrs. Cotton you'll be late. All right, sweetie?"

"Thank you, Sister Margaret." Betsy smiled back. *Someone's finally being nice.* Sister Margaret, however, had always been nice to her. As the director of religious services, she had worked with Betsy since freshman year, preparing for Friday masses and other holy events at the school. During that time, Betsy felt as though she had become her quasi-third grandma, who was a hundred times kinder than her real ones.

"You're quite welcome. I'll lock the door, so no one interrupts you. Take all the time you need." She placed a cold hand on Betsy's arm as she passed her then continued to the door. "Have a blessed day."

"You too," Betsy said, still smiling. She turned around and walked to the first pew. When she heard the door shut, she genuflected then moved into the pew and sat down on the maroon cushion that lined the hard wood. With a deep breath, she made the sign of the cross. "In the name of the Father, the Son, and the Holy Spirit. Amen. Oh, Lord, Jesus Christ, please f-f-f-forgive me. I have committed a horrible s-s-s-sin." She paused. "Well, it wasn't *that* bad. I slapped Kathleen, but I was mad. She kept saying I gave Luke a b-b-b-blow job."

At the word "blow," a creak echoed through the stuffy room. Immediately, Betsy looked up and locked eyes with the sad, skeletal Jesus that hung behind the table. *Oh, God*, she thought, realizing she'd just said "blow job" in front of Jesus. "I'm so s-s-s-sorry. I didn't mean to say 'blow'—that word." Studying the statue—his head thrown back and his eyes fixed to the top of his sockets as if he were rolling them in frustration—Betsy imagined he wasn't the right person to talk to about her boy drama.

She made the sign of the cross again. "Hi, Mom. I'm s-s-s-so sorry to bother you, b-b-b-but I need you. I had a fight with Kathleen, and I slapped her." She continued without a breath. "I didn't want to slap her, b-b-b-but she was s-s-s-saying awful things about how I...how I..." She heaved a sigh. She didn't want to say it again. Not in the chapel or to her mother.

"She said some really awful things about me," she went on. "I know she's mad, but I didn't mean to get her in trouble with Daddy. It just sort of p-p-p-popped out of my mouth. I didn't know he was g-g-g-going to come to my r-r-r-room and-and-and..."

Betsy let out a second, heavier sigh as she bowed her head and closed her eyes. She remained still for a moment, trying to relax her anxious tongue, then opened her eyes and said, "I'm sorry, but this is just too much for me. Everything seems like it's happening at once, just like when you died. First I watched while you got really sick, which was *horrible*; then Daddy started drinking, so I had to stay with Grandma and Grandpa"—she let out a short, bitter laugh, remembering the endless nights of split pea soup and *Wheel of*

Fortune as an angry Jesus statue stared down at her—"and then Kathleen became this totally different person. Like she secretly hates me b-b-b-because...everyone's nice to me and not her."

She took a quick breath, sweeping the paranoid crumbs into a back nook of her mind. "I don't know how we've stayed friends all this time. Maybe I put up with her because I was afraid of losing my best friend, but she's taken things too far. I really like Luke, but I feel like she's going to ruin everything. I mean, he's the first boy who's showed me this kind of attention." She paused, mulling over her next words. "Maybe he likes me because he wants...certain things. I don't know." She shrugged. "I'm not sure if I like him anymore. He was so mean to David this morning...and I didn't say anything."

She huffed in frustration, then asked, "So should I stop talking to Luke and apologize to Kathleen and David? Or should I forget about them and give Luke a second chance?" She gazed at her fingers, which were folded in prayer, waiting for that warm weight-off-the-shoulders feeling that would let her know everything was going to be all right. "Mom?"

Suddenly an odd vibration ran along her sides, as if a ghost were trying to tickle her. As she looked up, her enormous eyes questioned the room; she'd been in this chapel so many times—collecting liturgical items for Mass or sneaking in a quick prayer—that it felt like her own private hideaway, a hidden sanctuary to spend a quiet moment with God or her mother. At this moment, however, she felt as though she were sitting in another dimly lit, cornflake-smelling room in the school, all by herself.

"Please, Mom. I really need you. I've been pretty strong through everything that's happened, but now I don't know what to do." She went quiet, hoping for some sort of divine wisdom, but the room remained a dust-filled abyss. "Okay. I've uh...probably been asking for too much. Sorry." She made the sign of the cross again. "In the name of the Father, the Son, and the Holy Spirit. Amen."

Unfolding her hands, she looked down at the carpet and then, after a minute of pensive silence, she decided she had a choice: she could stay in the chapel and enjoy an entire period of quiet solitude, or she could go to study hall and be beaten to death by Kathleen.

The choice was simple. She stayed in the pew, vacantly eyeing the carpet, while her tongue slowly traced the ridge between the bottom row of her teeth and gums.

16

David, 9:15 a.m.

Standing at his locker, patting his jeans with sweaty palms, David scanned the hallway while a herd of girls dressed as slutty animals passed by. "Where the hell is she?" he said, watching the opposite end of the hall until the first bell rang for second-period. As the pack of trampy mice, cats, and a red-horned bison dispersed, he laughed, narrating the scene in a faux David Attenborough voice. "Migration season has started. Leaving their nesting areas, the flocks of wild Dullen prostitutes scamper in a multitude of directions in search of gum and attention. Will Kathleen, the fiercest of the female predators, make a rare appearance to feed on these young girls' vulnerable self-esteems? The answer is...no." He whacked his pants, leaving a pee-looking blotch below the crotch. "C'mon, Kathleen. We're going to be late for study hall."

He paused, checking the hallway for a third time, but again no Kathleen. "Jesus Herbert Christ. She'd better be making up with Betsy." He let out an airy laugh. *Yeah, right,* he thought, imagining it was more probable—no, definite—that Kathleen was bent over one of the bathroom sinks, trying to pop her cyst with a thumbtack.

"Hey, sexy," Alice said, walking up from behind and brushing her shoulder against David's. "What are you dressed up as? A hunky stripper man?" She fired a rapid fifteen-round bullet laugh as she squeezed his twig-like arm.

"Yeah." David smirked. "I'm serving hairy nerd fantasy. What's your costume?"

Alice turned to her side and stuck out her plump buttocks. "I'm a piece of sushi!" She flashed him a lascivious grin. "Don't you wanna take a bite of me?"

He rested his hand on his chin, striking a silly "I'm thinking about it" pose while trying to suppress the image of Alice's complicated womanhood.

I don't eat fish was riding the tip of his tongue, but instead "I don't know if I can handle such a big piece of sushi" came out.

With another M2 Browning laugh, Alice slapped David's arm. "Don't worry. You can save some for leftovers."

David responded with a timid chuckle. "Oh, Alice. You'll be my Moby Pussy."

"Oh, I certainly will." She batted her humongous fake eyelashes.

"Um, yeah." David's mouth warped into an uneasy smile as her eyes stayed on his. *What the tomfuckery is going on here?* Suddenly his eyes made a suicide jump off his cheeks as she licked the vampy lipstick covering her lips. "Okay. Sorry, Alice, but I have to get to study hall. I'll see you at lunch, all right?"

"Yup. See you there, babe." Alice's pearly whites made a cameo. Then she turned around and sashayed away.

David shook his head. *Does she actually think I'm straight or is this some sort of inside joke I'm not getting?*

He contemplated the question for a moment, then shrugged, stashing it away in his "Gay Questions That Are Too Hard to Answer" mental file. "All right, I can't take this shit anymore," he said, looking down the hallway to watch his future beard for the prom disappear down the art wing. "I'm waiting one more minute, and then I'm going to study hall."

Four minutes later, the second bell rang. "Fuck," David said, still standing at his locker. "I gotta go, or Mrs. Cotton's going to give me detention." He then headed to the cafeteria, a gigantic gray space with the drab, depressing lighting of a prison mess hall. After sneaking through the back entrance, he took a seat at the last table (one of the few empty ones of the two rows of long, beige tables). On the opposite side, Mrs. Cotton, a tall woman with frizzy blond hair, was staring at her cell phone, trying to find her ex-husband's profile on Tinder.

As soon as he sat down, a low chorus of moronic, apelike laughter erupted. *Shit, I'm sitting right next to the clan of jock monkeys, aren't I?* He took a glance over his shoulder. He was right; Mike and Luke and all the other hairy-knuckled cretins who made his life a miserable hell were sitting at the table across from him. Immediately he looked down, tightening his frail body in frightened-turtle mode. After the candy incident in religion class, there was no doubt they were planning some sort of idiotic prank.

He waited for their juvenile revenge, but a full two minutes passed without a study hall hate crime. *Huzzah*, he exclaimed, smiling inwardly. *A Halloween miracle.*

Just then something nicked his cheek—something round and lime green. He looked down at the table and found a Skittle. The stupid monkeys laughed as though they'd flung poo at the zookeeper's back.

All right, David told himself, his face putting up a hard shield. *It's just one tiny Skittle. Skittles can't hurt you.* "Ow." A lemon Skittle struck his nose. More laughter ensued.

"Okay," Mrs. Cotton said into a handheld microphone that played over the cafeteria's sound system. "Let's get attendance done as quickly as possible, so I can find my loser ex…" She pretended to cough in her hand. "I mean, so I can get to my work, and you can do yours…or talk or whatever. I don't really care, as long as you're not too loud. Aaron."

A strawberry Skittle hit David's neck. "Here."

"Abbott." Another Skittle. "Here."

"Bond."

As Mrs. Cotton called the last names of the students sitting sporadically throughout the cafeteria, David continued to be the silent dartboard in the monkeys' Skittle game. *Fuck my life*, he thought after the fifteenth name. *They definitely didn't get the fun-size bag.*

"Ecklund."

David raised his hand. "Here."

"I'm here! I'm queer! Get used to it!" Mike said with an exaggerated lisp, then threw a grape Skittle at David. His fellow primates went nuts, hooting and hollering.

David tossed a hopeful look at Mrs. Cotton, imagining she'd heard either the homophobic remark or cackling, but nope, her head remained fixed on the sheet of names she was reading off. Clenching his teeth, David took a deep breath. *It's okay*, he reassured himself. *Only about fifteen more names and*—he glanced at the wall clock—*thirty more minutes to go.* He sank into his chair. *You are so fucked.*

And then, as if the Halloween miracle he'd wished for had come true, Kathleen strutted into the cafeteria, mentioned something to Mrs. Cotton, then continued toward David's table. *Oh, God, thank you*, he silently prayed as he cracked a smile. *Thank you so much!*

"Great," Mike said. "Here comes Jabba the Hutt."

The apes laughed but went quiet as soon as she approached David's table. His smile grew, grateful that he was friends with the girl who had kneed Sean Butler (Monkey 14) in the nuts for asking her if she could reach her vagina.

"I'm going to fucking kill Betsy," Kathleen spat out as she sat down at the table.

David gave a dubious chuckle. "Um, okay." *I guess they didn't make up.*

"I'm serious. I'm going to run that *fucking* cunt over with my *fucking* car after school."

A squiggle of surprise and confusion snaked across David's forehead. "All righty then. Did something happen in the bathroom?" He lowered his voice. "Did you pop your cyst?"

"*No*," Kathleen responded. "Betsy slapped me with her gigantic man hand." She turned her face and pointed to a faint oval mark on her cheek.

David gasped. "Holy shit. Why?"

"I don't know. Maybe because I told her she's a slut and her mother thinks so too."

"*Kathleen*," David said with a scoff-snort combo. "Don't you think that was, *you know*, a little harsh?"

"Uh, no. She *is* a slut. She gave Luke a blow job at her party."

"How do you know that?"

"I figured it out from our fucking bathroom powwow. The bitch basically admitted her dad caught her giving Luke a blow job, so she told him I was drinking, and that's how I got in trouble."

David squinted in doubt. "That doesn't make sense. If Betsy's dad caught her giving Luke a blow job, don't you think he would've been more occupied with that than with you drinking?" His lips pursed with banshee-girl attitude. "And you still haven't told me *why* you were drinking, but that's neither here nor there. We're just soul mates and all."

Kathleen was silent for a moment, her heavy eyes contemplating his statement (or the speed of a car needed to crush a human skull, he couldn't tell), then thrummed the table with her right hand. "I can't tell you right now." She turned toward the table of apes, huddled together as if they were planning their next act of misplaced aggression, then turned back to David. "Maybe later, all right?"

He grinned. "Hey, I like later. Later's all right."

"Uh-huh," Kathleen said. "I'm not sure about Betsy and Luke." She shook her head, signaling a hint of doubt. "Maybe she was in the middle of giving him a blow job, but then she chickened out, and then—I don't know— her dad came into the room, and that's when she sold me out."

"Hmm. I guess that makes more sense." David paused, thinking how he could use the moment to make peace between the two frenemies. "Well, now you know what happened, so you can just let it go." He started singing: "*Let it—*"

"No," Kathleen said curtly. "Fuck that. And fuck Betsy. First, she betrayed me and then she freakin' slapped me in the face. I'm going to kill that slut."

David slouched in his chair. *My, my, my. Troye Sivan, just take me away.* "All right, Kathleen. I know you're mad, but can't you think of something a little subtler than murdering her? I don't want you to go to jail. At least not until I graduate."

Kathleen raised one thick eyebrow in a silent no.

"Please," David said in a baby voice. "*Pweety pwease.*"

Kathleen laughed, rolling her eyes. "Jesus, you're gay." She ejected a low grunt from her nose. "Fine, I won't steamroll the bitch with my car. Do you have any better ideas?"

"*Oh*, I don't know. Let me think about it..." David tapped his front teeth, trying to think of an idea that would delay Kathleen's inevitable future as a lifelong prisoner. "Hey, wait a minute. Where *is* Betsy?"

Kathleen shrugged. "She ran off like a little bitch after she slapped me. Hey, were you eating Skittles?" She picked up the lime green Skittle from the table and popped it into her mouth.

David gagged. "Ill, Kat. Don't eat those. Those assholes over there were throwing them at me."

"What!" Kathleen exclaimed, curling her lip. "Who the fuck eats Skittles anyway? They should've thrown some Starbursts. I fucking love Starbursts." She ate another Skittle.

David bowed his head in frustration. *No, don't worry about me*, he complained to himself then said, "Please stop. God only knows what they did to them."

"What would they have done to them?"

"I don't know. Shove them up their asses?"

"Mm, kinky," Kathleen said, then wiggled her tongue over the strawberry Skittle in her fingers.

David let out a queasy laugh. "Okay, well, that's...not sanitary, so I'm just going to keep my head down while I think of a better plan. All right?"

"Yup," Kathleen said, popping the red Skittle into her mouth.

"Mm-hmm," David said with a mocking smile, while his eyes drifted over the words carved into the table: "I pray to Satan because he listens," along with the WWE logo. *Oh, my God. People still watch wrestling?* A moment later, he looked up to see Kathleen finishing the last of the rogue

Skittles. "I'm really sorry, but I'm fresh out of revenge plans. Do you wanna come over after school and talk about it there? We can watch the horror movie my mom just bought me."

"What is it?"

"I don't know. I didn't get a chance to look at it, but I'm sure Eli Roth produced it."

"Eh," Kathleen said. "Do you have anything else?"

"Of course. I have a whole crate of DVDs we still haven't seen. *Re-Animator*, *Psycho Head*, *Chopping Mall*—"

"What the fuck is *Chopping Mall*?"

"Are you serious?" David huffed. "You've never heard of *Chopping Mall*? It's a classic."

"What's it about?"

"Isn't it obvious? A bunch of teenagers get chopped up in a mall. By a killer robot."

Kathleen's nostrils flared as if she'd caught a whiff of the creamed beef being defrosted for lunch. "Sounds like the dumbest fucking thing ever."

"*What*? It's a killer mall robot in the eighties. That's like my dream job."

Kathleen stared at him without blinking. "What other movies do you have?"

"You're no fun. Um, let's see…"

They continued to plan their potential horror movie marathon, listing the movies they wanted to see (and which ones they'd save for their upcoming religious retreat) until the bell for third-period rang.

"All right, so we'll watch *Motel Hell* and *The Blob* tonight," David said, "and save *Nekromantik* for the retreat?"

"Sure," Kathleen said, standing up.

"Fantastic. See you at lunch."

"All right, but you'd better come up with a plan for Betsy, or I'm running her over."

"Don't worry. I'll make sure I come up with the revenge—"

Suddenly Mike ran up to David and poured a large bag of Skittles over his face. "Enjoy the rainbow, fag," he said, as the candy rained down with a flash hailstorm sound, then raced out of the cafeteria. As the apes went wild, David sat frozen in his chair, his lap filled with a colorful arrangement of humiliation.

"Plot," he finished, staring past Kathleen into the imagined realm where his self-worth hid from the cruelty of the real world.

•   •   •   •   •

Grimacing, Kathleen looked down at David's expression of horror, his hazel eyes casting the heartbreak wreaking havoc on his gentle soul. *How could anyone do something so wretched to such a wonderful human being?* she asked herself, then realized the answer was simple. "You vile, little shits," she said, as Mike's asshole friends walked past her. "Don't any of you have any goddamn decency?"

"Shut the fuck up, fat bitch," Luke said, following the others out of the cafeteria.

A dark crack ran down Kathleen's smooth forehead, making it look like a dessert plate split by a Californian tremor. *What the fuck did he say to me?* "I'm going to fucking—"

"*Hello?*" Mrs. Cotton called out. "The period's over."

Kathleen turned to her, her pale face flushed with questions. *Are you a fucking mute? Didn't you see my best friend get assaulted or do you not give a shit about anything other than—* She sighed instantly, remembering the disheveled teacher was more concerned with catfishing her estranged husband on Tinder. "Yeah, we're going," she said, then underneath her breath added, "Detention Nazi." She turned to David. "C'mon, we gotta go, or Mrs. Cotton will come over here and write us up for the Skittles."

"I don't care," David said, his eyes glazed over with a dark sheen.

"Yes, you do." Kathleen grabbed hold of his arm. "You want a perfect record so you can go to Fordham and leave me forever. Now let's go."

David shook his head. "No, I don't."

"C'mon, you two," Mrs. Cotton shouted. "I need to get to my next class."

No, you need to get over your divorce, she thought, then turned to Mrs. Cotton, who stood by the entrance. "David hurt his leg in gym this morning, so he needs a couple minutes to stand up."

Mrs. Cotton blew out a frustrated breath. "All right, whatever," she said, as she left the cafeteria. "I don't have the…"

Kathleen chortled. "I hope your ex-husband gives you crabs again." She turned back to David. "C'mon, you need to get to class."

This time, David said nothing.

"All right, fine." Kathleen crossed her arms. "If you get up, I'll tell you why I was drinking at Betsy's party."

David's blank expression heated into a gaze of excitement. "You will?"

"Yes."

"Promise?"

Kathleen stomped her right foot. "Oh, my God, *yes.*"

"All right." David sprang up from his chair.

"Shit," Kathleen said with a small laugh. "I didn't think that was going to work."

David shot her a thin, sarcastic smile. "Well, it did. So you gotta tell me."

"Goddamn it." Kathleen started for the door. As David raced to her side, she said, "All right, but you need to promise me you won't laugh. Or get all gay and start gasping and shit."

Entering the hallway, David let out a cross "Huh?" then added, "I don't get all gay!" Kathleen turned to him with a tight lip and an arched eyebrow. "Okay," he responded with a groan. "Sometimes I can get a little gay. Can you just tell me why you were drinking that night?"

"Yeah, fine," Kathleen said, then took a deep breath. "So um...I had this tiny crush on Luke—"

Immediately, David stopped and expelled a "They're making a sequel to *The Devil Wears Prada*" gasp. "What?"

Kathleen turned around, bringing her hand to her head and massaging a fake headache. "*See?* This is exactly what I meant about you getting all gay."

David remained still, paralyzed by the news he'd just received. "Well, yeah, you just said you have a crush on *Luke!*"

"Hey!" Kathleen swiped at his arm. "Turn down the gay before one of those little rats hears you." She gave a quick look at the peevish, rodent-looking seventh and eighth graders streaking through the hallway. "And I said I *had* a crush on Luke. You know I've got the worst taste in men. I've had two scumbag boyfriends in the last three years, and both of them cheated on me. Now c'mon."

Glaring, David placed his hands on his hips and tilted his head. "Mm-hmm," he said, then started walking again. "Luke isn't your neighbor who sells cocaine to children or"—his mouth flattened into a line of pure disgust—"that guy who worked at T-Mobile. He's pure evil."

"I didn't know that at the time," Kathleen said as they merged into the stream of babbling lower classmen. As she plowed through the crowd, the red-cheeked little students jumped out of her way as if the legend of the Freshmen-Eating Senior were true. "One day I was waiting for basketball practice to start and he'd just finished, so we started talking and um"—she exhaled a small breath—"I don't know. He was actually nice to me. Good-looking guys like Luke aren't usually nice to me, so I developed a little crush on him."

"Um, okay. So how's your little crush connected to drinking at Betsy's party?"

"Well," Kathleen went on, "I told him he should come to the party, but he said he didn't want to because he knew there wouldn't be any alcohol since Betsy's father is Sheriff Hitler. So I told him I'd bring a bottle of Jack Daniels and he said he'd go. Then I asked Betsy if he could come. She said no, but then I told her I liked him and she said okay."

"Ah, I get it now," David said as they headed down the freshman wing. "So you got mad when you saw Betsy and Luke at the party together and decided to drink a whole pint of Jack?"

"No. I was so nervous that I drank about a third of the bottle before I got to Betsy's house. I don't even remember seeing them together."

David stopped again, puffing out another sigh. "Wait! So you didn't even *know* they were together at the party until I told you this morning?"

Kathleen stopped, her eyes rolling into the back of her head to say, "Goddamn it" to her brain. "No, David. I didn't."

"Oh, well, that's just fantastic. I'm thrilled I was the catalyst in this petty drama."

Kathleen laughed. "You weren't the catalyst, you attention queen. Betsy started this bullshit when she ratted me out to her dad, and that's why we need to get the bitch back. Along with Luke and all those other assholes who treat you like shit."

David snorted. "Yeah, Kathleen," he said, shaking his fist in the air. "Let's get 'em all back!"

Kathleen bowed her head into a cold gaze. "I'm serious."

The second bell rang for third period. "Yeah, I know," David said with an uneasy nod. "All right, I have to get to physics before this turns into a reboot of *Glee*."

"Uh-huh," Kathleen said through a quick giggle. "Are you going to be all right?"

"Little, old me? Oh, I'll be fine. Because..." He started singing the chorus of Destiny's Child's "Survivor." After the last line, he flashed a toothy grin then turned and headed for his next class. "Peace!"

Kathleen laughed again. *He is so fucking gay.* She paused, remaining still while a pair of sophomores dressed as *The Dark Knight* Joker and *Suicide Squad* Joker scampered around her. *And smart and funny and extremely talented. He definitely deserves better than this shit town.* She looked down, shuffling her feet as she dove deeper into her thoughts. It was inevitable;

David would graduate and start his exciting New York City gay adventures, and she'd stay in Syracuse, settling into a long career as an SSI couch whore.

She stared at the path of dirt footprints trailing down the tiled floor, and then, knowing very well what was about to happen, she bit her bottom lip and discharged a long, noiseless fart. "Fuck," she said to a short, bucktooth freshman boy speed walking past her. "My ass is a busy beaver today."

The boy stopped and turned to her. After his hooded eyes screamed, *It's the Freshman Eater!* he ran off to share his terrifying encounter with the infamous beast.

17

The third-period bell rustled the stale calm of the chapel. Betsy's eyes wrenched themselves from the carpet, and she looked up, her tongue wedged in the space between her upper lip and teeth. "All right, I guess it's time to get killed by Kathleen," she said under her breath.

Remaining in the pew, she let out a hard "Ha," imagining the statement wasn't too far from the truth, then murmured, "Maybe you could just stay here the rest of the day." She laughed again. "Yeah, right. Sister Babcock would call the main office, and then Ms. Cheryl would announce your name over the loudspeaker, and you don't need any more attention." She shook her head. "No. Just go to religion and make sure you avoid Kathleen at all costs, all right?"

She gave a discouraged nod of agreement. "Yup," she said, then moved out of the pew, genuflected toward the "I'm so over this crucifixion" Jesus, and left the chapel. As soon as she stepped into the hallway, she stopped, seeing Luke heading in her direction with a big dimpled grin centered on his olive-skinned cheeks.

"Hey," he said, stopping in front of her.

"Oh, hey," she said, then returned his grin with a faint smile.

"I was looking for you in study hall. Where were you?"

"Oh, um..." Betsy looked down. "I was in the chapel."

"Why?"

Focused on the scuff marks on her light pink slip-ons, she wondered whether she should tell him the truth. Would he think it was unladylike that she had slapped Kathleen or would it be a turn-on? *Straight men are basically gay because they only watch lesbian porn,* she remembered David saying at lunch last year. "I uh...had a f-f-f-fight with K-k-k-kathleen."

Surprise scrambled Luke's beautifully trimmed features. "Really? Were you guys screaming at each other or was it like a *fight* fight?"

"Uh..." Betsy's mouth turned down in unease. *Is he turned on or not?* she wondered, then glanced at his crotch for any signs of a boner. Nope—his jeans were too baggy. "No, we were just arguing, but then she said some really mean things, so I went to the chapel to, you know, be alone for a little bit."

Luke frowned. "Oh, man, I'm really sorry that happened." He placed a strong hand on Betsy's arm. "You don't need to worry about Kathleen. I shot her down hard in study hall."

"You did?"

"Yeah. She was about to open that big, fat mouth of hers, but I told her to shut the fuck up."

Betsy gave half a smile. *Good. She needs to shut up for—*

Luke let out a deep, sinister laugh. "You should've seen what Mike did to that faggot friend of hers. He poured..."

Betsy's smile dissolved into a sludge of disappointment. *Not again.* Looking on with a glassy stare, she wanted to tell him the F word wasn't funny, but before she had time to think of what to say, he was already on the next topic. "So am I still coming over to your house after school?"

Betsy's faced reddened. "Oh, uh,...no. I'm really sorry, but my f-f-f-father called and s-s-s-said I have to go to my grandparents' house."

"Why?"

Betsy shrugged. "I don't know."

"Shit. That sucks."

"Yeah, I know."

An awkward moment of silence passed between the two seniors, supported by the giddy roar of a dozen overexcited underclassmen until Luke broke it with a boyish chuckle. "Maybe you can sneak out for a couple of hours and come with me to Mike's party."

Betsy gave a quick laugh, a hint of "Are you crazy?" in the delivery. "I'm not sure I can do that."

"Yes, you can," Luke said, slinging an arm around her shoulder. "It'll be easy."

Betsy's shoulder clamped up, worried that the small exchange of affection would fuel a perverted collection of rumors among the group of younger students. "I don't know. My f-f-f—" From the corner of her eye, she spotted Kathleen and David walking out of the cafeteria. *Shit,* she thought, envisioning her two-hundred-pound ex-best friend charging her like an angry bull and pummeling her head with her bulky, basketball arms—

exactly like she had when she found out her first boyfriend, Zhong, was texting another girl. "Can we talk about it at lunch?"

Luke's dimples twitched. "Sure."

"Thanks." Betsy broke away from Luke's arm then turned left, headed for the senior's wing. "Sorry, but I forgot my book for Religion."

"Oh, okay," Luke said, following her. "Can I walk with you?"

"Yeah, sure." Betsy bowed her head in an attempt to create a magical shield of invisibility. She then sped off with Luke, escaping Kathleen's sight in the nick of time.

18

"Dr. Bonesteel!" Sheriff Coleman cried out, turning the corner of the massive yellow house. "You can't just—"

"Sh!" the doctor whispered as he knelt underneath a wide double-hung window, a narrow stone path positioned between him and the edge of a plot of cherry trees. "I think I saw something move inside the house."

Sheriff Coleman transformed from behind-the-desk sheriff to cop in action, bending down into a squat, his hand on the Glock 22 in his holster. "Okay, stay still and keep quiet," he said in a soft but commanding tone. "I'm going to slowly walk over to the window and look inside. I repeat: stay still and keep quiet. Nod if you understand."

Dr. Bonesteel nodded, his blue eyes igniting underneath his wispy eyebrows. Sheriff Coleman nodded back, then slinked toward the window in slow, carefully placed steps. He stopped at the side of the window. Then, his fingertips flirting with the butt of his gun, he inched his field of vision toward the spotless glass reflecting the grim woods across from it. His bright-green eyes contracted into a dark pair of binoculars. Covering the window was a white lace curtain, concealing the lightless contents inside, but with a hard squint, he could make out the basic outline of a large room— a brown bookcase covered the entire right wall; a short wooden cabinet furnished the left; and a collection of love couches and armchairs filled in the center, arranged in a circle as though it were time for an English tea party.

The sheriff studied the room, waiting for the flash of movement Dr. Bonesteel had mentioned but detected nothing until—*bam!*—a small, leopard-like cat rammed into the window, discharged an ugly hiss, then raced away, as though its sole purpose was to scare a middle-aged sheriff and a semi-insane psychiatrist. "Jesus Christ," Sheriff Coleman shouted, shuffling away from the house. At the same time, Dr. Bonesteel fell onto the stony path, letting out a sharp "Ah!"

After shaking off the surprise cat attack, Sheriff Coleman turned and chuckled nervously. "Geez," he said, offering his hand. "That was quite a scare."

"I'd say." Dr. Bonesteel took the sheriff's hand and returned to his feet with a bashful smile. "But it's a good sign that Nick isn't here."

"Why's that?"

"I imagined he would've killed the cat already. I gave him a black-and-white kitten for his fourteenth birthday." Dr. Bonesteel turned to the window, cutting the cool air with his laser-beam gaze. "I was either too naïve or too stupid to know what the monster was capable of, but after ten minutes with the animal, Nick snapped off its head, then dug his hand into the back of its skull and tried to stab one of the male orderlies with its teeth."

Sheriff Coleman's top lip flittered.

"Yeah," Dr. Bonesteel said. "I got a hundred more bedtime stories like that to keep you awake at night." His pensive, saucer-like stare stayed on the sheriff for a moment then relaxed into a look that was about ten percent less invasive. "So what's the next step? Should we break one of these windows and search the house?"

"No. We can't do that."

"Why not? Nick could be in there with a knife to Jamie's throat."

Sheriff Coleman released a discouraged breath. "Yes, I know, but we can't search the house without a warrant from the judge, or my department could be sued, and I could lose my job."

The fire returned to Dr. Bonesteel's eyes. "What about exigent circumstances? Nick stabbed a man then broke out of a psychiatric hospital for crying out loud!"

Sheriff Coleman raised a palm to calm down the doctor. "Again, I know, but the state is very strict about property searches. I'd need more probable cause. Like a report that Jamie Strode is missing. Not just an account that Nick escaped the hospital. For all we know, he could be in another state." His voice rose when he saw the flames in doctor's eyes burst as if someone had poured gasoline onto them. "If we saw something like a broken window or an open door, then yes, we could search the house."

"Well, we haven't searched the other sides—"

"Hold on," Sheriff Coleman said, grabbing the sleeve of the doctor's coat as he took a step toward the back of the house. "Let me go first. If he's hiding out in the woods, then I'll be able to protect us if anything happens. Unless he's invincible to bullets." The muscles in his slim cheeks prepared to tighten into a subtle smile but remained loose when he saw Dr. Bonesteel's wide-eyed glare. His eyes were like two oval windows, granting access to the thought possessing his mind: *You can't kill the Devil with bullets.*

The sheriff didn't wait for a response, reverting to his cop-in-action role as he tiptoed to the back of the house. Stopping at the corner, he unbuttoned his holster and grasped the handle of his gun with one hand then signaled the doctor to stop with the other. For a moment he listened to the gentle autumn air, trying to catch any hint of an intruder, but hearing nothing but the occasional bird chirps, he took a fast in-and-out peek around the corner. The peek revealed no sign of homicidal maniacs seeking babysitter revenge, so he pivoted quickly with his gun aimed in front of him.

A survey of the backyard—a long green square, lined with yellow shrubs around the perimeter of the neighboring woods—confirmed that no maniacs were standing out in the open in broad daylight. "Wait there," Sheriff Coleman ordered, then moved forward for a closer inspection. Aligned with nine fixed windows and one large peppermint-green backdoor, the back of the house was the perfect model for a two-page spread in *Better Homes and Gardens of Child Killers.* "Okay. No signs of forced entry."

They continued to the third side of the house. Again, everything was in pristine condition—no broken windows, busted doors, or demon cats. "All right," Sheriff Coleman said, walking around a set of plastic trash cans and continuing to the front of the house, "I guess we'll wait here. If he isn't still on the road, he's probably—"

Boom! Hearing a sudden, rubber-against-ground smack behind him, he spun around and drew his gun, imagining Nick had leapt out of the woods and tackled Dr. Bonesteel to the ground. He was half right. "Sorry," the doctor said, bent over one of the trash cans while the other rolled back and forth like a Tilt-a-Whirl car. "I was looking at the woods and ran into these darn bins." He mumbled something underneath his breath (Sheriff Coleman made out the words "tools" and "Devil"), picking up the trash cans as he stood up. "I'm okay. I'm a bit of a klutz. What were you saying?"

Gawking at the red-faced old man, Sheriff Coleman answered in a ruminating tone. "I was saying if he isn't still traveling, then he's probably hiding out somewhere, waiting until it gets dark so he can make his move." His stout body sagged into a flimsy stack of confidence. How was this clumsy fool supposed to go up against the so-called Devil of Manlius when he could barely survive a couple of trash cans? "Yeah. You know what? I'm going to order a town curfew."

He marched directly to his car. Once there, he opened the driver-side door and reached for the hand microphone. "Sergeant Bill, do you copy?"

"Yes, Sheriff," Sergeant Bill said in his spunky voice. "Loud and clear."

Again he ignored Bill's ill-suited tone and went straight to business. "I'm ordering a countywide curfew. No one's allowed out of their houses after ten o'clock. Get a team from Information and Publicity together to call all the TV stations and schools to get the word out. Got that?"

"Yes, Sheriff. What should I tell them to say?"

Sheriff Coleman's lips crumpled into a tight ring. *Good question*, he thought. The wrong words could turn a mild night of childish pranks and street fights into *The Purge*. Or fool everyone into a false sense of security. "Tell 'em...tell 'em there's a man named Nick Roesch who escaped from an upstate psychiatric hospital this morning. You should add a physical description of Nick, but please, for the love of God, don't mention the whole gates-of-hell eyes, okay?"

Sergeant Bill answered with a light laugh. "Understood. Anything else?"

"Let me think." Sheriff Coleman paused for a moment. "Yeah, you can also say he's considered extremely dangerous, and therefore we ask all citizens of Onondaga County to obey a ten-o'-clock curfew." Another pause. "The sheriff's department is working diligently to apprehend the patient, but uh...all citizens should follow basic safety precautions: children should be accompanied by a guardian; all doors and windows should be locked; no one should open doors to unsolicited visitors, and anyone with information should call 911." He summarized the statement in his head then mentally nodded. It was good for the time being. "Did you get that?"

"Yes, John."

"Good. Any word on Jamie Strode's whereabouts?"

"I got in touch with one of the neighbors, who gave me the number of a family friend. I called, but they weren't there, so I left a message. I'll update you as soon as I get something important."

"Okay. Ten-four."

"Over and out. And praise—"

Before Sergeant Bill could finish, Sheriff Coleman dropped the microphone onto his seat and shut the door. He turned the noiseless house, his face taut from holding in a long mental groan. *Where the hell is this girl?*

"The curfew's a good idea," Dr. Bonesteel said by his side. "It'll keep the kids off the streets."

"Yeah." Sheriff Coleman kept his eyes on the house. "It'll be good for the younger ones. But the teenagers"—he let out his mental groan as a slow sigh—"they won't listen. Two weeks ago my daughter had her birthday party at my house. I told her I didn't want to see any alcohol there, but sure enough, someone showed up with it."

A low "tsk, tsk, tsk" snaked its way out of Dr. Bonesteel's lips. "Despicable."

"Yeah, well, she's getting to that age." Sheriff Coleman paused, considering the thought. Betsy wasn't a little girl anymore. She was eighteen, a woman in the eyes of the law. He cleared his throat, ramming the idea down his head like trash at the rim of a garbage can. "I think we should wait in the car before these horseflies"—he slapped the tickle of a mosquito landing on his hand—"eat us up."

"Sounds like another good idea," Dr. Bonesteel replied, swatting his bald head. As he started for the passenger side of the car, Sheriff Coleman scanned the windows of the house, each cloaked in a black veil. A tame wind blew through the surrounding trees, allowing a stream of sunlight to fall upon the shaded face of the house.

As the stream of light bleached the black sheets covering the windows, his eyes swept over the rows of glass, hoping he'd uncover Nick's hiding spot. Finding nothing, he waved an annoyed hand at the house. Today was going to be a painfully slow game of hide-and-seek.

19

Nick, 10:30 a.m.

"Ninety percent of my trips are salmon trips, and the other ten percent is smaller stuff—sea bass, catfish, tarpon—but I still use the twenty-pound spin rounds for everything because—"

Stupid cock-sucking, shit-eating pigs, Nick screamed silently while he lay in the same spot of the parking lot, his meaty extremities sprawled across the pavement like a Vietnam soldier in the last moment of his life. *Stop talking about fishing and leave!* Closing his eyes, he brought his veiny fists to his head and pulled on his tufts of curly black hair until it felt like a helmet of needles had been shoved onto his scalp. *Leeeeeave!*

As the Eeyore-like cop droned on, Nick sent telepathic knives at the man's throat, ordering them to tear the cylinder of muscle and tissue into a shredded mat of gore. Then, suddenly, there was silence. Nick opened his eyes, a wormy smile wiggling through his bulging chin. It worked. He was free of the policeman's torturous babble.

"What about you, Barry?" Eeyore said. "Have you been getting in any fishing lately?"

Nick bowed his head, baring his sharp teeth and growling through a salty slop of drool. He stopped, catching sight of the shattered pieces of glass from the rearview mirror he'd broken off the red Jeep parked across from him. As he stared at the shards, a buried memory ejected from the deepest chasm of his mind and played on the makeshift screen in his inner forehead. The flick: *Faces of Death: The Home Movies.*

The opening scene started with thirteen-year-old skin-and-bones Nick standing in the corner of his living room. The cavernous space was almost in total darkness except for a beam of muted orange streaming from a streetlight into the adjacent garden window. The dandelion-colored beam cast a hazy spotlight on the mess of pink glass pieces (previously his mom's rose-patterned Tiffany lamp) sprinkled around Nick's feet.

Suddenly a muffled exchange of voices came from his parents' bedroom upstairs, followed by a door swinging open then a round of quick footsteps. A second later, the upstairs hallway light came on, revealing a curved wooden staircase at the opposite side of the room. A lean seventeen-year-old boy with wavy black hair raced to the staircase as he put on a varsity jacket over his bare chest. "Hey," Steve said, looking down into the dark living room. "Who's there?"

Nick remained silent as he slowly bent down and picked up the longest piece of glass.

"Is that you, Nicky?" Steve said, heading downstairs. "I'm sorry, man, but you can't be here right now. Jamie and I are busy studying. Why don't you just uh…go back over to Jamie's house, and then, when we're done here, we'll come get you, and we'll do whatever you want, all right?" When he reached the bottom of the staircase, he turned on the lights, revealing an enormous lounge designed with the finest unwelcoming decor old money could buy. Steve's close-set eyes swelled with fury as they fell directly onto the broken glass. "Goddamn it, Nicky! What the hell did you do?"

Holding the piece of glass behind his back, Nick glared at him.

"We're gonna be in so much trouble," Steve said, running over to the heap of glass. "C'mon, man. Help me pick this up before your parents come home." He grabbed the embroidered pillow from the nearby chaise and started sweeping the shards into a pile.

Nick continued to watch the teen clear away the lamp bits like a self-powered broom, and then, in one sudden thrust, he jabbed the piece of glass into Steve's right eye. Immediately he sprang backward, letting out the squeal of an overexcited cheerleader. Nick followed him, slashing his muscular arm as it reached out for mercy and then his hollow pink cheeks. Each time, blood splattered across the granite floor, creating a Halloween-themed Pollock painting.

"What's going on?" Jamie asked, running into the hallway. The peach-faced girl stopped at the top of the staircase and shrieked, "Steve!"

For a second, Nick looked up at Jamie then returned his black-pitted eyes to the trembling boy, his back pressed against the wall with the slashed arm covering his face. "Please," Steve wheezed, raising his free hand toward Nick. "Stop."

Why's it talking? Nick asked his conscience. *Brooms don't talk.* He then leaned over and, grabbing the boy's blood-covered neck, stuck the piece of glass deep into the flesh and ran it across the entire width. A low gurgle dispensed from the back of Steve's throat before his body dropped to the floor with a lifeless smack.

"Oh, God. Steven!" Nick looked back at Jamie, her long, delicate hands trying to keep her horrified face from lunging off her skull. With an earsplitting scream, she turned around and fled the surreal scene.

Taking in a string of steady breaths, Nick straightened up and slowly walked up the staircase. At the top, he caught the back of Jamie, who was hurrying into his parents' bedroom at the end of the sterile hallway. As she closed the door behind her, Nick stood there, his glass shiv dripping warm blood onto his hand, and listened as she sprinted to the other end of the room. There was a second of silence, and then she yelled, "Help! My name's Jamie Strode, and I'm at 332 Wheeler Avenue. Oh my God, please come quickly. He killed my boyfriend, and now he's coming for me!"

Tightening his hand around the makeshift weapon, Nick headed down the hallway and—

Ring! Ring! Shaking himself from the memory, he looked up from the broken rearview mirror and turned to the school. *The bell*, he thought, but which one? Was it almost the end of the day? He remained still, listening for an answer.

"Hey, you guys wanna hear a joke?" Eeyore asked.

The three other cops agreed in unison.

"All right. So these two fishermen—"

A purplish crisscross of veins popped onto the surface of Nick's forehead. *No*, a deep voice roared through his electrified nerves, and then he threw his head against the bumper of the white pickup truck he was sitting against. *Stop. Talking. About. Fucking. Fishing!*

20

David, 11:30 a.m.

The lunch bell rang.

Finally, David told himself, ripping his eyes away from the clock. He swiped his backpack, threw it over his shoulder, and scampered out of health class. "Of course Kathleen isn't here," he said as he approached his locker. "Why would today be different? With all the girl slapping and cyst picking." He tossed a weak sigh into his invincible jar of frustration then plopped against the door of his locker and waited in silence. After four minutes, Kathleen arrived. "Well, *hello*, did anyone else slap you?"

She let out a short "Yeah, right" laugh. "No."

"Good. Because I came up with a plan for your revenge, and it's fucking awesome."

"Is it better than running over that cunt?" Kathleen asked, her face fixed in an emotional flatline.

David bulged out his eyes and hiked his skimpy shoulders into an exaggerated shrug like a vaudeville comedian. "Well, we can certainly hope. Right, boss?"

Kathleen showed the barest hint of a smile. "What is it?"

"All right," he said, as they started for the cafeteria, "remember when we watched *Halloween* with Betsy like two years ago, and she got really scared?"

"Yeah."

"Well," David went on, "she said she's grounded, so I was thinking, we can go to my house after school and get my Michael Myers mask. Then we'll go to Betsy's house and scare the shit out of her." A wide, optimistic smile popped onto his face. "Is that a great plan or what?"

A wrinkle of "Eh" ran through Kathleen's brow. "Yeah, I guess."

David sighed "You guess? Um, hello. She's terrified of Michael Myers. She'll piss her pants."

"Yeah, I know."

"*Okay*. So what's the problem?"

"I don't know. It's all right. But what about you?"

David snorted. "What about me?"

"How are we going to get back at Luke and Mike and all those other assholes?"

"Who cares? Let's not worry about them, all right?"

Kathleen stopped. "Why?"

"*Fughhhh*," David said, turning around after the second it took to notice she wasn't next to him, "why are we always stopping in hallways? C'mon, Kathleen. They're serving tater tots today. *Tater tots.*"

"I don't give a shit."

"Why not? You *live* for the tots."

"Because I want to know why you don't want to get revenge on all those fucking dickweeds."

"Are you like serious right now?"

"Yes."

"Um, okay. I'll tell you. Because I don't want to fucking die."

Kathleen blew a raspberry. "Please. They're not going to kill you. They're a bunch of pussies."

"No, they're not, Kat. If we did something to them and they caught us, they'd come after me. Not *you*. Me. And I'm pretty sure they wouldn't just call me names like fag or fudge packer. They'd pound me into queer hamburger, and they'd probably get away with it because, *well*...white people have been getting away with a lot of things lately, don't you think?"

Kathleen snickered. "You're white too. And trust me, I wouldn't let them get away with it. I'd run all those assholes over with my car, and I wouldn't give two fucks if I went to jail."

David smiled faintly. "That's very nice of you, but I don't want to go to college as a paraplegic. I can barely handle stairs now. So can we just, you know, focus on Betsy?"

A vacant gaze reflected off Kathleen's bowling-ball face. "Fine," she said, reaching behind and scratching her right ass cheek, then started walking again.

David followed, continuing with his plan. "All right, so I was thinking, we could park a couple of streets away from Betsy's house, and then I could run up to her door, knock on it, and go hide." He let out a mischievous giggle. "Then I'll do it again, so she gets really freaked out, and then you can go up to one of the windows, wearing the mask—"

"What?" Kathleen barked. "Are you stupid? I can't be Michael Myers."

"Why not?"

"Because I'm fucking three hundred pounds."

David scoffed. "Stop. You're not three hundred pounds. Not even close."

Kathleen was silent for a second. "Well, no. I'm a big girl, though, so it won't be scary. It'd be like seeing Mama Cass in a Michael Myers mask."

David dismissed the statement with a quick laugh. "Okay. So what do you want to do?"

"I don't know. Why don't you be Michael Myers?"

"Me? Oh, no, I can't."

"Why? You're tall and pale, and you hate women."

David sucked his teeth. "I'm not pale." He paused. "Am I?"

"You're whiter than my twat," she said, then stopped as they entered the food line. "Fuck!"

"What?"

"Betsy's right there."

He turned to Betsy, who stood at the cash register with a tray of pizza and applesauce, wearing a vacuous expression on her usual lively face. He couldn't decide if she was trying to ignore their presence or was lost in an invisible dimension of worry. "Okay," he said, then turned back to Kathleen. "So?"

"*So?*" Kathleen snapped. "I'm going to throw a fucking tater tot at that stupid slut." She grabbed a crisp tot from one of the Styrofoam cups on the food line.

"*Don't!*" David said, grabbing her arm as she prepared to hurl the tater tot.

Kathleen pulled her arm away. "Why the fuck not?"

"Because we're better than that. Or did you forget the whole Skittles incident, hmm?" His hazel eyes met Kathleen's, giving them a motherly stare down. As she stared back in silence, he nodded. "Yeah, I didn't think so. And plus, do you want to get detention? Because if you get detention, we won't be able to, you know"—he lowered his voice—"do what we're planning to do. Understand?"

Kathleen let out a careless titter. "Do you know how many times I've gotten detention?" She left no time for a response. "About a million. Do you know how many times I've gone?" Another immediate answer. "Zero." She then popped the tater tot into her mouth. "Besides, I'd never waste this golden deliciousness on that stupid slut."

David laughed. "Okay," he said, grabbing a burger and fries. As Betsy walked away, he waited for the three junior girls from Manga Club, their faces covered with black, *Uzumaki* spirals, to get their food, then continued to the cash register and paid the ancient lunch lady, Mrs. Grimson. He then headed to the silverware and condiments table with Kathleen on his heels.

"Hey," Mrs. Grimson said, moving her long, spindly arm in front of Kathleen. "Where are you going, young lady?"

"Down the rabbit hole," Kathleen replied. "Wanna join me?"

Mrs. Grimson's lips, lined with a dusting of gray hair, disappeared into a cheerless fold. "You owe me a dollar fifty."

"*What?* No, I don't."

"Yes, you do," Mrs. Grimson said. "I saw you take a tater tot. You're paying for the container."

"Are you serious?" Kathleen asked with a puff of frustration. "It was *one* tater tot."

Mrs. Grimson pointed one of her witch-like fingers as though she were casting a curse on Kathleen. "Every day I see you steal something. This is the last straw. Either you pay me, or I'll call the principal down—"

"I'll pay for it," David said, turning to Mrs. Grimson. "Let me pay for it."

"No!" Kathleen balked. "You're not paying a dollar fifty for a greasy-ass tater tot."

"What the hell?" Sam Duncan, the school's Most Likely to Stay a Little Bitch (awarded by Kathleen), shouted from the back of the line. "What's the hold-up?"

"Yeah," Peter Hammer, the school's Biggest Closeted Homosexual (awarded by David), agreed. "Move out of the way!"

Before Kathleen could verbally assault them, David stepped in front of her and said, "I'll pay for the tater tots. So why don't you get the container, so we don't get in trouble, *okay?*"

Cocking her head forward, Kathleen eyed him down then let out a dismissive laugh. As she turned around and walked back to the lunches, she mumbled something that David speculated to be "Tater Nazi" or "Tot Cunt"—something related to Nazis or the vagina or both.

"She's lucky she's got you," Mrs. Grimson said.

David turned to her with a gracious smile. "Yeah," he replied, then quickly added, "but I'm lucky I've got her too."

•　　•　　•　　•　　•

Maybe Luke was angry with David for laughing at him, Betsy argued with herself, as she waited in the lunch line with her pizza and applesauce. *He was nice to him at the party. He said hello, didn't he?* Her tongue pushed against the roof of her mouth as she stared blankly at the faded DON'T BE A ROTTEN APPLE. THROW AWAY YOUR TRASH! poster taped to the eggshell-colored wall. Suddenly a new thought pushed a grimy paw through the roof of her mouth and seized her tongue. *Yeah, but maybe he was just being nice t-t-t-t...* She lowered her tongue, making way for a heavy sigh. *Great, now you're stuttering in your head. Ugh, it doesn't matter anyway. I can't sneak out of Grandma and Grandpa's house. That's just crazy.*

Betsy's muscles tightened into "All right, time to die" mode when she heard a shrill, evil voice she instantly recognized. "Fuck!" Kathleen said.

"What?" The second, slightly feminine voice that followed was David's.

"Betsy's right there."

"Okay. So?"

Betsy's chest relaxed as the muscles in her legs remained ready to flee. "So?" wasn't much, but it felt like he was at least trying to keep Kathleen from murdering her.

"*So?* I'm going to throw a fucking tater tot at that stupid slut."

Betsy grimaced, digging her nails into her food tray. *Why does she keep calling me a slut?*

"Two dollars and twenty-five cents."

Betsy turned to Mrs. Grimson, who was sitting on her red stool, her sunken gray eyes demanding payment of Betsy's lunch or soul—it was difficult to decide. "What?" she asked the woman.

"Your lunch. It's two dollars and twenty-five cents."

"Oh, sorry." Betsy reached into her pocket, paid the two twenty-five in quarters, then bolted out of the lunch line, a crimson rash creeping up her neck. *Why the hell is Kathleen being so mean? Is she jealous of me or something?* As she rushed through the main aisle between the tables, each a boisterous mix of costumed and non-costumed characters, she laughed to herself. *Yeah, right. There's no way she likes Luke. She was just joking when she—* She flicked the thought away with an angry breath. *Stop it. You like Luke, and he likes you, and that's all that matters. Right?*

"Right," she said, sitting at a table on the upper left corner of the cafeteria.

"What?" Luke asked, taking a seat across from her.

Betsy shivered as she asked herself, *How the hell did you get here?* Ever since sophomore year, she had sat with her core group of friends (Kathleen, David, Alice, Samantha Patchett, Lindsay Cerul, Joe Solpietro, and Eddie Summers) at the table in the opposite corner. For the last two weeks, however, she had been sitting with Luke and now, blindly navigating the cafeteria in anger, she still found their table as if she had developed some sort of animal migration sonar for mating. "What?" she asked, coming back to the real world.

"Did you say something?"

Feeling the heat of her rash rise to her cheeks, she shook her head. "No."

"Okay," Luke said, smiling. "So did you decide if you're coming to Mike's party with me?"

"Oh, uh...no. I can't s-s-s-sneak out."

"Yes, you can. I used to do it all the time when I was younger."

Betsy smiled curiously. "You did?"

Luke leaned forward, his vibrant eyes seductively teasing hers. "Yeah, I'd wait until my parents went to sleep, and then I'd sneak out the window so I could sleep in my tree house."

Betsy giggled. "Really?"

"Yeah," Luke answered with a playful quirk of his eyebrows. "Are you making fun of me?"

Betsy's face turned vampire-victim white. "No."

"Good," Luke said, then licked his pink engineered-for-kissing lips. "You'd better not be, or I'll tickle you in front of the entire cafeteria."

"Oh." As Betsy looked down, the rash returned in spurts across her entire body, as if her trembling flesh were hosting a Fourth of July fireworks display. Imagining Luke tickling her in front of two-thirds of the senior class (as well as a handful of juniors, two teachers serving as lunch monitors, and one half-in-the-bag janitor), she would've run away in a virginal embarrassment if it weren't for the tiny, deep-down pleasure she got from the idea. *How exciting would that be*, her loins bellowed, *if everyone knew the hottest, most popular boy in school liked you?*

"So is there a room at your grandparents' house with a window you can sneak out through?" Luke asked.

Without thinking, she looked up and said, "Yeah. They have a b-b-b-bedroom on the first floor where I usually s-s-s-sleep."

"Good. So I'll drive you over there after school, and you'll tell them you're tired and want to take a nap. Then you'll go to your room, sneak out the window, and run back to my truck so we can go to Mike's party."

Betsy laughed nervously. "Um, I don't know."

"Trust me." Luke placed his warm, cinnamon-bun-soft palm on hers. "It'll be easy."

Once again, Betsy's loins screamed. *Do it!* they told her. "Mmmm," she replied, then chewed her lip as if it were a pre-lunch snack. She didn't know what to say; she wanted to go, but there were so many unanswered questions. Did Luke really like her or was he just pretending so he could get certain things? Could she sneak out of her grandparents' house and what kind of tracking device would her father implant in her head if she got caught?

"It's okay," Luke said, removing his hand. "You don't have to go. I know how your dad can be." He snickered. "Man, I'd never heard someone so angry when he burst into your room."

Betsy released the salty bit of lip she was working on and let out an anxious huff. "Yeah, it was pretty bad."

"Yeah." Luke laughed again. "But it's all right. We can always hang out some other time, right?" He gave a wide, dimple-connecting smile as he returned his hand to Betsy's. As he gently massaged her fingers with his thumb, her eyes glistened with excitement. *Oh, my God, he's asking you out. He likes you. He really—* Catching an "Are you going to answer my question?" squint from Luke, she pretended to cough.

"Oh, um...yeah."

"Good. Can I still give you a ride home today?"

"Sure," Betsy said, tucking her hair behind her ears, then picking up her pizza. "Do you want to meet—"

"Good afternoon, students," the principal recited over the loudspeaker. "This is Mr. Miehan with an important announcement."

Suddenly someone—Betsy couldn't tell who—baaed like a sheep. The entire cafeteria erupted with laughter, including Luke.

Mr. Miehan continued. "The police department has just informed me that there will be a county-wide curfew. All residents must be in their homes by ten p.m., and—"

An explosion of boos came from Mike Barrett's table—the same table where Luke usually sat. A collection of groans and whispers followed.

"Police officers will be monitoring the streets," Mr. Miehan went on, "but I trust that you, as Bishop Dullen students, will represent the school as the moral institution that it is. Let me remind you that all of you signed the Oath of Virtues and..."

As the principal reiterated the oath all students were required to sign at the beginning of the year (two-thirds breaking it in the first month), the noise in the cafeteria grew louder, and then, without warning, Mike Barrett slammed his hands on his table and shouted, "No curfew!" He repeated the phrase, inciting a roar of applause and laughter throughout the room. Other students, including Luke, joined in. "*No curfew! No curfew! No curfew!*"

While the chanting continued, Betsy stared into space, her fingers melting into the doughy pizza slice in her hand. *Goddamn it*, she cried internally, her arms and legs pulsating with anger. *I bet Daddy did this just to make sure I don't do anything tonight. But why? I didn't do anything to deserve this!* As her head dropped, she stopped herself from breaking into a sob. *No, you did*, her conscience reminded her. *You did something horrible, and now you're being punished.*

Her body sank into the hard plastic of her chair. Her conscience was right; she had committed a handful of sins, and now—no matter how many times she prayed to God or apologized to her mother—she had to accept her punishment.

"Thank you," Mr. Miehan said. "And remember: God loves you."

Betsy snorted. *No, God hates me. He lets everybody else get away with everything, but when I do something wrong, I get punished for it!* Suddenly she looked up, her furious gaze aimed at Kathleen, who was sitting at her old table. As Betsy watched her participate in the chant with the rest of their friends, her eyes replaced the anger with outright hatred. She couldn't read lips, but it looked like Kathleen was mouthing, "Betsy's a slut." A squirt of marinara sauce slid down her arm as she crushed the pizza slice in her hand. *Fuck you, Kathleen. I don't care anymore! I'm going to have fun.* "Hey, Luke," she said.

Laughing, Luke turned to her. "Yeah?" Concern erased the joy from his chiseled face. "Oh, shit. Your pizza—"

"I want to go to Mike's party," she interjected, as a glob of cheese plopped onto the table. "And Ashley's party too."

21

Staring at the rearview mirror, Sheriff Coleman's droopy eyes focused on the sun-filled opening on the other end of the driveway. For the last forty minutes of their three-hour stakeout, he had watched the blood-orange leaves fall from the neighboring cherry trees, tallying their direction of flight. *148 right, 62 left*, he counted in his head after a minute of monotonous studying, then let out a long "feel it all the way down to the toes" yawn. As he continued his endless game, his eyes opened and closed in slow motion, signaling the need for a solid, dreamless nap, when suddenly his head jerked up, feeling its cantaloupe-like weight. "Oh, man," he said, shaking off the fatigue. "I need a drink."

"Me too," Dr. Bonesteel said and then, a second later, added, "Pshaw, where is it?"

Turning to find the doctor foolishly search his coat once more, Sheriff Coleman opened his mouth to release a sigh but stopped himself. *It's okay,* he said in his head as he cracked out the arthritis in his knuckles. *He's a clumsy old man, but that doesn't mean he can't—*

"Here's the old SOB," Dr. Bonesteel said, feeling around in his front left pocket. He extracted a silver flask, unscrewed the top, and took a long drink. He then gave a deep, satisfied "Ah" when he was done.

Sheriff Coleman did a Laurel and Hardy double take. "What the hell are you doing, Doctor?"

"Having a drink," Dr. Bonesteel answered, his eyes narrowing in confusion. "Didn't you say you wanted one too?" He offered the flask to him.

"I meant coffee," the sheriff said, draconian eyes carved into his stony face. "Why the hell are you drinking at"—he looked at his watch—"twelve thirty?"

With those last two words, his mind pressed "pause" on the doctor's drinking and switched to Betsy. Lunch was either starting or ending—he couldn't remember—and he wondered whether she was still angry with him.

A harsh laugh from Dr. Bonesteel disrupted this line of thought. "Why am I drinking, Sheriff? Because I'm fighting my demons before I face the Devil." He paused, aiming his own monster sneer at the house. "Do you know what it's like to watch a disturbed young man turn into a total creature of evil?"

Great, John, Sheriff Coleman thought, expecting another Devil-laced rant from the doctor. *Now you've done it.*

"No, you don't," Dr. Bonesteel said, setting his fierce gaze on him. "For a year I tried my best to rehabilitate Nick, but then I realized it was hopeless. That beast was born without empathy for any living thing. Do you know what he did after he turned his cat's head into a gloved weapon?" The answer followed without a pause. "He almost spooned out the eyes of a poor, breathtakingly beautiful *nurse.*"

The doctor's voice cracked. Sheriff Coleman turned to him, surprise swatting his face as he caught sight of a tear trickling down the doctor's sagging cheek. *Beautiful? Did you know this nurse?* he wanted to ask, but the doctor quickly returned to his campfire story about the legend of Nick Roesch. "So we took away all the utensils and let him eat with his hands like an animal. We thought we were safe, but *oh, no*, he found a way. Can you guess how he stabbed the orderly and escaped this morning?"

Sheriff Coleman didn't respond, knowing the doctor would do it for him. "He grew out his fingernails, waiting until they were long enough, and then *bam*"—he snapped his stubby fingers—"he dug his demon claws into the man's face and ripped off his cheek so you could see his teeth."

Sheriff Coleman's lips kinked into a horrified twist.

"That's right," Dr. Bonesteel continued. "I have four more years of such fond memories, and this"—he raised the flask—"is the only thing that helps me forget them." He took another long swig.

Goddamn it. Stop that, Sheriff Coleman was about to scream, but stopped himself with a disappointed head bow, knowing what it was like to wash away memories with a drink. He kept his head down for a moment, suppressing those memories by multiplying a pair of double-digit numbers (a strategy he had learned from AA), then looked up and said, "All right, I understand it's difficult, but please take it easy. I'd like you to be coherent when we find Nick. Okay?"

"Don't worry, Sheriff," Dr. Bonesteel said, his eyes growing even wider. "The sight of the Devil will straighten me out."

Sheriff Coleman turned to the large yellow box of a house. *For Christ's sake. I'm sick of all this Devil talk. Nick's nothing more than a mentally challenged individual.* He wrestled with the thought of telling the doctor that, then decided he didn't want to agitate the old man any further. Unfortunately, he was their only hope of stopping this cat-killing, fingernail-stabbing young man.

As a discouraging tension fell between the two men, the sun shifted through the trees, forming a new pattern of spirals on the hood of the cruiser. And then, hoping to break the daunting silence, Sheriff Coleman cleared his throat and said, "I wasn't able to read the entire police report. What happened the night Nick killed Jamie Strode's boyfriend?"

"It was horrible," Dr. Bonesteel replied, returning the flask to his coat. "He took a broken piece of glass from one of his mother's lamps and hacked away at the boy. He stabbed him three or four times before he slashed his throat."

"Oh, God. Why did he do it?"

"That's what I tried to figure out, but after the heinous acts of violence Nick committed at the hospital, I realized he was devoid of human emotions. In fact, after he murdered the boyfriend, the cops found him in his room, lying in bed, reading a comic book like nothing had happened."

"That makes sense. I've read that a good percentage of murderers have certain disorders that cause them to lack emotions."

"Yes, they're personality disorders like APD—antisocial personality disorder," Dr. Bonesteel explained. "Which is exactly why I went to you when Nick escaped. I know he's come back for Jamie, and he'll kill anyone who gets in his way."

"Right," Sheriff Coleman said with a pensive nod. A pair of yam-colored leaves spiraled down and landed on the windshield of the cruiser. "So where's his family in all of this?"

"His parents left as soon as their son was committed to Summer Hill. They packed up and moved out of the state without even putting a FOR SALE sign on their house." Dr. Bonesteel paused, swallowing a gulp of air and saliva. "When I found out Nick had escaped, I called them immediately, but no one picked up. So I left them a message. When I tried them twenty minutes later, I got a message saying the number was no longer in service."

Sheriff Coleman passed a sour laugh through his mustache. "That's pretty disgusting."

"Yes and no," Dr. Bonesteel responded. "Something hellish happened, something no one could fully explain—not even the best doctors or child psychiatrists." His mouth puckered, activating a ripple of deep lines on his forehead. "And it frightened them, so they ran. Wouldn't you?"

As the doctor held on to an unblinking stare, Sheriff Coleman looked back with the last five years running through his head like a slide projector of large-scale disasters. First, there was Patricia's battle with cancer, and then there were the two years he'd been off the force, drinking himself to sleep some nights, drifting further from his daughter. *Yeah*, he answered in his head, *I was frightened enough to run away too.* "Yeah, maybe. So did they live close by?"

"Across the street."

Sheriff Coleman raised his bushy eyebrows. "What?"

"They lived across the street. That's where the murder happened."

"It did? I thought it happened here."

Dr. Bonesteel shook his head. "No, Jamie was babysitting Nick at her parents' house, but then her boyfriend came over—and you know how teenagers are—so they sneaked over to Nick's house, and eventually Nick came over and...well, you know the rest."

Sheriff Coleman sucked his teeth. *All this time...* "We need to take a look at Nick's house."

"Why?"

"Because," he said, and then the next words popped out of his mouth without a moment of logical thought. "Sometimes the Devil's work is done at home." *Jesus*, he thought, as soon as the unexpected statement came out and stirred the dreary air with a supernatural spark. *Now I'm starting to talk like Dr. Frankenstein here.*

Dr. Bonesteel smirked. "You're right. We should check it out, but I don't think we'll find anything."

Sheriff Coleman started the car. "Yeah, but we still have to take a look."

22

Betsy, 12:15 p.m.

"As adolescents begin to assert their independence and find their own identity, many experience behavioral changes that may seem bizarre and unpredictable to them. These changes include..."

As Sister Babcock rattled off the text in the religion book with her choppy John Wayne voice, Betsy doodled in the margins of her notebook while her tiny, inner rebel glowed with a new confidence. *I did it*, she praised herself as she drew the basic "I'm bored" cube on the upper left-hand corner of the page. *I'm going to two parties with Luke, and it's going to be so much fun.*

Her growing excitement climbed up her throat and tried to escape her mouth as an involuntary squeal. Fortunately, her full lips caught the noise, and it came out as a low hum. *Calm down,* she thought, resting her chubby cheek on her knuckles as a precautionary cover. *Don't get in trouble. You only have two more classes. Government and creative—*

"Shit," she mumbled into her hand, remembering she had creative writing with Kathleen and David at the end of the day. "She's going to kill you."

"As adolescents develop their identity, they receive feedback from the people around them, including their peers," Sister Babcock continued. "Unfortunately the peer culture many teens find themselves in can promote values and behavior that contradict Christian values. This includes experimentation with illicit drugs, alcohol, and sexual activity."

A crackle of laughter came from the class. "C'mon on, guys," Sister Babcock reprimanded them. "Let's be more mature about this." There was a moment of silence, and then she went on. "Teens who do not conform to peer culture..."

Betsy let out a slow, unsteady breath. *Stop,* she scolded herself. *Everything's going to be fine. You just gotta think of a way to get out of creative writing.* As she brainstormed an escape plan, her pencil took on a life of its own, scribbling across her notebook. *Why don't you say you're having female trouble so you can go to the nurse's office? Kathleen does it about three times a month.*

"Whatever adolescents face," Sister Babcock said, then slowed down to exaggerate the importance of the passage, "they must always remember to follow the Christian teachings of honesty and respect. Two important commandments to remember are: 'Thou shalt not bear false witness' and 'Honour thy father and thy mother.'"

"Damn it," Betsy said as the tip of her pencil broke off.

"What was that, Betsy?" Sister Babcock said, looking up from her book. A couple of snickers came from her classmates.

"S-s-s-sorry," Betsy said, looking back at the nun. "My pencil broke."

"Mm-hmm," Sister Babcock replied, a pinch of agitation on her face. "All right, let's continue to page forty-five."

Betsy looked down at her book, her cherubic face contoured with streaks of red. *Can this day get any worse? Like seriously, I want to die right now.*

23

Kathleen, 12:25 p.m.

"And that which rather thou dost fear to do, than wishest should be undone. Hie thee hither, that I may pour my spirits in thine ear and chastise with the valor of my tongue all that impedes thee from the golden round, which fate and metaphysical aid doth seem to have thee crowned withal." There was a knock on Lady Macbeth's door. "What!"

Kathleen giggled. *This bitch is fucking crazy*, she thought, then turned from the projection screen (Mr. Rooker, the English literature teacher, was showing 1997's *Macbeth* off Confickerfreeasiangirlsflix.net) and whispered to David, "Hey, did you think of something better than that stupid Michael Myers idea?"

"What?" David whispered back, furiously writing in his notebook.

"Did you think of a better idea...for Betsy? Are you taking notes on the movie?"

"Um, yeah," David said with a slanted right eye that said, *Why wouldn't I?* "And no, I haven't. I was too busy in AP Calc."

Kathleen pressed her lips shut, muzzling the words that were clawing away at her tongue: *Who the fuck does math their senior year, you goddamn overachiever?* "All right," she said instead. "Why don't I just punch Betsy in the face in creative—"

"Hey, quiet down, guys," Mr. Rooker said in his nasally voice.

Kathleen let out a snide laugh at the elfish-looking man with his black goatee and square hipster glasses. *You look like fucking Frodo at Coachella*, she thought, then turned back to David. "Maybe I should write a story about a girl who gives a blow job to a guy at her birthday party and share it with the class. The guy's name will be Duke and the girl's name will be Betsy Coleman."

David dropped his pen and whipped his head over to Kathleen. "Are you crazy?" he said under his breath. "You *cannot* do that. Besides, we have to work on our next story. It's due Wednesday, and we haven't even decided on an idea."

Kathleen shrugged. "Why don't we write the story about the girl with the possessed cyst?"

The bottom row of David's teeth rose out of his mouth like ten cream-tinted protest signs. "That's a little too gross, and—"

"Kathleen and David," Mr. Rooker said in a loud, pixie-ish voice, "I'm not going to say this again. Stop talking, or I'll give you detention."

"Sorry, Mr. Rooker," David said, then cowered over his notebook.

As Kathleen glanced at the teacher, her eyebrows rose in rebellion, preparing for a fight. Normally she would've dismissed the tiny man's threat and happily received detention, but not today, she told herself. She needed revenge more than she needed to tell off Frodo, Lord of the Cock Ring.

Eat a dick, you dumb fuck, she mentally broadcast to the gremlin-looking teacher then turned back to the movie. As she watched Lady Macbeth talk to herself, her hand moved to her pajama pocket. A soothing breath left her nose as she pulled out a safety pin.

"Come, you spirits," Lady Macbeth wailed, "that tend on mortal thoughts. Unsex me here, and fill me from the crown to the toe, top-full of direst cruelty. Make thick my blood. Stop up the access and passage to remorse, that no compunctious visitings of nature shake my fell purpose, nor keep peace between the effect and it!'"

Kathleen smiled maliciously as she plunged the metallic point into the tip of her thumb. *Ditto.*

24

David, 2:00 p.m.

"Girl gets cyst. Cyst is possessed by a demon. Cyst shoots puss into people's faces and kills them."

David frowned, rereading the last three sentences he had written. *This is like the worst idea ever.* Staring at the page, he expelled a breath of frustrated writer's block. *What the hell makes a good horror story?*

He continued staring then said, "Duh. Good horror stories are scary." He wrote the statement in his notebook, then jotted underneath it, "They're scary because they're based on real events." He gazed upon the new sentences, hoping for a spurt of Dickens inspiration. Feeling a prick of cafeteria pizza pre-gas in his stomach, he shifted in his chair then resumed brainstorming: *What are people afraid of?*

He created a list: "Ghosts, killer dolls, killer animals, children possessed by demons, men." He laughed at the fifth item, then drew an arrow next to it and continued: "Big, silent Michael Myers–like psychos who are immune to every deadly weapon except for a sweet, virginal girl." *Yes*, he thought with a stroke-of-genius gasp, whispering while writing down this new insight. "Good horror stories have a final girl!"

"Hey, kiddo," Mrs. Kolinski, an older leathery-skinned woman wearing a Hawaiian shirt and purple lei (which was her usual "I'm the fun teacher" wear rather than a costume), said from her desk.

As David looked up from his notebook, his cheeks stretched into a smile as he watched Kathleen enter the classroom. "Hey, Mrs. KO," Kathleen said, as always, then headed toward him, scratching her crotch. Snorting with laughter, David returned to his notebook and scribbled, "Kathleen Strife is the opposite of a final girl." His eyes screamed with excitement as they bounced from the newly written sentence to Kathleen, then back to the sentence. *Hairy Mary. I've thought of something totally scary.*

"Suck my twat," Kathleen grumbled as she sat next to him. "Now my pussy's on fire."

David's eyes snapped shut, trying for the second time to block the image of a vagina—especially what Kathleen's looked like—from entering his subconscious. "*Okay.* Do you think you have another cyst?"

"No," Kathleen replied. "It's probably just another UTI. Did you come up with a new revenge plan?"

"Um…" David took a deep breath then puffed out his chest, trying to build the courage to tell her he didn't want to commit any acts of revenge (especially now that there was a curfew in effect), but unfortunately, he chickened out and gave the first excuse that came to mind. "We had like four minutes since our last class. I hardly had a chance to sit down. I've got great news, though."

Kathleen's eyes took on an eerie glow. "Betsy's dead?"

David let out a chuckle, trying hard to believe that she was kidding. "No."

"Then where is she?"

"Oh, I don't know," David answered, searching the wooden desks arranged in a "Kumbaya" circle. In the last two weeks, Betsy had opted to sit ten desks away, among the beer-bellied jocks and their blond cumdumps who couldn't write a story as simple as an Eric Carle book. She wasn't there; however, his news trumped her absence. "I think I figured out an idea for our story," he said, turning back to Kathleen. "Do you know what a final girl is?"

"Never heard of it."

David rolled his eyes, ignoring her obvious sarcasm. "Uh-huh. So I was thinking, we could write a traditional slasher story but with the opposite type of a final girl. Kind of like a final girl who's bad. A final girl gone bad!"

"A final girl gone bad?" Kathleen asked, a trace of doubt on her face.

"Yeah. Imagine *you* in a horror movie, running away from Michael Myers."

"Shit," Kathleen said, then launched a hard laugh from the back of her throat. "That does sound scary. My fucking fat ass would be dead in two seconds."

As the second bell rang, Mrs. Kolinski shuffled a stack of papers on her desk, then walked to the podium. As she greeted the class, David sucked his teeth then whispered, "I didn't mean it like that, Kathleen. You'd be a total badass. You'd be like, 'Leave me the fuck alone, Michael. Go kill the other bitches.'"

"Yeah, he'd probably make me suck his dick, though."

David clenched his teeth. "*Yeah,* I think we both know you've sucked dick for less."

"Well, hello, kiddo," Mrs. Kolinski said from the podium. "Thanks for being on time."

"S-s-s-sorry."

"Hey, speaking of sucking dick," Kathleen said, turning toward the front of the class.

David frowned as he looked at Betsy standing in the doorway, her round face stamped with a red blotch of grief. *Oh, man, she looks terrible.*

"Come in and sit down," Mrs. Kolinski said. "The chairs aren't comin' to you."

Everyone except David laughed. *Well, that wasn't very nice,* he thought.

"I uh…" Betsy stood still for a second, hesitating, then walked over to Mrs. Kolinski and whispered something in her ear.

"All right," Mrs. Kolinski replied, her sunburned face wilting in disappointment. "You can go."

"Thank you," Betsy said before hurrying out of the room.

"Wow, what's wrong with Betsy?" Sarah Edwards, the eternal dumb blonde, asked David and Kathleen from two seats away. "She got the Friday blues or something?"

"The only thing that's blue is Luke's balls," Kathleen stated mechanically.

Sarah's perky cheeks deflated. "What?"

"Okay, let's get started," Mrs. Kolinski said. "Who's got a story idea?" The room was silent as she scanned the campfire circle of airheads. "Goodness gracious, don't talk all at once. We wouldn't want a *Lord of the Flies* situation." David and Kathleen were the only two who laughed. "What about you, Steven?"

Mrs. Kolinski turned to Steven Bonds, a five-foot-two scrawny soccer player whom Kathleen and David called "The Curious Case of Steven Button." "Uh, I was thinking about writing a story about some kids who start their own boxing club."

"Okay. And what happens?"

Steven's small face shrunk into a bewildered speck, clearly indicating he wasn't aware that stories needed a plot. "Well, I think it would be funny if the kids beat each other up until the smallest kid is left."

David's mental critic howled in amusement. *Oh, Steven Button. Someday you'll be big enough to write real stories.*

"All right," Mrs. Kolinski said, sounding equally unimpressed. "David, do you have something for us?"

David sat up with a nervous laugh. "Yeah, kind of."

"What does 'kind of' mean?"

Another nervous chuckle. "Well, Kathleen and I were talking about writing a horror story."

"In honor of Halloween," Kathleen interjected.

"Right," David agreed.

"So what's this horror story about?"

David turned back to Mrs. Kolinksi and brushed his shaggy hair away from his forehead, gifting himself a moment to put together his half-baked idea. "Well, we thought it would be fun to write something that sort of...plays around with the final girl character. That's a pretty big trend in horror movies right now. You know, the whole 'subverting the trope in a meta way' thing."

"What's a final girl?" Amanda Oropallo, her strawberry-blond hair tied up with a red bandanna, asked from the other end of the circle.

David's eyes landed on her orange stomach beneath a short blue top. *Is she supposed to be a sexy Rosie the Riveter?* "She's the last character in a horror movie who ultimately kills the serial killer. She's usually a beautiful, innocent girl, so Kathleen and I thought it would be cool to make her the total opposite. You know, she's loud and rude—"

"And fat," Amanda interrupted. Her diamond-shaped cheeks produced an innocent smile.

"*Yup*," Kathleen said with a mocking smile. "And her skin isn't bright orange either."

"Um, okay," Amanda said, then laughed off Kathleen's blatant reference to her heavy spray-on tan. An awkward silence followed as Kathleen's exaggerated smile bore into the girl's fried skin.

"So yeah," David said, breaking the silence, "that's what we'd like to do." He looked back at Mrs. Kolinski, his face flushed from guilt by association. "Does that sound okay?"

"There's only one way to find out," Mrs. Kolinski answered. "Do you know what that is?"

"Start writing it?" An apprehensive smile cleared the embarrassment from his face.

"Bingo." Mrs. Kolinski turned to the other students. "Does anyone else have anything?" Again the class was silent. "All right, you banana heads. Everybody start thinking of ideas. Your stories are due on Wednesday."

As the other students conversed with their writing partners, David opened his notebook to a new page. "All right, Kathleen. Let's brainstorm.

Should we start thinking about our final girl gone bad or start with the homicidal maniac?"

Kathleen scoffed. "Are we not best friends? Obviously the homicidal maniac."

"Okay," David said, laughing. "What should he look like?"

"I don't know. He should have a big horse face and wild greasy hair and um...razor-sharp teeth that could rip a man's dick off in a single bite. Or, you know, look exactly like Betsy."

David bent his head forward and dispensed a "Let's stop talking about Betsy" look. "*Kathleen.*"

"What?"

"C'mon. Our homicidal maniac *cannot* look like Betsy."

"Why not?"

He shrugged. "Because we need our homicidal maniac to be a little bit more...unique. Don't ya think?"

"Mm-hmm." With a restless exhalation, Kathleen looked straight ahead, her enormous eyes casting a smoldering gaze until an evil chuckle erupted from her dark reverie. "What if our homicidal maniac looked like Garfield with tits?"

Knowing she was referring to Amanda, David snorted. "I would say that's *too* unique...and not very scary."

"I do like the female killer angle, though," Kathleen said, "especially if we fool the reader into thinking she's some sort of sweet final girl."

"Yeah! That sounds—" A throaty groan ceased the end of David's sentence.

"What?"

"Well, that's a big trend in horror too," David explained in disappointment. "The final girl turns out to be the killer. *Scream 4*, *High Tension*—it's been done to death." He expelled a puff of air to vent his frustration. "Shit, I want to do something along those lines, but I don't want to copy someone else's idea. Do you think they're too similar?"

He turned to Kathleen, hoping her fuck-them attitude would persuade him otherwise. She delivered, blowing a dry raspberry. "Who the fuck cares about other people? Every horror movie in the eighties was a rip-off of *Halloween*. And *Halloween* basically stole from *Psycho* and *Black Christmas*."

David nodded. "True." He paused, reconsidering his idea of the final girl gone bad. "And besides, we've got a crazy sense of humor, so whatever we write will be a smashing good time." A jazzy smile exorcized the worry in his face.

"Exactly." Kathleen hoisted her cheeks into a brief smile, then released them into their usual swampy form. "There needs to be more stories with fucked-up women in them anyways. I'm so sick of female characters having to fit that sweet-and-sexy mold. Women are cunts. My mom's a cunt. I'm a cunt. And Betsy's the biggest, hairiest cunt of them all."

David laughed nervously. *Does the American Counsel of Labia Studies pay her every time she says that word?*

"So like I said," Kathleen continued, "Betsy should be our final girl gone wild or whatever because she's a stupid cunt."

"Uh, okay," David said, his voice wavering with uncertainty. "It's a pretty interesting idea. I'm going to start brainstorming some backstory for our 'Betsy the Cunt Killer'"—he made air quotes—"all right?"

"Sure."

"Okey dokey." David gave a friendly "Everything's good" grin, then looked down at his notebook with an internal "This is totally stupid" sneer. Yes, they had their final girl gone bad, but he couldn't imagine sitting in a theater watching Betsy Coleman slowly stalk a cast of big-breasted cheerleaders and their shit-for-brains jock boyfriends.

Or could he?

Feeling Kathleen's eyes push a metaphorical gun against his back, he grabbed his pen and wrote, "Betsy: who does she kill and why?"

25

Betsy, 2:05 p.m.

Pulling a stray thread from the sleeve of her shirt, Betsy walked up the art wing from Mrs. Kolinski's class toward the main hallway. *You're fine*, she told herself, as she wrapped the thread around her pointer finger. *Just say you're having cramps and Nurse Clare will tell you to go to the back room and lie down.* She arrived at the chapel then continued around the circular room until she suddenly froze, her eyes bursting from the sockets as though she had passed Jesus wearing a purple leopard-print pimp costume. *Wait, what if she calls Daddy?*

Ripping the loose strand from her sleeve, she turned to the nurse's office across from the chapel. *No, she wouldn't tell him I'm on my period, would she?* She stared at the doorway for a moment then shook her head. *Don't. It's too risky.*

Then where are you going to go? Her first thought: *The chapel.* She quickly turned, rushed to the front of the chapel, and tugged at the doors. They were locked. "Damn it," she mumbled, looking away. Her flesh bubbled with goosebumps as she spotted Ms. Cheryl through the large glass window of the main office. Without thinking, she fled to the right of the chapel, toward the senior wing. As soon as she turned the corner, she saw the door to the guidance office open and raced into the girls' bathroom.

Immediately she checked underneath the stalls. Finding no one in them, she moved to the same mirror she'd stood in front of right before she'd slapped Kathleen. A disgruntled moan crawled into her mouth as she stared at the slovenly ghost of the overly excited girl she'd known at lunchtime. "God," she said, grabbing the cold porcelain of the sink. "This is...this is just too much. You can't sneak out. D-d-d-daddy will find out s-s-s-somehow and lock you in the basement for the rest of your—"

A hand slammed against the bathroom door. "C'mon, Kierstin," someone said—it sounded like the bubbly voice of Melissa Horn—from the hallway. "Grab the makeup. Mr. Underwood is going to see us."

Dashing into the first stall, Betsy finally noticed the acidic stench of tater tots wafting from the toilet and gagged on a faux burst of vomit. "*Kathleen!*" she hissed as she looked away from the unflushed mountain of brownish-green shit.

"Calm down, Melissa. We've got like thirty minutes." Betsy was right; it was Melissa and her best friend, Kierstin Beadel, two-thirds of Dullen's Mean Girls, scampering into the bathroom.

"Yeah, but that isn't enough time to—" There was an abrupt lull, followed by, "Gross. It smells like shit in here."

"Ill. It does." Kierstin gasped, then whispered, "Someone's in that stall."

"This is so *disgusting*. Let's go to the other bathroom."

"Yeah."

Erupting into the loud neighs of two sadistic horses, Melissa and Kierstin left the bathroom. "Holy shit. Who do you think—"

Keeping her hand over her mouth and nose, Betsy waited until their voices trailed off, and then, as quickly as she could, she pushed down the toilet seat and flushed the week-old-broccoli-smelling mess Kathleen had graciously left behind. "That fucking bitch!" Betsy shouted, choking back her tears. "I'm going to k-k-k-kill her!"

26

Sheriff Coleman returned his gun to his holster and sighed as he completed a full circle around Nick Roesch's parents' three-story brick house. *Well, now we know he's not here*, he thought, stopping in the paved driveway directly in front of the French-style garage. *Son of a bitch is probably halfway into Canada, laughing his ass—*

"I guess he's not hiding outside in the open," Dr. Bonesteel said sarcastically behind him. "C'mon, Sheriff. I'm sure he knew how to get into the house without breaking anything. Isn't that enough for you to crack open the door?" He stopped next to the sheriff and swatted his arm. "Or how about we smash a window and say it was a burglary?"

Sheriff Coleman's clouded eyes drifted over to the doctor. *This man is the bane of my existence.* "We can't do that."

"Why not?"

"Because one, it's illegal, and two, we wouldn't be able to do it without stirring up trouble."

Dr. Bonesteel stared at the sheriff, his baseball-size eyes studying the man's stale expression. "Yes, we could."

"No, Doctor," Sheriff Coleman said, turning to the impressive edifice, probably designed by Frank Lloyd Wright's second cousin and blessed by an archbishop who had once shared a plate of fries with the pope. It was a sparkling-clean model of perfection. "Look at this place. There isn't a single chipped brick or piece of bird shit. And take a look at the yard." Behind him, he pointed to the enormous green square that looked as though it had been cut from a professional baseball field. "Do you notice anything?"

Dr. Bonesteel placed his wild eyes on the yard. Following the vertical stripes to the edge of the street, he replied, "It's been mowed." He turned back to the sheriff. "I guess a new family's living here."

"I don't know about that. I'll have to double-check with my sergeant, but I'll bet Nick's parents never sold the place."

"What?"

"I have a feeling they were afraid the neighbors would talk to the rich stiffs and sully their reputation, so they moved away, but hired people to keep the place up. And it looks to be heavily guarded. Did you spot the ADT sign in the window?" Sheriff Coleman pointed to the blue octagon sticker in the corner of the large picture window near the front door.

"Son of a gun," Dr. Bonesteel said. "You're one hell of a sheriff."

Sheriff Coleman raised the right tip of his thin lips, suggesting half a smirk. "Thanks. I imagine they have one of those light timers too, but like I said, we can't touch the house. Believe me, I'd like to, but as soon as we crack open one of those windows, ADT will notify the local police and the family, and they're probably the type of people who'd sue my department for destruction of property and invasion of privacy. And that'd cost a lot of jobs."

"Yeah," Dr. Bonesteel said, his zealous stare shrinking into disappointment. "You're probably right."

"Yup," Sheriff Coleman replied with a solemn nod and then, preventing the doctor from devising any other illegal activities, continued without a pause. "C'mon. Let's get back to the cruiser and check whether Nick's parents sold the place." He started for his car, which was parked alongside the road. "If they did, maybe we can contact the new residents and see if they'll let us inside."

"All right." Dr. Bonesteel followed the sheriff. "We can certainly hope the Devil isn't home, playing damnation on the innocent."

Yeah, let's hope, Sheriff Coleman thought flippantly as he approached his vehicle. He got into the driver's seat and grabbed the hand microphone. "Sergeant Bill, do you copy?"

As Dr. Bonesteel climbed into the passenger's seat, Sergeant Bill said, "Yes, Sheriff. Loud and clear."

"Have the patrols found anything suspicious?"

"No, Sheriff."

"What about the schools?"

"Nothing there either. But I have confirmation from every school in the county that they've told their students about the curfew."

"Good. Have the TV stations been informed?"

"Yes, they're running alerts every thirty minutes, and they're going to make an announcement on the six and ten o'clock news."

"All right, great. Keep the patrols going, and could you find out about Nick's parents' house? It's 332 Wheeler Avenue. That's 332 Wheeler Avenue.

I want to know whether it was sold, and if it was, let me know who the new homeowners are."

"Will do, Sheriff."

"Thanks. I'll—" Sheriff Coleman's stomach growled the monstrous roar of a 1950s B-movie crustacean.

"'There's nothing better for a man than to eat and drink and tell himself that his labor is good.' Ecclesiastes two twenty-four." Sergeant Bill gave a jolly laugh. "Sounds like you could put silverware to a plate."

"Yes," Sheriff Coleman answered, a heated prick of embarrassment poking through his cheeks. "Could you send a patrol over to relieve us for lunch?"

"Sure thing, John. Ten-four."

"Thanks. Over and out."

"Over and out." As Sheriff Coleman lowered the microphone, Sergeant Bill finished with a mirthful "And praise be to God."

The bones underneath Sheriff Coleman's cheeks pushed against the skin as though they were preparing to pop out Predator style. *Bill and his goddamn religion. Wasting my time while there's a nutjob on the loose. He's going to get a piece of my—* His eyes caught onto the doctor's, their aggressive shine shaded by a desperate need. *Please, Sheriff,* the dusky blues pleaded. *You can't fight the Devil without God on your side.*

Sheriff Coleman relaxed his jawbone. "Praise be," he said, then returned the microphone to the radio. As a calming mist lightened the doctor's despairing gaze, Sheriff Coleman took a deep breath, then made a mental note to talk to Bill about the God chatter. "Do you mind if we get something to eat?"

His shoulders immediately tightened, as Dr. Bonesteel turned to Nick's house with a long, rustic inhale. *The Devil doesn't take a lunch break,* the sheriff imagined him responding, but instead, he coughed a dry old-man cough and said, "Not at all."

"Good." Sheriff Coleman relaxed his shoulders, then glanced at his watch. "It's almost one. There's a diner about ten minutes from here."

"Sounds good."

With a friendly tip of the chin, Sheriff Coleman turned to the window and looked out at the long stretch of road slithering into the distant woods. *I'll call Mom's house at three and talk to Betsy. She'll probably be calmer by then...or maybe not...* His sea of thoughts drifted through a smoky fog of doubt until his policeman instincts took over. *Snap out of it,* he thought, clearing the fog with a shake of his head. *You need to concentrate so you can catch this lunatic and end this madness.*

Examining the road with an eagle-eye watch, he attempted to find something interesting to keep his head unclouded. The road was a light gray like the feathers of a pigeon, he noted, but unlike the dirty rat birds, it was immaculate, free of tire marks or oil spots. Maybe the residents hired a private service to clean them, he thought. Or did the town foot the bill? *If Betsy's still angry with you, maybe you could tell her what's going on,* a wee voice called from the back of his mind, interrupting his thrilling thoughts on street cleaning. *No. She'll get angry you didn't tell her earlier, and you don't want to destroy your relationship with her. Whatever's left of it.*

"So," he said, turning to the doctor to escape the dark path his boredom was taking him down, "where are you from, Alfred?"

27

Nick, 2:45 p.m.

Blasted by the sound of the shrillest school bells, Nick opened his eyes with a swift jump. *Goddamn lizard scrotum*, he mentally croaked, as he looked around the parking lot filled with brand-new and early '90s shit cars. *Home, home, hoooooome.*

A wave of panic swept across his chunky face as he remembered the two cop cars blocking his escape. As he pulled himself off the pavement, his panic transformed into a fleshy jubilance when he spotted only one cruiser in the parking lot. *This is it*, he thought, arching his thick body into a tiger-like attack, and then started for the two policemen inside. Suddenly a squeaky male voice screamed from behind him, "Happy Halloween, motherfuckers!"

The words dug into his back and yanked his throbbing veins, prodding him to turn toward the school. Holding a murderous scowl, he growled as a dozen students poured out the front doors, their faces brimming with dangerous excitement. As they made their way toward the parking lot, Nick swiveled back to the cop car, his venomous sneer swallowed by the uncertainty of what to do.

He scanned his surroundings, searching for an escape route until he caught sight of the black tarp covering the back of the truck he'd been hiding behind. Smothering the feral grunts and growls that accompanied his movements with a bite of his tongue, he slipped silently into the back and hid underneath the plastic covering.

While a babbling stream of students moved past the truck, cheering their idiotic need for white-people danger, Nick constructed the next step of his escape: he'd wait until the driver left the parking lot, and then, as soon as he or she stopped, he'd jump out, kill whoever was inside and drive away.

Home, he thought, a wicked smile slicing through his doughy cheeks. *Bed, sleep, comics—*

His eyes became two saucers of terror. *No!* he howled from the murky chambers of his mind, as his swampy memory brought up a question: *Is this truck an automatic or stick?*

28

Betsy, 2:45 p.m.

At the sound of the last bell, Betsy lifted herself from the toilet seat and darted out of the bathroom, her round cheeks bent into two red neon signs broadcasting a forty-minute marathon of furious crying. *It doesn't matter*, her mind dictated to her legs. *Get the hell out of here.*

She moved down the empty hallway like a rabbit scurrying toward a hidden thicket of safety until she suddenly stopped on the left side of the chapel, the timid creature realizing she'd left her book bag in her locker. "Fuck." She turned around and headed to her locker.

"What the hell?" she said, after throwing her bag over her shoulder and closing her locker. Within the three seconds it had taken her to retrieve her bag, the senior wing had gone from a deserted wasteland to a madhouse of costumed teenagers.

All right, just go, she thought with a hard exhalation, then started down the hallway again. Trailing the row of lockers, she carefully zigzagged through the disorganized groups of kids chatting about their plans for the night. Repeatedly saying "Sorry," she pushed through the crowd until she reached the corner of the hall and—*bam!*—Mr. Ghostface jumped out, his cloaked arms raised above his head in mock attack. Surprised, Betsy let out a scream that shut down half the student body and all the staff except Mrs. Cotton, who had left early to become "Lola" for her first date with her ex-husband.

"Oh, shit," Kevin Prescott, the senior class clown, said as he took off the white mask. "Sorry. I thought you were someone else."

"That's all right," she said, laughing off the scare. *God, it's like everyone's celebrating Halloween for the first time*, she thought, as she turned away and continued through the hoard of wild students in the main hallway. Power walking toward the front doors, she gave a small smile, remembering the first time she'd gone trick-or-treating: It was with Kathleen. They were seven years old. They both had dressed up as Disney princesses. Betsy was

Ariel from *The Little Mermaid*; Kathleen was Belle from *Beauty and the Beast.*

Betsy released a loud rip of laughter. It was the first and last time she'd seen Kathleen in a dress.

Walking out the front door and down the front steps, Betsy let out a curious "hmm." *We used to be best friends, and now we hate each other. Just because of a stupid* party. The last word was weighted with mistrust, bending her thin smile into a suspicious hook. *No,* she corrected herself. *We used to be best friends until Mom died, and then we started...drifting apart.*

The thought unfolded from a side pocket of her long-term memory. After four months of lying spiritlessly in bed, eating one or two spoonfuls of her grandmother's smoke-flavored soup per day (to keep alive or kill herself, she wasn't sure), Betsy returned to school and a new Kathleen. Once a bubbly "Let's get matching unicorn folders" type of girl, she had turned into a dark entity, more miserable than the entire Trench Coat Mafia. Even worse, while most of the students smiled and asked Betsy if she needed anything, Kathleen treated her with an unsympathetic coldness—as though her mother's death had initiated a secret war between them.

Because they still talked at school and hung out (whenever her grandparents allowed it), Betsy didn't think too much about it at the time. Maybe Kathleen had changed because her parents had gotten divorced during the time she was gone, she thought. Then they had befriended David in eighth-grade English when he had persuaded them that his pen was a mini camera. After several hands-on-the-hips, hyperextend-those-elbows poses from the two wannabe models, the three of them burst into a giggling fit when David broke the news that the "camera" was, in fact, a BIC Cristal ballpoint.

Lovers of everything horror, David and Kathleen had turned into an inseparable platonic couple, leaving Betsy as the third wheel. At first, Betsy was jealous of the self-appointed "soul mates," but eventually she realized they had become different people and perhaps she had the chance to make friends with people who were more...un-Kathleen-like.

Still, she thought they would remain friends until graduation. Before that morning, she'd never thought beyond that, but now she had no idea what would become of their friendship. Would they somehow make up or stay mortal enemies, taking their high school drama to their graves?

"Hey," a robotic voice called out. "Are you getting on or *what?*"

Wrenched from the existential theatrics running through her brain, Betsy turned to the sterile voice and found Ms. Swanson, her pole-with-a-brown-wig bus driver, looking down from the driver's seat with her electrolarynx against the small hole in her throat. With a pissed-off squint, she removed the electrolarynx, took a drag of the Virginia Slim in her other hand, then blew a puff of smoke from her throat hole.

"Oh, I'm s-s-s-sorry," Betsy said, laughing nervously. Lost in the voluminous novel of her past, she somehow had made it through the swarm of students who were scuttling to the line of buses parked on the side of the school and had found her own without getting trampled or run over by the cars speeding down the adjacent road. "I'm...um...um..."

Betsy looked down at the gum-covered pavement. She wanted to go to the parties with Luke, but could she disobey her father?

"C'mon!" Ms. Swanson shouted through the electronic voice box.

"I'm going to walk," Betsy blurted out as she looked up at the yellow-skinned driver blowing smoke rings from her throat hole. "Thank you." She smiled briefly then turned away and headed back to school. Maybe she could call her father, she reasoned, and ask him if she could go to Mike's party. His house was much closer than Ashley's, and she'd be back before the curfew. She stopped in front of the parking lot, laughing. *Are you crazy?* she reprimanded herself, then turned to the parking lot and released a crabby breath. *He'll probably ground you for a month just for asking.*

Catching sight of Kathleen in her beat-up car, she quickly looked away. "Fuck," she wheezed with the remaining air in her lungs, then turned around and headed back to the bus. *All right, it's fine. You can just...call Luke when you get to Grandma and Grandpa's and tell him you've got a stomachache or something.*

Two steps from the curb, Betsy was struck with an invisible bat of disbelief as she watched her bus speed away. "Are you kidding me? This is... This is just..." Her mind scrambled for the best response to the Rube Goldberg machine of shit she was trapped in. "...a big slimy fuckturd!" She felt a soft tap on her shoulder. "What?" she barked, turning around. "Oh!" She blushed as Luke stood in front of her, a towering, breathtaking creature, just like the spiky hair vampires and werewolves in the fan fiction she read as a tween.

"Everything all right?" he asked with a glower that intensified his young beauty. "I was standing at your locker for like five minutes."

"Oh, s-s-s-sorry. It was...really wild in there, s-s-s-so I just came out here."

Luke chuckled. "Yeah, everyone's acting pretty crazy. It must be the curfew."

"Yeah." Betsy nodded and then, in the moment of silence between them, locked eyes with his. Drifting into his sweltering gaze, she imagined wrapping her arms around his muscular back, closing her eyes, and leaning in for a slow "stranded on Labia Island with Pirate Fabio" kiss.

"Suck my big beef!" Vincent D'Azzoto, a twenty-year-old super senior, screamed as he ran past Betsy in his hot dog costume. The abrupt declaration catapulted her from her romantic daze to the chaos of the parking lot.

Throwing his hands into the air, Luke let out a rambunctious "Woo," watching Vincent run through the throng of students toward the corner store across the street. "What a fucking idiot," he said, turning back and laughing. "So are you ready to go?"

"Oh, uh..." Looking down, Betsy tucked her hair behind her ears, asking herself for the hundredth time if she could defy her dad and sneak out of her grandparents' house. "Um, yeah."

"Are you sure?"

She looked up and nodded again. "Mm-hmm," she said, but she still wasn't sure. She didn't want to get into trouble, but she wanted to go, badly. She was so confused.

"All right," Luke said, his dimples appearing from a wide smile. "Let's go."

"Okay." Betsy returned the smile with a weak smirk, then walked with him to his white pickup. *Holy mother of God*, she yelled in her head as a blast of adrenaline rocketed through her. *You're going! You're really—*

"Hey." Luke stopped abruptly. "What's going on?"

Mike, standing next to his Jeep as a quivering blob of aggression, looked up from the plastic object in his hands. "Someone broke my fucking rearview mirror," he said, then held up the deformed shell in his beefy palm.

"Holy shit," Luke replied. "Who the fuck did that?"

"I don't know. I walked out here and saw it on the fucking ground."

"Fuck," Luke said and then, after a short pause, added, "Maybe it was David Ecklund."

Mike's fat forehead bent into a V. "You think that fag did it?"

The excitement on Betsy's rosy cheeks wilted into two gray sacks of frustration. *Seriously, can you guys stop calling him a fag? I mean, that word.*

Luke shrugged. "I don't know. It's possible. Why don't you tell the cops over there?" He gestured to the other side of the parking lot. "I'm sure David won't mind going to prison. Heh-heh."

Sploosh! As if God had ordered a freak shit storm over the parking lot, Betsy's robust frame constricted into a taut shell of disgust and anger. *What the fuck?* her mind rattled off. *Did Daddy send them to spy on me?* Her milky forehead folded into a hateful scowl. *Are you stupid? Of course he did.*

"Fuck the cops," Mike scoffed. "I'm going to beat the shit out of that flamer the next time I see him."

"Good. I'll help you," Luke said, then delivered a mock punch to Mike's arm in a manly display of support. "We'll see you later. We're going to Ashley's party first."

Mike's chunky cheeks, which were squeezed like a threatening fist, softened into wanting strands of putty. "Oh, okay. That's cool… Could you um…say hi to her for me?"

"Yeah, sure." Luke turned to Betsy with a cross-eyed look, then turned back to Mike. "I forgot. What's your address again?"

"330 Wheeler Avenue. In Manlius."

"330 Wheeler Avenue, Manlius," Luke repeated. "All right. See you there."

"Yeah, you too," Mike said, then looked at the broken mirror in his hands again.

"Ready?" Luke asked Betsy.

"Yes," she said with a hard nod, as she shot an evil eye at the police cruiser, imagining the two pigs inside were recording her every movement. *Fuck you, Dad,* her mind thundered. *And fuck you, Kathleen, if you're watching me too.*

"Okay. Go to the other side, and I'll unlock your door."

"Okay." Removing her furious glare at the cop car, Betsy walked around the back of Luke's truck to the passenger side. As he climbed into the driver's side, a tinge of confusion delved between her eyebrows. For a second it looked like something, or someone was lying underneath the black tarp in the back of the truck. And then, with a sudden creaking sound, the passenger door opened. "Thanks," Betsy said, ignoring the bizarre thought, and hopped into the vehicle.

"No problem." Luke let out a quick chuckle. "Mike's so funny. He's got a huge crush on Ashley, but she thinks he's annoying as hell."

"Really?"

"Yeah," Luke said, starting the truck. "He also looks like a dog's ass and smells twice as bad." Pulling out of the parking lot, he giggled like a toddler hearing the word "wiener" at a family picnic. "Hey, do you need to stop at your house for your costume?"

Betsy's insides sprang into her throat, forming a quivering roadblock of blood and tissue. "What?" she croaked out.

Luke turned to her, his amber eyes shooting a beautiful but serious stare. "Ashley's having a costume party."

"I'm sorry. I d-d-d-didn't—"

"I'm just messing with you, Betsy," he said through a burst of heterosexual-bro laughter. "I got a mask as a joke, though. Wanna see it?"

Betsy swallowed, forcing her guts back into her lower half, then smiled with the hope they'd return to the right places. "Sure."

"*All right.*" As he drove toward the parking lot exit, he reached back, pulled out a large mushroom-looking hat from behind his seat, and placed it on top of his head. "I'm a *huge* dick!"

A surprised "Oh" ejected from Betsy's mouth, as she looked upon the cheap polyester cock crowning his forehead. "I thought it was a mushroom or something."

"Nope, it's a penis," Luke said, then reached behind his seat again, "and I got the balls to prove it!" He positioned a pair of foam balls underneath his chin.

Betsy replied with a soft laugh. Not because she was a fan of crude sexual jokes, but because there was a hidden computer chip connected to some sort of outdated area of her brain that had programmed her mouth to entertain the vulgar humor of cute boys. "Oh, wow. That's...s-s-so funny."

"Thanks," Luke responded. "I'd put the balls on, but it's kind of hard to do with one hand. It's even *harder* with two!" Tossing the balls onto the dashboard, he belted out a deafening cackle.

The brain chip forced Betsy to laugh again, but a small voice in her head—one she didn't recognize—asked, *Is this what you really want? This future frat boy whose vocabulary consists of "balls" and—*

Suddenly, as they drove past the police cruiser, Betsy silenced this strange voice and returned to the icy tone bred by her growing rage. *Go to hell, you fucking spies,* she thought, as they exited the parking lot and peeled down the road.

●　　　●　　　●　　　●　　　●

Hunched over the steering wheel, Kathleen watched Betsy and Luke with a set of piercing death eyes. As she observed the lovebirds standing side by side, talking to Mike the Bull Dyke, she aimed her penetrating glare, attempting to sever the silly idea that they were a couple. After two minutes she gave up.

To any of the costumed morons passing by, Betsy looked like one of those pathetic, brainy bitches waiting to get back the pen the handsome meathead had borrowed in English (hoping he'd throw her a thankful wink so she could later masturbate to the image). However, as she'd been Betsy's best friend for more than ten years, she noticed the cherry-colored excitement tinting her pasty skin and the scared-but-still-determined expression stretching out her face and knew with one hundred percent certainty, the silly girl didn't want to get back her pen. No, she was thinking of the different places he could stick it in.

Spotting the bulge pushing against the crotch of Luke's jeans, Kathleen knew he was thinking the same perverted thoughts.

That fucking bitch, she griped, continuing to stare. *We've been friends since first grade, and this is the shit she plays?* A malevolent laugh echoed through the recesses of her heart. *Don't worry, you backstabbing cunt. I'll get you back.* She took a drag from her cigarette, blew out the smoke, then tapped out the ashes.

"Hey," David said, his body squeezed into a pretzel as he crouched underneath the dashboard on the passenger side. "You're getting ashes all over me!"

"For crying out loud," Kathleen said, dropping her fiery watch on him. "Would you get the fuck up?"

His hairy chicken legs pushed into his chest. "No! I don't want to be incriminated."

Kathleen rolled her eyes. "You're not going to be incriminated."

"I don't know about that. I thought we were going to get my Michael Myers mask, but I guess not since we're still here. Surrounded by the police, mind you."

The Lovecraftian monster in Kathleen's soul stirred in its abiding hibernation. *Lose the pussy and kill those fuckers*, it snarled, but she ignored it, wanting David's support (and an alibi if needed), and said, "There's one cop car. And of course, we're still here. Betsy's getting into Luke's truck."

"She is?"

"Yes."

"Okay. Maybe he's giving her a ride home."

Kathleen shook her head as she watched Betsy stand at the passenger side of Luke's truck. "No, I've got a feeling something's up, and I'm going to find out what it is."

"Oh, good," David said sarcastically. "Nancy Drew's on the case."

Kathleen chortled. "If Nancy Drew was a big, fat crackhead..." She took another drag off her cigarette then threw it out the window. "All right, they're leaving. Shut up so I can focus." She started the car, turned up the radio (which was playing the second chorus of Talking Heads' "Psycho Killer"), and sped out of the parking lot.

"*Kathleen!*" David shouted, pushing himself farther into his hiding den. "Are you crazy? There's a cop car right there!"

"Fuck the cops," Kathleen said, her eyes set solely on Luke's truck.

"Oh, okay, fuck the cops," David said, a queasy fear overpowering the lisp in his voice. "What about Luke and Betsy? They're going to know we're following them."

Kathleen's eyebrows responded, arching into a perverse hook. *I could ram into Luke's truck right now and kill them both, but that'd probably scar you for life. Or kill us, I guess.* "All right, fine," she said, easing her foot off the gas. "I'll slow down."

"*And?*"

"And what?"

"And you should probably turn down the music, don't you think?"

"Oh, my God." An exasperated puff of air rattled the sleeping beast inside Kathleen. For a moment, she imagined waking it up by blasting Talking Heads and driving into one of the towering cherry trees on the side of the road. Then she thought, *What good is death without revenge?* "Fine, I'll turn it down. Happy now, you fucking old man?"

"Yes. As happy as one can be before getting arrested for stalking."

Kathleen laughed. "Don't worry, honey. This wouldn't be considered stalking. Trust me."

"Unfortunately I do."

"Fantastic." With a malevolent study, she kept a forty-five-mile-per-hour crawl on the truck. Ten minutes later, she turned off the radio and stopped at the corner of a long suburban road, each sidelined with a continuous row of brown cookie-cutter ranches that looked like a world-record BM courtesy of Ronald and Nancy Reagan.

"Are we at Betsy's house?" David asked, poking his head out from beneath the dashboard.

"No." Kathleen's eyes were still locked on Luke's truck, which was parked about two-thirds down the road. "We're at her grandparents' house."

"*What?* I'm not scaring no old people."

Kathleen expelled a furious dragon's breath through her nose. "You don't have to scare anyone, David, because she isn't staying." Her eyes tapered into bat slits as Betsy stepped out of the truck and headed to the cramped, chestnut-colored box that was her grandparents' house. Kathleen cracked a triumphant smile. "Yup, they're not staying."

"How do you know?"

"Because Luke pulled up to the driveway and stopped. He's obviously waiting for her."

"*Oh*," David said in surprise. "Wow. Good work, Crackhead Nancy!"

Kathleen snorted. "Thanks." She missed the beastly eyes peering out from underneath the black tarp in the back of Luke's truck, as she kept her watch on Betsy standing at the centuries-old door of her grandparents' house. *She's sneaking out*, Kathleen settled. *But where to? Ashley's party or the KFC parking lot where Luke takes all the dumb sluts he screws?*

The snaggletooth on the left side of her mouth took hold of her cheek and slid its hard point into the wet tissue as though she was driving the serrated edge of a knife into Betsy's back. *That ugly whore is going to let him fuck her tonight, isn't she?*

29

The Sheriff, 1:00 p.m.

"It was an unsuccessful first year," Dr. Bonesteel said, sitting next to Sheriff Coleman, his eyes coated with a ruminating, Clarice Starling glaze. "All my attempts to rehabilitate Nick had failed, and I was losing faith in my practice and myself." He paused, shedding his disappointment with a heavy breath. "And then something happened that made me lose my faith entirely."

As Sheriff Coleman's gaze drifted aimlessly over the opulent neighborhood, he passed an undetected sigh through his pointed nose. *I asked the guy where he's from, and he can't go twenty minutes without talking about Nick. He's obsessed.* His tired eyes, a stroke of lavender darkening the bags underneath them, dipped down for a time check. *Where the hell is the patrol to relieve us? I'm ready to pass out.*

Dr. Bonesteel continued. "I made the unfortunate mistake of developing feelings for one of the nurses at Summer Hill. Her name was Maria, a very lovely woman. She had the most radiant red hair I'd ever seen…and a pair of knockers that could give a breast man arthritis." He let out the raspy laugh of a dirty old man. In return, Sheriff Coleman smirked, happy that the doctor was starting to sound more human and less Van Helsing. "It wasn't anything serious. We were only talking to each other—you know, little conversations in passing. However, one day, I finally mustered the courage to ask her out. I was planning on doing it after a session with Nick, but then he stopped that from happening. Do you know what he did, Sheriff?"

Sheriff Coleman sucked in an apprehensive breath. *What did the lunatic use for a knife this time? His toenails?* "No."

"He attacked her with a spork."

"Are you kidding me?"

"No," Dr. Bonesteel said, his eyes spaced out on the distant line of trees. "It happened about three years ago. Maria and a male nurse were handing Nick his lunch when he took the spork from his tray and stabbed the male nurse in the eye. He then grabbed Maria from behind, put the spork up to her eyes, and led her out of his room. He was planning to jump from the fire escape, but fortunately, he slipped down the main staircase, and Maria was able to run away."

Sheriff Coleman's mouth hung open, teasing the millions of dust specks falling through the stale air of the car. "Wow," he finally said, "I've been on the force for a long time, and I've never seen—or even heard of—someone attacking another person with a spork."

"That's because you haven't come across anyone as malicious as Nick," Dr. Bonesteel said flatly. "Until now."

Sheriff Coleman nervously shifted in his seat, keeping his initial response to himself (*The asshole's probably enjoying a hockey game in Toronto by now*). "Right," he said instead, then turned back to the windshield. "What happened after that?"

"Well, I learned two important things from the incident: one, it was impossible to rehabilitate Nick, and two, the hospital needed to take every precaution to keep the staff safe." The doctor paused, unleashing an airy sigh of what could have been. "Unfortunately Maria was so traumatized that she left that day and didn't return. I called her apartment, but she didn't answer, so I went there, but again no luck. I guess she didn't want to be bedfellows with the Devil's counselor." Silence ended the short speech, but the heat of Dr. Bonesteel's words charged the air with an electric tension. An odd, elephant-like roar pushed through his sinuses. "Gee Rover cripes," he said, frantically searching the right side of his coat, then the left. "This coat has too many pockets!" After two more attempts, he triumphantly pulled out his flask. "Finally!" He opened it and took a swig. Following a brisk "Ah," he took another gulp.

"All right," Sheriff Coleman said, reaching for the flask. "I think you've had enough."

"No!" Dr. Bonesteel cried, pulling it away in a Gollum-holding-his-precious tantrum. "I need this. It's the only thing that keeps me from running away!"

"No, it doesn't."

"Yes, it does," the doctor shouted.

"That's horseshit!" Sheriff Coleman shouted back. "You're an alcoholic, and I would know. I'm a recovering alcoholic myself."

Dr. Bonesteel slowly lowered the flask.

Sheriff Coleman looked over at Nick's house, burying his outburst in the freshly cut lawn. *Jesus, you shouldn't have told him he's an alcoholic. Now he's going to leave...* He mentally laughed, imagining the doctor escaping to the surrounding woods, living on snails and mud water until he found Nick. Feeling the man's stern gaze poke his back like a sewing-machine needle, he gave a relenting sigh and turned back to him. "I'm sorry, Doctor. I...shouldn't have yelled at you like that, but like I said, I'm a recovering alcoholic, and I get nervous when I see the signs in others."

"I-I had no idea. I'm very sorry."

"It's all right," Sheriff Coleman said, then tore the stale air with a deep groan as his stomach growled for the second time. "For crying out loud, where's that patrol car?" He grabbed the hand microphone. "Bill, where the heck are the guys who are supposed to relieve us? I haven't eaten anything all day!"

"Sorry, Sheriff," Sergeant Bill replied, less chipper than usual. "They should've been there by now. I'll radio and see where they are."

"Please do," Sheriff Coleman said, then returned the microphone to the radio without a proper sign-off. He turned to the windshield and looked out at the flawless road again, chewing his caterpillar-like bottom lip. *Shit*, he said to himself as silence settled in the car. *As if this weren't awkward enough... An alcoholic doctor and a recovering sheriff on the lookout for a runaway killer. Just like one of those silly crime shows on Fox.*

30

Betsy, 3:00 p.m.

Betsy marched up the stairs to the screen door of her grandparents' small brick house—the same door she'd been told to not slam shut or else it would break (at least three times a day, for about two years)—and knocked on the door with a row of strong, confident knuckles. *There*, they told the glass, carelessly shielded by the torn yellow-encrusted sheet of mesh. *How do you like me now?* A wicked smile stung the soft muscles in her cheeks as she imagined the two cops—probably a pair of senior officers too old for the downtown beat—sitting in the school parking lot talking about fishing or farts or whatever old men talk about. *Assholes. I hope they get fired.*

There was no answer. Rolling her eyes, she remembered her grandparents couldn't hear anything but the raccoons getting into their trash cans at night, so she knocked harder. Again, nothing. Her evil smirk melted away with the rest of her confidence as she stood there, a frumpy sack of stupidity, staring at the wreck of a door until the rustle of autumn leaves crept into her consciousness.

Suddenly a cold chill rushed through her body, inflating the blond hairs on her arms into tiny spears of fear. She felt eyes—the meticulous beam of a crow hunting for worms—on the back of her head. *Luke's*, she first thought, then a second, violent chill shook her rib cage. *Did the cops follow us here?*

Her head started to turn to the street, but she stopped herself then looked down at her right foot tapping against the concrete. *It doesn't matter*, she thought as the computer chip plugged into her brain ran a new program: "Don't Let the Cute Boy Down." *You gotta sneak out or Luke will get mad and tell everyone you chickened out.* Her hand shot up to her mouth as she sucked in a terrified gasp. *Or maybe he'll lie and tell everyone I gave him a blow job at my birthday party.*

"Grandma!" Betsy threw her palms against the glass pane in rapid succession until she finally heard the slow sway of slippers approaching the door.

"All right, already," the old lady said after a brief round of smoker's cough. "I hear ya." Grandma Coleman, a short oval-shaped woman with a handful of white streaks hanging from her purpled-spotted head, opened the door and stared out with the same surly glare she usually wore. "Oh, right," she mumbled, then clasped the green cardigan sweater she was wearing over her floral muumuu with her ghostly finger nubbins. (How she had lost her fingertips Betsy still didn't know and probably would never ask.) "I forgot you were coming over. Hello, Betsy."

"Hi, Grandma," Betsy said with an uneasy smile, then hugged the portly woman, making sure she kept her hands above the elbows like always so she wouldn't catch nubbin fingers. "How are you?"

"I'm fine," Grandma Coleman answered curtly. "Why don't you come in? It's freezing outside."

Betsy, her frayed nerves stoking a bonfire underneath her coat, dismissed the chilly breeze prickling her exposed neck and slowly stepped into the dark foyer, telling herself, *You can do this. Just try not to stutter and go straight to—*

Occupied with the spur-of-the-moment pep talk, she made the silly mistake of breathing in. With one innocent inhalation of the oppressive stench (fresh pea soup seasoned with mothballs and nicotine), a heavy wretch blasted out of her mouth. "Jesus, Mary, and Joseph," Grandma Coleman snapped as she turned to her granddaughter from the doorway. "What the heck is that racket? Your grandfather's trying to relax."

Betsy's eyes, cleansing themselves in a salty solution of tears, dropped to the plastic liner covering the oak floor to hide the pissy sneer on her face. If the eighty-six-year-old, phlegm-filled man hadn't choked on the toxic fumes from her cigarettes, she thought, he would've been able to sleep through a nuclear explosion." "S-s-s-sorry, Grandma," she said, scratching the tears from the corners of her eyes. "I think—"

Betsy swallowed two lungs of pure terror as she looked upon the crucifixion of Jesus—the man's skeletal body supported a shrunken goblin face with two orange glowing eyes—hanging over the living room doorway. Years ago, the statue was propped on top of the glass cabinet in the dining room. When Betsy was younger, she'd sat through holiday dinners of over-salted ham and asparagus, contorting her spine into a candy cane so she wouldn't have to look at Jesus H. Boogeyman. However, a two-hour meal in the daylight with a roomful of adults was a daydream of warm blankets and fluffy puppies compared to the nightmare she'd have to endure each time she stayed at her grandparents'.

A month after her mother's death, she was shipped to their house so her father could cope from the loss of his wife. It started as a weekend here and there, and then gradually, as he slipped further into his "widower's sickness" (as her grandparents had called it), it became a permanent stay at the wax museum of religious horrors. Every night, in her room/Grandpa's fishing storage, when she was supposed to be sleeping off a day's worth of crying and aimless staring, she lay on her twin-size cot with a flashlight aimed at the door.

Her eyes fixated on the brass doorknob; she was scared Jesus with the Scary Eyes would resurrect from his frozen state of torture and lead Grandma and Grandpa's other religious paraphernalia (a holy army of glass angels, plastic saints, and ceramic ducks) to march to the door and then what? Plunge her grandfather's fishhooks into her hands, creating a nasty case of trout-smelling stigmata?

Her horrific visions always ended before she was murdered—maybe because the idea of Jesus as the leader of a killer parade was too sinful. Still, the image of Jesus and his pals stalking the hallways of her grandparents' house, slowly making their way to her room for an unimaginable horror, had kept her awake for two years.

Grandma Coleman coughed up a dry gust of lung cancer, breaking Betsy's train of thought. "What's wrong with your face?" she asked Betsy. "You okay?"

"No," Betsy said. Her mind—knowing this was a golden opportunity to escape to her room—had ordered up a sickly grimace. "I have a really bad headache. Could I go lie down in my room?"

"Oh, my, yes," Grandma Coleman said, the crinkles on her meatless cheeks molded into biohazard symbols. "We don't need any more fevers, or it'll be our time with the Almighty. Go!" She shooed Betsy away with her nubbins. "Your grandfather set up the cot, and I left a pillow and a couple blankets on top, so you're all set."

"Thank you, Grandma." Betsy flashed a polite smile, then headed for her room. Lightly treading past the living room (where the holy army stood attention on a mix-and-match of marigold- and mahogany-colored cabinets) and continuing down the adjacent hallway, she kept an air of sickness, holding her face in a foul tweak until she got to the last door. *Keep going,* she told herself as her face relaxed into the start of a hopeful grin. *You're doing great.*

As she opened the door to her "bedroom," her face straightened into a plank of timber. At first glance, the room looked like it belonged in a convent of nuns who secretly fished; the walls, painted in cream, donned a single cross on the right, and the floor, covered by a mosslike carpet, was furnished with a navy folding cot, a dark-brown dresser, and a collection of her grandfather's fishing poles and tackle boxes stacked in one corner. However, this modest decor was a disguise to anybody other than Betsy. To her, the glorified closet she had just stepped into was a prison cell.

Quickly, she closed and locked the door, then threw her book bag on top of the cot, next to the water-stained pillow and crepe-colored wool blanket she'd be sleeping with for the night or—God forbid—the entire weekend. Without hesitation, she went to the small, square window by the simple black cross on the wall and tried to lift the bottom pane.

As the bottom rail dug into her fingers, sending a line of sharp pain across them, she let go and screamed into her lips. Realizing she needed something to protect her hands, she headed to the dresser and pulled out a frumpy pink cardigan she'd worn once for her grandmother's "We Need Ten Thousand Dollars for the Anti-Abortion Billboard" church fair. As she did, a small laminated card slipped out and landed on the carpet. Betsy's eyes feasted on the picture of the Virgin Mary on the face of the card until her hands grew hungry for a touch. She picked it up and turned it over. Underneath the Hail Mary, was the following text:

In Loving Memory of
Patricia Elizabeth Coleman
December 9, 1964–November 21, 2009

Betsy's tongue sped into overdrive, practically scraping the enamel off the back of her teeth. Was this a sign from her mother, telling her not to go? *Mom,* she asked, closing her eyes and folding her hands in prayer, *are you here? Do you want me to s-s-s-stay—*

"Harold," Grandma Coleman yelled as though she were standing on a distant planet. "I'm heating up some cream of mushroom. You want some*...eckkkkk...*" She hacked a warm course of coughs as if the soup were being served from her mouth.

"No, Maude," Grandpa Coleman barked back. "I'm trying to re-*eck-eck-eck—*"

"Nope," Betsy said, opening her eyes as her grandfather coughed up the rest of the sentence. "I'm sorry, Mom, but I have to go to these parties tonight. I think I deserve to have fun for once in my life. Don't you?" She listened to the heavens for a divine response but received the tail end of her grandparents' gagapalooza. With a flinch of disgust, she kissed the card, placed it in the back pocket of her pants, and headed back to the window.

After grabbing the bottom of the window with the ugly sweater, she slowly opened it until it was all the way up, then crawled out one foot after the other. When both feet touched the ground, she pulled down the window until a sliver of space was left, then turned around and pussyfooted to the corner of the house. A mousy peek found no trace of the cops on either side of the street, prompting a record-breaking sprint to Luke's truck.

•   •   •   •   •

Kathleen clapped her hands. "See, I told you! I fucking told you!"

"What?" David asked.

"She's sneaking out of her grandparents' house!"

David moved up and poked his head over the dashboard. "Ha! Betsy's a badass bitch!" He turned to Kathleen, his face full of feminine glee. "I kind of like it."

She turned to him, a clear message written with her eyebrows: *Are you fucking kidding me?*

David quickly wiped the excitement off his face. "What do you think they're going to do?" he asked in a robotic tone.

"I don't know, but I'm going to find out." Kathleen turned the key in the ignition and started down the street as Betsy returned to Luke's truck.

"Um, Kathleen," David said hesitantly.

"What?"

"I'm a little concerned about the curfew."

Kathleen felt the urge to grab his petite neck and strangle the weak bitch out of him, but suppressed the impulse, deciding she didn't have any more time to babysit him. She was on a mission to kill her former best friend. "Don't worry about the curfew. I'll get you home in time. All right?"

David remained silent for a moment, the decision to fight or flee ping-ponging between his almond-shaped eyes, then mumbled, "Fine." He moved up to the seat. "But I'm not sitting on the floor anymore. It smells like tater tots and shit down there."

"That's because I farted like ten times."

"*Kathleen*! For fuck's sake, I didn't even hear them. How's that possible?"

"I don't know," she said, laughing. "I've got skills to pay my grocery bills."

David stuck out his tongue and made a nonsensical string of tongue garbles. "God, I think I can taste them."

Kathleen laughed again. "Good," she replied, "you paid for them."

"Well, isn't that lovely," David said, then turned to the windshield and watched the back of Luke's truck driving down the next street. *At least she's keeping a good distance*, he thought, then settled into a silent roost of safety. Unfortunately, it took only fifteen minutes to shake him out of this false sense of security. "Oh, yeah, uh," he said, clenching his teeth, "I'm not too sure about this, Kat."

"What?" she said, focused on the road. Heart's "Barracuda" was playing on the radio.

David shifted nervously as Kathleen drove up the on-ramp to the highway. "Well, we're kind of getting on the highway, *soooo...*"

"So what?"

"So I think I should probably...not go."

"Okay," Kathleen stated mechanically and then, without warning, jerked the steering wheel to the right. The car roared across two highway lanes and then, stomping on the brake, she brought the car to a quivering halt onto the shoulder. "Denny's is right over there," she said, keeping her eyes straight ahead of her. "Walk over and call your mom. I'm sure she'll pick you up."

David took a deep breath, sucking his colon back into his body, then shot an angry-old-man stare at Kathleen. "Are you fucking crazy? You could've killed us with your little car stunt, and for what? We're following Luke and Betsy like we're spies, and we don't even know where they're going!"

"They're going to Ashley Rathburn's mega-cabin in Baldwinsville."

David let out a dubious scoff. "Megacabin? How do you know that?"

"Because you said Luke invited Betsy to Ashley Rathburn's party, and this is the way to the fucking castle where she has all her parties."

"And how do you know *that*?"

"Ashley and I were on the basketball team together until I was kicked off and lost the only opportunity at a future. Because of Betsy. Remember?"

"Oh." David frowned, disappointed that he had forgotten such an important detail. He took a chance at lightening the mood. "Wow, you've made another brilliant deduction Crackhead Nancy."

The thin line drawn underneath Kathleen's steely gaze didn't tear away for a laugh. "Mm-hmm. You can get out and walk to Denny's or whatever. I don't care."

David's bony chest caved in. "Kathleen, I..." He stopped and turned to the window, sighing at the grassy hill between the road and Denny's, the late-night drag-queens-and-stoners diner. He was afraid, but at the same time he felt bad for her. Basketball was Kathleen's niche; a fierce and energetic power forward, she'd been the star of the girls' varsity team. Having attended the majority of her home games, he understood why the jock apes at school hated her. Yes, she was a bitch, but she could probably beat all of them at their manly sport for men. And that, all of a sudden, had been taken away from her. "All right, I'll stay," David said, turning to her with an innocent look of surrender, "but if we're going to scare Betsy—"

"No," Kathleen said, cutting him off. "Fuck that scaring shit. I'm going to crash that motherfucking party and kill the bitch!"

David snorted. "Oh, c'mon. You don't really want to kill her."

Kathleen turned, directing the murderous, white mask molded over her face at David. "Yes, I do," she said with a strong hold on each word. "When someone betrays me, I fight back, and you should too. Those stupid assholes like Mike the Bull Dyke have fucked with you for the last..." She raised her hand in protest. "Actually, no, I take that back. I don't want you to come with me."

"What? Why?"

"Because you deserve much better than this, David. You're going to go to Fordham and become a really successful writer, and I'll probably stay in this shit town for the rest of my life, sucking dick for tacos."

David exhaled an ugh of frustration. "That's not true. You're going to go to Manhattan with me, and we'll *both* be successful writers."

Kathleen turned toward the passing traffic and laughed. "No, the only chance I had of leaving this town was getting a sports scholarship, and now that's gone to shit." A pause followed, injecting a sadness into the air. She then gave a second, softer laugh. "I'll be lucky if some hoodlum from my neighborhood knocks me up and I'm in a good mood to keep the thing. At least then I'll be able to get government assistance."

David opened his mouth to reassure her they were going to New York City together, but then he thought there was some truth to what she'd said; Kathleen was an amazing basketball player, but other than that, she'd never really applied herself in school. She was a talented writer (so talented that it made David jealous sometimes), but sadly she rarely finished anything she started. So what was she going to do when he left for college? *Probably nothing,* he answered in his head, then took a deep breath and straightened up, mustering every ounce of courage he possessed. "All right, I'm going."

Kathleen shook her head again. "No, you're not."

"Oh, yes, I am," David responded in his best sassy gay tone. "And do you know why?"

"Why?"

"Because you're my soul mate, and soul mates have to stick together." David nodded, putting a stamp of truth on the statement. "And you're right about the fighting-back thingy. I *have* to learn how to stop being such a sad sack of sperm because...well, what if I go to college and I run into the same type of assholes? Will I let them walk all over me like I usually do?" He swiped his head to the right, and in a baby's voice said, "*No*, I don't want to be afraid for the rest of my life."

Kathleen stared at him for a moment, her prominent eyebrows saying nothing in particular. "Are you sure you want to go with me?"

David didn't hesitate. "I'm one hundred percent sure. But uh...maybe we could do something a little bit different than killing the bitch."

"Like what?"

"I don't know. Can I think about it?"

Kathleen blew out a puff of laughter, cut with a trace of annoyance. "All right, I'm giving you one more chance, and it better not be dumb. And I fucking mean it!"

"All right," David said, laughing back. "Thanks for the motivation."

"Uh-huh." Kathleen turned up the volume on the radio, pulled away from the shoulder, and continued along the highway.

David winced as the Beastie Boys' "Sabotage" blasted through the car. "Mm, I'd probably do a better job thinking if we were listening to the radio at a reasonable volume." As he reached for the knob, Kathleen gave his hand a hard smack. "Hey," he said, pulling his hand away. "Why'd you do that?"

"You know you're not allowed to touch my radio."

He rubbed his hand. "Bitch. I'm going to pop your fucking cyst."

Kathleen snickered. "You don't want to do that."

"Why not?"

"Because it'll spray demonic puss at you."

David chuckled along with her. "Right, I forgot about our movie. Hey, if we do write it, who do you think should play you?"

"I don't know. Christina Ricci would be cool, but I'm such a fat ass that they'd probably get Rosie O'Donnell."

David let out a quick "Oh, you" laugh. "Stop it with the silliness," he said, waving a limp hand at her. "Who should play the cyst?"

"Um...Shia LaBeouf."

"Oh, my God, that's like the perfect choice!" He paused, getting out a few more giggles, then asked, "What about me? There has to be a gay best friend, right?"

"Of course. How about...Paul Rudd?"

"Oh, God, *yas*! I'd definitely have sex with myself."

Kathleen threw her head back and released a hearty laugh. "Jesus Christ, you're too much."

He smiled, considering it a compliment. "Yeah, I know. That's why we're soul mates." Suddenly his face brightened as if someone had turned his inner excitement dimmer to 'New Idea.' "Hey, we should totally have a gay best friend in our final-girl story!"

"Yeah, we should," Kathleen said nonchalantly. "You should probably start thinking about what we're going to do to Betsy, though."

David rolled his eyes. "*Yes, Mother*," he groaned, then turned toward the woods outside his window. Watching the late-afternoon sun weave through the crisp leaves, he gave a small breath, then hummed the opening lines of Roxette's "Joyride."

31

The Sheriff, 1:15 p.m.

For the fifteenth time, Sheriff Coleman looked through the TV-size window, checking his cruiser in the parking lot of J.R.'s Diner. He knew his car was safe; there were two other cars, which he assumed belonged to the staff, and a Mono Transit eighteen-wheeler, probably operated by the bearded loner at the corner table, but checking his car for scratches was a hard habit to break. Especially since there were only two diners near the police station—The Little Gem and No-Name Café—and both were havens for cop-hating street thugs. Every two months he found a key line scratched into one of the doors or, from a literate punk, even a word or two. Mostly it was FUCK U PIG.

The car's fine, he reassured himself. *Maybe it'll even be cleaner by the time we're done.* He laughed in his head, viewing the distant field of untainted ryegrass that could've been the front picture of a postcard reading, "Welcome! You're Not in Shit Town Syracuse." Fifteen minutes from Nick's house, the tiny diner was far from the dirty streets of the city, past the rich snobs of Manlius, resting in a quiet little pocket of a five-hundred-acre plot of cow-tipping country.

Heaven, his subconscious said to his nose, prompting his thin nose to take a big sniff. Even with the odor of cooked hamburger and hot coffee, he could still smell—almost taste—the batch of pines trees standing along the rye field. It was a sweet but powerful scent, like a cup of sawdust drenched in maple syrup. *Man, I'll have to bribe some hillbilly kids to light some firecrackers or something, so I can come here and—*

The sharp sound of a glass cup nicking his table disrupted his thought. Slowly his eyes moved down to the checkered tabletop and Dr. Bonesteel's veiny hand holding his tumbler of water. Sitting across from him, he sensed the doctor's intense stare, a dopey, invasive instrument from the sci-fi movies of his youth, trying to extract the thoughts from his brain. Or perhaps they were gazing wildly, constructing the rabbit's snare he would use to trap the Devil. Sheriff Coleman's eyes stayed on the table, slightly embarrassed from his outburst in the cruiser. "You're an alcoholic, and I would know. I'm a recovering alcoholic myself" wasn't professional sheriff talk. It was a confession from one of those cheesy, daytime soaps: *As My Children Turn* or *One Day to Live*.

"Here you go, baby," said a young woman with a voice dipped in raw honey.

The pet name drizzled into Sheriff Coleman's stew of thoughts and took hold of his human functions, rendering him into a goofy slab of meat. Ever since Patricia's death, he imagined he wouldn't have been a "baby" for the remainder of his life (he didn't have the time or the courage to start dating in the twenty-first century), but Sarah, the short, but padded-in-the-sweet-spots woman, who had led them to their table, taken their food orders, and was now pouring him a hot cup of coffee, had called him "baby" not once but twice.

Sheriff Coleman smiled politely while he threw it in the "Don't think about it" bin. *Nope. She's a cute little chipmunk, but "baby" is just waitress speak for "I want a decent tip."*

However, as he watched the perky brunette serve him his coffee, the horndog inside him rattled out of a long nap. *C'mon, buddy*, he barked. *She wants you. So which part do you want? Those big breasts or ass?*

Immediately another part of his mind pushed him away. *No*, it whined. *Someone as young and pretty as her would never—*

Sarah suddenly bent forward and reached out as though she were about to climb the table and show off her impression of Tawny Kitaen in Whitesnake's "Here I Go Again" video. "Here you go," she said, placing a saucer of creamer tubs and sugar packets next to the sheriff's coffee, then winked at him.

Awoooooo, the horndog replied, then whacked his brain to say something smooth. "Thank you," he croaked out.

"Of course," she said, then pressed her bee-stung lips—coated with a ruby lipstick—into a flirty peck. "Anything else I can get for you?" Keeping her sultry gaze on the sheriff, she poured a cup of coffee for the doctor.

"No, I'm good," Sheriff Coleman replied with a far-too-jolly nod—a subconscious effort to show off his gentleman demeanor. "Thanks again, ma'am." *What?* his horndog howled. *You can't bag this chick with "ma'ams."*

Sarah giggled lightly. "No problem, sweetie. Your food will be ready in a couple of minutes. All right?"

"Okay," he said, then smiled politely again, fighting his horndog's loud protests. Sarah smiled back, then turned and walked away with a confident wiggle. *Oof,* he thought as he watched her vanish through the swinging aluminum doors behind the counter. *I'd like to bite into that beautiful...ass.*

As the thought faltered, his smile disappeared into a limp noodle. He'd never had a sexual thought—about his wife or any woman—as graphic as that. Was it too much? Should he not be thinking of other women? He certainly loved Patricia, but was a naughty thought in a six-year-and-counting stint of celibacy so sinful?

A dry cough from the doctor put a hold on his line of questioning. *Damn it,* Sheriff Coleman said to himself; he'd been caught red-handed, thinking in front of a jittery therapist who'd lost the concept of private thought. Sheriff Coleman, following social norms, tried to fumble through the awkward silence by starting a conversation. "This is a pretty nice diner," he said, then chuckled as he scanned the room; it was nothing special. A pair of tables with matching checkerboard tops stood in the center; a row of red booths lined the paper-mache walls; and for ambiance there was a simple old barn-painting nailed above the door. "I'm surprised more people aren't here."

"Yeah, me too," Dr. Bonesteel said, then fashioned his old mouth into a smirk that hinted, sooner or later, he would pry the thoughts from Sheriff Coleman's head.

Blanking on a response, the sheriff occupied the lack of conversation with a drink. "Oh, God!" he said after a sip of his coffee.

"What is it?" Dr. Bonesteel asked, stirring his own cup of coffee.

"This is damn good stuff." Sheriff Coleman laughed, then took another sip. "Almost as good as my wife's." His hefty shoulders dropped as he released an inaudible groan. He looked at the doctor, hoping he'd ignore what he'd said, but Dr. Bonesteel looked back with an unblinking gaze that said, *I ain't forgetting nothing.*

Sheriff Coleman sighed in defeat. "I'd like to apologize again for calling you an alcoholic. I had no right to say it. I was just...worried, you know. You're probably the only who can to talk to Nick. Lord knows this town would go straight to hell if I had to do it." He let out a wry laugh.

Dr. Bonesteel's stare didn't relent, exceeding the human body's capacity to keep its eyes open without internally combusting. Sheriff Coleman cleared his throat. "So yeah, I'm sorry," he went on. "Like I said, I'm a recovering alcoholic, so I know what it's like to try to suppress bad memories. Believe me, I've been doing it for years."

"Would you like to tell me about it?" Dr. Bonesteel asked. He blinked, and then his eyes returned to their replicant beam.

"Oh, um..." Thinking, Sheriff Coleman licked the residual coffee from his mustache. He wasn't sure if he was comfortable sharing his story in a truck-stop diner, but then again, he thought it might help Dr. Bonesteel. His therapeutic skills needed to be sharp to confront the Devil. "All right, well...I started drinking about six years ago when my wife was diagnosed with stage IV stomach cancer." With the sudden weight of those words, he puffed up his chest, preparing himself for a wrestling match with his emotions. "It was difficult, especially since I knew she was going to die. When she was admitted to the hospital, her doctor told us she had about six months to live.

"Patricia was a strong woman. She had to be in order to put up with me throughout our marriage." He let out a short, bitter laugh. "She tried her best to pull through—she really did—but...it was just too much. After four months, her body deteriorated until it was basically nothing." He paused, remembering his wife's skeletal body and the sad death mask she had worn for the last two months of her life. As a darkness started to sweep through his mind—the same darkness that had waged war on his psyche after his wife's passing—he took a deep breath, then told himself, *No, you're not going down that path again.* Holding the darkness at bay, he started again. "So yeah, it was hard. Of course, my parents didn't make it any easier. They're very religious people, so they kept telling me a miracle would happen, and Patricia would live."

Another deep breath. "I knew she wasn't going to make it, but I didn't tell my daughter that because, you know, how can you tell your child her mother's going to die? So, like a coward, I ran away. I took time off work, asked my parents to take my daughter for the weekends, sometimes for a couple of weeks, and then"—once more he sighed—"I started drinking."

Dr. Bonesteel made a quick sound of displeasure. "You shouldn't think of yourself as a coward, Sheriff. First, there isn't a rulebook for these types of situations, and two, you were trying to handle your daughter's emotions while dealing with your own. That was very selfless of you. Of course, there were consequences."

"You got that right," Sheriff Coleman said with a hard nod. "God, I used to sit and stare at the wall, drinking can after can of beer." Shaking his head, he added, "I could finish off a case of Natural Ice in an afternoon."

Dr. Bonesteel brought his pointer fingers to his lips and suppressed a giggle.

"What?"

"I'm sorry," he said, lowering his fingers. "The orderlies at the hospital drink Natural Ice. I tried it once. It was like drinking a cup of horse piss."

Sheriff Coleman chuckled. "You don't drink Natural Ice for the taste."

"Unless you're a madman."

"Exactly." The sheriff laughed again, then ran his tongue against the inside of his cheek, recalling the crude aftertaste of Natural Ice.

"So how did you become sober?" Dr. Bonesteel pressed.

Shifting to serious mode, the sheriff hid his cheer behind his mustache and answered, "I guess you'd say I hit rock bottom. I was driving to the store for beer while intoxicated. Thankfully I didn't crash or anything, but Bill—the sergeant working the front desk today—pulled me over on a routine stop. He's a terrific guy; he told me he wouldn't arrest me if I joined the AA program at his church, so I did." The ends of his lips tipped up in pride. "That's when things started turning around. I got sober, started going to church, and went back to work. I was so focused that I worked myself up to sheriff."

"Wow," Dr. Bonesteel replied, leaning back in awe. "I'm very impressed."

Sheriff Coleman's shoulders flinched in uncertainty. "Mm, thanks. But I'm pretty sure my drinking caused a rift between my daughter—"

Just then a plate with a western-style omelet and two crispy bacon strips appeared in front of him. Looking up, Sheriff Coleman found Sarah's grapefruit-size breasts saying, *Hello, sugar* to his face. "Here you go," she said, then placed a bowl of cream of wheat and two poached eggs in front of Dr. Bonesteel. "Is something wrong with your coffee"—she bent down to read the sheriff's badge, her breasts returning to his line of sight—"Sheriff Coleman?"

"What?" he asked, staring into her cleavage as though it was the vortex of colored light from *2001: A Space Odyssey*.

"Your coffee, babe," Sarah responded, straightening up. "Doesn't look like you touched it."

"Oh, uh," Sheriff Coleman choked out as he yanked his vision away from her extravagant space show. "We were just talking." He gulped a large breath of suppressed horniness. "Actually the coffee's excellent."

"Good," Sarah said, then squeezed her lips into her signature flirty peck. "Because I made that pot."

"Oh, well, compliments to the chef!"

She laughed a hearty, cowgirl laugh. "Why, thank you, Sheriff. I don't usually get compliments for my coffee." She paused, flitting her petite cinnamon-colored eyes. "So do you two need anything else?" she asked the doctor while placing a hand on the sheriff's shoulder.

As the doctor replied with a "No," Sheriff Coleman felt his penis snake its way over to his gun and lift the barrel from underneath his pants. *That's right*, his horndog whistled. *Show the little lady how you handle your—*

Catching sight of the burly trucker in the corner, wide-eyed with fear from the sheriff's gun pointing directly at his forehead, Sheriff Coleman threw his hand over the erected gun and bowed his flushed cheeks. "Okay," Sarah said, patting the sheriff's shoulder then starting for the back. "Enjoy, boys."

Ask the pretty girl out before it's too late! his horndog hooted.

No, the sheriff replied, biting into the bristles of his mustache. *I love Patricia, and what about Betsy? She'll probably never talk to me again.* He brooded over the thought until he realized he must have looked like one of the doctor's patients, chewing on his mustache instead of the hot plate of food in front of him. He let go of the tiny hairs and unanswered thoughts and dug into his food.

A slow order of chewing and swallowing weren't good deterrents from stopping a busy mind, and he quickly returned to his thoughts. *Sarah seems like a sweet girl*, he ran through his head. *And she's pretty chatty, too. Is there something wrong with getting to know her?*

Hell no, his horndog hollered back.

"What the heck is going on?" he said when she returned to table to refill his coffee. "You've got the best coffee and omelets in town. Why isn't this placed mobbed?"

"Because we don't sprinkle gold into our food for the Manlius housewives," Sarah retorted.

Sheriff Coleman gave a booming laugh. Check one: she had a sense of humor, and check two: she wasn't a snob.

When he finished his coffee, he asked for another refill and the apple strudel in the display case with the other freshly-baked desserts. "I hate to be a stereotype, but I need sugar."

Sarah let out a light laugh. "To heck with stereotypes. You fight crime. You deserve anything you want."

Check three: She respected him, which was a radical change from the waitresses at the downtown diners. *How much cigarette spit can someone digest in a single year without getting a fatal stomach condition?* he often wondered. Sarah then told him her father, a retired lieutenant in the navy, had several friends on the force, so she'd always had a fondness for cops and authority. Sheriff Coleman received an erection that could rob the tiny diner.

Sarah left then returned ten minutes later, asking if they wanted anything else. "Of course," Sheriff Coleman had already planned to say. "Could I get a meatball sandwich for the road?" He wanted to jokingly add "I could use a delicious sandwich for the long night ahead of me," but he worried the mad doctor would interject with, "Because we're going Devil hunting."

Sheriff Coleman was amazed that Dr. Bonesteel had gone an entire meal without mentioning Nick. Staring out with his blue eyes set to normal human, he sipped his coffee through an uncatchable smile more puzzling than the Mona Lisa's. *Maybe he's giving me a break*, Sheriff Coleman thought. *Since he lost that nurse he liked.*

Or maybe he's daydreaming about newspaper headlines: "Badass Doctor Catches Satan."

Sheriff Coleman's meatball sandwich arrived ten minutes later. "Here's your sandwich, babe," Sarah said, her brown eyes sparkling like two pots of her creamy, hot coffee. "And be careful. This sandwich is so scrumptious it might make you lose your head."

They laughed at the same time. "Well," Sheriff Coleman said, carrying on the banter, "I promise I won't eat and drive." His soul shuddered. *That was a tasteless joke*, it scolded. *People die from drinking and driving. You could've died.* And then, as though his confidence had hitched a ride with the cold sweat pouring down his forehead, he pressed the abort-talking-to-the-pretty-waitress button. Switching to sheriff in charge, he wiped the teenage joy off his face and said, "Could I get the check, please?"

Sarah's eyes lost their twinkle. "Yeah, sure," she said, replacing her kittenish singsong voice with the official, J.R. Diner–approved tone. "I'll be right back." She took his cup, leaving a ring of coffee on the table that he almost licked off, and walked away with a sturdy march.

Sheriff Coleman's eyes darted, reaching out with invisible hands. *No, come back*, he wanted to scream out, but he wasn't brave enough. He lowered his head, angry that he'd let one silly joke ruin his chance for...what? A "Sorry, I have a boyfriend"? A thirty-minute dinner followed by a five-minute "Sorry, I haven't done this in six years" bang? A second chance at happiness?

"Shit," he exclaimed, looking at his watch. "We've been here for two hours!" He looked up at Dr. Bonesteel, who was staring back with an enigmatic smile.

"Have we?" he asked.

"Yes," Sheriff Coleman replied quickly, recognizing the man's charity. "I'm going to step out for a second to check on my daughter. Then I'll come back, pay the check, and we can go straight to Nick's house. Okay?"

Dr. Bonesteel answered with a quiet "Okay."

"Thanks," Sheriff Coleman said, standing up and walking to his cruiser. There, he took his track phone from the glove compartment and dialed his parents' number. After three rings, Sheriff Coleman's mother answered with her rough "It had better not be a salesman" voice. "Hello?"

"Hi, Mom. It's John. Did Betsy get to the house yet?"

"Betsy? Yeah, about ten minutes ago."

"Can I talk to her?"

"Okay, but...*chhhkkkk...*" Grandma Coleman's raspy voice rumbled into a wet cough that sounded like one of her lungs had slapped the receiver. "She's in her bedroom, lying down. She said she doesn't feel well."

Sheriff Coleman's eyebrows lifted up like two red flags. *She didn't sound sick on the phone earlier*, his inner detective reminded him. *Let me talk to her anyway* was traveling from his brain to his mouth when his inner father interjected. *Maybe she's still angry with you. Wouldn't it be better if you gave her some more time to calm down?*

He shifted his chair, wiping the coffee-soaked strudel crumbs from his lips, as he mulled over the question.

"Hello?" his mother said. "Those damn squirrels better not have eaten the telephone lines—"

"No, Mom," Sheriff Coleman said, still undecided. "I'm here. I was just thinking. I'll...call back later, all right?"

"Okay. Bye."

"Bye." Returning the phone to the glove department, he turned to the windshield, his focused thoughts turning the diner into a blurry red square. *Yeah*, he thought after a minute of mental tug-of-war. *It's best to give her some time.*

His decision fizzled into the rose-colored wood beams of the diner's entrance. "All right," he grumbled. "Let's get this over with."

Stepping out of the car, he went over the plan in his head: *Go in, pay the check, and say goodbye to sex for the rest of your—* Suddenly he stopped in the doorway of the restaurant, wadding his hands into "Don't grab your gun" fists, as he caught Dr. Bonesteel sneaking whatever was in his flask into his cup of coffee. "Goddamn it. I told him not to..." His voice, like a train burning its last shovel of coal, slowed to a small sigh. "Fuck it. You owe him one." Watching the doctor guzzle the coffee, he gave a brisk shrug. "Maybe it'll help the poor guy. Like Popeye's spinach or something."

II.
Slasher Crasher
Presents:
The Senseless Murders
of
Six Insignificant
Characters

32

Nick lay in the trunk bed of Luke's truck, trembling like a young doe sidelined by an oncoming tractor trailer. His thick purplish veins slithered through his gigantic fists, and his cracked lips squeezed together as tightly as a new inmate's asshole. He was trapped in brutal torture, far worse than listening to the four policemen talk about fishing. He was stuck listening to teenagers.

Shut up and go, his riled nerves begged, as the two boys beside the truck kept blathering about their cars. *C'mon. Go home. Home.* As he tightened his stocky throat around a lungful of air, a crimson streak spread across his forehead. *Shut up, shut up, shut up! Or I'll choke both of you to death!*

An abrupt silence answered his mental death threats and then:

"Fuck the cops," one of the boys said. "I'm going to beat the shit out that flamer the next time I see him."

Nick's body relaxed into an eye-of-the-storm calm. *All right*, he slowly planned in his head. *I'm killing these stupid, fucking kids, and then I'm going to kill those goddamn cops. I don't fucking care if—*

"330 Wheeler Avenue. In Manlius."

Did one of the little cunts say "Wheeler Avenue?"

"330 Wheeler Ave in Manlius," the other boy repeated. "All right, thanks. See you there."

Nick drew a wide, enthusiastic smile from the tough fold of his jaw and pierced it through the top of his cheeks. His luck had returned. He finally was going home!

33

Betsy, 3:50 p.m.
Betsy watched the blurry row of passing maple trees with a thin line drawn across her mouth, the ends curved slightly in excitement. After passing through the small town of Jamesville (its seemingly only functions were selling snow tires and condemning sinners), they were now working their way through an infinite stretch of woods, a blanket made of gray evening slowly covering it.

Speeding into a world she didn't know, Betsy usually would've been afraid of such an adventure, but at this moment, exhilaration was overcoming her fears. The seed of rebellion had been planted in her—perhaps when her father had ordered her to grandma and grandpa prison, perhaps even earlier than that—and now it was pushing through the rigid soil of her father's rules, preparing her for her first real party.

Of course, she had been to plenty of "parties" with Kathleen and David. However, they usually consisted of the three of them—sometimes one of Kathleen's short-lived "boyfriends" would be there too—at David's house watching a terrifying horror movie or something even more disturbing. An obese woman with the worst makeup eating dog feces or a group of teenagers, naked and chained, eating human excrement. Whatever it was, it always involved eating poop.

Betsy looked down at the smooth, sateen legs of her pants and expelled a low breath, a subconscious attempt to shed those vomit-inducing images from her adolescent memories. "Nervous?" Luke said, placing his strong hand on her right knee.

"No." A micro flinch in her forehead asked, *Do I look nervous?*

"Good," he said, then turned to her with a boyish smirk. Receiving a shy smile back, he turned to the windshield, his left hand on the steering wheel and the other remaining on Betsy's knee. Creeping up with a steady crawl, his hand found her thigh and started to caress the soft muscle with his pointer finger. "God, there's nothing out here," he said, as a wave of electric tension flew from one hormonal teenager to the other.

"Yeah," Betsy said, looking out her window, trying to ignore his impromptu massage. Luke was right; there were no signs of civilization except for a row of crooked telephone poles and an occasional opening in the trees suggesting something was hiding in the woods—like an abandoned castle or Buffalo Bill's Museum of Wells. Following the nothingness with an anxious stare, Betsy counted the number of passing trees while Luke's fingers weaved a thin coat of gooseflesh over her body.

Her flesh sizzled like a steak on a hot pan until Luke splayed his fingers and slowly rubbed her inner thigh. *No*, her genitals gurgled, as if a spoon of hot oil had been poured over the sensitive organ. *No, no, no, no...*

Her womanhood squirmed in the sweltering, almost painful sensation, alternating between *No* and *Please stop*. Using the *Fifty Shades of Grey* dictionary, this translated as: *Yes. More please. Keep going until our tongues...*

Suddenly Betsy's Christian guilt took hold of her heart, which was pumping like a train piston, and scolded her. *Stop it, child. You're disgracing God with your naughty thoughts.*

I'm s-s-s-sorry, she pleaded with a silent gasp of ecstasy. *I'll think about...about the party.* A modest smile attempted to appease her guilt. *It's going to be really fun. I hope everyone...*

Her inner dialogue fell silent at the mention of "everyone." In the two weeks since Luke had invited her, she had focused her mental energy on going, and in the chaos that had happened earlier, she'd never taken one second to think about who would be there. *Ashley's the most popular girl at school*, she thought, ignoring Luke's palm moving closer to her sex, *so it'll probably be all the popular people.*

As she mentally listed the popular seniors at Dullen, a low, snakelike voice in her head whispered, *Nervous?*

No, she thought, imagining the blond airheads and equally brainless jocks who would be at the party. *They're dumb as rocks, but they're not mean to me.* The snake-like voice hissed, suggesting that wasn't entirely true. Sure, they weren't mean to her now, but they had been. On the first day of seventh grade, Mrs. Halem, her arithmetic teacher, had asked each student to take the first letter of their name and come up with an adjective that described their personality. Her mnemonic name was Beautiful Betsy, but her nervous tongue turned it into B-B-Buttfull Betsy.

For the entire month, she was called Buttfull Betsy by Ashley and her newly formed clique of the most beautiful students in the grade until her mother passed away. When she returned to school after her hibernation of mourning at her grandparents', the name-calling was replaced with "Hey" or "How are you doing?" Betsy noticed they never followed it up with "Wanna go to the movies or something?"—as if they were fulfilling the bare requirements of their parents' agreement: fifty dollars for civility, one hundred for real friendship—but Betsy didn't say anything. As long as they weren't bothering her, she didn't care.

What if they break their promises to their parents? she asked herself. *What if they're actually planning to play a Halloween prank on you?*

"All right, we're here," Luke said. As the truck slowed, Betsy's eyes traced a path from her window to her leg (sans Luke's hand now), then to the driver-side window. Outside, along an endless barrier of maples, she saw the beginning of a long brick driveway with a wooden gate—as tall as the entrance gate to Jurassic Park—opened to the side.

"Oh, wow," she said with a child's gaze of wonder. She'd only seen houses with gates on *Desperate Housewives.*

Luke chuckled. "This is nothing," he said, pulling into the driveway. "Wait till you see the house." As he continued down the narrow path, Betsy sat up and looked for her first glimpse of the cabin, her growing anticipation overpowering her nerves.

A moment later, her mouth opened in a big O. Ashley's cabin...wasn't a cabin. It was a megastructure. Constructed entirely out of massive cedar logs that could've only been cut and erected by the gods, the gigantic building looked as though it were made of four attached houses: three two-story homes on the bottom and a glass A-shaped standing on top of them.

Scanning the surrounding maples and their royal red tops, which extended to the overlooking hills, Betsy laughed to herself. *This place looks like a supervillain's lair.* And then, triggered by those words, the pesky nerves returned—this time more vicious, as if they were a pack of cannibalistic mutants lurking in the hills, waiting for lost travelers to feed on. *Do you think you belong here?* they asked. *You don't. This place is too good for you, and so are the pretty teenagers inside. You won't get out alive!*

Luke parked his truck next to a pink convertible Beetle. "Hey," he said, his good looks taken hostage by a mischievous smirk. "Can you do me a favor?"

Betsy hid her anxiety with a tight smile. "Um, yeah. What is it?"

"Could you knock on the door while I go hide? I want to jump out wearing my penis hat and scare whoever answers the door." He let out a piglike squeal. "Wouldn't that be awesome?"

Not really, Betsy responded automatically. She wasn't a fan of pranks. They were like name-calling's brain-dead cousin, and having been Buttfull Betsy for a month, she felt a prank could rip someone's self-esteem into shreds as easily as an unwanted nickname. However, the quick insight went through the cute-boy program in her brain and came out as a perky "Sure."

"Great." Luke grabbed the penis hat and foam balls. "I'll run over and hide behind that bush next to the door. And then you come up and knock. Okay?"

Betsy nodded. "Okay."

"This is going to be fucking hysterical," Luke said, then produced a second, juvenile squeal. He put on the penis and balls, got out of the truck, and raced over to the left pine bush, its brother standing on the opposite side of the horseshoe-branded front door. Crouching in a ready-to-pounce position, he turned and nodded. Interpreting the nod as the go-ahead sign, Betsy reached for the door handle in the truck, but her back, layered with a fresh spread of terror sweat, stayed attached to the blue vinyl seat. A second of hesitation challenged the boy program—*Do you really want to do this?*—but then it responded with a *beep-bop-boop-boop*. In English, that meant, *You disobeyed your father. You want to go to the party. You want Luke. He's a silly boy. You can change him.*

Pressured by a "C'mon, let's go" wave from Luke, Betsy stepped out and headed for the front door. Plodding the pebble runway on her tippy-toes, she succeeded in making as little noise as possible, but at a high cost. The woods lay silent, allowing her paranoia to creep out of the sunless cavities and continue their savage taunts. *They're not going to like your little prank. They're going to get mad and tell you to leave. Go, Buttfull Betsy! You're not wanted here. You're not as pretty as we are.*

She approached the door, reaching out to knock, but stopped. From behind the door, cutting through the deep bass of a hip-hop song she didn't recognize, she heard an orchestra of laughter, perfectly timed to her imagined humiliation. *What if they don't like me? Will they—*

Luke snickered. "Go ahead," he whispered.

Betsy's legs tightened, preparing to flee, but the rest of her stayed planted in front of the Log Cabin of Gozer as she received the next message from the boy program. *Beep-beep-beep-bop-bop. Luke will tell everyone you chickened out. Your life will be over.* "Okay," she forced through her shaky lips, then knocked on the door as quickly as she could.

The music stopped, followed by a string of whisperings and someone shouting in a sugary voice, "Coming!" After a bunny hop of footsteps, the door opened. "Oh, my God, I was wondering when—" Ashley Rathburn froze. Or was it the other way around? Did Betsy take a mental snapshot of the tall blonde, her perky breasts and large-for-a-white-girl hips posed perfectly in her plaid boyfriend shirt and denim stripper shorts? Betsy's nerves hissed in her ear, *You won't survive.* "*Oh*, Betsy Coleman—"

"I'm a giant cock!" Luke shouted, jumping in front of Ashley. Immediately the blond girl jumped back with an overly dramatic scream that informed the forest animals and one cocaine-fueled trucker in the surrounding area that a white teenage girl was scared. Luke stood up, laughing a wild roller-coaster laugh. "Oh, man! I totally got you!"

"You jerk!" Ashley shrieked, then slapped his arm with a weak palm.

"Sorry," Luke said between his coming-down giggles. "I had to."

"That was fucking gay," a blunt, angry-man voice said from behind Ashley. Betsy turned to the amphitheater-size living room (deep-fried and super-sized in everything—hanging lassos, bull's horns, and all the signs of classic Republicanism) and stopped dead, her nerves squeezing out every ounce of life in her body with an "I told you so" grip. Four of the most popular and wealthiest students in their class (or "Hitler's Youth of Dullen" to Kathleen and David) were sitting on the two half-crescent leather couches in the middle of the room. Seated were Jeff Storrie, a sour-faced pit bull of a boy in baggy blue jeans and a Raiders jersey (his barely visible lips glued together in a cocky smirk from the homophobic insult he'd just directed at Luke), and his plain popsicle-stick friend, Matt Borodinsky (wearing the same Lucky Brand jeans and Patriots jersey as Jeff), sitting next to him.

Shit, Betsy mouthed as she turned to Melissa Horn and Kierstin Beadel, a set of dirty-blond "twins" with a twenty-pound size difference. They sat on the other half crescent, their faces decorated with beige lip gloss and copper-colored foundation that blurred the line between their typical pancake faces and hookers hired for an Oompa Loompa bachelor party. *They don't know it was me in the bathroom, do they?*

"*You're* fucking gay," Luke told Jeff.

"Please," Jeff barked back. "You're gayer than David Ecklund!"

The nerves on Betsy's wrinkled face settled into a flat pond of "Really?" *Do you hear him?* a small voice protested from a distance gorge of her mind. *This is who you're going to die for?*

Luke laughed. "Oh, really, faggot? I'll show you who's gay." He ran over to Jeff, mounted his left leg, and dry humped it like a horny St. Bernard.

"What the fuck, dude?" Jeff said, pushing him away. "You really are gay!"

"No, I'm not," Luke said, staying on Jeff's leg. "I'm just a cock who likes hot thighs."

"Get the fuck off me, man," Jeff shouted, standing up and pushing him harder. Luke took a couple of clumsy steps backward and knocked into the coffee table, made from two reclaimed wooden beams. A pig-shaped candle fell from the table and hit the floor with a Play-Doh-sounding smack.

"Would you guys stop it?" Ashley screeched. Stomping to the table, she let out a neigh-like groan as she picked up the pig candle in two pieces—its upper body had split from its rump. "Great. You broke my mother's favorite candle."

"Shit," Luke said, straightening up. "I'm sorry, Ashley. I was just joking around."

Sighing, Ashley looked up, her dark-orange cheeks relaxing into resting bitch face. "It's okay. It was an ugly candle anyway."

"I'm sorry too," Jeff said, reaching his stubby paw for her petite golden arm.

"Mm-hmm," Ashley said, returning to full-blown bitch face. She headed to the dark wooden cabinet that stretched from the edge of the log-style staircase to the corner of the room and placed the broken candle in the top drawer. As she turned around, she stopped, her cunt-shaped eyes locking onto Betsy's. She let out a quick laugh, hardened by her black heart. "Um, you can like come in now."

Betsy's shoulders shivered as the rest of the group turned to her. Was she still standing in the doorway? *Damn it*, she thought; she was. "Oh," she said with a crooked smile. "I'm s-s-s-sorry." Before she stepped into the living room, she hesitated—a second in reality, but in her head, it felt like the endless trip of a penny rolling around a spiral wishing well. In this slow-motion version of time, the mammoth living room, trying desperately to keep upstate New York as red as the Confederate flag with its good ol' country tchotchkes, became a hunting lodge with a dark agenda.

Behind the couches stood a brick fireplace the size of a Southern megachurch altar, with a collection of animal skins above the firebox. In the middle of these mock trophies was a space left for the only animal not displayed: human.

It's too late now, Betsy told herself. *Just relax, keep your mouth shut, and don't look that mean bitch in the eyes again.*

After closing the door, she walked into the house with a modest pace, keeping a cautious gaze on the other guests. Flushed from the embarrassment of her poor first impression, she stopped next to Luke, wanting to collapse into her abdomen like Transformer Barbie, but she held her head up, continuing to watch the others as they did the same. Perhaps they were planning the shallow incisions needed to skin her soft flesh. Perhaps not. She couldn't tell.

There was a moment of awkward silence. Then Luke turned to her and said, "Do you want to sit down?"

"Oh, uh...sure," Betsy said with a nervous laugh, then took a seat next to Matt.

More awkward silence followed the odd introduction of Betsy Coleman, the stuttering nobody, to the popular students of Bishop Dullen. "So," Luke said, taking the penis and balls off his head and placing them on the coffee table. "Is anyone else coming?"

"No," Ashley responded, then rolled her poor-princess eyes. "My fucking mom said I could only invite five people if I didn't want her here, *sooo* this is it." A long grimace sharpened her resting bitch face, but then it dulled with a burst of happiness. "Oh, hey. Do you want something to drink? My brother bought us a ton of stuff."

"He did?" Luke said.

"Yeah. There's like four bottles of Absolut and two cases of Bud." She smiled, knowing they were his two favorites, then quickly added, "By the way, you'll have to spend the night if you're going to drink." She rolled her eyes again. "Another one of my stupid bitch of a mom's rules."

"Oh, I uh...don't think I can. I have to drive Betsy back, and we were planning on going to Mike's party."

As if someone had poured a beaker of acid over Ashley's head, the joy melted from her face, revealing a skull missing its toothy grin. "Really?"

"Yeah and—"

"Good," Jeff interrupted. "We're going to play beer pong tonight, and I don't want to catch AIDs."

Luke made an angry squeak. "What the fuck, man? Are you still pissed about the leg thing?"

Jeff stared at him with the lifeless brown eyes of an average, lacrosse-playing teenage boy, then shattered the tense silence with an unsettling clown laugh. "I'm just fucking with you, homo."

Betsy sighed internally as she stared at the polished oak floor. *Why do they have to keep calling each other those names?*

"We can play, but I need a cigarette first," Jeff said, standing up. "You want—"

Ashley spun her head in a quick, almost 360 *Exorcist* fashion. "You can't smoke in here, Jeff, or my mom will *fucking* flip."

The nasty pit bull retreated into a teacup Chihuahua. "Oh, yeah, of course. We'll go outside to the patio, so you don't get in trouble, okay?"

"Mm-hmm," Ashley said through a dismissive smile. "And make sure you close the door."

"You got it," Jeff said, then pulled his cheek muscles into unknown territory, creating a disturbing smile that could frighten the most demonic spirit. The world's greatest magician, he made the disturbing smile vanish as he turned to Luke and Matt. "Are you guys coming?"

"Sure," Luke answered, then placed his hand on Betsy's shoulder. "You wanna come with us?"

"Oh," Betsy said, then looked up at him with a tight smile. She had developed a strong hatred for smoking. Not only did she suffer through her grandparents' secondhand smoke, but she also endured the rancid smell and unplanned trips to 7-Eleven whenever she hung out with Kathleen. There was no escape from the dirty habit she didn't even possess.

At that moment, though, she imagined ten minutes of inhaling the putrid stench outweighed the uncertain horrors of sitting with the Mean Queen of Dullen and her bitch minions. "Yes" was circling the rim of her lips but then she remembered her father had super bloodhound smell (He always knew when she'd been with Kathleen because he could smell the difference between Kathleen's Slims and her grandparents' cigars.) "I'm sorry, but I can't," she finally said. "My dad will probably s-s-s-s-smell the s-s-s-smoke on me."

"Right," Luke said, then pouted. "Okay. Well, we'll be back in a few minutes."

Betsy opened her mouth to respond with a sweet "Okay," but Ashley beat her to the punch. "We'll set up the beer pong." A naughty-girl smile, injected with inexperienced tease, led to, "And don't worry. If you're not going to play, you can still watch me destroy everyone."

"You're not going to destroy me," Jeff interjected.

"*Go fuck yourself!*" Ashley barked. Immediately the large room filled with an icy tension, and all eyes turned to the beautiful, blond girl as she stood soberly like a Paris Hilton Pez dispenser. She coughed into her hand. "Just make sure you close the patio door, okay?"

"Okay," Jeff said quietly. He turned and marched off toward the red door with the steel pentagram—bought as a barn star, but it was actually used in hundreds of black Masses around the Canadian border—located at the back of the room. "Don't worry, bitch," he grunted as he disappeared behind the door. "I'll destroy your vagina with my big dick."

Luke chuckled, warming the chilly silence. "I guess somebody needs a nicotine fix," he said, then started for the satanic door. Matt, remaining a deaf-mute, followed him. "We'll be back in a few minutes."

Again Betsy prepared to say "Okay," but Ashley won the second race. "All right," she said in a lighthearted receptionist's voice. "See you in a few minutes."

Are you in love with him? Betsy grumbled in her head, directing a nasty sneer at Ashley's suede fringe ankle boots. *Stay away from him. He's mine.*

As Luke and Matt headed outside, a stale air, infused with the softest day-to-night hum, settled over the all-female party. "So um...I left the cups in the kitchen," Ashley said, turning to Melissa and Kierstin. "Can you guys help me get them?"

"Sure," Melissa and Kierstin replied in unison.

"Great." Ashley turned to Betsy with a smile less enthused than those she had gifted to Luke. "We have to go downstairs to get the cups for beer pong. It'll just take a minute, okay?"

Betsy nodded meekly. "Okay."

"Okaythanks," Ashley said as one faux-friendly word then walked away with Melissa and Kierstin behind her. As they filed through the door (revealing a glimpse of a long, Lincoln Logs hallway), they erupted into a coven of cackling witches.

Placing a cold hand on the warmth rising up her neck, she looked at the spotless fireplace and frowned, imagining she'd easily win a million-dollar bet guessing who they were laughing at. "Well," she spoke in a hushed chagrin, "at least they're gone."

34

Nick, 4:10 p.m.

Nick's patience was running on the burnt fumes of an empty gas tank. Sprawled across the bed of the white truck, his plastic tub-of-fluff body, exposed to the cold evening air, wiggled against the metallic mat. His pumpkin-size head, wrapped in the black tarp like a massive lollipop, followed along as he clawed the tarp with his razor-sharp nails, mumbling a nonstop train of hate. "Fucking shit brain lizard taint teenagers," he whispered through his teeth. "Get in the house, or I'll fucking chop you up into little pieces and then—"

Calm down, his common sense chirped from the steel cage buried deep in a mesh of malfunctioning neurons. *You don't have to kill anyone. The kids will go into the house soon, and you can take the truck.*

I'd better, he sneered. *Those assholes stopped once, and there was a fucking car following—*

"Um, you can like come in now," Female #1 said in the distance.

"Oh," Female #2 responded. "I'm s-s-s-sorry."

A second later, Nick heard a door close shut. With that marvelous sound of freedom, he threw off the tarp and sprang up from the hard trunk bed, his back freshly loaded with sciatica. Sweeping the miles of surrounding woods, his hunky face scrunched into a five-pound sandwich of confused turkey meat. Why was he in the middle of the woods again?

Spitting out a glob of blood-tainted mucus, he leapt out of the truck bed and moved to the driver-side window. His lips flexed with mild satisfaction; there were no keys, but it had an automatic transmission. He tromped over to the pink convertible parked next to the truck and peered through the window. Discovering it had a manual transmission, he kicked the front wheel, headed to the enormous log cabin, and stopped at the wide picture window next to the front door. The curtains, a watermelon red, teased him with a faint outline of the inside.

He leaned in, hoping he'd catch the whereabouts of the truck's keys.

"So," Male #1 said. "Is anyone else coming?"

"No," Female #1 said back. "My fucking mom said I could only invite five people if I didn't want her here, *sooo* this is it." She paused. "Oh, hey. Do you want something to drink? My brother bought us a ton of stuff."

"He did?"

"Yeah. There's like four bottles of Absolut and two cases—"

Nick placed the side of his fist on the glass of the window. *Keys! Or I'll bust through this window and destroy every one of you!*

"We can play, but I need a cigarette first," Male #2 said. "You want—"

"You can't smoke in here, Jeff, or my mom will *fucking* flip."

"Oh, yeah, of course. We'll go outside to the patio, so you don't get in trouble, okay?"

"Mm-hmm. And make sure you close the door."

"You got—"

Patio, Nick huffed, then went straight to the right-hand side of house, turned the corner, and continued down the tidy dirt path until he reached the patio, half a football field of gray and gold flagstones with a brick fireplace in the center. There, he crouched behind the stone wall that wrapped around the patio, waiting for whoever was coming outside to smoke. Two minutes later, three boys—a trio of white trash bags—stepped out of the house and headed toward the back end of the patio.

Gritting his teeth, Nick watched them. He knew one of the walking bags had the keys to the truck, and he was going to get them no matter what.

•　　•　　•　　•　　•

Luke stopped at the edge of the patio and squinted, his delicate eyes offended by the big ball of fuck-you yellow lounging on the endless forest that was Ashley's backyard. *Fuck, man, the sun's out, and it's still dead-ass cold*, he thought, reaching for the back pocket of his jeans. "Shit."

"What?" Jeff asked, taking a cigarette from the pack in his hand.

"I left my smokes in my truck."

Jeff's sausage neck jerked as he coughed up a hard laugh. "Well, you'd better get them," he said, then placed the cigarette in his mouth. "Because I'm not giving you one of mine." He lit his smoke with a blue BIC lighter.

"Thanks, pillow biter."

"Sorry, cock gobbler," Jeff mumbled with the cigarette in his mouth. He removed it and blew a ring of smoke into the nipple-hardening air. "These little fuckers are a bitch to get. I had to drive all the way to the reservation in Oneida. They don't card there."

"Want one of mine?" Matt asked, offering a cigarette in his breadstick fingers.

"Um, yeah," Luke said, taking it. "Thanks, bro." He brought the cigarette to his mouth but stopped, his small smile of gratitude crooked in apprehension. "Mm, I probably shouldn't."

"Why?" Matt asked.

"I don't know. I don't want to get Betsy in trouble."

"*Oh, how sweet*," Jeff said, his raspy voice dripping with sarcastic romance. He took a second drag off his cigarette, then expelled the smoke through his nose, his mouth occupied by an evil grin. "So I wanna know...does her pussy stutter too?"

Luke's mouth sprang open like a defective bear trap. "Fuck, dude. That's *way* too much."

Jeff hocked up another sausage-neck laugh. "Shut the fuck up, man. I was just kidding."

"Uh-huh," Luke said. "At least someone's interested in me. How many times has Ashley rejected you?"

Matt opened his vanilla wafer mouth, letting out an "Oh, shit!"

Jeff turned to him, his flabby cheeks pulled up into an angry pit-bull bite. "What the fuck are you laughing at, queer? You're so scared of pussy, you haven't said one word to the girls." He turned back to Luke. "And don't worry about Ashley. After I tell her my dick tastes like butter, she'll gobble it down. Trust me."

Luke chuckled a wordless "Whatever."

"I'm not fucking playing," Jeff continued to shoot off. "Besides, I don't see you getting anything from Betsy. Shit, you had the chance to fuck her, and you passed. What's up with that? You scared or does your dick only like it when it's up a guy's ass?"

Matt threw his hand around his mouth and said, "Goddamn. That's savage."

Ignoring the gawky virgin and the rumor that he had swallowed his own jizz at baseball camp last summer, Luke kept his jade-colored eyes on Jeff. He'd been served a down-to-the-tendon, race-to-the-emergency-room burn, and in the competitive world of teenage jocks a response was mandatory. Or one would receive a ruthless litany of sexually oriented humiliation equivalent to a Cambodian back-alley castration.

"Fuck off," Luke planned to say. "As a matter of fact, Betsy and I..." *Stop*, his conscience instructed. *You like Betsy. She's sweet. Not like the other prissy bitches at this school.* "Okay, you know you've got some competition for Ashley, right?"

Jeff's light-blue eyes went dark. "From who?"

Luke smiled triumphantly. *Game, set, and match, bitch.* "Mike Barrett. But I don't think you two losers have a chance in hell." He started for the house. "Sorry, I gotta take a piss."

As he headed for the sliding glass door, Jeff watched him, his eyes charged with a thunderstorm of hate. "Go fuck yourself, you...you...sperm-burper," he shouted as Luke walked into the stadium-size cabin. "Ashley's sucking my dick tonight!" He turned to Matt, who again was laughing at him, and punched his bony shoulder.

"Hey," Matt said, his oblong head peppered in red and white patches as he rubbed his shoulder. "What was that for?"

"*What was that for?*" Jeff mocked him. "'Cuz you're laughing like a little bitch."

Matt let go of his lean shoulder. "No, I'm not."

"Yes, you are."

"*No!*"

"All right, shut the fuck up," Jeff said, turning to the girthy shaft of sunlight trying to cock-slap his face. *Fucking sun*, he thought, adjusting his eyes, then took another drag off his cigarette. The cheap, cardboard-tasting smoke floated to his head, filling the gaps left from his thoughts. *She wouldn't go for Mike... She needs a big dick like mine... A horse dick to fill that huge mouth of hers... How are you going to get that snobby little bitch's attention though...* As he brainstormed, his mouth slowly opened and released a waft of smoke like the coffins in every Hammer film. And then, as the perfect idea struck him, his sparse lips popped out a Crypt Keeper grin.

"Hey," he asked Matt, "wanna go scare the girls?"

"Yeah," Matt said immediately, scared that a second of hesitation would invite a joke about the jizz incident at sports camp.

•　　•　　•　　•　　•

Crouched behind the stone wall, Nick watched the tallest of the three flesh bags return to the house. *Fuck, fuck, fuck, fuck, fuck*, he thought, digging his long nails into the muddy earth. Now there was one less chance to find the keys. Swiveling his head, he planted his owl-like eyes on the two other bags and rethought his plan of attack. On the count of three, he'd slowly sneak up to them and then...what? Snap their necks? Crack their skulls open? *Which one should I do first?* he wondered as he eyed the two bags. *The one who looks like a dog or the really skinny one? Maybe I could—*

Just then the two bags scuttled off to the opposite side of the house. "Go," he ordered, then walked up the steps to the patio, his ponderous upper body bent over like a gorilla on the warpath, and followed them to the ten-foot totem pole—the faces of older country music stars carved into the wood—in the corner. As he glanced around the totem pole, his sweaty palms on Reba McEntire's smiling face, he spotted the two boys—dog boy on the right, white twig on the left—creep alongside the house, snickering to each other. *Get keys*, growled his inner serial killer. *Now.*

Nick's nostrils flared. *No. Need weapon.*

He turned around and searched the patio for anything sharp or heavy. There were four wicker chairs with a horse-shaped pillow on each of the seats and an herb garden with a ceramic gnome holding a sign that read, WORKING LIKE CRAZY TO SUPPORT THE LAZY. He stopped and made a goofy grin as he caught sight of a cast-iron trowel plunged into the circular garden. He walked over to the garden, and as he pulled out the trowel, his conscience, grasping the bars of its cage with the last of its strength, wheezed out, *Please don't do this. They're just boys!*

No, they're garbage bags, Nick interjected, then took the trowel with a pre-hacking grip and lumbered back to the side of the house. As the white twig fell a step behind the dog boy, he tiptoed over the rotting autumn leaves as though they were landmines until he caught up to the tall boy. And then, in one quick movement, Nick covered its mouth and ran the slanted side of the trowel across its neck. A hot spurt of blood shot out, making the same spritzing sound of a child spitting out a mouthful of watermelon seeds. Dog boy turned around and opened its mouth to scream.

Nick dropped the white twig onto the floor of orange-reddish leaves, then cut off the garbage bag's scream by jamming the pointed end of the trowel into its larynx. With a squishy gush of blood, he pulled out the trowel then went for its chest, stabbing it repeatedly until its legs gave out. With a "thick piece of pizza dough pounded against a marble counter" thud, dog boy joined the twig in the pile of leaves and torn flesh.

Nick tossed the trowel to the ground then bent down and searched their pockets for the keys to the truck. They were empty. "*Fuckkkkkkkk*," he hissed, kicking dog boy's head with his black high top. "Where. Are. The—"

The squirrely laughter of two girls in the distance disrupted him. *Girls?* he said to himself as he followed the log-stacked wall of the house, searching the second-floor windows. Scanning the empty windows, he quickened his pace, a line of confusion trailing through the splash of warm blood on his face. "Where are they? I know I heard them!"

His right foot slipped on the edge of a square opening in the ground. Gaining his balance before he fell into the unknown darkness, he exhaled a deep, close-call breath then looked down with wild eyes and followed a dusty staircase winding through the opening until it reached a plain, wooden door. At that exact moment, a second round of girlish giggles erupted from behind the door. *Get the trowel,* the killer inside him ordered, *and find those keys.*

35

Wrenching herself from a mental swamp of misery, Betsy shook her head. "It's fine," she muttered, then scanned the living room from the couch. "They don't really like me anyway." She exhaled a large breath of wonder as her restless gaze landed on the three-tiered chandelier, a row of diamond-shaped cowboy hats dangling from each arm. *My God, Ashley's father must be a multimillionaire.* Her delighted awe pulled back into a taut display of loathing as if a demon had reached out from the underworld and grabbed the back of her forehead. *I wish Daddy was a millionaire instead of a drunk asshole.*

She looked away from the chandelier and discharged a guilt-ridden moan. "Sorry, Mom," she whispered. "I didn't mean that. I know Daddy's been sober for a long time now." She paused, sighing. "It's just, why does he have to be so mean? If he just told me why I had to go to Grandma and Grandpa's house, then I'd be fine." A second pause. "Well, I guess that depends on the reason."

The gears in her head, rusty from this morning's drama, turned steadily, attempting to produce a plausible reason. They suddenly stopped when she spotted the penis hat on the coffee table. *Luke's a child*, said the strange voice from earlier. *You need to go before...*

"What?" she said, as her eyes moved down and found something on the floor near the bottom right leg of the coffee table, something metallic. Curiosity overriding a moment of rational thought, she leaned forward and picked up the silver object. It was a ring of five keys, each marked with a different colored cap, except for the last large key, its black head too big for any cover. *Oh, no. Are these Luke's?*

Glazing over the BMW logo on the head of the large key, she gave a nod of recognition, assuming he'd dropped them when he was fighting with Jeff. *Yeah, they're his.* The boy program relaunched with a series of *beeps* and *boops. Return these keys to Luke. Repeat: return these keys to Luke. He will be happy with you.*

Betsy stood up and walked to the red door with the pentagram. *Wait,* her brain ordered her body, and she stopped, her palm touching the tool of the Devil, unbeknownst that the cold center was filled with a dozen souls of lost American hikers. *Is this okay or will Ashley get mad at me?*

Betsy released a sarcastic snort. *What's she going to do? Kill you for leaving the room?* She opened the door to the hallway, then took a couple steps and stopped once again. Which way was the patio? Down the hall, behind the wall of sliding doors, or did the three boys take the curved staircase to her right?

She chose the hallway, heading down the bare corridor until she reached the sliding doors. "Wow," she breathed onto the glass as the immense stone patio, basked in a blood orange glow from the sun, bewitched her eyes. Pressing her round nose against the warm glass, she envisioned a summer wedding with Luke. And then, as she realized the patio was empty, the vision popped out of her head.

"Maybe he's upstairs," Betsy said, then turned around and headed back to the curved staircase. She started up the wooden stairs toward the towering, observatory-like room at the top. *We can have the reception here,* she thought, then stopped when she heard the faint clacking of boots from below.

Don't, the strange voice shouted as she took a peek down the staircase, but the rebel in her said, *Go.*

36

"Oh. My. God," Ashley said, her hay-colored nails stabbing the soft flesh of her palms as she stormed into the cave-like kitchen. "What the fuck is she doing here?"

"I know," Melissa said, trailing behind her with Kierstin.

"No," Ashley said, stopping at the stone island topped with a slab of green marble and turning to them. "I mean, like, *seriously*. Why the fuck is Betsy Coleman at my party?"

Melissa and Kierstin looked at each other with a Tweedledee and Tweedledum exchange of stupidity, then turned back to Ashley. "I don't know," Melissa said, shrugging. "Maybe she's trying to crash your party. You know, like *Wedding Crashers*."

"*Yes!*" Kierstin told Melissa with a high-pitched laugh. "Remember when we saw that at Ed's house?"

"Ha-ha-ha! Yeah! We got *sooo* drunk on Mad Dog."

"I know," Kierstin said. "That shit was so nasty. And then Ed's friend—what was his name? Rodney? Ralph?"

"Eric," Melissa answered.

"Yeah," Kierstin continued. "He tried hitting on us with the lamest pickup line." She switched from her Minnie Mouse voice to the deep register of a twenty-five-year-old phone salesman. "*Do you girls like Cricket phones?*"

Melissa's pear-shaped face winced. "Oh, my God. He was so stupid. Do you remember when..."

Closing her eyes, Ashley returned her nails to her palms and dug for the blood vessels. *Please, make it stop*, she thought, imagining taking one of the knives from the bamboo block from the island, ripping off the sleeve of her shirt, and adding a new notch to her arm. Pressing her nails until she felt eight pricks of hot pain, she erased the thought and replaced it with her daily mantra: "Popular girls aren't cutters." "Okay," she said, opening her eyes, then freeing the pulsating skin of her palms from her nails. "Betsy isn't crashing my party. It's pretty obvious Luke invited her."

"Ill," Melissa said, her beaklike nose crumpling up. "Why?"

"I don't know," Ashley huffed. "That's what I'm trying to ask you guys." She paused, worried the next sentence would expose the tiny, insecure mutt hiding behind the vicious Rottweiler bite of her too-cool-for-school persona. However, as the two dimwits watched her, the urgent need to ask the question finally came out. "Do you think he likes her?"

"Oh, *hell* no," Melissa said. "She's, like, really gross."

"And she stutters too," Kierstin added.

"Yeah, I know," Ashley replied, crossing her arms. "So why did Luke bring her?"

There was a minute of more moronic staring, and then Melissa said, "Maybe it's a prank."

Ashley's face shone with a rare glint of hope. "Is it?"

"I don't know," Melissa answered with another shrug.

"Oh, my God," Ashley said. "No one said anything in the car. Did the guys say anything at school?"

Melissa and Kierstin turned to each other. "*Um, no,*" Melissa said doubtfully.

"*Yeah, no,*" Kierstin said with the same tone of uncertainty. "At least I don't think so."

Ashley's eyes retreated to the back of her head. *Fucking idiots.* "All right, I guess I'll have to find out myself," she said, starting for the door. "The cups are in the cabinets by the door. Could you guys find them and set them up in the living room? Thanksloveya."

Ignoring their empty-headed stares, Ashley left the room and continued down the hallway, which was divided by four sections of wooden arches, each decorated with overpriced Aztec artifacts bought during one of her parents' illegal prescription runs to Mexico. *All right,* she told herself, as she headed toward the next hallway. *Luke cannot like Betsy. Really, I'm a hundred times prettier than her. And plus, he likes me. I know he does. This definitely has to be a prank.* As she pressed pause on these thoughts, a dark cloud formed over the scared pup inside her. *And if it's not, I'll fucking kill myself.* She let out a quick laugh, recognizing the truth to that statement, then turned the corner at the end of the hall and—

Bam! She collided into Luke's broad shoulder. "Oh, God, I'm so sorry," she said, then laughed off the hard blow to her chest. "I thought you were outside smoking."

"No, I decided not to. I need to go to the bathroom, but um"—Luke chuckled—"I can't find it."

Ashley laughed again—too hard for what she would've considered a dumb mistake made by any other person. "You're too funny. There's a bathroom down the hall." She pointed to a mahogany door—among a dozen other identical doors—at the other end of the hallway.

"Thanks," Luke said.

"You're welcome." Ashley fashioned her pouty, wet lips into an "I like you. No, I love you. Please don't leave me or I'll cut myself" smile. However, as Luke started for the bathroom, the lingering thought that he liked Betsy threatening her life, she let instinct break through the emotional wall she'd been building since childhood. She threw her arm in front of him and said, "No, wait! Can I, uh...talk to you for a sec?"

Luke stopped, an innocent expression intensifying his boyish charm. "Sure. What is it?"

Ashley glanced at him, her yellowish-green eyes glazed with a watery sheen, then looked down at the multicolored, multi-triangular carpet—bought in Guadalajara, made in Taiwan—beneath her feet. "Um..."

•   •   •   •   •

Her mouth open like that of a mounted trout, Melissa gaped at the double-door refrigerator built into the stone wall across from her. Finally, after a minute of clueless silence, she shaped her thin lips into a puzzled ball and said, "Uh...what were we supposed to do again?"

Dead-eyed, Kierstin looked away from the French-top stove, the charcoal-colored rectangle that dominated the other side of the room, and turned to Melissa. "I think we're supposed to get like cups or something."

"Oh, yeah," Melissa said. Her face lay like a flat spongy pancake. "Where are they again?"

"I don't know," Kierstin said, walking over to the row of wooden cabinets standing on her right. "Maybe they're somewhere in here." She opened the first door, took a lightning-quick look inside, then stopped and exhaled an irritated breath. "God, Ashley's such a bitch."

"I know," Melissa said, watching idly, as though she were Kierstin's soon-to-be-fired supervisor. "Can't she get the cups herself? I mean, they're just like cups, right?"

Kierstin turned around and tittered the inaudible laugh of a field mouse. "I know. She's like so ridiculous. I bet Luke doesn't even like her."

"Oh, my God, definitely," Melissa said. "It's obvious he likes Betsy, for whatever reason."

"I know," Kierstin said, turning back to the cabinets. "Ashley's a fucking imbecile. She should just settle for Mike Barrett."

Melissa's pancake face hardened into a rusty plate of iron. "What?"

"She should settle for Mike Barrett," Kierstin said again, grabbing a package of Chips Ahoy from one of the cabinets. "He talks about her all the time."

"Oh." Melissa turned to the stainless-steel refrigerator. A tawny oval, frozen in heartbreak, stared back at her.

"You've never heard him talk about her?" Kierstin said, ripping open the package of cookies.

Melissa remained still as the heartbreak manifested as a sharp ache in her chest. "No, I, uh—"

A sudden, loud knock came from across the room. Throwing out her hands, Melissa performed a frightened shuffle backward while Kierstin let out a quick scream. "Jesus Christ," Melissa said. "What the hell was that?"

"I don't know." With a guilty look, Kierstin returned the cookies to the cabinet then took two steps back. "It sounded like someone knocked on the door."

Melissa turned to the large block of hickory next to the row of cabinets. Her reddish eyes, drawn with the fearful guess that it was some hillbilly meth-head, remained on the door then deflated into an annoyed sulk. "It's probably the guys trying to scare us." Her voice rose in anger. "Okay, dickweeds! Ha-ha. You knocked on the door. *Soooo* scary."

No response. A second later, another loud knock came.

Melissa heaved a deep sigh, producing a small crack in her caked forehead. "Goddamn it," she cried out. "Just answer the door, Kierstin, so they'll stop."

Kierstin turned to her, a frenzied fear stifling her delicate features. "I'm not opening it," she said, imagining it was a pair of forest ghosts. "You do it."

Melissa stared at her, trying to figure out how she could get the idiot to open the door (as punishment for not telling her sooner about Mike), then rolled her eyes, deciding it wasn't the dumb bitch's fault (It was Ashley who deserved the punishment.) "Fine, whatever," she said, starting for the door. "No, wait." She stopped and turned to Kierstin with a wicked smile spreading across her cheeks. "I have a *great* idea." She went to the stove and grabbed a copper pot that hung from the wall. "I'm going to fill this pot with cold water, and then, when I say 'Go,' you open the door, and I'll throw the water at the guys. Okay?"

Kierstin's flat stomach slightly lifted as she released the world's softest giggle. "Okay."

"Good." Melissa moved to the sink, filled the pot with water, then positioned herself at the side of the door. "All right. On the count of three. One...two...three...go!"

As Kierstin opened the door, Melissa took a step back and swung the pot of water forward. The cold water flew into the air and landed on the lifeless body sprawled facedown on the concrete floor at the bottom of an old, wooden staircase. "Oh, my God," Kierstin said, moving toward the doorway. "Is that Matt?"

"I don't know," Melissa said, placing the pot on the kitchen island then walking over to Kierstin's side. "I think so..."

"Is he okay?" Kierstin asked, stepping forward.

"Wait," Melissa said, taking hold of her wrist. "They're just tricking us. Jeff's probably hiding somewhere, waiting to jump out—"

Suddenly something long and heavy swung at them, hitting Melissa squarely in the abdomen and throwing her to the floor. After hearing a piercing shriek from Kierstin, she slipped into a vortex of darkness that lasted for five, noiseless seconds. Regaining consciousness, she found Jeff's stiff two-hundred-pound body pinning her legs to the stone floor. With a blood-chilling cry, she tried to roll him off her, but she wasn't strong enough.

Her eyes erupted in godless terror as a fat, teenage beast raised something black and sharp into the air and brought it into her stomach. Letting out the loudest scream she could produce, she shook her legs in a second fruitless attempt to escape Jeff's weight. The pasty werewolf boy pulled the object out of her then rammed it into her stomach once again.

Her head jerked up toward the off-white ceiling as a tremendous stinging swept through her lower body. Quickly the ceiling became a collection of fuzzy gray dots, and then, after a direct strike to her small intestines, everything faded to black.

•　　•　　•　　•　　•

Laughing nervously, Ashley traced the line of fuchsia and aqua triangles in the carpet with an invisible laser of scared shitless. *Damn it*, she thought as the frightened mutt that lived in her consciousness stood still and whimpered. How was she going to ask Luke if he liked Betsy? She couldn't just ask him outright—then he'd know she liked him and what if, by some chance, he actually did like Betsy?

No, he likes you, she told herself firmly. *You just don't want to sound...desperate.* And then, with a stroke of luck, it hit her. "All right," she said, looking up with her typical facade of confidence, "so you have to promise you won't tell Melissa I asked you this, but...I have to ask you because she's been *dying* to know. Okay?"

"Uh, okay. What is it?"

"I don't know if you know this, but Melissa has a crush on you."

Luke's hazel eyes flew open. "She does?"

"Yeah." Ashley nodded. "A *big* one."

Luke giggled. "Wow. I had no idea. How long has she liked me?"

"Oh, I don't know." Ashley took the longest strand of her hair and twiddled it nervously. "I think she said something at the St. Patrick's Day dance last year."

"The St. Patrick's Day dance?"

"Yeah. Don't you remember? I went with Jared, but he left with some stupid slut from another school, so you gave me a ride home." Letting go of the curled strand and placing her hand on his arm, she gave him a "Pleeeease love me. I have no one else" smile. "That was really sweet of you."

Luke stared at her, blankly or full of thought (Ashley couldn't tell which), then returned her smile with a smirk. "Oh, yeah. Of course." A moment of silence passed between them as she slowly stroked the back of his hand. "So why hasn't she said anything?"

Ashley removed her hand from Luke's arm. *God,* she thought with a mental sigh. *He's so stupid.* "I don't know. Maybe she doesn't know if you like her back." She paused, the worry building a flash thunderstorm in her mind. "Or maybe she thinks she isn't good enough for you because sometimes she feels...not good enough for anyone."

"What?" Luke said, laughing again. "That's crazy."

Ashley let out a soft laugh and shrugged. "I don't know. I'm just guessing." She shook her head; she was being too honest. "It doesn't matter. She likes you, so she wants to know if you're dating Betsy."

Luke's handsome face flickered. "Oh, um, I don't know. Nothing's official. We're just, you know, hanging out."

"Oh, okay," Ashley said cautiously. "So you're just hanging out?"

"Yeah, I guess."

Yeah, I guess. Ashley wasn't satisfied with that response. She had to press him further. "Okay. So do you want to go out with Betsy...or something?" She feigned a ditzy laugh. "Sorry for being nosy, but Melissa will get super pissed if I don't find out if you two are dating."

Luke chuckled. "No, it's okay. Uh, yeah, I think I'd like to go out with her."

The storm clouds broke open, releasing a flood of hurt over the weak mutt inside her. "Oh, my God, *why?* She's so..."

"So what?"

"Gross, okay," Ashley blurted out. "Betsy's really gross. One day in eighth grade, she was stuttering so much in math class that she drooled onto her desk and wiped it off with her *hand.* And plus she's kind of ugly—"

A sharp scream came from the kitchen, followed by a loud crash at the other end of the hall. As Ashley turned toward the crash, she caught a glimpse of Betsy disappearing around the corner.

"Fuck," Luke said, looking in Betsy's direction. "Betsy!" he called out, racing down the hallway.

Ashley scoffed. "Luke? C'mon. I'm sorry. I didn't mean to..." She followed Luke to the end of the hallway then stopped, watching him run up the curved staircase to the living room. *All right, whatever,* she said to herself. *If he likes that ugly bitch, then fine. I don't—* "Goddamn it," she barked, looking down at the floor. Her mother's favorite ceramic vase from Mexico—retailing for six hundred dollars, worth fifteen—was scattered into a dozen shards. "Are you fucking assholes going to break *everything?*"

Another loud scream erupted from the kitchen. "Oh, my God. What the fuck is going on in there?" Heaving a quick, exasperated sigh, she started down the hallway for the kitchen.

37

Betsy, 4:25 p.m.

Betsy's eyes shook with tearful waves, but tapped out from her two outbursts that morning, nothing came out of the tear ducts. As they pulsated like diesel engines drained of fuel, she sped through the wide, brightly lit hallway, hell-bent on getting to the farthest place possible from Luke and Ashley. She turned the corner and found an exact replica of the same hallway as if she were Alice trapped in the Queen of Heart's royal labyrinth. Powered by a full tank of embarrassment, she moved through the maze without hesitation, hoping she'd find the outside of the massive cabin and wake up from the nonsensical dream in which she believed that anyone as good-looking and popular as Luke could like her.

Racing through two more similar-looking hallways, she finally found the staircase that led to the living room. She took the stairs in twos, headed straight to the front door, then hurried toward the driveway. Forcing a moan through her dry throat, she suddenly stopped, stung with the realization that she wasn't waking up from any dream. Her senses were flooded with the nightmare of her reality—smelling the thick, mold-like scent of dead leaves as she scanned the boundless forest, she knew she couldn't escape this humiliation.

"Fuck!" she roared, the muscles in her stomach strained with exhaustion. "Why is everything happening to me?"

"Betsy!" Luke shouted as he ran out of the house.

No, no, no, Betsy thought, hunching over into an embarrassed hook. *Please don't let him—*

"Betsy," Luke panted, stopping in front of her. "Are you okay?" Her legs wobbled as she held on to her flustered hunch. "*Betsy,* are you okay?"

Just go, she thought with a straight line of sight on the red floor of leaves.

Luke placed his hand on her shoulder. "Betsy—"

"No!" she shouted through a dry whine, trying to shake his hand off. "I'm not okay. Everybody thinks I'm ugly and g-g-g-gross."

"Oh, Bets. C'mon." Sliding his hands down her arms, he lowered himself into a squat. "Nobody thinks you're gross. And you're definitely not ugly. Ashley just said those things because she's jealous of you."

While her blond strands of hair blocked her peripheral vision of Luke, Betsy laughed at the shaggy carpet of leaves. "Why would she be jealous of me?"

"Because I think she likes me," Luke answered. "But I don't like her. I like *you*."

She looked up at him. "You do?"

"Yes, I do. Not only are you pretty, but you're also one of the nicest girls at school." Luke's dimples made a second cameo from a deep smile. "And I was about to tell Ashley that, but then someone screamed as loud as *fuck*."

"Yeah, I know." Betsy straightened up, remembering the scream. It was so loud that she'd bumped into the small table behind her and knocked over what looked like an expensive vase. "Who was it?"

"I don't know." Luke paused with a pensive gaze. "Jeff and Matt are probably trying to scare the girls or something." He smiled again and giggled. "I guess they got 'em pretty good."

Betsy feigned a light laugh. "Yeah." They shared an awkward exchange of mindless stares and then, as she searched for something to say, Luke broke the silence with a chilled breath.

"I'm really sorry I brought you here. I didn't know Ashley was going to say those things about you."

"Oh, no, it's okay," Betsy replied. "I wanted t-t-t-to c-c-c-come." She stopped to take a breath. "It was...my choice."

Luke frowned. "I guess. Would you like to get out of this dump?"

Betsy laughed, for real this time. "Okay."

"Great. Do you want go to Mike's party or back to your grandparents' house?"

"Oh, uh..." Betsy wasn't sure what to say; she was done with Halloween parties for the night (and probably the next decade), but she didn't want to go back to her grandparents'. *Could we take a ride somewhere?* she was building the courage to say, but the strange voice from earlier asked, *Is that what you really want?* "Is it okay...if we go back to my grandma and grandpa's house?"

"Sure," Luke said. "Let's get out of here."

He placed his hand on her back, directing her to his truck. "Okay," she said, then stopped dead in her tracks. "Wait. I found your k-k-k-keys on the floor in the living room." She fished the ring of keys out of her pocket and showed them to him.

Luke's silky forehead folded in confusion. "Those aren't mine."

"They aren't?"

"Nope," he said, then took out his key of rings—a Pittsburg Steelers pendant attached—to show her. "Those are probably Ashley's. Shit!" He looked away, groaning. "I guess I have to give them back to her, right?"

Betsy smirked. "Yeah, I guess."

"All right," Luke said, then took the key ring from her. "I have to get my penis and balls anyway." Their eyes met while they laughed in unison. "Damn it, that made me sound super gay, didn't it?"

Betsy made a quick sound of displeasure.

"What?" Luke asked.

Hesitating, she looked down at the wooly carpet of leaves, the sight of an empty condom wrapper among them lost to her thoughts. Again she didn't know whether to say something or not. *No*, the strange voice screeched. *You need to listen to your gut and speak up.* "I'm s-s-s-s-sorry. I don't really like it when people use...that type of language." She looked up at Luke, expecting him to laugh at her.

"Shit, I'm really sorry," Luke said, frowning. "I didn't know."

"It's okay. I just...don't like it. I think it's really mean."

"Oh, well, I don't really mean anything when I say it. It's just, you know, something you call your friends when you're fucking with them."

"David Ecklund is your friend?" Betsy asked.

Luke smiled unevenly. "Well, no, that's different. Pat Kearny told me David wrote this skit in their creative writing class that said jocks are stupid. I mean, if he wants to use some dumbass stereotypes to make fun of me, then I'll do it too."

Betsy sighed inwardly. She told David and Kathleen that their skit— *Yo, Jocks Are Mad Dumb, Son*—would get them in trouble. "Wait," Luke said, knitting his brow, "I thought you weren't friends with him anymore."

"Yeah, we aren't." Betsy paused, giving it a second thought. "Well, I don't know. We might be. Could you just, um...not call him names anymore, please?"

Luke gave a casual nod. "Yeah, of course."

"Thanks."

"You're welcome." A romantic moment settled among the two budding lovers—each of them smiling warmly, as though they had settled their first argument like an old married couple. For the second time, Luke broke the sweet exchange with "You're really pretty."

Pretending to tuck her hair behind her ears, Betsy lowered her head and secured the strands already pressed to her ear with sweat, while her baby cheeks flushed with excitement. She returned his compliment in true teenage girl fashion. "No, I'm not."

"Yes, you are," Luke said, placing his hand on hers. "You're the prettiest girl in school."

Still looking down, she shook her head. "No, I'm definitely not—"

"No," Luke interjected, moving his fingers to her chin. "I think you're the prettiest girl in school and you... Hey, could you please look at me? I want to see that beautiful face of yours."

Betsy looked up with two swollen cheeks.

"There, that's better," Luke said with a butter-melting smirk. "I think you're the prettiest girl in school and you should too. Got it?"

This time Betsy didn't leave a second for the strange voice in her head to question her. She simply nodded and said, "Yes."

"Good," Luke said, then delivered a soft peck on her lips. "Okay. So I'm going to bring back Ashley's keys really quick. Do you want to wait in my truck?"

Betsy nodded, trying to contain the happiness engorging her entire body.

"All right," Luke said, starting for the house. "I'll be right back."

Mumbling something that resembled "Okay," Betsy stood still and watched as he continued to the front door, his perfect, olive-colored skin reflecting in the waning sunlight. "I love you," she whispered, then turned around and headed for his truck.

38

Ashley, 4:25 p.m.

Ashley stomped toward the kitchen, the venom of rejection consuming her *You're a loser*, the venom hissed as it hungrily devoured her self-esteem. *You're ugly. Everyone hates you. You couldn't even outrun that tub of lard Kathleen last month during basketball practice. Kill yourself.*

The scar tissue on her wrists tingled with goose skin. *Yes*, she thought, relishing the thought of going to her room, grabbing her crystal nail file, and raking the end against her inner forearm. Deep enough to release the hurt but staying away from the major arteries. She didn't actually want to kill herself. Her family's wealth outweighed her emotional pain.

For the time being.

"Why are you guys screaming so loud?" she said, bursting through the kitchen door. "Can't you handle a simple task...?" Her insult trailed off from the confusion of an empty kitchen, the lights turned off. "Um, hello?" she called out, as she moved slowly into the room. "Where the fuck—"

She stopped again as she looked down and saw two streaks of...blood? *Yes*, she told herself. It was blood. After three summers of volunteering at her father's medical practice, she had the uncanny talent of recognizing blood by its musty, metallic odor. But why was it here? Was it part of some elaborate prank to humiliate her even more?

Ashley let out a prissy laugh. *Yeah, right. How'd they get real blood?* Her eyes followed the streaks to the back door of the kitchen. A normal curiosity would've taken her to the door, but she was transfixed by the wispy, cherry-colored trail. Eyes fixed, tongue resting lazily in her cheeks, she was transported to two weeks ago when she had missed the winning shot against Dullen's basketball rival, Fowlham High. That night she had gone home, prepared a bath that could cause blistering, and with a disposable razor stolen from her father's shaving drawer, felt the sweet release of pent-up misery with the slow trickle of her blood.

The sensation was so good, so freeing, that she wanted to get on all fours and feel the mysterious blood. Would it have the same enchanting effect? How would it taste?

Just then she heard a slow creak from the pantry door behind her. *Listen,* she commanded, as a surge of fear warned her that someone she didn't know was there, someone who had something to do with the blood on the floor.

Again the normal instinct would've been to run for the door, but Ashley was an orange belt in Krav Maga. One Saturday morning, while she was filing patient reports, a heroin addict, looking for needles, attacked her. Although she was able to escape without any major harm, she received several bruises and a fear of filing cabinets. Even worse, Ashley's father wanted her to stop volunteering, which meant their deal—if she volunteered for three years, he'd buy her the pink convertible she'd wanted since she was five—was in danger of being postponed.

Ashley had panicked. She already had spent countless hours of hard work, filing and restocking the cutlery in the break room. Plus, there was absolutely no way she wasn't going to be the first student in her grade to have a car. So she came up with a proposition: if her dad allowed her to continue to volunteer, she'd take a personal defense class. After two weeks of research, he agreed, but on one condition: she wasn't signing up for Divas in Defense '80s Jam Night at Kickbutt Academy. She was going to learn Krav Maga, the militaristic boxing/wrestling/judo-fighting technique, with UFC featherweight champion Sarai "The Tough Brisket" Aronstein.

Remembering her training, Ashley went into the basic stance, stepping back with her left leg, heel raised, both knees slightly bent. She then tipped her forehead and raised her hands to her face in a pseudo judo chop, waiting for her attacker. Half a minute of silence passed, and then, bursting through the pantry door behind her, the assailant quickly came up and grabbed her neck with his furry claw-like hands. Her first thought: *Bigfoot?* The subsequent thought: *Attack the hairy bitch!*

Raising her right hand, she spun around and pushed his right hand from her neck with hers. Then, balling her left hand into a fist, she punched the weak spots of his face with three quick jabs: *bam* (nose), *bam* (ear), *bam* (chin). Immediately, as the wooly attacker staggered in pain, she took his sweaty shoulders and pushed him into the back door. As soon as his slimy weight lifted away, she turned around and ran out of the kitchen as though she were trying out for the varsity team all over again.

From the imaginary sidelines, her coach, mother, and everybody else who had judged her wretched life watched as she sprinted down the hallway with silent determination. There was no need to scream, she guessed. Everybody was probably dead, looking for cups, or dry humping each other's legs. Besides, she already had concocted a solid plan: head straight to the panic room in the basement, trap the robber or whatever he was with the house's insta-lock system (a push on a panel of buttons locked any door of her choosing), then call the police.

She locked eyes with the sliding barn door at the end of the hallway that led down to the panic room and picked up speed. Halfway down the hall, she heard her mysterious attacker pop out of the kitchen and charge after her.

For such a huge guy, he was fast. His heavy footsteps sounded like exploding landmines set on no-man's-land speed until *boom!* About ten feet away, he lunged forward with an inhuman growl and his long nails set to "murder." Ashley, utilizing the wrestling component of Krav Maga, went for the floor and performed a one-shoulder roll. As the disgusting beast crashed into the barn door, she shimmied backward, grabbed a cylinder glass lamp from a side table, and threw it at his oversized head. "Fuck," she wheezed, missing him, then turned around and dashed for the end of the hallway. Hurtling over the shattered pieces of her mother's vase, she tried again at "Hit the Random Lunatic" and took the shell mask representing the Mexican god Quetzalcoatl (fifteen hundred dollars retail, an art project of the seller's daughter) from the wall and flung it like a Frisbee. Again she missed.

She let out a hoarse grunt, hearing the invisible crowd of spectators shouting, *C'mon! Can't you throw a lousy Quetzalcoatl mask?*

Fuck off, she yelled back. *I'll do something amazing, I swear.* Continuing through the hallways of the lower level, with the man only an arm and a half away, Ashley searched her database of Krav Maga counterattacks for something out of this world. Something that would make *everyone* love her.

As she approached the curved staircase, "Eureka!" in neon pink flashed across her eyes. She had her something amazing—but it wasn't anything she had learned from Krav Maga. It was from her elementary-school years of "Mom's forcing me to do this" cheerleading. This is what happened: when she was halfway up the stairs, she jumped up to the inner railing, grabbed the banister above her head, and as soon as she felt the wild man run into her feet, she wrapped her legs around his thick neck as though she were setting up for a shoulder sit. Squeezing every hard-earned muscle in her thighs, she pushed him forward until his heavy gut hit the railing, forcing his upper body over. With a front flip, he fell to the floor, landing on his back with a titanic smack.

"Suck a dick, you fat *slob*..." For a second she thought the tub of goo with the pale, squash face was Gordon McCann, the creepy junior who had stalked her Instagram until she got a restraining order. *That can't be Gordon. Didn't he move to Ohio?*

As the white blob wriggled from his floor plank, Ashley shook off the thought and headed upstairs to the living room. "What the fuck?" she shouted, searching the coffee table for her phone with a pair of red-hot coals for eyes. There was nothing but Luke's stupid penis hat. "It was right—"

The red door swung open with an explosive blast, flinging the pentagram into the air and revealing her superhuman assailant. Producing a horse scream from her lungs, Ashley started for the door, but with his supernatural speed, the hairy man was already behind her, grabbing her neck with a murderous hold. Instinctively she spun her head out and bit his fingers as hard as she could. As the man moved back with a pained howl, she scrambled free from his hold and started for the door a second time.

She took three steps forward, and then, in one swift movement, the beast jolted up and threw what she thought was a cotton bag over her head. Ashley tried to bite his hand again as he covered her mouth, but the bag was too thick. Resorting to panic mode, she kicked her legs in a wild frenzy, trying to escape his grip, but again no luck. He held her with the strength of the jaws of a great white shark.

And then he tightened his sausage hands and broke her neck with a brisk snap. Immediately Ashley's legs stopped kicking. She hung from his arms like a sick lamb being carried to the cutting stump.

•　　•　　•　　•　　•

Holding Ashley's keys in his right hand, Luke stuffed his own keys into his pocket, then opened the front door of the cabin. "Hey Ashley, I—" He jumped back, half surprised, half scared to see...Gordon McGarbage? He had hardly noticed the kid except for the time Gordon had knocked into him at last year's homecoming game (he had made sure to return the favor by pushing him into a garbage can at lunch the following Monday), but he fit the description of what he remembered: a fat, curly-haired slob with a creepy sneer that made him look like he was always about to murder someone.

But why was *he* there, and why was Ashley dangling lifelessly in his arms with the penis hat over her face? Luke snorted with laughter. "Holy shit, guys," he said, imagining this was payback for his door prank. "You got me, but Ashley forgot to yell, 'You're a big, flaccid cock!'"

He waited for Ashley to rise up and scream the punch line, but she remained still. And so did Gordon.

Luke laughed nervously. "Okay, McGarbage. So is that it or is there more to this stupid prank?" Again there was no surprise "You're a flaccid cock" scream. "All right," Luke said, stepping forward. "I found Ashley's keys, so—"

"Gordon" took a quick step, throwing Ashley's lifeless body at him. Without thinking, Luke reached out and caught her as she crashed into his chest. "Fuck," he yelled, falling backward into the door with what felt like a duffel bag filled with fifty-pound dumbbells. And then it hit him: he wasn't holding Ashley. It was a mannequin—perfectly matching her buxom figure—with weights attached to the legs. "What the fuck, faggot?" he screamed, dropping the dummy to the floor. "That fucking hurt—"

Gordon grabbed him by his wavy curls and rammed his head into the door. The hard blow felt like a rod—made of brain freeze and extraterrestrial noises—had spiked his brain. Luke's animal reflex reacted with a lazy swing to Gordon's flabby arm, but he missed, resulting in a limp-wristed gesture that said, *Girl, I just got the face crack of the century.* Gordon responded by taking a firm hold of his hair and beating his bleeding head on the door until Luke couldn't feel the rod in his brain anymore. Or see. Or breathe.

Ashley's key ring fell from Luke's hand, and then his lean body followed, landing on top of her as if they were preparing to have sex in the afterlife.

39

Betsy, 4:40 p.m.
While Luke's skull was being cracked open—a spritz of brain shooting out like an Epcot water fountain—Betsy was sitting in his truck, chewing her thumbnail with a giddy smile that circumnavigated her round face. *He said he liked me*, she thought, looking out the passenger window and imagining herself floating through the evening sky in a magical love bubble. *Me! Not Ashley. Or Kathleen—*

The bubble stopped midair and its wall, a rainbow-colored sheen, converted to fart green. "Shoot," she said, looking down at the collection of cigarette butts on the floor. She was so preoccupied with the party that she'd forgotten about Kathleen. What would happen when she returned to school on Monday? Would Kathleen forget the whole thing or would she be waiting at her locker, prepared to finally go to jail for murder?

Betsy laughed. "Are you stupid? Even if you apologized..." She inhaled the demented notion of apologizing to Kathleen. "No, she doesn't deserve an apology. She's a horrible human being who deserves to be miserable for the rest of her life."

Shame seized her growing anger as she imagined her mother and the notorious "eyes swollen with grief" expression she used on the rare occasion when they got into an argument. "I'm s-s-s-sorry, Mom," Betsy said. "I know I shouldn't stoop to Kathleen's level. I should probably forget everything and just...pretend like she doesn't exist, right?"

Right, Betsy felt her mother answer. However, her soft pinkish lips rebelled, raising the right side in doubt, then whispered in the secret pocket of her mind where her mother couldn't hear her thoughts, *If only Kathleen could do the same.*

At that moment, she heard the driver-side door open and turned to...

Confusion grabbed hold of her mouth—*Gordon McCann?*—and then horror pushed its rotted, skeleton hand down Betsy's throat and seized her frightened heart. It wasn't Gordon who had entered the truck, but the crazy beast-man who had chased her to school, his greasy pumpkin-head splashed with...red paint? *Wh-wh-what's going on?* she thought in a stiff state of shock. *Why's he here?*

The mysterious psycho tried to put the key he was holding into the ignition. It didn't fit, though. He tried it once more, but again, it didn't go in. And then, suddenly, he squeezed his large hands into hammers of rage and pounded the steering wheel in a follow-up to his "destroy all cars" rampage from earlier.

The violent jolt from the steering wheel popped Betsy out of her happy bubble of forever love and sent her on a four-hundred-foot vertical drop to hell. Pushing every ounce of air in her lungs, she let out a "Could this be my last" scream, causing the beast-man to spin around and release a cry of "I thought I was alone." Silence followed, diffusing the tension between these terrified strangers as the large man stared at Betsy, his head slanted to the side like a terrier trying to place a familiar voice, while Betsy stared back with a clear view of his pasty face, thinking, *Wow. He really looks like Gordon.*

The man's hand, a five-pointed harpoon, sliced through the silence toward Betsy's throat. With a second scream, she grabbed the door handle, pushed open the door, and fell out of the truck. Her back hit the soggy ground with a hands-clapping smack, but powered by a rush of adrenaline, she got to her feet as fast as she could and ran straight to the cabin.

As she raced into the living room, her knees turned to putty, and she dropped to the floor, which was littered with greasy bits of gore and blood. Her heart, cradling the last strands of young love, imploded in an end-of-the-world explosion as she saw Luke—the gorgeous but silly senior who had granted her first kiss, whom she loved and would someday marry—slumped into a permanent sleep with his head cracked open like an egg. "Jesus. Fucking. Christ!" Betsy shouted, catching sight of Ashley's limp body sprawled underneath his. "He's mine, you slut!"

As she leaned forward with the intention of dragging Ashley's skanky, dead body to the garbage where she belonged, the sound of dry leaves crushed by charging footsteps halted her plan.

40

Kathleen, 4:30 p.m.

Speeding down an endless stretch of road, Kathleen gripped the steering wheel with two sweaty woodworker's clamps for hands and scowled at the windshield, ignoring the rich foliage encompassing the road. As well as the road. *Fuck that stupid cunt,* she ranted in her head. *She didn't like Luke before I told her I did, so why now? Did she get a sudden craving for dick or was she just jealous that a fat bitch like me could get a boyfriend before her? Why the fuck does he like her any—*

"Um, Kathleen?" David said from the passenger seat.

"What?" she snapped, thrown out of her thoughts.

"I just checked my phone. It's a miracle that I get service in cousin-fucking country." David gave a quick laugh. "But um...it says it's about to get dark soon, *so...*"

"So?"

"So I'm worried we'll get into a *Hills Have Eyes* situation." Another quick laugh. "You know?"

No, I don't, Kathleen thought, her eyebrows erected in big exclamation points. *Are you serious?* they asked his proud "I made a horror reference" smile.

It immediately vanished, and he answered, "I don't see Luke's truck. Unfortunately, I was looking out my window, admiring the *beautiful* foliage. So I have to ask: did we lose them or are you going slow like I asked?"

Kathleen wanted to tell him, "Shut up, we haven't lost them" and return to the riddle of the hour: why would Luke date an ugly bitch like Betsy? However, he was her best friend who had stuck with her through the hardest of times—the two scumbag boyfriends who had cheated or suddenly left, the fits of depression—and so she felt like she shouldn't reward that type of loyalty with lies.

Unfortunately she didn't know when she had lost Luke's truck, how long she'd been driving since then, and whether she and David were even still in

New York, so she responded with the first fact that came to her. "There's a large gate in front of Ashley's driveway."

"A large gate?"

"Yeah, it's wooden."

"*Oh, you don't say,*" David responded, impersonating his favorite *RuPaul's Drag Race* queen, Alaska Thunderfuck 5000. "*I'll start looking for Ashley's large wooden gate.*"

Kathleen snickered. "Mm-hmm." Her cow eyes squinted, transforming the road into a notepad and imagining the title "Why Luke Likes That Bitch" written on the horizon. After a moment's thought, she asked herself, *Maybe because she's practically the only cherry at Dullen that Luke hasn't popped?* She paused. *Has Alice gotten fucked?* Another pause. *Yeah, Joey Duffer got deep in her fried rice last—*

"Kathleen?"

Bite my dirty, white twat, she shouted in her head, ripping out the list from her imaginary notepad. "What?" she said stiffly.

"Are you still mad at Betsy?"

Kathleen grasped the steering wheel, fighting the temptation to shove his stupid question up his ass. "Of course I'm still mad at her. She sold me out for fucking cock. Why would you even ask that?"

David shrugged. "I don't know. You look really mad and...I was just hoping you'd forget about Betsy, and then, you know, we could go get some frosty chocolate milkshakes!"

Kathleen chortled. Not because she wanted to, but his naïve humor—though she expected he had slipped in some truth—was too charming. "No, I didn't forget," she said, then let out a careless sigh as she turned back to the road. "I've been thinking about something else, though."

"What?"

"I..." She hesitated, afraid he would laugh at what she was about to say, then remembered he had kept his cool (relatively) when she told him she liked Luke. "I just don't get it. I know I'm like fifty pounds heavier than Betsy, but I think I have, like...a prettier face than her, right?" She looked again at David for a sign of agreement.

Without delay, he nodded. "Oh, yeah, definitely."

"All right," Kathleen said. *He agreed a little too fast, didn't he?* "And I wasn't being a total sarcastic bitch when I was hanging around Luke, *so...*"

"*Soooo?*" David drew out like Alaska Thunderfuck.

"So why did Luke pick Betsy over me? I mean, what the fuck? Why does she get the nice guys, and I get a Chinese pedophile and an asshole with a six-year-old brat?"

David chuckled, remembering her last boyfriend, Kevin Maloney, was a fry cook at McDonald's who had a five-year-old son David had nicknamed Happy Meal. "How's Happy Meal?" he'd ask Kathleen, then jokingly add, "Did you teach him the importance of perseverance?" or "Are you allowing him to experience the natural consequences of his actions?"

I'm sure Happy Meal remembers you as a positive female mentor was ready to shoot from his mouth, but recalling the night that Kathleen had rammed Kevin's car with her bumper when she had found out he was sexting Happy Meal's mother, he chose honesty over a lame wisecrack. "Um, I don't know, but Luke isn't a nice guy. He called you a fat bitch, *and* he isn't so keen on the gays, no?"

"Yeah, okay," Kathleen agreed. "He's an asshole. So what about you?"

"What about me?"

"You're a nice guy. Would you go out with me?"

David laughed. "Um, yeah. As long as I never saw your *vagina*!" He stuck out his tongue and made a low "I'm about to vomit" groan.

Kathleen rolled her eyes, finding no charm in his response. "C'mon, I'm serious. What if you weren't gay? Would you go out with me?"

With an innocent, toddler-like pout, he stared at her for a moment, then gave a wide smile that looked like he was using every muscle in his mouth to support it. "*Yeah, of course...*"

"Oh, my God, you're such a fucking liar."

David laughed again. "Well, what am I supposed to say, Kathleen? You're—"

"A fat, ugly bitch," Kathleen finished for him. "Yeah, I know. I get it."

"Oh, Kourtney, Kim, and Khloé! I was *not* going to say that."

"Uh-huh," Kathleen replied with less focus on the road than the anti-abortion assembly that happened every spring at Dullen. "Then what were you going to say?"

"*Well*, I was going to say I wouldn't go out with you because...honestly, you're different than me."

Kathleen snorted. "Exactly. I'm a fat, ugly bitch."

David huffed a powerful puff of air. "Goddamn it, would you stop saying that? I mean you're different because you don't give a shit about school; you drive like a fucking maniac; and you listen to music really, really loud." He squealed in frustration. "We're complete opposites! You're a total badass, and I'm a fucking…goody gay shoes." Suddenly an invisible terror tore open his eyes. "Shit! I forgot to text my mom."

Out of habit, Kathleen eyed the backseat in the rearview mirror. (*That's David for you*, the glance would communicate to Betsy, but this time, she wasn't there to return an "I know" smirk.) "Why do you have to text her?" she asked, looking back at the windshield with the mental warning: *Do that shit again and no more Kerouac.*

"Um, one: I don't want her to call the FBI," David said, taking his phone out of his jacket. "And two: I love her, so I want to make sure she isn't worrying about me. *Heyo*, I got a bar!"

Kathleen laughed again. "You're right. We definitely wouldn't work as a couple."

"Told ya," David said, texting away on his phone. "We're homies for life, yo, but you'd kill me if we ever went out."

"Why's that?" A small smile crept out of her steel-trap mouth, preparing for more of his ingenuous humor.

"Because you're fucking Kathleen Strife," David said, returning his phone to his jacket. "You deserve a badass motherfucker and not a whiny little bitch like me."

Kathleen exhaled a quick breath that was somewhere between a laugh and scoff. "You're not a whiny little bitch."

"Yes, I am. I'm a prissy little snob, and we both know it. Now say you're going to meet some sexy, badass motherfucker and fall in love with him."

Kathleen pushed a crow-like squawk from the back of her throat. *Yeah, right*, she thought. She was a fat, ugly bitch who was perpetually stuck with McDonald's workers and baby daddies.

"*Kathleen*."

"What?"

"I want you to say you're going to meet a sexy, badass motherfucker and fall in love with him!"

Kathleen shook her head. "No."

"Why the hell not?"

"Because…" She took a glimpse of him, the poster child of squeaky-clean queers trying to squirm their way into *Fox & Friends'* America, then turned away, thinking, *No. He wouldn't understand. He's too…normal.* "Shit!" she said, spotting a wooden structure from the corner of her eye.

"What?"

"I think we just passed Ashley's cabin."

"Oh," David said, looking behind him. "We did?"

"Yeah. It's all right. I'll just turn around."

"Oh, fuck! Kathleen—" With a sharp cry for help, David shot his hand out and reached for the passenger-side grab handle as Kathleen jerked the steering wheel and made a sudden *Grand Theft Auto* U-turn.

41

Betsy screamed as the obese psycho, his X-Acto-nails raised in rip-to-shreds mode flew toward her. Hurtling over Luke and Ashley in their frozen missionary position, she raced through the living room, back through the red door and down the curved staircase, returning to the labyrinth of hallways. There, she flew through the corridors until—*bam!*—she collided into a mahogany table against the wall, nearly avoiding a face plant into the shattered vase she'd knocked over earlier.

"Shit," she mouthed, hearing the heavyset lunatic run down the staircase, then looked down the hallway. Confronted with a dozen choices of doors, she heard the strange voice in her head urge her to hide underneath the table rather than play *Let's Make a Deal*, serial-killer edition. She followed the voice's suggestion, dropping to the floor, crawling underneath the table, then pressing her legs against her chest as hard as she could.

As the man's heavy *klomp-klomp-klomp* footsteps approached, she sucked in a quick breath and held it at the top of her lungs, hoping her body would forget it needed to breathe. The man's massive legs ran in front of the table then stopped. Why? She didn't know, but as his legs stood stiffly, she covered her mouth with her shaking hands and prayed. *Please, Lord, protect me. I know I've sinned. I've disrespected my father, and I let Luke...I let L-l-l-luke—*

The humongous creep walked away from the table, toward the opposite end of the hallway. *Oh, God, thank you,* Betsy thought, uncovering her mouth and releasing a hard breath that might've been her last if she'd kept it in for a second longer. *Thank you so...* A worried hush spilled out of her mouth, as she realized she was still underneath the table. *D-d-d-damn it! How am I s-s-s-supposed to get out of here...*

Luke's keys, the strange voice offered. *Go back to the living room, get his keys, and drive his truck to the nearest house.* A veil of confusion encased the fear carved deep into her face. Whose voice was it that kept speaking to her? Was it her own? Or her mother's?

She guessed her mother's. *But I don't know how to drive, Mom. Daddy never taught me.* She paused. *Well, he tried but—*

Do you want your skull bashed into your brains like Luke's? the voice snarled in a biting tone that was less Mom and more Dr. Kornberg, her speech therapist from middle school, whom she despised for his drill sergeant tactics. *No, you don't. You need to sneak off to the living room and get those keys... Now!*

Okay, okay. She listened for the sound of the man's footsteps, and then hearing nothing but the gentle hum of the never-ending house, she poked her head out and looked down the hallway.

It was free of psychopaths. *All right, go,* the voice commanded. A second shot of adrenaline swept through her body, convincing her leg muscles to start moving. Slowly Betsy crept out from underneath the table, took a step forward, and—*crunch!*—stepped on a shard of vase camouflaged by the baby-oil shine of the wood flooring. A booming growl resounded from the end of the hallway, and then, once again, she heard those heavy footsteps sprint toward her. Releasing a scream, she bolted in the opposite direction, backtracking through the maze of halls and then upstairs to the living room. Heading straight to Luke's spiritless body, she bent down to try to grab his keys from his pocket. She didn't have enough time, though. The mad giant burst into the living room and darted toward her.

With another horrified scream, Betsy made a panicked dive to the right then continued to the staircase with the giant on her heels. At the top, she headed to the first room she saw and reached for the faux pink diamond doorknob. As she turned the doorknob, the man's bearish claws grabbed her hair and pulled her backward. "No!" she cried, her hands instinctively grabbing for something. She got hold of a metallic picture frame—a glamour shot of Ashley, age seven, as Little Miss Crisco—from the wall and swung it over her shoulder with a harder-than-expected, Little Leaguer swing. The wild beast-man immediately let go of her, releasing a shrill bellow.

Quickly Betsy entered the room and locked the door behind her. "What the hell?" she rasped, as her fleeting sanity was slapped with a bigger, more bizarre shock. The oval bedroom, painted in thick coats of hot pink, was a fanatic shrine to Hello Kitty. At least fifty idols of the Japanese bobtail-cat-inspired character—lamps, rugs, the white tail of a vibrator sticking out from underneath the plush pillow—surrounded the canopy bed in the center. "Is this...Ashley's room?"

The ends of her mouth twitched, trying to break the stone-cold misery on her face with a smile, but then—*whap!*—a sudden thud thrashed the door. Startled, Betsy vaulted toward the other side of the room, screaming. "Why are you doing this? I don't even know—"

Shut up! Dr. Kornberg instructed. *He's not going to listen to you. You need to get out of here.*

How? Betsy asked.

Check the window. Maybe you can climb down the roof.

What? I can't climb— A second, harder thud attacked the door. Betsy's solid thighs rattled with fear. *Okay, I'll climb down.*

After moving to the wall across from her, she ripped off the pink-and-white Hello Kitty curtains from the small picture window and threw them to the floor. "Yes," she exclaimed; the roof, a mild slant tiled with California redwood shakes, looked like an easy climb down to the gutter and then a short drop to a padded field of dry leaves. She grabbed the bottom rail of the window, but as she started to pull up the lower panel, the murderous hulk rammed into the door, producing a tremendous thump infused with a quick cracking sound.

"Oh, God," Betsy whimpered, turning to see a thin split running down the middle of the light-pink door. Turning back, she clutched the rail with an impatient grasp and lifted the window, leaving a square space for her freedom. She took hold of the sides and crept through the window frame until—*boom! crewkkkkkkk!*—the door broke open with a thunderous crash.

Propelled into do-or-die hysteria, she pushed herself headfirst through the window. And then, after successfully maneuvering her right leg through the small space, she attempted the left but slipped on a soggy clump of leaves and fell onto her back. As she rolled down the roof, a stream of obscenities spurted from her mouth, paused as she swung over the gutter, then returned even louder until she dropped onto a quilted mat of leaves—a soft blow to her entire body except for the back of her head, which landed on the rim of a tree stump.

A torrent of pain and dizziness flooded her skull, sweeping the rest of her into a gelid sleep. In the second she was still conscious, she looked up at the patches of blue sky scattered among the skyscraper-like trees and softly said, "I'll see you soon, Mom."

42

Kathleen stomped on the brakes, stopping the car about a foot from pile driving into the gate to Ashley's cabin. "All right," she said, turning to David. "What did you come up with?"

David, folded into a protective cocoon of arms and legs, released an infuriated jumble of sounds. "Goddamn it, Kathleen! You need to stop driving like a maniac, or you'll wind up killing someone!"

"Uh-huh," Kathleen uttered carelessly, as she smoothed down the wild strands of her hair in the rearview mirror. "Did you think of a new plan?"

Sitting up, David grumbled in his head, *One of these days, Kat, you're not going to be so lucky*, then said, "*Yes*, I did."

"Okay. Are you going to tell me it or not?"

"Oh, my God, yes," David answered. "Jesus, just give a minute for my nuts to pop out of my ass!" He let out a snippy laugh as he adjusted the crotch of his jeans. "All right, my balls are still here. So we know—or we've *surmised*—that Betsy was giving Luke a blow job at her party, but it was cut short by her dad, right?"

"Right."

"Okay. So I'm guessing that those two hornballs are going to go at it again at this party since Daddy isn't in the picture, don't you think?"

Kathleen shrugged. "Yeah, probably."

"So I was thinking we—or, you know, perhaps *you*—can sneak up to the house, take a pic of Betsy and Luke getting their freak on, then text it to her. She'll feel guilty for being a hypocrite and apologize to you, and then we can all go back to being best friends. Yay, friends!" He gave a wide, comical smile, knowing Kathleen didn't want to speak or even pass gas in Betsy's direction ever again.

He was right. As Kathleen titled her head in a half crook, her eyebrows grew thick with rage.

"Um, Kathleen?" David said, then laughed anxiously. "Is that a sign that you don't like my idea?"

"No," she said flatly.

"No? Um, okay. So is that a 'No, it isn't a sign, and you do like the idea' or 'No, you think the idea is complete shit'?"

Kathleen groaned. "Quit it with the constant need for approval, you brilliant cocksucker. I like the idea. Except for one thing."

"What's that?"

"Well, I like the idea of taking a picture of Betsy giving Luke a sloppy bee-jay, but we're not going to send the picture to her. We'll send it to her dad so we can let that hypocritical cunt know she shouldn't fuck with me ever again. Sound good?"

David's eyes widened in alarm. *Ruh-roh*, he thought, then looked down at the dingy floor of the car. *You probably should've known she was going to turn your idea into something evil.* "Um, are you really sure you want to do that?" He looked up and clenched his teeth, thinking of how he could reason with his cold-hearted friend. "What about...fem-i-nism?"

"Oh, suck my dick. Just because she's a girl doesn't mean I can't get back at her for what she did. We're getting back at Luke too, aren't we?"

David released a small laugh. "How? All his ape friends will probably give him a pat on the back."

Kathleen opened her mouth but said nothing. "Yeah, maybe," she said after a couple seconds. "But the basketball teams have a morals clause, so once Coach Lynn finds out Luke had sex, he'll kick him off the team. And I'm sure Betsy's dad will notify Coach Lynn as soon as he finishes cutting off Luke's dick. Okay?"

"Um, *okay.* I guess that's...fair." David sighed internally. What else could he do or say? Pretend to have a stomachache? Pull off his shoe and beat her over the head until she was out cold?

"All right," Kathleen said, adjusting her bra, then opened the door. "Are you ready?"

David's anus clenched as though he'd heard his gym teacher, Mr. Morris, blow his whistle for changing time. "Oh, uh...Kathleen?"

"What?"

"I...um...um...I..."

"For fuck's sake, you sound like Betsy. Spit it out!"

"I'm sorry," David exclaimed, "but I can't go! I just can't. I'm really, really, *really* sorry." He turned away and pushed his head against the window in embarrassment.

Kathleen closed the car door, mumbling something—the words "fuck" and "vulva" were heard—underneath her breath. "C'mon, man. Don't tell me you're still fucking scared!"

As the sweat from David's forehead collected into a warm slime against the window, he looked out at the calm woods surrounding the car, wondering how he could the describe the complexity of his emotions. "Yes, I'm scared," he finally said, "but uh…"

"But what?"

"But there's more to it than being scared." David took an apprehensive breath, fogging the glass against his chin. "I don't want to go because…well, you know how I said we're complete opposites?"

"Yeah."

"Okay. So we're different in many ways. Like…you tend not to care about what people think about you, and I…well, I kind of do."

Kathleen narrowed her eyes. "Okay, but these people hate you."

"Yes, I know," David said, shaking his head at the irony of the situation. "I'm the big pile of shit from Jurassic Park to them, but I still want them to like me." He laughed, remembering his dream about Mike Barrett that morning. "God, I probably shouldn't tell you this—or anyone, except the shrink I *know* I'll have when I'm an adult—but uh…it'll be good to get it off my chest." He nodded. "Yeah, it'll be good. Do you want me to tell you?"

Kathleen shrugged. "Sure."

"All right. So I have this dream every couple of months or so. In it, I'm running away from a masked serial killer like I'm the final girl in a horror movie." He paused, rethinking his statement. "I guess it would be more like the final gay, which is better for us queers. We haven't had many final gays in horror films."

He gasped, slapped with the backhand of a new idea. "Oh, my God, that's what our story should be about! A final girl gone bad—you—and a final gay—me—trying to kill some homicidal maniac because…because he killed the final girl and we're the only ones left. Holy shit, doesn't that sound amazing?"

Kathleen chuckled. "Yeah, it does, but I should probably be called the final fat girl."

"Oh, stop," David scoffed. "We're not going to call you the final fat girl."

"Mm-hmm. Could you get back to your dream?"

"Right," David said, laughing. "So anyway, in my dream, I'm the *final gay* who's running from this Michael Myers-esque serial killer until we have a final showdown. Of course, I kill him, and then—and this is the really weird part—Mike Barrett appears out of nowhere, and he's really happy that I killed the guy. You know, we're high-fiving and hugging and um...that's when I wake up with a huge hard-on." His eyes popped out as he gave a nervous giggle. "Fuck, I'm a total freak, aren't I?"

Kathleen smiled in return. "Pretty much. But that's good. I was starting to think you were too fucking normal."

"Well, we can't have that, can we?" David said, then smiled back. "But...I'd like to clarify that I'm not sexually attracted to Mike, like, at all! I think I just..." He blew a messy fart sound through his lips. "I don't know. I guess I just like the idea of being accepted, you know?"

"Yeah, I know, but people aren't always going to accept you, and you're gonna have to deal with that. You said you don't want to be afraid for the rest of your life, right?"

David sulked, realizing she was right. "Yeah, I did, but I...I just can't do it right now. I'm definitely not ready for something like this. Is that all right?"

"It's fine," Kathleen said, sounding dejected. "I'll just go myself."

"Are you sure?"

"Yeah. Whatever."

"*Oh, my God, Kathleen—*"

"Stop it," Kathleen said in a gentle but stern tone. "I said it was all right and I meant it. You're not ready, so I'm not going to push you. Okay?"

"Um, *okay.*" David smiled innocently, worried she would deposit his cowardice into a deep-seated reserve of resentment to cash out later. "Thank you. I really appreciate it." He paused. "And hey, now I can be your getaway driver—"

"No," Kathleen said immediately. "Nobody can drive my car but me, and I'm not just speaking metaphorically. This fucking car literally won't move unless I occasionally finger bang it."

As she reached for the door, David looked down the long, empty road ahead and squeezed his ostrich-shaped neck into a hairy tightrope. "Wait," he blurted out. "So you're probably going to hate me for saying this, but...I think you should park the car somewhere down the road."

Kathleen spun around, shooting an evil glare she would only give to most of the student body and half the staff at Dullen. "Why the fuck do I need to do that?"

"Well, it's a party, and we're literally *right* in front of the driveway, so yeah, it might be best to get out of the way. Unless you want one of the apes to come by and try to beat the gay out of me."

Kathleen kept her malevolent glare on David. "All right, fine," she acquiesced, as her dark horse eyes softened into a cold look of indifference. "I'll move it, but that would have to be a pretty hard beating."

"Thank you," David replied, ignoring the homophobic diss. "And please, could you try not to—"

Kathleen stomped on the gas pedal and sped forward.

43

Betsy, 4:50 p.m.

Lying on her back, in a motionless straight line, Betsy witnessed a universe stretched across an infinite belt of darkness, thronged with thousands of disembodied voices calling out to her. Each one was unique—some were soft and meek, while others were loud and harsh. The loudest of the voices sounded like Dr. Kornberg's. *Get up, Betsy*, it instructed. *I didn't teach you to be a quitter. Now wake up or suffer the horrible—*

You gotta stand up, the mellow voice of an older woman cut in, *and run away as fast as you can.* Hypnotized by the darkness, Betsy remained on her back. *Please, Betsy. You gotta get up. I don't want that man to hurt my sweet angel.*

"Mom," Betsy said, bolting to an upright position and opening her eyes. Two red-hot pricks, heated by a surge of sunlight, punctured her corneas. "Ow," she hollered, closing her eyes, but the sharp pain burrowed through the soft tissue of her brain and drilled the back of her head for a way out.

"My head," she said, as she moved her fingers through her damp, frizzled hair, right below the round bone of her skull. She rubbed the crusty paste of something that had collected in that spot until her eyes were free from the two pricks of scorching pain. *What?* she thought, opening her eyes to a crisp autumn day, and then looking down at the blotch of blood and brown crust on the tips of her index and middle fingers.

Her mind was bombarded with questions: Why was she bleeding? Was she hurt? Did she need to call 911? Where was she? A survey of her surroundings revealed a scant amount of information, leading to more questions. She had hit her head on a tree stump, but how? She was in the middle of a forest, populated with tall trees and a mountainous cabin she'd never been to or seen, but how did she get there and why? And where was her mother? That was her mother's voice she'd heard, wasn't it?

"Mom?" Betsy scanned the woods a second time but, finding nothing except a sprawling wasteland of shriveled leaves and rotting wood, looked toward the side of the cabin, a lofty wall made of amber-colored logs each about the size of her garage. *Maybe my mom went inside*, she thought, focusing on the door painted the same light orange as the logs, then stood up.

A wet hiss shot through her teeth as a pang exploded in her lower back then ran down her right leg. "*Owww*," she said again, freezing in place. She stood still until the pain subsided into a dull tingle, then continued to the door, a slight limp melding into her cautious pace.

"Hello? Mom?" she said, approaching the door. "Are you...alive?" She stopped once again, her memory injecting her mind with the sad reminder that her mother was dead. Her face, glazed with a tepid concoction of sweat and tears, puckered into tiny folds of bewilderment. "Wh-wh-what's going on here?"

Just then, a monstrous roar—half human, half dinosaur—erupted from the second floor of the cabin. It was followed by a heavy crash of glass and metal that stamped her backside with a blazing branding iron that read, "Run, bitch!" Without thinking, Betsy zoomed along the side of the house until she reached the corner and fell into the giant cedar post that stood there. Ignoring the fierce sting that returned to her leg, she peeked around. When she spotted the white truck in the brick driveway, her eyes, fogged with the frightening feeling that she was lost forever, shone with recognition.

"That's Luke's truck." Her eyes brightened even more. "He gave me a ride to Ashley's party. This is Ashley's cabin!" She stepped out and turned to the massive house with a big smile. The smile dissolved with a new set of questions. Who had made that horrible noise? Was it one of the boys? Or was it Luke, performing another one of his stupid pranks?

"That's so mean!" As she stormed toward the front door, her bright eyes dimmed until they were black with rage. "I almost cracked my head, and he's—"

Luke, lying on his back, his left eye open in a calm stare and the right one kneaded into a puffy, blood-covered dough of forehead and brain, restarted the real-life horror movie that starred the petrified and possibly concussed Betsy Coleman. In an instant, she remembered everything: Kathleen and David, Luke and Ashley, and—

Like an overweight, straggly haired bull, the crazy man who had chased her earlier charged down the stairs and tore through the living room. Everything in reach—the coffee table, the gaudy *Hee-Haw* decorations—he knocked down or over or off, dismantling the country-style mansion into a trailer park struck by Hurricane Psycho.

"*Him!*" Betsy rasped, as she watched the foul thing with two silver dirks for eyes—one aimed at his throat, the other at his balls.

Run, Betsy's mother, Dr. Kornberg, and all the other voices from the dark universe shouted in unison. *Or he'll kill you.*

Layered in a film of exhaust and cold fright, Betsy's brain told her body to flee, but her heart—upon seeing the only boy she'd ever liked who actually liked her back was gone, forever—sprouted a thorny vine of fury that traveled down her legs and planted her feet into the stone steps underneath them.

C'mon, Betsy, her mother bawled louder than the other voices. *You have to—*

No, Betsy stated matter-of-factly, as the vine multiplied into a network of hate, swallowing the frightened girl who wanted to run and hide. *I loved Luke, but this fat asshole killed him*—she was tempted to look again at Luke's mangled body but stopped herself—*so now it's time for payback.*

Betsy, no. You—

"Hey," Betsy barked, stepping into the house. "Come and get me, you f-f-f-fucker!"

The beast-man froze at the coffee table and turned to Betsy with a dopey, caught-by-surprise stare and a leather pillow shoved in his mouth.

"Are you s-s-s-stupid or s-s-s-something?" she asked after a couple of seconds, then raised her empty hands. "I've got nothing on me, so come and get me, you dumb bastard!"

With the pillow hanging from his teeth, the man stood perfectly still. The surprise faded from his huge eyes, but the idiotic stare stayed glued to his pupils. *C'mon,* Betsy growled within. Falling deeper into this radical beast version of herself, she waited for the man to attack, trusting her primal instincts to figure out what she would do in return. *Is this man an idiot or is he just looking—* A sinister smile soiled her face as she remembered the man's tirade against Luke's steering wheel. "Hey, moron! I know where the keys to the truck are."

Immediately the man spat out the pillow then jumped off the table and rushed at her. Betsy, like a young cadet running into battle, countered with a war cry and dashed for the enemy without an inkling of what she would do when she got to him. And then, as the disheveled psychopath approached her with two thick hands held out for a murderous choke, Betsy's inner rage gifted her with super-ninja abilities. With the speed of a gray blur, she used the coffee table to hop onto the man's sourdough loaf of a chest and pummeled his head.

She scored about ten punches, and then thrusting his long nails into the soft flesh of her upper arms, the man threw her off him. Crashing onto the leather couch cushions piled against the coffee table, Betsy ignored the sharp blow to her back and the hot splash of blood on her arms and rolled away, her wrath ushering her straight into the next offensive. After shooting to her feet, she grabbed the golden ruby floor lamp standing at the end of the couch and swung it like the racket of a determined tennis player, Maria Sharapova grunt included.

Betsy whacked the brute in the side of his gut, halting his bloodthirsty charge. She attempted a second swipe at the monster's stomach, but he caught the lamp and, after a six-second match of tug-of-war, snatched it away. As he plowed forward with the shattered light bulb aimed like a bayonet, Betsy backed away blindly until she bumped into the fireplace.

Quickly tapping into her ninja powers, she climbed onto the mantle like a spider monkey, ripped the stuffed raccoon off the wall, and bashed the man's wooden block of a head with its over-starched back. As he released the lamp and stumbled from the fireplace, Betsy grabbed the deer antlers that hung next to the raccoon, then leapt off the mantle and dropped onto the man, driving the ice-pick tips of the animal bones into his shoulders.

Together they collapsed to the floor screaming—a blubber of pain from the man and a motivational wail from Betsy—as she pushed her entire weight into the plague of antlers. However, Betsy's weight was no match against the live sack of angry cement blocks she was wrestling. She lasted about ten seconds before she was flung into the fireplace with a mighty kick to the groin.

Receiving a stiff slap to the back of her head, Betsy couldn't ignore the pain this time. Like a power tool with a headache attachment, it felt as though the fireplace had drilled a do-it-yourself migraine into the middle of her brain. The blow blinded Betsy with a milky circle of stars that drifted aimlessly in her central vision until the sound of sneakers scraping against the wooden floor shook her out of her daze.

She screamed, watching the deranged blob—sans antlers—slither to her feet, and then she reached out to her right and grabbed the first thing that came in contact with her hand: a short wooden handle. Clueless as to what was at the end of that handle, she lifted it into the air then brought it down on the man's murderous stare. An awkward silence paused the chaotic scene; the man, about an arm's length away from ripping Betsy's foot from her leg, was lying on his stomach, his egg-shaped face covered by the granola-colored straw of a fireplace broom.

With a muffled snarl, the man spurted forward, his right-hand claw opened for a toe dinner. Betsy performed a back handspring from the floor, pulled out the cast-iron fire poker from the matching stand where she had snatched the ash sweeper, and drove the pointed end into the man's tree trunk of an arm.

Releasing a howl of pain, the man attempted to crawl to his feet, but Betsy—receiving an extra dose of crazy from her superhuman rage—withdrew the poker from the quarter-size gash on his pudgy bicep and doled out a Lizzie Borden smackdown on his back. Neglecting the man's scream-laden convulsions, she gave him five consecutive whacks, then suddenly stopped, holding the poker midair, with the blow poke aimed directly at his piggish head. "Go to hell, fucker!"

Tightening her grip, Betsy wondered whether she could get the poker through his head in one stab, but then a sudden blast of Christian guilt halted this brutal thought. *You can't do this*, a tranquil voice told her. *You can't kill him. He's a human being. He's...* Her face, soft in its moment of doubt, squeezed back into a Pazuzu glare as she caught a whiff of Luke—a pungent combo of Axe body spray and splattered brains. "No. You don't deserve to die quickly. You deserve to bleed to death."

She exploded like a medieval cannon. Accompanied by a mighty roar that permeated the extravagant room, the pointed end of the poker launched through the air then penetrated the man's right thigh, cutting through the top muscle. As he unleashed a piercing scream, Betsy held on to the poker, watching a pool of purple shock flood his cheeks. Her eyes, tinted with a subtle red from the fading sunlight streaming in from outside, moved to the man's black eyes and gave a tenacious stare that vowed, *If you try to get up, I will jam this poker through the bone.*

The man obliged, his body clunking against the floor in a wild fit until his arms and legs stopped and flopped to the floor like a net of dead trout. Hoping he was still alive, Betsy backed away, leaving the poker sticking up from his leg and a trickle of bright-red blood oozing from the perimeter of the gash. *That's right*, she thought, turning to the door. *Bleed a very slow death.*

She locked on to Luke's mutilated corpse and stopped, holding the stern gaze she had used to warn his killer not to move. Her broken heart suggested suicide, as she was unable to imagine a life without her Romeo. However, the rage that had transformed her into a ninja assassin had encased her previous self with a suit of emotional armor. She was no longer Betsy Coleman, the sweet, bashful virgin of Dullen. She was a badass warrior, aka the final girl in any self-respecting, super-violent '80s slasher.

Although she had seen this quintessential horror trope in dozens of films (with the help of Kathleen and David), she had become more familiar with the back of her hands shielding her eyes during the terrifying grand finale between final girl and big, scary guy. She felt it, though. The warm, sympathetic sentiment she typically expressed to the world had been replaced with an aggressive coldness—as if she had been kidnapped by an international gang of terrorists, brainwashed into their army of child soldiers, then sent away to destroy the enemy.

However, she was done fighting. She had defeated the savage beast—whoever he was—and now it was time to go. She could've grabbed the keys from Luke's pocket and tried to drive his truck home or found a landline or cell phone and called 911, but she started for the front door, compelled to take a victory march in the last stretch of warmth and light of the day.

"Bye, Luke," she whispered, as she stepped outside to the autumn evening, which was about five degrees cooler and a shade darker than an hour ago. "I'll see you in my dreams." She headed down the brick driveway, her head bowed in a grim arc. "Or maybe my nightmares."

44

Kathleen, 4:50 p.m.

Kathleen's car came to an earth-crunching, brakes-screeching halt on the side of the road, about sixty yards from the driveway. "Happy now?" she said, turning to David.

Holding a hand to his chest, he let out a low moan that sounded like a drag queen's orgasm. "I swear to God, Kathleen, one of these days... *One. Of. These. Days.* You're going to kill someone. I mean, seriously. You're going to—"

Reaching into the backseat and searching through the piles of fast food wrappers, hoodies left unwashed for months, and emergency toiletries, Kathleen grabbed a Playtex Sport pad from an opened box and slapped him across the face. "*David!*"

He ended his rant with a hand to his cheek and an extra gay gasp. "Did you just slap me with a tampon?"

"It's a sports pad. We're away from the driveway. Are you happy?"

He turned to the windshield. "*Well...*"

"You gotta be kidding me. What the fuck is wrong now?"

David's lips wiggled like the flaps of an old man eating creamed corn. Kathleen, knowing he was wrestling with his thoughts, sucked in a puff of the musty car air. Sensing a vicious tirade and/or punch to his stomach with her diaphragm, he spat out a response in one breath. "I was thinking, it would be better if you parked *past* the driveway"—he pointed behind him—"instead of here."

Kathleen looked around, scanning the typical, upstate New York *Blair Witch* woods. "Why?"

"Well, if one of the dumb-jock apes drives up, he'll probably come in our direction, and we wouldn't want him to see me or we'd be fucked, right?"

"But I'll be gone for less than a minute."

"I know, I know. But what if they show up and beat me to death with their gangsta visors? We really should park past the gate, behind us."

Kathleen's jaw clenched like she was biting down on a steel rod. *Bitch-slap him. Bitch-slap him until he's knocked out cold so you can get this shit over with.*

She lifted her hand from the steering wheel, her fingers pressed into a "I saw the sexts, Kevin" slap, but stopped as she caught the nervous twitch at the ends of his innocent smirk. *No,* a calm voice stated, a voice she would only listen to for David. *He's scared. Give him a break. He needs to find his courage in baby steps. Very slow baby steps.* "All right, I'll move the car." She put the car in reverse and hit the gas.

"Holy shit," David said, reaching for the dashboard. "Kathleen?"

"What?" she asked with an exasperated breath. *This mofo better not ask me to drive back in time.*

"We're going in reverse. Like really fast."

"*Yeah,*" Kathleen said, turning from the rearview mirror with a crooked eyebrow-lip combo that read, *And that's a problem, why?*

"All right. I guess this is one way to drive." Dropping his concerned look into a salty gay man's critique, he added under his breath, "Even though it isn't very safe."

Kathleen clicked her tongue. "It's safe."

"Oh, yes, Kathleen. You're the epitome of safe driving. Those dents in the back of your car prove it."

"Please," she said, a flash of images sparking her memory; first she saw the back of Kevin's Pontiac Aztek, a bottle of Bowman's Vodka, and then the faded teal ceiling of the psychiatric ward at Crouse Hospital—her second time staring at the same, mind-numbing spot. "Those dents are the results of a crime of passion."

"Mm-hmm," he said through a small smile. "I don't know why you don't let me drive. I'm a much better driver than you are."

Kathleen snorted. "Yeah, right. You can barely parallel park—" There was a sudden, loud thud against the back of the car. "Fuck!" she shouted, slamming on the brake.

In that same moment, David jumped up from his seat in a hysterical shake, screaming, "Oh, my God! Did you hit something?"

"I don't know." A spike of pain shot up Kathleen's right ass cheek. "But I think my cyst popped." She shoved her hand in the back of her pants and searched for the throbbing sac of puss. "Nope, it's still there."

"*Kathleen!*"

She snapped her head at David, the thought of bitch-slapping him warming her hand. "What!"

"It sounded like you hit something!" David's sweet, cinnamon-colored eyes watered. "What if you hit a deer?"

Kathleen checked her rear-view mirror. "I don't see anything. I might've just nicked it, and it scampered off."

"Well let's hope so," he said, shooting an angry scowl at Kathleen. "I'm going to check for any mutilated deer, you savage!" He opened his door and stormed away.

Kathleen turned to the windshield, exhaling her pent-up frustration. "My God, this is what I get for being a fag hag to the biggest queen in—"

David let out an earsplitting scream, announcing to the woodland animals and the same truck driver that heard Ashley scream from Luke's prank, that there was a frightened, sexually fluid grandmother in the area.

"What the hell?" Kathleen said, then stepped out and headed to the back of the car. Her mouth unlatched into a big O when she saw Betsy's lifeless body sprawled across the pavement, her clothes torn and splattered with blood, as though she had set her period to lawn sprinkler. "Wow," she said, after a minute of chilly silence, "I actually killed the bitch. How...ironic."

45

The Sheriff, 3:12 p.m.

She's in her bedroom, lying down. She said she didn't feel well. Hearing his mother's tobacco-tainted voice in his head, Sheriff Coleman took a deep breath as he walked down the short aisle of the diner, then exhaled a long sigh when he sat down at his table. "Is something wrong, Sheriff?" Dr. Bonesteel asked, pouring a dribble of half-and-half into his Irish coffee.

"No, not really," Sheriff Coleman said, watching the doctor take a sip of the spiked drink. "I just wasn't able to speak to my daughter, that's all."

Dr. Bonesteel frowned. "I'm sorry. Is everything okay?"

"Yeah, she's lying down. My mother said she's not feeling well."

"Well, I'm sure she'll feel better after a good nap."

"I guess," Sheriff Coleman said, looking down at the mess made from his two-hour lunch. *Is Betsy really sick or is she still mad at me?* Grumbling internally, he realized the answer was obvious. *Jesus, I'm always the bad guy. I'm just trying to keep her—*

Feeling a soft tap on his hand, he looked up. "Sheriff Coleman?" Dr. Bonesteel said.

"Yeah?"

"I asked if your daughter was going out tonight." Dr. Bonesteel's deep-set eyes squinted. "Are you sure you're all right, Sheriff?"

"Yes, I'm fine," he said with a sharp nod. "I was just…thinking about Nick. I want to make sure we catch him before anyone gets hurt." He paused, contemplating whether or not to answer the doctor's first question. "And uh…no, my daughter's staying at my parents' place. I definitely don't want her going out tonight."

"Good," Dr. Bonesteel said, then took another sip of coffee. "That was a very wise decision."

"Indeed," Sheriff Coleman replied with a hint of sarcasm. He checked his watch. It was 3:15. "Are you almost done with your coffee, Doctor? I'd like to get back to Nick's."

"Oh, yes, me too," Dr. Bonesteel replied. "Let me take one more sip. It *really* is good!"

"I bet." Sheriff Coleman pushed his chair from the table. "I'll get the check."

"Beat you to it, sweetie," Sarah said, appearing from behind him. Her entire chipmunk face was a square-tooth smile as she placed the bill on the table.

Sheriff Coleman gave a nervous school-boy laugh. "Oh, thanks," he said, picking it up. "I would've gone to the cash register, *though...*" The last word faded into an airy breath as his eyes scanned down to the bottom of the check. Underneath the total, Sarah had written, "Call me, good-looking. 315-555-6390."

"Oh, no, I was *happy* to bring it to you," Sarah said. "I hope you enjoyed your meal."

Shit, Sheriff Coleman thought, keeping a bewildered gaze on the receipt. *Does she want me to ask her out? What do I say? Do I do it now or later?* He then looked up at the waitress with two reddened cheeks. "Definitely. Everything was delicious."

"Good," Sarah said, then licked her glossy red lips. "Hope to see you again soon."

Sheriff Coleman's heart pumped like a gas station fuel dispenser, forcing a gallon of blood to his growing erection. *Go on*, his horndog ordered. *Give her a wink. She wants you.*

"Well, I guess I should start cleaning up before the dinner rush. Have a good night, boys."

Sheriff Coleman opened his mouth—what he was going to say, he didn't know—but the doctor beat him to it. "You too, Sarah," Dr. Bonesteel stated. "And make sure you lock your doors and windows when you get home. The Devil's close, and he'll hurt you."

The flirtatious cheer disappeared from the waitress's supple cheeks. "Um, *okay...*"

Goddamn it, Sheriff Coleman thought, casting the doctor a steely look. He turned back to Sarah with an explanation, but she was already racing for the kitchen, no doubt to tell the cooks about the perverted cop and his Satanist friend. *Whatever*, he said in his head, as an invisible snare of disappointment tugged at his face. *Everything eventually ends anyway.*

"How much do I owe you?" Dr. Bonesteel asked.

"It's okay," he said softly, reaching for his calfskin wallet. "I got this."

"Are you sure?"

"Yeah, we uh…had a good talk," Sheriff Coleman said in earnest. He placed twenty-five dollars on top of the receipt, covering the waitress's number, and stood up. "All right, let's go," he said, then added in his head, *I can't stand this place anymore.*

•   •   •   •   •

Thirty minutes later, he was sitting in his police cruiser, his head bent toward the radio, hoping Bill would tell him the good news: Dr. Bonesteel, a retired vacuum salesman, had escaped from an old folks' home and was recapping early episodes of *Unsolved Mysteries.* That call never came. Instead, the doctor sat next to him, rattling off his horror epic, *More Scary Stories to Tell About Nick.* "…It seemed like he was trying everything to escape. One time, during the winter, when he first arrived, he saved his milk cartons and filled them with his urine. Then he tied them to the bars of his window with his shoelaces and hung them outside. He didn't tell us why he did it, but I suspect he was attempting to freeze them so he could make some sort of weapon. Thankfully one of the nurses found them in a state of slush during her evening inspection. Unfortunately, Nick later tried the *other* waste product."

Sheriff Coleman's cheeks wrenched, slapped by the disgusting visuals his imagination was creating. *Nope,* he thought, blinking away the image of a poop-filled pillowcase. *This has to stop. You got to tell him no more—*

Suddenly his broad shoulders shook, feeling the feathery lick of a cold chill along his spine. It wasn't your ordinary "I need a sweater" chill, though. There was magic in the icy sensation. A magic hinting that something was happening. Something that involved Nick.

"What was that?" Dr. Bonesteel asked.

"It was…" Sheriff Coleman turned to the doctor and hesitated, seeing his eyes in their gigantic white-saucer state. "…just a cold chill. Excuse me for a minute." He grabbed the hand microphone from the radio. "Bill, do you copy?"

"Ten-four," Sergeant Bill said in an unusually depressed tone.

Sheriff Coleman went stiff with attention. "What is it? Is something wrong?"

"Yeah, kind of. I was able to track down Nick's parents. They live in Anchorage, Alaska." Bill gave a rare bitter laugh. "Nick's father, Frank, runs the only printing press in the state, so you can only imagine the money the family has." Another cutting laugh. "Anyway, I called the company and got a machine. I left a message, but I haven't heard back."

Sheriff Coleman sank into his seat. It wasn't bad news, but it wasn't good either. "All right. Keep checking the number until you get someone, and when you do, don't let them go until you get a home number, cell phone, address—anything that'll get us in contact with the parents. Got it?"

"Yes, Sheriff."

"Good. Have you heard anything from the patrols?"

"Nothing relating to Nick."

"Okay. Make sure to update me with anything suspicious."

"Yes. Ten-four."

"Over and out."

"Over and out."

Sheriff Coleman returned the hand microphone. *I felt it,* he argued with himself. *It wasn't just a cold chill. Some bad shit is going down.*

"That summer," Dr. Bonesteel broke in, "Nick took a handful of his own feces and—"

"My knees are hurting," Sheriff Coleman interjected. "I need to stretch them."

Dr. Bonesteel's eyes flared as though he were offended that the sheriff didn't want to hear his poop anecdote. "Oh, okay. Maybe I should do the same."

At the word "same," Sheriff Coleman barked, "No! I uh"—his mustache danced for an excuse—"need you to stay here to listen to the radio. If Bill comes on with an update, call for me. All right?"

Dr. Bonesteel smiled pleasantly as if he'd been upgraded to official sidekick. "Will do?"

"Great." *I probably won't be able to eat for a year, thanks to your stories,* the sheriff quipped, as he stepped out of the car. He headed to the pristine sidewalk, where the street started its gentle slope downhill, and performed a series of stretches from his police training days—a right and left knee hug, a cross-body pull, and four pinwheels. *Maybe the chill wasn't about Nick,* he said to himself, as the air popped from the space between his heavy bones. *Maybe it was about Betsy. She couldn't still be mad at me, could she?*

Probably, he answered, then scanned his memory for moments when she'd been angry with him. There were very few moments that could compete with this morning's stone-cold treatment—except for one. Betsy was ten years old. Inspired by that day's school lesson on pollution, she had taken his collection of shoes from underneath the couch and brought them outside to the recycling bin. They weren't new—just six or seven pairs of work shoes that were chafed down to the soles—but they were still good for housework. *How dare she throw away my shoes?* he had thought. *What if I did the same to her toys?*

His temper, the coldhearted monster he had inherited from his father, answered that question. Grabbing a trash bag from the kitchen, he marched off to his daughter's room and started throwing away his daughter's dolls. Betsy, watching the rampage in hysterics, ran to the bathroom and locked herself inside. Patricia, also watching, attempted to stop him.

As soon as he turned, she moved back to the wall with a yelp. He immediately lowered the bag to the floor and closed his eyes, realizing she had slunk back in fear. Exactly like he had done every time his father had passed him after a night of drinking.

This isn't me, he thought, as he replayed the worst of those nights. *I hated that mean son of a bitch.* He went straight to the bathroom door and told his daughter that he was sorry, he'd let his temper get the best of him, and he'd never let it happen again. There was no response. After a moment of thinking, he remembered he had oinked like a potbellied pig, Betsy's favorite animal, whenever she got fussy as a toddler. Clearing his throat, he performed his best impression of a baby pig wrestling in a puddle of mud. Giggling, Betsy came out of the bathroom and hugged her father.

Sheriff Coleman smiled. *Maybe I could call and oink like a pig. That might cheer her up.* He looked at his watch. "She's got to be up by now," he said, then turned toward the cruiser. "Hopefully she'll have a good laugh, and then I can talk to her about this morning. Maybe even explain what's going on—"

"*Partyyyyyy!*"

Sheriff Coleman groaned automatically. Having patrolled hundreds of St. Patrick's Day parades and college basketball games, he knew that word was the rallying call of drunken idiots looking for trouble. "Shit," he said, directing his worried gaze downhill and seeing two high school boys—a hefty pair destined for fraternity life—walk to the back of a red Jeep parked in the driveway of a faux cobblestone McMansion.

As the black-haired, bulldog-looking boy opened the trunk, Sheriff Coleman chanted, "Please don't let it be alcohol," but judging by their reckless smiles, he knew he was doomed for disappointment. Bam, disappointment it was; the boy took out two double-bagged plastic bags— Sam's Liquors written on the front—each containing a boxlike shape similar to a case of beer. "Of course it's Sam's," he said, as the dark-haired boy handed the bags to the blond, heavier boy. "Fucking mob must be running the place after all the times we've closed it down."

Sheriff Coleman chewed the inside of his cheek as he watched the bulldog boy take two more bags out of the car, close the trunk, then lead his larger friend to the front door of the gigantic, mundane house. *Maybe you should let them have their party,* he told himself, assuming the ninety-six cans of beer weren't for a relaxing night of chess. *Because if you tell them to stop, the damn kids will take it as a dare to drink even more.* He looked at the car for the license plate. *And it's probably best they're indoors instead of—*

"Nope," he said, spotting a bundle of wires sticking out of a small hole where the side mirror should've been. "Fucking kids are accident prone." Hitching up his gun belt, he stomped down the hill with a serious, *Dirty Harry* grill. "Okay, boys," he asserted in his no-nonsense sheriff's voice. "What are your names?"

The two thickset teenagers turned around and simultaneously dropped the bags in their hands. When the cases produced the unmistakable sound of beer cans slamming into the pavement, Sherriff Coleman laughed in his head, thinking, *They won't be drinking those fizzy bombs anytime soon.* Maintaining his serious expression, he turned to the larger boy and asked, "What's your name?"

The kid, an out-of-shape wrestler, gulped a meteor-size breath through his chubby neck. "Um, Pat Kearny."

Sheriff Coleman turned to the other boy. "What about you?"

This one, staring at the bags, looked up with a "Fuck you" glare. "Mike Barrett."

Sheriff Coleman's stiff expression didn't relent. "All right," he said. "And what's in the bags, Mike?" The boy's chapped lips were sealed shut, but his purple eyes screamed, *Suck a dick, pig.* Sighing, Sheriff Coleman looked down at the smooth, charcoal-colored driveway. "If you don't want to tell me here, I can take you to the police station—"

"Natural Ice," Mike blurted.

Sheriff Coleman looked up with a curious right eye. "Natural Ice?"

"Yeah," Mike said, his cheeks freckled with embarrassment. "You can take them, though." He picked up the two bags and offered them to the sheriff. "It tastes like jockstrap sweat anyway."

Sheriff Coleman lowered his head in a tight-lipped bow like a child holding in a bad case of church giggles. *Don't laugh,* he ordered the cackle caught in his throat. *It's a sign of weakness.* Searching for a quick distraction, he turned to the house and said, "Are your parents home?"

"No, they're not," Mike answered.

"Hm. Are you having a party?"

"Um—"

"The answer is 'No, Officer,'" Sheriff Coleman said, turning back to Mike. "'We were just about to take these cases of beers, dump them into the kitchen sink, and then call our friends to tell them the party's off because there's a curfew at ten, and if we don't, then we'll both be spending the weekend in jail.' Isn't that right, boys?"

Both boys nodded.

"Good." Sheriff Coleman nodded back. "I'm going to have a patrol car stop by in a little while, and if you're having your party—"

"Sheriff!" Dr. Bonesteel shouted from the top of the hill. "Sergeant Bill wants to talk to you! He says he found something!"

The sheriff stood attention as if a surprise mugger pressed a gun into his back. "Get in the house, boys," he said, pointing to the eyesore, then started for the hill. "*Now!*" After reaching the top, he got into the driver's seat and grabbed the hand microphone while the doctor moved into the passenger's side. "What is it, Bill?"

Sergeant Bill replied in a bleak tone, "Highway patrol found a dead body—a seventy-two-year-old male—about ten minutes from Summer Hill. Looks like someone ran over his head."

Sheriff Coleman's face tightened. "Was there any sign of Nick Roesch?"

"Maybe," Sergeant Bill responded. "The man's car was stolen, but we tracked it down. The vents are all smashed up—"

"It's him!" Dr. Bonesteel interjected. "I know—"

Sheriff Coleman raised a stiff palm to the doctor's face, silencing him. "Was it a manual transmission?"

"Yes, Sheriff."

"Shit. It's him, Bill. It's Nick Roesch."

"Yes, I figured," Bill said. "There's more, though."

"What?"

"We found the car a few blocks from your house."

"You did?"

"Yes, on Leonard Street—"

"I gotta go, Bill. It's urgent." Sheriff Coleman dropped the hand microphone and went for his phone in the glove compartment. *I knew it*, he told himself, as he called his parents' house. *I felt something was—*

"Hello?" his mother croaked over the phone.

"It's John. Can you go to Betsy's room and see if she's there?"

"What? Why wouldn't she be there?"

Sherriff Coleman squeezed his eyes closed. "I don't have time to explain, Mom. Could you please just check on Betsy?"

She sighed a wet breath so heavy he could almost feel it on his ear. "All right, just a second."

As Sheriff Coleman heard his mother put down the phone, he turned to the windshield, unable to handle the wide-eyed 'I told you so" stare from Dr. Bonesteel. *Goddamn it, John*, he hammered into his head. *Why didn't you ask Mom to check on her before? Now she's probably...she's probably...* "God grant me the serenity to accept the things I cannot change," he said loudly, "the courage to the things I can, and the wisdom to know the difference." He raised his voice, as he heard the doctor start to say something. "God grant me the serenity to accept the things—"

"Dear God, John," his mother wheezed, returning to the phone. "Betsy isn't here!"

Dropping the phone, Sheriff Coleman collapsed into his seat. *Oh, God*, he thought. *She's dead...*

III.

The Gay, the Fat Bitch, and the Final Girl Gone Bad

46

Nick, 4:50 p.m.

Coated with a fresh layer of sweat and blood, Nick lay across the oak floor of the living room, his puffy raccoon eyes closed and chicken-gristle body sprawled out. The poker, standing straight up from his right leg like a radio antenna, picked up the loudest screamo song ever produced by a band of skinny-jean-wearing liberal arts majors from Purchase College.

Blasting from the button-size gash as waves of sweltering pain, this music traveled through his lifeless body and ordered his heart to mosh. The fatty muscle followed orders, thrashing around the tightly packed space like a drunk Juggalo at Woodstock '99. "Raaaaage," the music belted. "Fasterrrrrrr. Harderrrrrrr. Until the darkness takes you underrrrrrrrrrrrrr."

Nick remained an undisturbed mound of flesh while the music grew louder. "Don't stoppppp! You're all aloooooone! The darkness is now your hoooome!"

A small bundle of neurons in the back of his mind twitched from the mention of "home." *No!* they revolted. *You want to go to your room. Your room is home.*

The music ignored his quiet protest, becoming louder and angrier. "Beat that fucking heart uupppp! The darkness is now your hooooooome!"

Nick's broad shoulders jerked as the rebellion spread through his head. *No!* he shouted back. *My room—*

"You're never getting hooooooome!"

Fuck you!

Absorbing a field of energy from the surrounding air like Omega Red, his favorite mutant from the X-Men universe, Nick torpedoed through the scorching pain with a new, superhuman strength. With a mindless grab, he opened his blood-spotted eyes and pulled out the poker.

"Motherfucking lizard clit!" he screamed, dropping the poker, as a geyser of agony gushed out from the stab wound with a tangy squirt of blood. "I'm going to kill that *stupid* ninja bitch!" After raising himself to an upright position, he reached for the sunflower runner on the coffee table and wrapped it tightly around his bleeding wound. He then stood up using the armrest of the leather couch and headed for the two worthless sacks of organs stacked by front the door.

Keys, keys, keys… "Fuck" tore from his mouth as a bolt of fire shot up his injured leg. He stumbled to the floor and landed on his healthy leg. "Goddamn it," he cried. "I wanna go—"

An elderly woman's scream came from the end of the driveway. *People*, Nick thought, turning toward the noise. Spotting the bumper of a white car, his eyes glistened with excitement, then swiftly darkened into a determined grimace, remembering his day's record of good luck. *No*, he told himself. *I'm going home.*

He stood up with a hard grunt and hobbled toward the driveway, picking up the poker on his way.

47

David, 4:55 p.m.

"Holy fuck!" David shouted, holding his hands up to his face. "You hit Betsy!" He turned to Kathleen with shock piled on top of his customary anxious expression.

"I know," she said, as she stared at Betsy's disheveled body lying on the road like dumb-bitch roadkill. "I thought it would've happened sooner."

"Is she dead?"

Kathleen gave half a shrug. "I don't know." She got down on one knee and leaned over. "It doesn't look like she's breathing, but I'm not checking her pulse. I don't need my fingerprints on this dead cunt."

"Oh, my God, we...we have to do something!"

"I guess." Without emotion, she added, "Let's toss her body in the trunk and dump it somewhere. Do you know where the closest swamp is?"

David set his frightened eyes on his best friend, his mouth hanging open. "*Kathleen*! We have to call the police and tell them it was an accident."

Her enormous eyes lost their dark-humor glow. "Are you fucking crazy? They'll send us to prison."

"Oh, shit," David whimpered, finally breaking the tears collecting in the corners of his eyes. "I can't go to prison. They're *mean* in prison!"

Kathleen let out a restless breath. "All right, so what are we going to do?"

David shook his head, his eyes still wide with panic. "I-I don't know. Can't we just...put her in your car and wait until she's alive again?"

Kathleen cackled. "Yeah, sure. And then we'll tie a couple of strings to her body like fucking *Weekend at Bernie's.*"

David's face ignited into a Lite Brite with "Yeah" written in rainbow pegs. "Okay!" He gave a long, confident smile, held on to it for a good thirty seconds, then burst into tears. "We are *so* fucked!"

Kathleen rolled her eyes. *Extremely slow baby steps.* "We're not fucked, David."

"Yes, we are," he shouted back. "It's the middle of the fucking day. Someone's going to come and see we hit her, and then they're going to call the cops. And then-and then they're going to tell my mom!" His eyes exploded like two water balloons dropped from The Empire State Building before bending forward into a full-blown panic attack. "Oh, my God...oh, my God... I can't do this... I can't go to..."

Kathleen watched his meltdown with a half-irritated/half-disinterested glower. *Yeah, this is getting...stupid.* "For fuck's sake. Just go."

David pressed pause on the panic attack and looked up with a teary expression mixed with confusion and snot. "What?"

"Go. I'll take care of...this." She waved an invisible circle around Betsy's body.

David took a step back, shaking his head. *You gotta get the fuck out of here*, his instincts told him, but his conscience forced him to say, "No, I can't."

"Yes, you can, David. You've got a future." As David opened his mouth, Kathleen raised her hand and continued at a quicker pace. "Run away as fast as you can, and if anybody asks, say we went to the movies, and then I dropped you off at your house. Okay?"

David said nothing while his instincts and conscience wrestled with each other. *You can't leave. She's your best friend.*

Hello! Do you want your first try at anal in prison? Get the fuck out of here!

But what if—

"Are you decorating your prison cell in your head?" Kathleen hollered. "Go!"

David exhaled a big puff of relief. "Oh, my God! Thank you, Kat. Thank you so much. I'll never forget this as long as—"

She raised the back of her hand. "There'll be two dead bitches if you don't get the fuck out of here!"

"Oh, shit, sorry," he said with a nervous laugh, then turned around and started down the country road. He made it about ten feet from the driveway then slid into a clumsy stop, the quick prick of guilt stinging his conscience. *Meryl fucking Streep*, he thought with a mental groan. *Don't tell me—*

"What are you doing?" Kathleen yelled at him. "I said *go!*"

David turned around, mumbling through an unnerving sigh, "I can't."

"What?"

He stepped forward and said, louder this time, "I can't go."

"Why the hell not?"

He answered with a hard laugh. *That's a good question*, he wanted to say, but struck with a second voodoo prick to the heart, he replied with a courageous thrust. "Because we're soul mates, and soul mates don't leave each other. I'm staying here and helping you!"

Kathleen smiled uneasily. "That's very sweet of you, but I believe in you. You're going to graduate from Dullen with a handful of cum laudes, and then you're going to go to Fordham and—"

"I don't want to go to Fordham," David broke in with a stern determination.

"Um, all right. NYU."

"No, I mean I don't want to go to college at all. I want to be a writer."

"What are you talking about?"

"I don't want to college. I want to go to New York City and just...write." David paused, reviewing the plan he'd spent the last two years perfecting. "I've saved enough money for a deposit on an apartment in Hunts Point, and there are *plenty* of waiter jobs in Manhattan. I can write on the train and in my spare time." He nodded for self-assurance. "That's what I want to do, and I don't care what my mom says."

Kathleen recoiled. "Wow, I thought I'd never hear you defy your mother. Are you *sure* that's what you want to do?"

"Yes. I've been thinking about it a lot, and I don't want to go to college. What the fuck am I going to do? Pay a hundred grand to become a librarian's assistant?" A quick laugh shot out of his nose. "Fuck that, I'm a writer, and all good writers need some...slightly deranged experiences. I'm sure Jane Austen helped the Brontë sisters dispose of a dead body, right?"

Kathleen chuckled. "Actually Jack Kerouac helped his friend dump a body into the Hudson River."

"Really?"

"Yeah."

"Oh, well," David said with a small laugh, "let's get this body over to Onondaga Lake." He frowned. "No, that water's so disgusting. Maybe we could find a nice pond...or maybe we could place her body in front of a *hospi-tal*." Hearing the sound of footsteps slowly approaching, he turned to the driveway and saw a towering figure limp through the blinding sunlight. *Fuck my ass with a broom*, he thought, recognizing the broad shape as the homeless man from the school parking lot. *What's he doing here?*

The bum, splattered with a red liquid that looked a lot like blood, stopped at the foot of the driveway, daggers in his vengeful eyes and a fire poker in his grizzly fist—both pointed at David and Kathleen. David inhaled a terrified breath, his horror-laden brain instantly identifying the wild-looking man as a fatter Michael Myers sans the inside-out Captain Kirk mask. *Man up*, he thought, his frail body quaking from a boost of adrenaline. *You gotta...you gotta...kick this guy's ass before he hurts Kathleen.* As the man continued to stare with an evil set of red eyes, David released the frightened breath, planting his feet into the hard ground. *Yup. You gotta protect Kathleen. It's your manly duty—*

The poor man's version of Michael Myers took a step forward. "Run!" David screamed, reaching a Mariah Carey whistle register, then sprinted past the supposed serial killer and up the driveway. "Run, Kathleen! He's going to kill us! The homeless man's going to take us..."

•   •   •   •   •

"...and fire poke us to death! Oh, God, help! Someone, please help..."

As David's voice trailed off, Kathleen turned to the beefy stranger, her right eyebrow hoisted in a puzzled slant. *Who the* fuck *is this dude?* she asked herself, her eyes scanning down the man's blood-drizzled blue scrubs, stopping at his sunflower tourniquet, then returning to the homicidal glare on his gigantic mushroom face. *He's...kind of cute.* "Sorry," she said with a flirtatious smile. "That's my friend, David. He's um...gay."

Remaining silent, the husky man stared at her for a moment then looked down at Betsy.

"And that's Betsy," Kathleen stated matter-of-factly. "She's used to be my friend, but uh...she's dead. Period cramps can be a bitch." She laughed at the ridiculousness of the situation, hoping he'd do the same. His pudgy, white face held on to its chilling Son of Sam stare down. *Seriously, who is this dumb redneck?* she thought, erasing the black humor from her face with a thin frown. *Did he have a fire poker-sheep fucking accident?*

A spark of recognition brought a flush of cheer to her heavy cheeks. *Wait a fuck. He looks exactly like that kid from school who fingered me for Cold Stone.* She giggled in her head. *Chocolate Devotion. That was some good fucking ice cream.* "Hey, there's this guy from my school who looks like you. Are you like related to him or something? His name is...shit! Was it Gene or Gary? Juan?" She shook her head, sighing. "Whatever. Do you know anyone who looks like you and can't find a G-spot without Google Maps?"

Again, nothing. No chuckle or hint of a smile. Only the dead eyes of a man who was holding on to a dark secret. "All right, Helen Keller. I don't know sign language so you can go back to your barnyard orgy or whatever. Unless you have a pig that eats dead bitches—"

Without warning, the broad-shoulder man hobbled over to Kathleen's car, opened the driver's side door, and moved down to the seat. "Fuck," Kathleen said, remembering the keys were in the ignition, then ran over to the door. "Um, hello? Mute hillbilly? This is my fucking car!"

As she reached for the keys, the man swung the poker at her stomach. "Shit," she shouted, stumbling backward while throwing her hands up in surrender. "*Okay*, I guess the hillbilly is stealing my car."

The chubby animal fucker turned the key in the ignition. The engine cranked but didn't start. Kathleen snorted with laughter. "Or not."

With an incredible, deep roar, the strange hillbilly pounded the dashboard with his Betsy-size hands. "Holy fuck, man," Kathleen said. "Calm down. It's not one of your redneck stepchildren. It's a piece-of-shit car. You just have to hit the steering wheel on the right-hand side." The man viciously beat the side of the steering wheel. "Yup. Exactly like...that."

Hearing a soft rustle of leaves at the back of the car, she took two steps backward and stopped, squeezing her mouth shut to trap a rare Kathleen scream. *Fuck me*, she thought, as Betsy's head slowly lolled to the side. A quick whimper escaped from Betsy's mouth, and then, at once, her eyes opened and locked onto Kathleen's. The horrific stare felt like a ten-inch icicle shoved into Kathleen's ass, delivering a cold chill through her back.

"No," she said, quickly moving back toward the man. "You have to turn the key and hit the side of the steering wheel at the same. Fuck it, do you want me to do it?"

With a low grunt, the brainless bear-man sprang up from the seat, grabbed Kathleen by the neck, and pushed her into the driver's seat. He then pressed the tip of the poker against her throat. "Yeah," Kathleen said with a nervous laugh. "I guess you do." On her first try, the car started. "See, Bigfoot. That's all—"

The man returned to the driver's seat, pushing Kathleen into the passenger seat with a hard shove. "Jesus Christ," she screamed, struggling to sit upright. "I've got a cyst on my ass the size of a fucking peach, you dickweed! You can't keep throwing me around like that!"

Wordlessly, the greasy tub of illiteracy closed the door and sped off.

•   •   •   •   •

Ignoring the monstrosity of Ashley's cabin, David raced for the front door, continuing his high-pitched cries for help. "Please! He's coming! He's going to kill me! He's going…" Running into the living room, he stopped instantaneously, as if the glossy oak floor were coated with industrial super glue. As he'd been exposed to horror movie gore for the last eleven years, his reaction evolved from sleep-with-a-vile-of-holy-water fear to fifth-year-med student. However, as he lay his jittery eyes upon Luke's lifeless body slumped against Ashley's (his classmates' brains and blood drizzled around the crude pile like a distasteful garnish), he could do nothing.

There wasn't an awed gasp or exhilarated jump-scare laugh. Staring at the two mangled bodies, he stood there, sedated by a horror more powerful than the fear and excitement produced by demon-possessed houses or murderous gingerbread cookies. It was the horror of real life. *Run, you moron*, his inner Randy Meeks ordered him. *Find a place to hide and call the police. You've got a cell phone, stupid.* He continued to stand in the same spot, his back open to a brutal fire-poker stabbing. *Goddamn it*, he scolded himself. *At least close the door.*

Again, nothing. He remained at the foot of the death pile like the ex-Disney stars and swimsuit models of his beloved B-horror films he had screamed at a thousand times to "Get the fuck outta there!" And then, a wooden creak from behind him shattered his stupid-horror-victim daze. "Not me!" he screamed, while his mind sent a dozen commands to flee, resulting in a way-too-fast turn/get-the-hell-out-of-here bolt. A second scream escaped his mouth as he tripped over Luke and Ashley and fell into the leather couch. "C'mon, man," he said, turning around with the image of the homeless man standing in the doorway with an "Imma 'bout to murder you" stance. "Could you at least give me a head start?"

Looking down with a vacuous zombie stare, Betsy stood in front of him, her Abercrombie & Fitch ensemble streaked with blood and dirt.

"Oh, my God, Betsy! You're…not dead."

"No," Betsy said coldly. "I'm not."

David attempted a friendly smile, as she continued to stare as though she was contemplating eating his brains for a midday snack. "Cool…" *Okay, something ain't right*, he thought, imagining anyone—sweet, Christian virgin or not—would turn into a creature of murderous rage after being hit by a car, but there was no sign of emotion on her colorless, scratched-up face. "So uh…I'm *really* sorry about the whole car thing, but um…it kind of wasn't my fault. I told Kathleen not to—"

"Where's your phone?" Betsy asked.

"Oh, right," David said, then quickly retrieved his cell phone from his jeans. "I should call 911."

"No," Betsy said in a hard, authoritative tone. "Text Kathleen and find out where she's going."

David pushed himself up, his eyes trying to escape the sockets. "Oh, God, what happened to Kathleen?"

"That man—whoever he was—drove off with her."

David gasped. "Oh, no, we need to call the police!"

"No," Betsy commanded with a more heated tone. "Text Kathleen and find out where they're going."

David's button nose twitched nervously as he eyed Betsy, turned his attention to Luke's scattered brain matter, then switched back to Evening Zombie Betsy. "Um, maybe we should call 911 so they can make sure you're, you know, still alive and—"

"Goddamn it!" Betsy roared. "I told you to text Kathleen!"

Startled, David fell over the arm of the couch and landed on the torn cushions on the floor. "Oh, God. 1-1-1..."

Betsy stepped over the two, mutilated bodies and bent down until she was an inch from David's face, fixing her baleful eyes onto his while her hot, earth-smelling breath blew against his mouth. "I'm not going to say this again. Text Kathleen."

David nodded immediately. "Okay," he said, then looked down at his phone. *Where r u*, he wrote, hands shaking, then looked up at Betsy. "Done."

"Good," Betsy said, snatching the phone from his hand. "There's a key ring in Luke's pocket. Go get it."

David let out a frightened whine as the wet, beige-colored bits of Luke's brain popped into his head. "Oh, no," he said, shaking his head. "I c-c-c-can't—"

Grabbing the neck of his jacket, Betsy pulled him into her. "*Listen*, Buttercup," she growled. "You and your bitch soul mate hit me with a fucking car, and then I heard you guys talking about dumping my body in the lake. So please, listen carefully: if you don't do what I say, I'm going to ram my fist into your ass so hard you'll be wearing diapers for the rest of your life! Got it?"

David nodded automatically. "Yes, okay. I'll get the k-k-k-keys."

Betsy tightened her hold of his jacket. "*Are you making fun of my stutter?*"

"No!" David squeaked. "I love your stutter."

"*What?*"

Envisioning his decapitation by jacket squeeze, he felt a dribble of pee run down his right leg. "No, no, no. I'm sorry! I didn't mean it in a bad way. I meant it like...your stutter is great because it makes you unique. Nobody stutters like you!" Watching Betsy's face collapse into a fiery tunnel to hell, he felt the dribble of piss turn into the Mississippi River. "Oh, God. I'm sorry, Betsy. I thought I would've been better prepared for this kind of situation but, go figure, dead bodies are a lot more terrifying in real life." He laughed anxiously, then made an innocent smile with the remaining strength left over from nearly being choked to death. He hoped to receive a light laugh in return but was greeted with silent demonic possession. His smile died. "I'll uh...get the keys."

"Do it quickly," Betsy said, letting go of him.

"Okay." *There's something* definitely *wrong with her*, he thought with a micro grimace. As Betsy stepped away, he looked down at the torture porn scene at his feet, then slowly crouched to his knees. *Fuck me*, he mouthed, turning his head away as he got closer to *Leigh Whannell Presents Luke and Ashley*.

Focusing on the cartoon-rabbit-in-cowboy-hat painting on the opposite wall, he tried to decide if Betsy's hand up his ass outweighed his hand groping Luke's gore-slathered corpse. Suddenly he gagged, catching a whiff of the moldy hot-dog smell of his classmates' publicly displayed innards. "This has been the *worst* Halloween ever."

"C'mon!" Betsy barked, kicking him in the shin.

"Yes, okay, sorry," David said, ignoring the slight sting in his leg, as he brought his knees to the floor. He reached forward and then, looking away with a pinched frown, searched for Luke's pockets. *Okay, no...that's his hair...his neck...his...fuckety, fuck, fuck, fuck!* He pulled his hand away from the clump of crushed brain and moved down until he felt the soft cotton of Luke's sleeve. He then continued to Luke's left pocket. There were no keys. He checked the right pocket, but again he came away empty-handed. "Um, Betsy," he said, keeping hunched over in fear. "They're not here."

She expelled a satanic witch hiss. "They must've fallen out. Check underneath his body!"

Check underneath his body? All right, something's obviously wrong with her! You need to... Hearing a slow step toward him, he sucked in a deep breath and imagined himself walking down the red carpet of the Academy Awards (Nominated for Best Film, Screenplay, Actor, and Song for his first horror film), as he shoved his hand between Luke's and Ashley's bodies. *Wow. That. Is. Squishy.* He paused. *Whatever it is.*

Tightening his lips into a deeper frown, he replayed his walk down the red carpet while he wiggled his hand between his classmates' still-warm bodies until he found something hard. *The keys!* he exclaimed internally, but upon grabbing the mysterious object, it compressed into a ball and slipped into his sleeve. God only knew what it was, but it felt like a giant booger taking a sleigh ride down his arm. *I'm so sorry, hand,* he thought, closing his eyes, *but if I survive this night, I'm going to have to chop you off. Ash Williams style.*

"Jesus Christ!" Betsy screamed. "Do I have to kick you in the balls to make you go faster?"

"No!" David pushed his arm up until his chin was resting on Luke's buttocks. "I...I found them!" He opened his eyes to see a blood-covered key ring in his hand—along with a mass of hair and torn flesh. A gush of stinging liquid surged up his throat then plunged down from the sight of the gross souvenir.

"All right, Daisy," Betsy said. "Stand up."

David silently sucked his teeth. *Daisy,* he said in his head. *My God, she's so mean when she gets hit by a car.* He stood up and offered her the keys.

"What the fuck are you doing? You're driving."

"You want *me* to drive?"

"Yes," Betsy said with her teen-girl death glare.

David shook his head. "But I'm no good with big cars." Gritting his teeth timidly, he looked out the door toward the convertible Beetle. "Maybe we could find the keys to that cute, little car—"

Betsy stepped forward, meeting her eyes with his for the second time. "Get into the truck and drive," she said in an eerily soft tone, "or I'll kill you with my bare hands." She grabbed David's bony hand and squeezed it into the set of keys with her gorilla-size palm.

"Ow, ow, ow. All right," he said, as one of the keys punctured the soft center of his palm. "I'll go, I'll go." As soon as Betsy released his hand, David let out a pained moan, then started for the white truck in the driveway. *Good God,* he thought, stepping into the driver's seat of the truck. He didn't know where they were going or what his strange-acting friend would do when they got there, but he knew it wouldn't be good.

48

"Sheriff? Sheriff Coleman? Are you all right?"

Dr. Bonesteel waved his rugose hand in front of Sheriff Coleman's vacant line of sight. The middle-aged man sat in the driver's seat, sinking into a bottomless wasteland he hadn't traveled through since his wife's death. *Nick was there*, his dark cynicism swore, propelling him deeper into the cruel depths. *God only knows what the sick fuck did to her, but ten to one he ran into Betsy and...and...* He laughed the maniacal laugh of a man drowning in his worst fears. *That was the horrible feeling earlier, and you didn't even know. God, you really are a terrible father.*

"Speak to me, Sheriff," Dr. Bonesteel said, grabbing his elbow. "Do you need a drink?"

Sheriff Coleman looked out, watching the darkness engulf his waning spirit. *Betsy's dead, and now I've got nothing to live for.*

"C'mon, Sheriff." Dr. Bonesteel shook his arm. "You're starting to scare me."

Closing his eyes, Sheriff Coleman reached for his gun. *I'm sorry, Patricia.*

"John!" Dr. Bonesteel barked. "Snap out of it!" He let go of his arm and slapped him.

"You stupid cocksucker," Sheriff Coleman shrieked, catapulted back to sanity by the warm sting on his face. He then balled his hand into a fist and punched the doctor in his spongy, gray jaw.

"Fuck," Sheriff Coleman said, his bloodshot eyes strained with worry as the doctor, his wrinkled hand on his cheek, stared back, his pair of pumpkin eyes saturated with shock. "I'm sorry, Doctor. I-I lost it for a moment. My daughter..." He tried to vocalize the horrendous thought that Betsy's body had been brutally butchered by the big, bad claws of Nick Roesch, but he couldn't give power to the possibility that he'd been robbed of his family and would suffer a loveless eternity like a modern-day Job. Instead, as if he'd swallowed a pair of mind-numbing antidepressants, his mind made an immediate switch from misery to empty hope. "She snuck out of my parents' house so she could go to a Halloween party."

Yes, his brain asserted. *She's at the party, safe and sound. But where is it?*

"It's okay," Dr. Bonesteel replied. "You've been building up a lot of anger. It needed to be released." He let out a hiss of pain as he rubbed his cheek. "I just wished you weren't wearing your wedding ring. That thing felt like a lead bullet."

"Yeah, sorry," Sheriff Coleman said, rubbing his gold wedding band with his thumb. "I'm really sorry." *A boy*, he told himself. *She said she was going with a boy named...Lance or...Luke! His name's Luke!* "I'm really sorry, Doctor, but I have to find my daughter and make sure she's all right. Do you want to wait here or do you want a ride back to the station?"

"Oh, uh...I guess I'll wait here," Dr. Bonesteel answered. "We don't want to miss Nick when he shows up."

"Right," Sheriff Coleman replied. "And don't worry—you won't be alone. I'll have a patrol car come to stay with you, 'kay?"

"Yup. I'll wait on the side of the road here," Dr. Bonesteel said with a quick nod. "And no worries about me. I can take care of myself." He patted the bottom pocket of his coat then stepped out of the police cruiser. "Good luck with your daughter, Sheriff."

"Thanks," Sheriff Coleman said with a wary smile. *He's got a gun, doesn't he?* he asked himself but left the question unanswered. He had to find Betsy. He started the car, made a sharp U-turn, then grabbed his phone and called his mother again.

"Hello," she answered with a miserable croak.

"It's me, Mom."

"Jesus, Mary, and Joseph. What the damn hell is going on?"

"Everything's all right. Betsy snuck out to go to a party, but I'm getting her now. Make sure you lock all your doors and windows, okay?"

"Why?"

"Because...the Devil's loose tonight. I gotta go, Mom. Bye." Speeding down the hill from Nick's house, he hung up without hearing his mother's response, then dropped the phone onto the passenger seat and picked up the hand microphone. "Bill, are you there?"

"Yes, Sheriff. What's going on?"

"Betsy snuck out of my parents' house."

"Oh, Lord. Do you know where she went?"

"No," Sheriff Coleman said, "but I found some kids who might go to her school." He slowed down and stopped in front of the large vanilla house where he'd talked to the two boys. "They'll probably help me."

"Okay," Sergeant Bill said. "Do you need me to do anything?"

"Um, yeah. I need you to call a patrol car over to Nick's house to keep an eye out on Dr. Bonesteel. Get some extra cars to patrol my neighborhood, and uh...could you try to get in touch with my daughter's friend? Her name's Kathleen Strife."

"Yes, Sheriff. I'll do it ASAP. Does she have any other friends I could try?"

Sheriff Coleman opened his mouth and released a flabbergasted cheep. *She's got a ton of friends*, he thought, and then his mind went blank. *There's the gay kid with the shaggy hair. What's his name?* His cheeks tightened, turning to an irritated purple, as his mind frantically searched through the messy piles of information stored in his memory. *Jesus, this is why you're a bad father. You don't even know—*

"John?"

"Yeah," Sheriff Coleman responded, catching himself from slipping into a second shame spiral. "Let's start with Kathleen, all right?"

"Okay. Good luck and be safe. I'll be praying for you."

"Thanks, Bill. Over and out."

"Over and out. And God bless."

"Yes, God bless," Sheriff Coleman said attentively, imagining he would need faith on his side. After returning the microphone to the radio, he glanced at his watch, then turned to the cookie-cutter mansion, the waning sun hovering over its several, multi-styled roofs. *It's too early for parties*, he thought, staring at the driveway; there were no other cars beside the Jeep with the broken rearview mirror. *Which means Luke probably stopped somewhere so he could...so he could...* His mustache curled, disagreeing. *She's a good girl. She'd never do anything...bad.* He groaned, catching his hesitation. *Just go. You're wasting time.*

49

Nick, 5:10 p.m.

Guided by the sun's turtle crawl into the distant hilltops, Nick sped down the country road with one white-knuckle fist on the steering wheel and the fire poker in the other. *Stupid bitch bag,* he thought, glancing at the overfilled sandbag sitting next to him. He wanted to take the poker and stab the bag with the day's built-up fury, leaving it a shredded cloak of nothing, but no, he couldn't out of necessity. What if the engine died? Could he start the car again?

No, he thought. *Home. Wait until you get home to kill the—*

"So where are you taking me?" the bag asked. "The KKK's welcome lodge for a Trump rally?"

An icy tingle ran through Nick's injured leg. *Shut up,* he sneered at the passing road. *Sandbags don't talk.*

"All right," the talking sack continued. "I guess you lost your sense of humor from your decades of incest. Could you at least tell me what happened to your leg, or are you just going to keep bleeding all over my car?" Nick took a quick peek at the tourniquet, the sunflowers soaked in a rose red. He looked back at the road without an answer. "*Hello?* Are you going to fucking answer any of my questions?"

Fucking dirty shit bag, Nick thought, tightening his greasy hold on the poker. *Shut the fuck up, or I'm going to… I'm going to—*

Suddenly the sack reached out for the fire poker, or was it the steering wheel? Nick lunged the sharp tip of the poker toward its chubby hand. "Jesus Christ, man," it screamed, retracting its hand. "Chill the fuck out. I was just trying to turn on *my* radio. Is that all right, or do you rednecks only listen to 'Dueling Banjos' when you're buttfucking your pigs?"

A purplish, wormlike vein popped onto Nick's forehead. *Kill it,* the vein demanded, as the thick tube pulsated from an angry rush of blood. *Kill it, or it'll keep talking.* He gripped the poker, struggling with the desire to thrust the heavy handle straight through the frumpy top of the bag. *No,* he thought, stuffing the desire into another cage in his subconscious. *Home.*

As he lowered the poker, the vein returned to its soft, jelly state. The white sack scoffed. "Fuck this. I'm turning it on anyway." The bag leaned forward and switched on the radio.

"*It was a grave—*"

"Fuck no," the sack said, then turned the station.

"*You know it's—*"

"Nope." The bag changed the station again.

"*Who you—?*"

Each time it switched stations, Nick gritted his teeth as the icy tingle in his leg turned to a sharp pain, igniting his poker wounds over and over.

"*Ghost—*"

"Oh, my fucking God. All these songs are old-people shit."

Nick squeezed the poker, ready to swing it across the bag's head, then opened his mouth to say, "Then turn it off, you fucking shit sack," but stopped when he heard:

"*Aaaah! Aaaah! Aaaah!*"

Yes, Nick shouted in his head, then let go of the poker and reached for the volume knob on the radio. Surprise streaked across his stony eyes as his hand bumped into the bag's. "Oh, my God," it said, giggling. "You like Zeppelin too?"

Turning, Nick froze with a gaze of awe as the bag magically transformed into a young woman—not the small-waisted, plain-faced ladies he was accustomed to seeing at Summer Hill House, but a composite of his two favorite female comic book characters. The loudmouth girl had the buxom, Amazonian physique of Wonder Woman and big, brooding eyes and cunning smile of Harley Quinn.

"Um, hello? Do you like Zeppelin?"

Nick nodded, too shy to say Led Zeppelin was his favorite band, then turned back to the windshield.

"Well, at least my kidnapper has good taste in music," the girl said, then turned up the volume and sang along with the music. As she continued, Nick stared out at the road with a building-of-bricks expression until his lips crept along his cheeks, forming a small smile. He felt like he was already home, sitting in his room, reading one of his comic books. Only now he had the real thing—a voluptuous, kick-ass vixen—by his side.

While the rock song roared out of the radio, the stabbing pain in leg subsided as if he were bathing in a heated pool of crushed Valium. *Home*, he thought, as his left foot tapped along to the music. *Soon.*

50

David, 5:15 p.m.

David held the steering wheel with a sweaty post-masturbation grip, his elbows pressed against his lanky chest. *All right,* he reassured himself, keeping a catlike watch on the dusty country road. *You're doing fine. Just keep your hands at nine and three o'clock, stay in your lane, and don't do anything to fuck with Betsy!* His brain warned him not to look, but his cruel gay man's curiosity took over. Slowly turning his head, he caught a glimpse of Betsy in the corner of his eye. She was frozen in a horrific scene of torment like a Halloween cutout, staring back at him with a pair of reptilian slits for pupils.

What the Dullen locker room is going on? he thought, his eyes fleeing to the windshield. *Why's she acting so weird? And who the fuck is that crazy-ass man?*

Looking out at the two-lane road, the waning sun flickering through the massive pines, he tried to come up with reasonable answers to his questions. Suddenly a quick breath escaped his nose. *Oh, my God,* he realized with a jolt. *She's a pod person!*

She has to be, he continued, his mind reeling through the depths of his horror movie knowledge. *She's like the complete opposite of herself. 1) she isn't stuttering anymore, and 2) she's completely evil!* He gave a brisk nod. *Yup, she's a pod person, and the homeless man must've changed her*—his eyes widened—*because he's an alien!*

As the thought sank into his mind, his mouth twisted in repulsion. *Are you a fucking idiot? This isn't another stupid sci-fi horror reboot by J.J. Abrams. There has to be a reasonable*—

"David!"

Startled, he flinched toward the window. "Oh, God, no!" he shouted, loosening his grip on the wheel. "Please don't turn me into a pod person! I like who I am...mostly."

There was a second of silence. "Pod person? What the fuck are you talking about?"

Squinting, he turned and let out a short whimper, seeing those venomous eyes focused on his body as though she wanted to suck the life-force out of him.

"Um, hello?" Betsy said, her face hardened into a demonic threat. "Are you going to keep staring at me like a moron or are you going to tell me what the fuck you're talking about?"

"Oh, my God, yes. I'm so sorry," David said immediately. "I-I-I—"

"Jesus Christ! Stop stuttering and talk!"

David flinched again. "Yes, okay. I'm sorry." He took a deep breath then fired out in one frightened string of words, "I thought that creepy-looking alien dude turned you into an evil replica of yourself just like in *Invasion of the Body Snatchers*." He exhaled, imagining it would be the last time he did.

Another moment of silence followed, and then Betsy erupted into a diabolical laugh. "You've seen way too many horror films! That creepy-looking dude isn't an alien. He's just some random lunatic who killed everyone at Ashley's party then tried to kill me."

David's forehead compressed into a square of puzzled lines. *That's like the plot of every slasher movie.* "Um, okay. Well, I saw him in the parking lot at school this morning, but I didn't say anything because I thought he was just a homeless guy. But he don't look like he's asking for no spare change." He gave a nervous chuckle, then swallowed a big gulp of air as Betsy turned to him with an irritated "Does it look like it's time for jokes?" glare. "Do you know who he is?" David asked.

"No," Betsy stated. "I saw him this morning, too. He chased me, but I got away. As I'm sure you know, Kathleen almost ran me over before school, so I forgot about him until he showed up at the party and killed Luke and Ashley. He probably got the others, but I'm not sure. He tried to attack me again, but I stabbed him in the leg with a fire poker." She paused, looking out with the worn-out gaze of a soldier victorious in battle.

Wide-eyed, David turned to her fighting the gay urge to say, "*Yassss*. You go, final girl!"

"I thought I killed the guy," Betsy continued, "but nope, you fucking morons ran me over and now that asshole is on the loose."

Dodging another death stare, David turned to the road and squeezed his teeth, making a "my bad" wheeze. "Oh, God, I'm really sorry, Betsy. We were just trying to—"

"I don't fucking care. As soon as I find the fucker, I'm gonna kill him for good. ...And then I'm going to kill Kathleen."

Struck with an involuntary spasm in his arms, David jerked the steering wheel to the right, causing the pickup truck to swerve. "What?" he asked, the whites of his eyes inflated with shock. "Why?"

"Why?" Drawing an eerie ventriloquist-doll smile, Betsy leaned in and slowly said, "Because she ran me over with her car, planned to dump my body in the lake, called me a slut about a thousand times today, and most importantly because I hate that *fat*, fucking *cunt!*" Screaming the last word, she balled her hand into a fist and whacked the rearview mirror off the windshield.

David squirmed toward the driver-side door, evading the mirror by the length of a dog hair as it hit the seat and landed by his foot. *Okay*, he told himself, clinging to the door. *This is a dream. Yup, just a dream. I'm the final gay, and Mike Barrett is going to pop out of nowhere, and then I'll wake up with a boner.*

Suddenly something hit his crouch. "Ow!" he cried, then glanced down to see his phone lying on his lap. Scowling, he looked back at Betsy. "Why did you do that?"

"Text Kathleen again," she said, "and ask her again where she's going. And don't try anything funny. I'm sure the two of you have your own fucking cutesy-girlfriend language."

David opened his mouth to tell her they didn't have their own cutesy-girlfriend language but scared she would take the phone and force it through his urethra, he grabbed it without a response. *Where r u!!!* he wrote and then, keeping his fingers on the keypad, tried to think of something to warn Kathleen. *Damn it! Why don't we have our own cutesy-girlfriend language?*

"All right," Betsy said. "Now put the phone on the dashboard, or I'll rip your fingers off."

Murmuring a low "Okay," David placed the phone on the dashboard. *God, she's like the meanest final girl ever.* His mouth tightened immediately, holding back a gasp. *Holy Wes Craven! Betsy's the final girl gone bad!*

51

Kathleen, 5:15 p.m.

"Fuck me," Kathleen said, as the radio switched from "Immigrant Song" to a Miller Lite commercial. "That is the *greatest* song ever written, right?" Smiling, she turned to the burly fellow, his stiff profile revealing an intense focus on the road ahead. She lowered the volume. "Hey, I said something. Are you going to talk to me or not, you illiterate meth head?"

Again, nothing. Kathleen blew a soft snicker out of her nose. *Does this stupid hillbilly think he's bad because he stole a car?* she wondered, turning to the blur of sun and trees rushing past the window. *Well, guess what, Rain Man? You're fucking with the wrong bitch. Kidnapping is my foreplay.*

"Ow," she muttered, as her phone vibrated in her back pocket, pushing against her cyst. "I gotta find a pair of scissors so I can pop that little asshole." She took out her phone to see a text message from David.

Suddenly the man's arm swung up, bringing the poker to her throat. "Shit," Kathleen said, as the needle tip of the poker hovered in front of her neck. "Okay, calm down. It's just...my fucking mom. She wants to know where I am."

The poker remained at her throat.

"Dude, my mom's a fucking bipolar bitch," Kathleen went on. "If I don't tell her where I am, she's going to have the entire police force looking for me. Trust me. So just tell me where we're going so I can text her, and then I'll put the phone down. Okay?"

The hillbilly turned to her, his bushy eyebrows in a slanted funk, as though he didn't know three-syllable words existed. Pressing the poker tip into her neck, he turned back to the windshield.

"All right," Kathleen said, enjoying the slight sting. "If you think *I'm* a bitch, my mother's the queen of cunts. Last year, after my junior prom, she called my phone fifteen times, but I was too busy hanging out with my friends, eating, so she came down to the Denny's—fucking Tiger Woods drunk—and rubbed her old-ass tits against the windows. Then she came into the restaurant and started screaming—"

Grunting, the man lowered the poker and pointed out the window. Kathleen turned and laughed as they passed a road sign reading, MANLIUS ½ MILE. "Manlius!" she bellowed. "Fuck. I should be the one robbing your ass."

The man let out a short, mouse-like laugh.

Was that a laugh? Kathleen thought with a hard snort in return then texted, *Manlius* to David. "All right, done," she said, placing her phone on the dashboard, then turned to the heavyset man, his block forehead and small lips stuck in an overfocused *Sling Blade* curl. *Maybe he's one of those retarded kids who comes from money,* she thought, *and accidentally killed the pet dog...or Grandma... Or maybe he just likes stealing shit for attention.* "All right, I'm dying to know. Are you a dumb hick or Barron Trump?"

There was no response.

"C'mon, Barron. There's no hidden cameras here." She waited for an answer. "Barron?"

More silence. Kathleen sighed. *Do I always have to do something shocking to get a fucking reaction?* "Okay," she said, turning to the door. "I might as well throw myself out of the car. I'm sure someone will see my gigantic ass and come help me." She grabbed the plastic handle and opened the door, letting in a rush of whistling air.

"No," the man said in a surprising, Michael Jackson–like voice. "I was in a mental hospital until I escaped."

Kathleen's face illuminated into a pale slate of excitement. "Really?" she asked, slamming the door closed. "Which one?"

The man, hunched over the wheel, sat in silence for a moment then softly said, "Summer Hill."

Not recognizing the name, Kathleen gave a short "Hmm" then followed it with, "A couple of years ago, I was at Crouse Hospital for swallowing a whole bottle of aspirin. Actually, I *tried* to swallow the whole thing, but I chickened out and threw them up." She waited for a response. Receiving nothing in return, she continued, "I got really angry when my best friend's—wait, no, my *former* best friend's—mother died."

Kathleen paused for a reaction, but again the man said nothing. She bit down on her lip in frustration and then, letting go of the salty flesh, went on. "So anyway, my um...former best friend was getting all this attention when her mom died, and I was like, 'What about me?'" She laughed. "I know that sounds fucked up, but *shit,* I've been through a lot worse, and nobody ever cared about me. When I was nine, my psychopath mother told me she almost got an abortion because she didn't want me! And my father"—she laughed again—"he's a fucking drunk who sits at home all day doing nothing. So yeah, I've had a fucked-up life too."

Kathleen imagined she would've finally gotten something (a quiet "yeah" or subtle nod), but the chunky mute stared out the windshield through the battlefield of mosquito guts. She shrugged, turning to the passenger window. "It doesn't matter," she said. "When I was in the hospital, I decided I didn't give a fuck about anyone but myself. And I *still don't.*"

That's such a damn lie, she thought, as she mumbled those last words. *You give plenty of fucks about people, but the only one who gives a fuck back is David.* She let out a curt laugh. *Yeah, and he'll probably chicken out and go to college, leaving your fat ass behind. So you should probably just say "Fuck you" to everyone and go back to being good ol' Kathleen Strife.*

She smiled at her reflection. She liked good ol' Kathleen. "So what about you?" she asked, turning to the driver. "Why did you go to the hospital?"

He didn't answer. "Okay," Kathleen said, grabbing the door handle, "I guess I'm jumping. Good luck if this piece of shit breaks down—"

"I killed my babysitter's boyfriend," he quickly stated.

Kathleen let go of the handle. "*For real?*"

"Yes."

"Um, all right," she said with a hint of a smile. *I Am Sam* didn't seem like the killer type. "Why did you kill your babysitter's boyfriend?"

"Because I wanted to go to my room."

"You wanted to go to your room?"

"Yes."

"*Okay.* What's so great about your room?"

"My comic books."

"Your comic books?"

"Yes."

Stifling a laugh, Kathleen tightened her jaw. She'd heard some crazy things from other patients when she was in the hospital (one man used to tell her he sailed the stratosphere on a hamburger boat every night), but killing someone because of comic books was ridiculous. She continued with the interrogation, excited to find out how deep his crazy went. "So is that why you escaped Summer Hill? To go to your room?"

The man nodded.

"Oh, my God," Kathleen said, bursting out with laughter. "I'm sorry, but you're fucking crazy, man." She paused as the so-called comic-book killer turned to her with a blank stare. "Hey, no worries. I'm the poster child of fucked up. And besides, you're a thousand times more interesting than any of the assholes at my school." Hoisting a flirtatious smile onto her round jaw, she thought about adding, "And you're cute too," but she hesitated, worried he would go Lennie Small and pet her like his pocket mouse. Instead, she decided to test the waters to see if he liked a fat bitch like her (or bitches in general) and said, "I'm a pretty big comic nerd myself. Have you read *The Walking Dead* series?"

52

The Sheriff, 4:55 p.m.

Sheriff Coleman pounded on the McMansion's swan-colored fiberglass door. "Open up! Police!"

"Oh, fuck!" someone shouted from inside, then attempted to whisper, "Hide the beer."

The sheriff, his face sharpened into a staff of unsympathetic determination, pounded on the door again. "If you boys don't open this door right now, you're going to find out whether or not the rumors about jail are true!"

The door opened instantly, revealing the bulldog-faced boy Sheriff Coleman had talked to earlier (Mark or Mike or Muhammad; he couldn't remember his name.) "Hey," the pudgy kid said with a nervous laugh. "What, uh, seems to be the problem, Officer?"

Sheriff Coleman glanced into the cavernous, all-beige living room, the Crate and Barrel collection of furniture pushed to the walls, leaving space for a bare folding table. Sitting on the sandcastle sectional in the corner was the heavier boy (Peter or Paco or whatever) with a wide mechanical smile, unaware a red Solo cup was peeking its head out from behind his flabby ass. "I'm looking for my daughter," Sheriff Coleman said, ignoring their obvious attempt to hide their planned beer pong marathon. "Her name's Betsy Coleman. I think she went to a party with someone named Luke—"

"Luke Gerasi?" the bulldog asked.

Hope flashed through the grim lines across the sheriff's face. "Maybe. Do you know him?"

"Yeah," the boy said with childish innocence. "I go to school with them. They're going to Ashley Rathburn's party."

"Ashley Rathburn?"

The boy nodded. "Yeah."

"Do you know where it is?"

"I think it's in Baldwinsville."

"Do you know the address?"

"No, sorry." The boy faked a look of concern. "It's a really big house, though."

Sheriff Coleman's mustache flicked in disappointment, as he imagined this was all the kid knew about the party. "All right, thanks. Do you have Luke's cell number?"

"Uh, yeah," the boy answered, then took out his phone from his pocket. "Just a second. I gotta go through my contacts."

Sheriff Coleman rolled his tired eyes. *This is the generation that'll be taking care of me when I'm old.*

"Here it is. 315-555-3195."

"315-555-3195," Sheriff Coleman said, then repeated it in his head. Switching to stern-cop mode, he straightened up and pointed at the boy. "A word of warning: if you plan on playing beer pong, the cruiser policing the area will find out, and both of you will be locked up for underage drinking. Got it?"

"Yes, sir."

"Good." The sheriff nodded then turned around and started for his car. As he left the house, he heard the boy mumble something under his breath. He imagined it wasn't a jolly "Good luck, Officer," but he didn't care. He didn't even care if they had their party, as long as he found Betsy, unharmed. He got into his car, started the engine, and grabbed the hand microphone. "You there, Bill?"

"Yes, Sheriff. What is it?"

"I need you to find a house in Baldwinsville for me," Sheriff Coleman said, as he started down the road. "The last name is Rathburn."

"As in Rathburn Medical?"

"I don't know," Sheriff Coleman responded. "It's a possibility. Apparently, it's a big house."

"All right. I'm looking now."

"Good. Betsy might be at a party there, so as soon as you find the address, send a patrol over there then radio me. Okay?"

"Will do," Sergeant Bill said. "Anything else?"

"Yeah, I need you to try a cell-phone number for me. It belongs to a kid named Luke who apparently went with Betsy to the party. 315-555-3195. That's 315-555-3915. Got it?"

"Yup, I'll call it ASAP."

"Thanks," Sheriff Coleman said. "Did you get a hold of Kathleen Strife?"

"I found a house number, but no one picked up."

Is no one fucking answering their phones today? Sheriff Coleman thought, squeezing the steering wheel. He then took a deep breath, allowing his anger to pass through him instead of propelling his knuckles against the screen of his police laptop. "All right, keep trying it. Over and out."

"Over and out."

Returning the hand microphone, he turned on his siren and sped toward I-81 for Baldwinsville with a fierce belief that his daughter was far from Nick. Eating ice cream sundaes with Luke in the middle of a crowded, well-lit restaurant.

53

Dr. Bonesteel, 4:45 p.m.

The doctor stood in front of Nick's driveway, looking up at the sky with his dry, liver-spotted hand positioned over his eyes. Once a majestic king of the sky, the sun was slowly losing its power to the horizon. "It's going to get dark soon," he said, "and this game of hide-and-seek will get ten times harder."

Lowering his hand, he checked each side of the street then blew out a hot, impatient breath. "It's almost like Jamie and her family knew what was going to happen, so they ran away too." He stood still for a moment then double-checked each side of the street as he rifled through his coat pockets for his flask. "Yeah, they knew. So I guess I'm the only asshole left to face the Devil."

"For Christ's sake," he said, his flaky forehead turning red while he scrambled through his pockets. "I gotta get a coat with fewer pockets... Ah! Here it is!" Smiling the drunkard smirk of an old sailor, he uncapped his flask, took a swig of the fiery liquid inside, then returned the flask to his coat.

"I guess it's time to take matters in my own hands." Dr. Bonesteel marched forward, crossing the street and entering the wooded driveway of Jamie's house. When he reached the end, he stopped and stared at the yellow colonial-style structure, its elegant exterior remaining untouched, like an antique dollhouse stored in a closed-off attic.

"I know you're here, Nick," he said, ambling toward the house. "And you want to take that poor girl's life. I don't know why exactly, but I've got a lot of theories. Perhaps you were infatuated with her, but when you saw her with another boy, you felt rejected and sought payback. Or maybe it's an innate craving. Destroying life is a turn-on. The longer the tease, the more exciting it is." He stopped at the large bow window, cupped his hands against the glass, and leaned in, trying to see through the same lace curtains that donned the window on the side of the house. He squinted, making out the silhouette of a grand black-and-white staircase.

"You were able to kill my chance at happiness," he continued, "but I'm back for revenge, you evil son of a bitch, and I've planned quite the reunion—"

Crack! Reaching into his coat pocket, Dr. Bonesteel made a sharp turn and pointed his...flask at the twiglike snap that sounded from behind him. He gave a guttural laugh as he looked at the silver container aimed at the empty driveway. "Jesus Christ, Alfred," he said, straightening up from his wannabe-Kojak poise. "You gotta be better than that or you won't make it through the night." He took a sip from the flask and returned it to his coat. After a quick search of his other pockets, he pulled out his compact Ruger revolver.

Standing still, he held the gun out, keeping the barrel locked on the shadowy space in front of him. "C'mon, Nick," he called out with a hungry stare. "Come out and play with me."

54

Nick, 5:35 p.m.

"Some people say the TV show is better than the comics," the curvy, black-haired girl blathered from the passenger's seat, "but those motherfuckers can suck my dick. I think the show is good, but the Walkers were much more brutal at Hershel's farm in the comics. When Rick opened the barn, it was a fucking bloodbath, but on the show, it was like a choreographed execution, you know."

Digging his nails into the steering wheel, he allowed a brisk "Mm-hmm" to pass through his oily lips. During the last twenty minutes of driving, the tranquil numbness in his leg had traveled up his inner thigh, growing into a tight burn, as though his blood were cooling magma.

"But I like that they added the Daryl character," the chubby girl went on. "He is *such* a badass." She let out a hungry grunt. "God, every time that man busts a walker's skull, I swear I get wet."

Feeling the girl's soft hand brush his shoulder, Nick squirmed in his seat as an odd sensation—almost like an electrical charge—zipped through his hamstrings. *Smelly Cheetos aardvark shit,* he thought, his beady eyes questioning the passing road. *What was that?*

The girl giggled like a Hentai-unicorn girl. "I'm not going to lie. If there was a zombie apocalypse, I'd probably get so *horn*-ee. I mean, come on. There's no school or work, and unless there's a surprise attack from the undead or a stupid group of rednecks, most of the time your ass is sitting in a dark basement with no TV or Internet. Fuck, I'd make sure I'd have a copy of *The Kama Sutra* and master that bitch with the help of every passing stranger."

Suddenly the muscles in Nick's stomach contracted, and then his cock followed, hardening against his pants. *Fuck, fuck, fuck, fuck,* he thought, as his nails struck the metal frame of the steering wheel. *No hard-on. Home.*

As he pictured himself sitting in his room, reading his favorite comic book, *Watchmen,* his erection softened.

"I love other graphic novels: *From Hell*, *Sin City*, *V for Vendetta*... Oh, my God, I fucking *loooove Watchmen*. It's my all-time favorite!"

Fucking Christ! Nick shouted in his head, as his cock transformed into a rod of robotic flesh. *Home. You're going home. You're going—*

"The movie was all right," the girl prattled on. "It was a pretty typical superhero movie except for the sex scenes. *Gawd*, Nite Owl and Laurie's scene is so hot." She gave another Japanese-unicorn-girl-giving-Godzilla-a-blowjob giggle. "I've always wanted to try superhero role play."

As Nick's metallic erection rammed the crotch of his pants, he lowered his left hand from the wheel and pressed his bulky thumb into the burning wound on his leg. *You're going home*, he thought, while the light heat turned into a bonfire. *You're going home. You're going home...*

"My secret fantasy would be to dress up as Laurie and then have my boyfriend strip off his clothes, paint himself completely blue, and fuck me as Dr. Manhattan."

"*Fucking Fritos turkey hymen!*" Nick's stomach squeezed into a ball, shooting a warm vibration through the center of his stiff cock. Then he raised his hand from his poker wound and punched the middle of the steering wheel. A long, harsh beep emitted from the horn.

The girl snorted. "Holy fuck, man. Are you okay?"

Nick stared out in a silent daze, his hefty body combed with a heavenly lightness, as if his soul had been washed of its sin. He took a deep breath and turned to her with a heavy exhalation. "I just came."

55

David, 5:35 p.m.

During the last ten minutes of driving, the road had transformed into a blurry roller-coaster track that David maneuvered on autopilot while his thoughts commanded his attention. *This is…this is like a really fucked-up horror movie: Betsy's the final girl gone bad, and Kathleen's the final fat girl.* He winced. *No, that's horrible. Kathleen's the new final girl, and you're the final gay who's going to have to save her…from Betsy.* He paused. *And homeless Michael Myers.*

His focus turned back to the road as he carefully navigated a sharp curve. He then laughed to himself as he returned to his fantastical ideas. *This isn't fucking* Scream. *Betsy's not a final girl gone bad, and she's definitely not going to kill Kathleen. She's just…really upset.* He nodded almost imperceptibly. *You'd be super pissed if someone hit you with a car.* He paused again. *Unless it wasn't their fault. You can't blame someone for—*

Just then, his phone vibrated against the dashboard.

"Check it," Betsy said in her current "Do it, or I'll ram my fist into your ass" demeanor.

David immediately sat up, surrendering to his new screwed-up reality. "Okay," he said, then grabbed his phone and glanced at the text message he'd received.

"Is it from Kathleen?"

"Yes," he said, turning back to the road.

"Did she say where they're going?"

"Um, yeah. They're going to Manlius."

"Manlius? Where the fuck is that?"

David's lips flinched. "I'm not sure."

There was a beat of silence, and then Betsy tore the quiet moment with a lion's roar of a scream. "Then look it up on your phone, Princess!"

David closed his eyes, letting the homophobic remark cut through his sensitive soul, then opened his eyes and said, "Yes, okay, sorry." Grabbing his phone, he gave a mental sigh, imagining his mother was going to kill him for going over his data. He had only one gigabyte of the internet left, then countered the thought with, *Betsy's going to turn you into a hand puppet, David. Choose your battles*, and entered "Manlius" into Google Maps.

"In twenty miles," Ms. Google Maps declared, "take exit 3E from I-481 south."

David sucked his teeth. *Shit, that's close.*

"What was that?" Betsy asked.

Oh, you stupid banana, David thought, his entire body seized with pre-rigor mortis. *Why did you have to suck your teeth?*

"For fuck's sake! Why did you make that sucking sound?"

Keeping his hands latched onto the wheel, he tightened the rest of his scrawny body into a ready-for-impact clench, frightened that she'd finally tire of her verbal threats, take the steering wheel, and turn them into the millennium reboot of the spokes-dummies Vince and Larry. "I'm sorry," he said through a shaky whimper. "I'm just worried about you, Betsy. I really think you should go to the hospital."

"No," she snapped, shoving a dirt-covered finger into his face. "I'm not going to the fucking hospital!"

David scoffed. God only knew where he'd gotten the courage, but he replied, "But you were hit by a car! Didn't it hurt?"

There was no response. *Fuck, I'm dead*, he told himself, as his short, pathetic life flashed in his mind: 2001, he was born; 2006, he cried until he vomited in Toys"R"Us because his father wouldn't buy Fashion Fever Barbie for him; 2010, the family got their first computer; 2011, David discovered gay porn; 2011–2014, he masturbated about twelve thousand times; 2015, he met Kathleen and Betsy; 2016–2018, he masturbated another twelve thousand times. *Wow, I probably should've cleared my Internet history—*

He stopped midthought, wondering why he wasn't dead yet. Mustering the last bit of his courage, he braved a glance at Betsy, who was poised in a slight hunch, her blood-covered face contorted into a malignant sneer. "Oh, it hurts, but I don't care," she said quietly. "I'm going to kill that *fucking* disgusting, deranged lunatic. And then I'm going to kill that crazy serial killer."

Ignoring the subtle dig at Kathleen, David continued his bold pursuit to save Kathleen's life. "C'mon," he said with the calmest voice he could produce. "Do you *really* want to kill her? You guys have been best friends since...forever."

Betsy released a short, acidic laugh that came from the back of her throat. "No. We *were* best friends until my mother died, and she's treated me like a piece of shit since then. For fuck's sake, she was ready to kill me in the bathroom this morning."

"That's because she's jealous of you," David blurted out.

The murderous scowl disappeared from Betsy's face. "She's jealous of *me?*"

David nodded. Kathleen had never said those exact words (and never would), but he could sense it in the car ride to the cabin. "Of course she is. Just take a look at the losers she's dated. I mean, come on, you were there when she rammed into Kevin's car." His eyes bugged out, exchanging the terror they'd shared from the near-death experience. "I think she just, wants someone nice to like her. She told me she had a crush on Luke because he was talking to her at one of their practices. So she got upset when she found out you guys were dating."

He waited for a response but heard nothing besides the soft jangling of the wind blowing against the car's aluminum siding. Swiveling his head, he found Betsy staring aimlessly at her reflection in the windshield, a set of bewildered lines etched into her normal angelic face. *Dear Lord, I swear on my life I will pay for my porn from now on.* He quickly looked at the road then back at Betsy. *Just please let her turn back to normal.*

After a minute of tense anticipation, Betsy finally turned and said, "She should've said something to me, but no, she tormented me because she's a horrible human being."

David let out a hushed sigh. "She's not a horrible human being. She's just...a little crude at times. But what do you expect? She's had a pretty bad childhood. Her—" He was going to say Kathleen's mother wasn't Mrs. Brady Brunch, but he imagined he wouldn't get any sympathy from Betsy. Dead moms trumped bad moms. He had to think of something else, something equal to—or of greater value than—a mother's love. "What about God? I know you're upset, but you're a good Christian at heart, Betsy. Can't you just forgive her one last time? That's what the Bible says...in *Nu-mer-ol-o-gy?*"

"No," Betsy said in the calm but unsettling tone of a teenage member of the Westboro Baptist Church. "God grants me a helmet of certainty and a sword of salvation so I can smite that evil sow."

Stupefied, David blinked twice. *What da fuck she say?* Without thinking, he turned to Betsy with a sad, pleading look and said, "Are you seriously going to kill Kathleen?"

"Yes," she replied with a generous confidence.

His eyes started to tear up; he knew he was volunteering for a cell-phone-up-the-ass death ram, but nonetheless, he couldn't let Betsy kill his best friend. "But you can't, Betsy. You can't do it!"

"Yes, I can," she said softly. "I'm going to kill her—"

"Well, then you'll have to kill me first!" Immediately David felt his soul burst through his chest and flee from the idle terror he kept poking with a stick. *You stupid idiot. Why you gotta keep teasing Death?*

"What did you say?" Betsy asked with a hint of annoyance.

As David's hands shook against the steering wheel, fear contaminated his head with a brain fart fouler than Jason Voorhees's taint.

Raising a fist, Betsy shouted, "Answer me!"

In one final move of courage/stupidity, David cocked his head up and bellowed, "I said you'll have to kill me first!"

Keeping his head lifted in a half-proud/half-too-scared-shitless-to-move pose, he looked at Betsy, with her annoyed-white-girl-waiting-in-the-bathroom-line-at-Starbucks stare. *I know she's going to fist fuck my skull, but it'd be pretty cool if she fist bumped me, like right now.* Silence followed. *Riiiight* now—

Betsy burst into laughter. "Are you fucking with me? Even if you *did* try to stop me, I wouldn't kill you!"

David's brow scrunched up. "Why?"

"Because I feel sorry for you. Most of the boys in our class treat you like you're scum, and you never do anything about it. It's pathetic."

David huffed, his cheeks cooking into two well-done patties of embarrassment. "That's kind of mean to say."

Betsy shrugged. "It's the truth, though."

"Well, yeah, but..." He turned to the windshield, his mind far from knowing whether he was driving down the highway or barreling into oncoming traffic. And then, his brain once again on autopilot, he had a flashback of the Skittles incident. *She's right,* he thought with a cringe. *I am pathetic. I'm a pathetic little fag.*

As he barreled down the highway at eighty-five miles an hour, a lump of long-lost neck cartilage formed in this throat. *Goddamn it. This is... This is so...* Warm tears oozed out of his eyes with a quick burn. *Ugh. Who the hell cares anymore? Just let her kill Kathleen.* He paused, letting the tears stream down his flushed cheeks. *Fuck it. I hope she kills me too.*

56

Kathleen, 5:45 p.m.

Kathleen smiled as her hulky captor breathed heavily through a skittish gawk. "You came? As in...you jizzed your pants?"

With the moan of an alpha yak who had impregnated the queen of all lady yaks, he nodded. "Yes."

"Um, okay. Why?" she asked, looking down at the guy's pants. There was a wet dot on his crotch, right above the blood-soaked tourniquet.

Besides the low rumble of the brakes slowly breaking off, there was a moment of silence, charged with a strange tension between kidnapper and kidnapped. "I don't know," he finally answered. "You were talking dirty about comic books."

Kathleen laughed. "Wow, I usually have to work a lot harder than that." Her eyebrows rose while she traced the man's stiff sausage penis underneath his pants. "Wait, are you sure you came? You're still hard as a rock down there." She looked up at the running-back-size man, who was eyeing the windshield with a nervous stare as though a simple math problem was written on it. "Maybe it was just pre-cum."

The man frowned as if the two-plus-two problem was just too hard. "Pre-cum?"

Kathleen grimaced. *This guy's a real catch, isn't he?* "Yeah, pre-cum," she replied. "It's like your body's way of saying you need to jack it." She waited for a sign of recognition, but the man continued to frown as though two plus two was the algebraic formula to calculate nuclear radius. "All right, I'm guessing you don't have a lot of experience with masturbating. Did you get to jerk off at the hospital?"

The man-child shook his head. "No."

"Yeah, I didn't get to at Crouse either. There was another girl sharing my room, and I was too lazy to go to the bathroom, so I had to wait until the girl went to therapy or had a freak-out." She looked at the man, hoping he'd respond with a Dustin Hoffman in *Rain Man* quip, but she was greeted with yet another bout of awkward silence. She returned to the man's leg and exchanged an impartial sigh with his python-size dick. *Face it, Kathleen. The guy's a giant retard, but you're a fat-ass bitch who'll never do any better than the lowlifes of Syracuse. So you might as well as enjoy his horse cock while you can.* "Hey, I was thinking," she said with a flirtatious smile. "I should probably help you with this before it becomes a distraction." Reaching for his thigh, she let out a quick "I'm a little girl, and you're my big, strong man" giggle that her scum-of-the-earth boyfriends had loved. "Is that okay, big—"

As she placed her hand next to the man's foot-long penis, he let out a horrific scream louder than his surprise, pre-cum orgasm. At the same time, Kathleen also screamed, retracting her hand in panic. "Oh, shit. I'm really sorry, man. Did that hurt?"

Smashing the cup holder with his hairy-knuckled fist, the man squeezed his teeth into a muffled snarl. "Yes, you fucking bitch! That chubby blond girl stabbed me with a fire poker."

Kathleen's forehead bent into a V. *That chubby blond girl,* she repeated in her head, and then the answer hit her: *Betsy!* "That fucking cunt! Why did she stab you?"

"I don't know. I was trying to find keys to the truck in the driveway, and she attacked me."

Kathleen huffed, a vision of running over Betsy's skull invading her head. "That bitch is always getting into other people's business." She waited for a response, but nothing came out of the man other than a Forrest Gump dribble. As Kathleen looked down at the man's leg again, she gave a quick giggle at the sight of his shitake-shaped penis head poking out of his pants. *Okay, he clearly needs to jack off, so show the idiot what you can do, and he'll be eating from the palm of your hand.* "All right, I'm going to try this again because it looks like you could use a good milking."

The gigantic moron flinched as she reached for the sea cucumber hiding in the blue depths of his scrubs. "No, my leg—"

"It's okay," she said, placing her fingers on the waistband of his pants. "You don't want your balls to explode, do ya?"

Horror took over the gullible idiocy of the man-child's moon face. "Explode?"

"Yeah," Kathleen said in an exaggerated baby's voice. "If you don't jerk off after you pre-cum, your balls will burst like Pop Rockets. I read it in a science book." She almost snorted with laughter, then stopped herself as she received her first touch of the man's massive shaft. After her short-lived experiences with her pedophile neighbor and the thirty-five-year-old baby daddy, she expected guys to have a penis no bigger than a baby carrot, but *Good Lord*, she thought with apprehensive awe, *if I didn't play basketball, I might break my wrist.*

"I'll be very gentle," Kathleen said, pushing her hand underneath the elastic band of his scrubs. "Just keep your eyes on the road, relax, and imagine you're covered in blue paint—"

"Oh, shit!" the man-child shouted, stomping on the gas pedal. Kathleen's car blasted past a minivan of nuns who were on their way to a Katy Perry CD burning.

She let out the concealed snort. "Well, I guess you're into Dr. Manhattan play too," she said, then returned her hand to the man's scrubs. "Everything okay?"

The flustered man-child, his Minotaur hands fastened to the steering wheel and a "I'm not sure this sex swing can hold the two of us" gaze on the road ahead, heaved an exasperated pant. "Yup."

"Good." Kathleen inched her fingers into the man's pants, home of the world's only living Titanoboa. "Now imagine I'm lying on my back, my wet— Holy fuck!"

"Did my balls explode?" the man asked, as his thighs clamped together like clam shells.

Kathleen gaped, holding the biggest thing she'd held since she was seven years old when she had volunteered to hold a crocodile tail on a family trip to Gator World. "Um, no..." She then spat on her left palm and grabbed the extraterrestrial cock. "All right, now—"

Just then "Highway to Hell" came on the radio. "Holy shit, dude!" Kathleen squeaked in excitement. "This is like the *perfect* song for a hand job." Keeping her hand on the elephantiasis-infected wiener, she turned the volume up with her free hand then straightened up, readying herself for a workout. "Okay, now sit back and keep driving."

57

Sheriff Coleman curled over the steering wheel like a faceless gargoyle. With two barren eyes fixed on the road and his lips stretched thinly, he sped down the highway, the dread of his daughter's whereabouts contained in his head like a haunted dybbuk box. "Oh, God, please," he spat out, his eyes glistening with tears. "I'm a good man. I work hard. I've been sober for the last five years. *Please* keep my daughter safe, wherever she is." He went silent, allowing his prayer to settle into the Christian astral world.

As he resolved into a mindless calm, the absence of thought ushered in a torrent of unspeakable scenarios involving Betsy and the Manlius Devil. He told himself not to think, but the cruel psychology of the human brain forced him into a front-row seat to his little girl's torturous death. "No!" he cried, picturing the cold-blooded monster ripping apart her chest with his bare hands so he could see what a heart looked like. "No, no, no, no, no! Please, God. I can't lose her too. She's all I got!" His line of sight sank into the eternal loneliness of his future. "She's all I—"

"John?" Sergeant Bill announced urgently over the radio. "I have the Rathburns' address."

Sheriff Coleman picked up the hand microphone in one swift movement. "What is it?"

"7378 Bayberry Drive."

7378 Bayberry Drive, the sheriff memorized then asked, "Is that in Baldwinsville?"

"Yes."

"Did you send a car?"

"Yes. I'll let you know what they find as soon as possible."

"Good. Did Luke answer his phone?"

"No. It went straight to voice-mail. But I'll keep trying."

"All right, thanks," Sheriff Coleman replied, not expecting the boy to pick up.

"You're welcome," Sergeant Bill said, his voice returning to his lighthearted singsong. "And don't worry about Betsy. The Lord will protect his flock."

Sheriff Coleman shook his head. He had the feeling that Betsy was far from okay, and this time he wasn't going to let it slip away. "Yeah, I hope so," he said instead of "I know."

"Over and out," Sergeant Bill said gaily. "And Godspeed."

"Yup, over and out," Sheriff Coleman answered, less hopeful than after their last exchange, then placed the microphone on the radio. Continuing to drive, he returned to his gargoyle-like hunch, remaining motionless as he pensively watched the road through glassy eyes. Except for the handful of blinks, in order to keep his eyeballs from falling out, he was completely still until a small quiver moved through his lips. He tightened his mouth, trying to control the thin strands of skin from shaking, but with the ghastly thoughts of Betsy at the hands of the Manlius Devil rushing into his head, he was like a child with cerebral palsy trying to plug a pinhole in the Hoover Dam. And then, with a sudden, ferocious scream, he took the microphone and threw it at the windshield. "Goddamn it! She's just a little girl! You need to...to..."

Before he could finish his sentence, he exploded into an uncontrollable fit of tears that could only match the unexpected outburst when he had received the phone call from the hospital informing him of his wife's death.

58

Dr. Bonesteel, 5:30 p.m.

The doctor sat against the front door of Jamie Strode's house, his bloodshot eyes on the police car at the end of the driveway. For thirty minutes, the cruiser—only its trunk visible—had been parked there, its red and blue lights spinning silently. He wasn't sure why the two policemen in the car didn't come out to check the house—laziness or perhaps a lack of faith that the Devil had a playdate with their town—but Dr. Bonesteel didn't mind. *Good*, he thought, as he scanned the surrounding woods etched in a layer of approaching autumn night. *I'm not playing anymore waiting games with police. This is war.*

His overwrought mind suggested the mighty knight fighting this war of good versus evil needed another shot of courage. "You're right, old boy," he said, taking his eyes off the woods, then lowered the gun in his right hand and grabbed his chalice of valor at his feet. He took a long sip from the silver goblet, until he stopped, turned it over, and shook it. A small drop of Old Crow bourbon fell out of the mouth.

"Consarn it!" he said with an aggressive rasp, tossing the flask at the strip of pear-green grass between the driveway and him. He gave the container the evil eye (as if it were responsible for being empty), then turned back to the thicket of pines and maples adjacent to the house. His eyes followed a narrow path between two of the tallest trees until an unending screen of dead leaves and mossy branches, glazed by the fading sun, blocked his view.

"Jesus H. Rice," he said, turning the blame onto the peaceful forest with an odious scowl. "Where the hell is that girl? She should be getting *killed*"— he hiccupped—"by now. Shit." He looked down at his shoes—his vision blurring for a second—then took a deep breath, attempting to stop his hiccup fit. Holding his breath for a moment, he nodded, finding himself in a calm, hiccup-less heaven. "Good." Exhaling the breath, he sat in a silent stupor—his vision focusing in and out—then said, "Maybe I should try breaking"—another hiccup—"in."

His growing frustration sculpted a surly look into the pulpy flesh of his cheeks. "Goddamn hiccups," he mumbled, then picked himself up from the porch he sat on, carelessly swinging the pistol in his hand as if it weren't a loaded gun with the safety off. Staggering to the door, he tried the doorknob, but finding it locked, he fired out the grumpy spit of a drunk camel. "Guess I'll have to try the window," he said, taking a step back, then sideswiped to the large window on the left. "I *hope*"—he hiccupped again—"I hope this house doesn't have a dog. I hate houses! *What?*"

As his vision wavered, he leaned in, attempting to read the white letters on the blue, octagonal sticker in the corner of the window. *CBF*, he guessed. *TTA? RUH? FMUTA?* "Oh, c'mon, man," he said, his vision returning to read the ADT sign. "Why can't you be cool?" He blew a raspberry as he stepped away from the house. "Fine, I'll just find another way in." He continued to back away, keeping a drunken glare on the security sticker. "Fucking house. Why don't you...why don't you get a bigger security sign, so—"

Dr. Bonesteel's foot caught on something, and he stumbled forward. Fortunately, he quickly regained his balance, saving himself from a nosedive into the hard-packed ground. "What the fuck was that?" he said, turning around and looking down. An ADT sign was sticking out of the grass. He cracked up with phlegm-filled laughter. "Okay, house. You win this time. But I'll *get*"—another hiccup—"inside you!"

Nodding with drunken confidence, he continued to the side of the house, the handgun swinging to the beat of his intoxicated shuffle. As he turned the corner, he suddenly stopped, catching himself from running into the pair of trash cans he had crashed into earlier. "Aha!" he said with a cunning smile. "You tried to get me again, but I stopped you, stupid house!" When he looked up, the victory illuminating his wan face switched to a frozen gaze of cross-eyed stupidity. "*Ohhh!*"

The garage, a yellow two-door structure attached to the house by a windowless breezeway, was furnished with a round gable vent at the top. The doctor's dopey stare stayed on the vent then moved down to the garage and then to the breezeway. His eyes returned to the vent and followed the same path. When he finished, he did it again and again: vent, garage, breezeway. Vent, garage, breezeway. "Well," Dr. Bonesteel said, a bright expression of triumph landing on the trash cans, "this certainly is a no-brainer!"

He turned, getting confirmation that the cruiser was still at the end of the driveway, then stepped forward and quietly pushed one of the trash cans up to the garage, underneath the vent. Placing his free hand and the hand holding the gun on the rim, he climbed onto the lid with surprising ease for a man of his age and stout size. "Well, house, looks like I've won," he said, steadying his stubby legs. "But we knew that was going to happen, didn't we? Because I'm a *man*"—he hiccupped once more—"and you're just a dumb, little—"

Without warning, the lid caved in, and Dr. Bonesteel fell backward to the pavement, his finger accidentally pushing the trigger of his pistol upon landing. Following the explosive blast of the gun, he sent a tremendous howl into the chilly air, feeling the tip of the bullet rip through his shoe and continue its powerful blaze to his foot.

"You dirty, cock-sucking house!" he shouted, reaching for his foot. His sunken eyes gave their best wide-eyed expression of alarm for the day. His big toe was a piece of bone covered in blood and bits of gray flesh. "Oh, God! My toe! Where's my big—?"

He heard the quick *whoop-whoop* of a police siren. "Oh, fuck," he said, as he turned and watched the cruiser coming up the driveway. "What the hell am I going to do now?" The obvious answer was to flee, but the elderly man could barely jog—with or without a big toe.

The police car pulled up in front of the doctor and stopped. And then, a blurry pair of purple-and-green dots—the doctor's vision was an acid trip of fuzzy colors—stepped out. "What's going on, sir?" the purple dot asked. "Are you all right?"

"No!" Dr. Bonesteel screamed through the excruciating pain surging out of his bloody spigot of a big toe. "The town is in your Devil!" He squeezed his teeth and growled. "I mean the Devil is in your *toe*." He hiccupped again. "Goddamn it, I'm missing my big toe! Can you help me find it before a fucking raccoon runs off with it?"

The two dots looked at each other then turned back to the doctor. "All right, sir," the green dot—slowly stretching into a streak of pale light—said, "we'll get you an ambulance, but you'll have to tell us—"

"No!" Dr. Bonesteel shouted. "The Devil, *the Dev...*" His piercing blue eyes rolled into the back of his head, and then he blacked out.

59

Nick, 6:oo p.m.

As The Rolling Stones' "Wild Horses" played from the radio, steeping the car with a silky air, Nick drove down the long, suburban road of his childhood neighborhood. His giant penis, resting in his scrubs like a newborn anaconda in its den, radiated waves of warm energy through his slacken, post-ejaculate legs. His cracked lips were fashioned into a long, worn-out smile across his rotund jaw until they succumbed to the thoughts in his head and parted slightly, releasing a quick breathy laugh.

"What?" asked the dark-haired girl, master of hand jobs.

Nick flinched with uncertainty. Should he tell her that, at the precise moment he had ejaculated, he was scared because he thought the geyser of white liquid that shot out of him was his soul trying to escape his body? Should he tell her that this fear eventually had dissolved into a tranquil bliss so wonderful that he felt like he was in his room, underneath his bed sheets with *Batman: The Killing Joke*? Should he tell her that he couldn't wait to get to his house and lock himself away from all the loathsome people of the world and their accusatory stares and loud, condescending laughs?

He opened his mouth, but a police cruiser sped out of an invisible wormhole built by the Thought Police, cutting off the soft music with its roaring siren. Immediately Nick went into defense mode, straightening himself from his lax daze and reaching for the fire poker. Instead of feeling the smooth bulb of the poker's handle, he felt the plump flesh of the girl's hand holding his. *What hell?* he thought, glancing down at their hands, his hefty claw connected to the palm she had used to deliver the frightening but wonderful explosion from his cock.

The cruiser sped past the car, followed by an ambulance. The girl let out a hard laugh. "Jesus Christ, those motherfuckers scared the shit out of me." As she turned to him, he swung his head toward the windshield and locked his eyes on the road ahead, hoping she would turn away and let go of his hand. *Get off me!* he thought, continuing up the gentle hill in front of him. *Or I'll chop off your fucking—*

"Home," he said in dreamy awe, spotting the three-story brick mansion at the top of the hill.

"This is your house?" the girl asked.

Removing his sweaty hand from hers, he made the turn into the driveway, parked the car, and turned off the radio. "Yes."

The girl laughed again. "Fuck my pussy, it's a palace."

Ignoring the comment, Nick opened the door and took a step out. *Wait,* he thought, his Sasquatch-size sneaker hovering over the pavement. What about the girl? Would she call the police or, worse, grab the fire poker and stab him like the chubby blond girl had? *Kill her,* his pent-up rage commanded him. *Grab her by the neck and ram her face into—*

"So I know this is going to sound crazy," she said, breaking his train of thought, "but I've always had a thing for weird guys and uh...I really like you, so I was thinking, we could hang out as friends sometimes. Maybe even friends with benefits, no strings attached."

Nick turned his head to the girl, the deep lines on his forehead searching for the meaning of "Friends with benefits." *Strings,* he thought, as she stared back with a mischievous smile. *Does she want to tie me up?*

"Or maybe we could try something more serious, like girlfriend and boyfriend."

"*No!*" Nick shouted, bolting out of the car. He took two steps and then, as if his right leg had been struck with a sledgehammer, stumbled to the ground. "Oh, fuck!" he screamed even louder as he looked up at his house, the sturdy walls and dark window shades teasing him with their solitude. He tried to crawl, but as soon as his injured leg dragged against the driveway, the fuzzy sensation from the hand job transformed into an icy shot of pain in his spine.

He then dropped his head and groaned into the cold driveway, "Fucking Christ! I'm so close! So...*close...*"

60

David, 5:50 p.m.

"*You have reached your destination.*"

David looked up from the spotless road ahead of him, holding the joyless expression of a broken, gay teenager. *Oh, good,* he told himself, as he surveyed the neighborhood of tasteless tract mansions. *Betsy's about to go on her murder spree. Let's hope she gets a few of these Stepford Republicans—*

"All right," she interjected. "We're here. Now where the *fuck* are those two assholes?"

Slowing down, David turned to his window and searched the nearly identical baseball-field yards of the massive homes. He saw no signs of Kathleen or the lunatic.

Betsy slapped him across the arm. "Are you fucking listening? Where are they?"

David's body clenched into a one-hundred-fifty-pound pole of anger and pubescent hair. *What the fuck was that for?* he wanted to shout back, but like the pitiful little queer he was, he tightened his grip on the wheel, keeping his look of shattered self-esteem away from the final-girl monster, and said, "I don't know. I'm looking for them."

"Do you see them anywhere?"

"No," David replied, seeing no one on the streets or in the windows of the fully-lit *Home Alone* houses.

"Then what the fuck should you do, Princess?"

David wilted further into his hunchbacked depression, allowing the childish name-calling to drill into his confidence. "Text Kathleen?"

"That's right. And don't get any ideas or I'll rip your tiny cock off and ram it down your throat."

"Yup," David said, his slim face sagging hopelessly. He pried his right hand off the wheel, grabbed his phone from the dashboard, and texted Kathleen. *Hey where r u?*

A moment later, she responded: *@ that weird guys house*

What street is it on? he wrote back, without the slightest guilt that he was an accomplice to his best friend's murder.

Idk imma check, Kathleen replied. After passing a fifty-shades-of-eggshell McMansion, David received a second text: *Wheeler ave.*

David quickly wrote, *R u ok?*

Im fine this guys a fucking asshole tho

He smirked. *Yeah he kind of kidnapped u.*

Dont care he blew me off after i gave him amazing hand job not even a thank u

David burst into laughter. "Oh, my—"

"All right," Betsy said, snatching the phone out of his hand. "You girls have talked for long enough. Where is she?"

As his cheeks returned to their Droopy Dog sag, he coldly answered, "She says she's on Wheeler Avenue."

"Wheeler Ave," Betsy repeated. "All right, I'll put it into Google while you keep driving. Got it, faggot?"

David's slumped body bolted up as he gasped in silent rage. *Oh, hell to the fuck no. I'm going to slap this bitch until she's—* Suddenly he felt a spongy ball pop out of his armpit and slowly start down his arm, tickling his skin with a shiver. *Oh, fuck! Is that...Luke?*

"In two hundred feet, turn right onto Fairmount Street," Ms. Google Maps said.

That's it, David told himself. *I've had enough of this shit. You need to do something. Like right now.*

61

Kathleen, 6:05 p.m.

Standing at the top of Wheeler Avenue, Kathleen stared at the spider-cracked screen of her iPhone 6, the last trace of patience she possessed from this shit show of a Halloween bubbling under her cheeks. *Hello*, she texted David for the tenth time, while grumbling, "Did you fucking read my text? The asshole ran off like a little bitch as soon as I told him I liked him." She paused, looking down the hill. "Fucking come and run, like always."

While her face flushed with a peppery streak of frustration, she waited for a response until she finally reached her boiling point and exploded into a big bitch of "I'm done." "Fuck him," she said, returning her phone to the pocket of her pajamas. "And fuck everybody else. I'm going to Canada. Weed is legal there, and they've got plenty of gays."

Pulling her t-shirt down from its mysterious creep up her belly, she turned away from the hill and marched back to Nick's house. Stopping at the driver's side of her car, she snickered, spotting the cowardly glob of a man lying face down on the driveway, his hands covering the sides of his face. *Men are such pussies.*

As she stood watching him, a series of muffled bleats echoed against the pavement. "Is he...*crying?*" Her eyebrows arched in suspicion as she slowly walked over then stopped about an arm's length away from the man-child. *Yup*, she said to herself, as she heard a faint babble of man-tears. His chest, heaving up and down, was the second piece of evidence.

Wow, this is a whole *lot of pathetic,* Kathleen thought, watching the imbecile cry until a thought popped into her head. *Maybe he's afraid of commitment. Or maybe he's never had a girlfriend.* A wicked smile triggered a ripple of troublesome waves across her cheeks. *Oh, this is good. A couple more hand jobs and maybe a visit to my vagina, and he'll be my slave.*

She bent down. "Need some help?"

The man's pitiable crying ceased. After a moment of silence, he looked up at her, his bullish eyes whipped with wet desperation. "Yes."

"Okay," Kathleen said, reeling her devilish smirk into a look of concern. "I'll help you up, but you gotta say you're sorry."

"What?"

"Say you're sorry for being an asshole in my car, and then I'll help you up." As the man stared at her, his pale face a gigantic chalkboard covered with white streaks of confusion, Kathleen stared back, hands on hips and lips pressed in a cocky display of authority. *Go on, mofo*, she demanded with an unblinking glare. *Say you're sorry so I can get the upper hand for once in my goddamn miserable life.*

"Sorry," the man finally mumbled.

Kathleen leaned forward, holding her hand to her ear. "Excuse me. What was that?"

His mammoth nostrils flared in anger, and then he shouted, "I said I was sorry, you bitch!"

Bringing her hand to her chest, Kathleen let out an "Oh, really" snort. "Uh-uh. I'm not going to be treated with disrespect from a man—or anyone—ever again." She started for her car. "Enjoy the driveway, sweetie. Hope your leg doesn't get infected."

"No, stop!" the man shouted. "I'm sorry. I'm *really*, really sorry."

Kathleen stopped and turned to him with *Last chance* written across her taut lips. "Why are you sorry?"

"Because I-I-I was an asshole in your car."

Kathleen relaxed her lips. "Are you going to be an asshole again?"

"No," he pleaded. "I'll be nice, I promise. *Please*. I just want to go to my room."

Kathleen laughed through her nose. *What a fucking child*, she thought, watching the overgrown imp writhe in his own desperation. "Okay," she said, the devilish smile returning as she walked over to her dude in distress. "I guess I can help you now. Oh..." She frowned at the fresh patch of blood soaking through the man's sunflower tourniquet. "Uh, this is probably going to hurt like a bitch. I should get you like a gag or something. Hold on."

Heading back to her car, she searched through the backseat/garbage dump/bathroom vanity. "This should work," she said, grabbing the pink-and-yellow box of menstrual pads, then brought it to the man. "Here. Put these in your mouth."

"What are they?" he asked, taking the two cottony sponges from her hand and sniffing them.

"Playtex Sport pads. With wings."

"What's that?" he grunted, as he pushed the pads into his mouth.

"They're protective wear for athletes and lesbians. Here. Take one more." She crammed a third pad into the man-child's mouth then threw the box to the ground. She laughed, taking in the sight of the giant's mouth stuffed with sanitary napkins. "Shit, I could take a picture of you, put it on a shirt that says 'Feminists Rule, Boys Drool,' and sell it to Forever 21 for a million dollars."

The man looked at her, an emotionless human cotton swab.

"All right," Kathleen said, drafting a game plan in her head. "Try not to scream. We don't want to scare these rich white people." She bent down, wrapped the man's right arm around her neck, and slowly brought him to his feet. With a long, miserable moan through the pads, he lifted his injured foot off the ground and hobbled toward the house with the support of Kathleen's sturdy body. "Okay," she said, stopping at the front door. "What now?"

The man spat out the sanitary pads. "Open the door with my spare key," he said, then let go of her arm and leaned against the side of the door. "It's in my right shoe."

"*Your* shoe?" Kathleen said, imagining the pool of sweat and blood collecting in his clown shoes. "Why didn't you just stick it up your ass?"

Again the man stared back with a dead-eyed expression.

Kathleen snickered. "Jesus Christ, we'll have to work on that Ted Bundy stare," she said, then moved down to one knee and started to untie the man's blue sneaker. "This is going to smell like a bucket of clits, isn't it?"

Removing the man's shoe, she received an immediate answer; her nose was slugged with the horrendous stench of a thousand cat assholes she sometimes smelled from the Chinese restaurant four blocks from her house. "Fuck," she shouted, turning the shoe over and throwing it back at the man. "Wash your damn feet once in a while." She picked up the silver key that dropped from the shoe and turned to the front door. "Shit!"

"What?"

"There's an ADT sticker on your window." Kathleen pointed to the blue sticker in the corner of the large picture window on the side. "Should I open the door or should we try to find an opening or...something?" As she turned, the man-child slouched against the side of the door, ogling the house through a cross-eyed daze. "Um, are you all right?"

"Unnnhhhh," he said through his gaping mouth, his tongue slowly rolling out.

"'kay." *Maybe he needs to take a dump or something.* "Let's just chance it. If an alarm goes off, we can find a place to hide. All right?"

As the man nodded, a trail of sweat trickled from his chin.

"Cool." Before Kathleen turned back to the door, she glanced at her car, thinking, *Shit, if this house starts ringing, I'm getting the fuck out of here. I got priors.* She put the key into the lock, turned it to the right, and tightening the muscles in her power-forward legs, threw open the door. There was no alarm. "Thank fucking God," she said, releasing a sigh of relief as she relaxed her legs. "Your parents must've stopped paying the bill."

The man made the frail groan of a Carnival cruise guest coming from the three-mile shrimp buffet. Ignoring it, Kathleen walked into the capacious living room, enthralled with the gothic scene. Lit by the setting sun was a collection of furniture, each piece covered with a brilliant white sheet she assumed had been stitched by Karl Lagerfeld's sex slaves. A musty smell—not like the rotted ass funk of her house, but that of an ancient library—pervaded the spacious room. "Wow," she said, stepping through the abandoned remains of the Victorian-style living room. "Tim Burton would dry hump Helena Bonham Carter to death in this place."

She gasped as she uncovered a wingback armchair upholstered with a fern-green velvet. "Get the fuck out of here! I love reading chairs. My grandma had one of these, except it was orange and had a big shit stain on it." She turned around and bent down to sit in the chair.

"Please," the man moaned. "My room. I need...to lie...down."

Kathleen stopped, her plump ass grazing the soft velvet of the chair, and looked up at the hobgoblin propped against the door, dripping with sweat as though he'd just swum through a pool of Malaria. *Fucking men,* she thought with a romantic sigh for the beautiful chair. *I should try women again.* "All right," she said, walking over to the bloated rubber ball of grease. "Where's your room?"

"Upstairs. Second door on the left."

Kathleen let out a groan as she turned toward the L-shaped staircase. "*Upstairs.* Well, shit, are there any goddamn lights or do I have to risk breaking my fat ass trying to carry yours?"

The man, his heavy eyes fighting off whatever was clawing itself through his colon, shrugged. "I don't know."

"Awesome. I guess I gotta do everything," she said through a deep breath, then scanned the vast room until she locked eyes on a light switch to her right. When she flipped it up, the haunting scene she loved vanished into basic bitch air, replaced with a boring square living room lit by a hundred doctor's office lights. "Guess your parents are still footing the electricity bill."

She looked over at her enormous kidnapper, his hormone-fed cow shoulders bent into a stiff limp. "My God, the things I do for dick…"

Kathleen took another long breath, mentally preparing herself for the vag-ripping haul, then headed over to the man. After wrapping his sweat-soaked arm around her neck, she started for the staircase, keeping a watchful eye on his injured leg. "Actually this isn't too bad." She paused for a response, but the man-child stayed silent. "All right, I'll just shut the fuck up so you can be an asshole in peace."

More silence followed as they reached the top of the stairs and continued down the wide hall, its oyster-colored walls displaying two Monet reproductions bought on OverstockArt.com. Stopping at the second chestnut-brown door, Kathleen opened it, then turned on the lights. "Holy fuck," she said through a high-pitched squeal; the dimly lit square space was less bedroom—the only furniture was a folding bed pushed into the back corner—and more masturbation booth at a hipster sex shop. However, instead of Asian-girls-taking-selfies-with-Bernie Sanders porn, the room had hundreds of comic books stacked against three walls for dick-spanking pleasure. "I expected a decent collection, but this is just crazy…"

Her voice faltered as she turned to the man; his chunky face was a gray clump of damp hand towels, but his beady eyes were tiny portals of white light locked on the room as if he were a seven-year-old boy with terminal cancer whose Make-a-Wish was to see a shitload of comics. *I guess he really likes comics*, she thought, then said, "Would you like me to take you to your bed?"

"Yes, please," the man said through a strained breath.

"*Oh*, I like those manners," Kathleen said with a big, condescending smile. She brought him to the dorm-size bed and helped him onto his back. As he lay against the bare bed, his eyes flew straight to the popcorn ceiling and stayed on the tiny gray dots.

Kathleen watched him, a cruel chuckle tickling her throat until it was too much. "All right," she said, giggling. "Is the ceiling a Magic Eye of Cat Woman's pussy or something?"

The man-child's trance continued in silence.

"*Yeah, okay*," Kathleen said, nodding off the awkward romance between the dimwitted giant and his ceiling. She pivoted around and scanned the room, skimming the stacks of comic books with a growing smile. *I could fucking stay here all day and read every—*

Her nose crinkled, the nostrils finally catching the room's scent of mildew and mummified fart. *Christ, this room needs some Febreze—*she shivered, hit by the damp cold of the tight space—*and an electric heater, for fuck's sake.* "Sorry," she said, tucking the sleeves of her hoodie into her hands as a pair of makeshift gloves. "I need some fucking air."

She walked out of the tiny bedroom and walked to the wooden banister overlooking the living room. "Man," she said, relishing the beauty of the spacious room. "This looks like it could be my new *home!*" Suddenly a sharp pain shot through her cyst. She let out a loud "Ow," then followed it with, "What the fuck? I'm *literally* just standing here!"

She pulled down the waistband of her pajama pants, looked over her shoulder, and reached down for her cyst. "If this stupid sac hasn't popped yet"—her fingers searched her right ass cheek for the pocket of puss—"I'm going to do it myself."

62

The Sheriff, 5:45 p.m.

Edging eighty miles per hour, Sheriff Coleman's cruiser tore through the honey- and apricot-colored woods of Baldwinsville. The potent sun, barred by the passing pine and maple trees, threw out its rays of golden light at the speeding car, trying to showcase its power over the approaching night. Sheriff Coleman, however, ignored its dramatic attempt for dominance. Dry streaks of snot and tears ran along his cheeks as he gazed at the somber gray sky ahead of him. *Not again,* he told himself, remembering the same ashen sky the day when Patricia was laid to rest. *I can't watch them bury my little girl.* He gulped down a large breath through the tense bulb that had sprouted in his throat. *If Betsy's gone, then I'm going too.*

Reaching ninety miles per hour, he continued down the infinite stretch of road, the vibrant woods whipping past the car like the dizzying images of a five-cent zoetrope. Again, his pale-green eyes forbade a glance at the rushing background and stared into the stale sky he was racing toward with a joyless expression. As the car glided over the road like a war drone, there was a moment of silent tension, like the eye of a monstrous tornado, and then the sheriff exploded, envisioning a small tombstone next to his wife's. HERE LIES BETSY COLEMAN, it read, and then, underneath, someone had added in red spray paint, BECAUSE OF YOU.

"No!" he shouted at the grim image. "She's alive, goddamn it! She's alive..." He broke into a wordless fit, squeezing the wheel as though it were Nick Roesch's chunky neck, while a hot salty river poured over the dried stream beds of his snot and tears. This stormy outpour of emotions went on for five minutes until Sergeant Bill came on the radio.

"Sheriff?" he said without the Christian cheer.

Sheriff Coleman snatched the hand microphone, his marble eyes on the grim world barreling toward him. "Yes?"

"I just got word from the Rathburn house. It's...bad."

Sheriff Coleman's sopping face turned translucent. "What happened?"

"There are six bodies, John. Three girls—"

"Is Betsy there?"

"We don't know—"

Sheriff Coleman threw the microphone at the dashboard and screamed. "Jesus Christ, I told her not to go there!"

"The officers haven't identified the bodies yet. They're waiting for your orders."

"I told her not to go there," Sheriff Coleman repeated, then punched the laptop attached to the dashboard, cracking the black screen. A short sting pierced the back of his hand, but he continued smashing the computer with his hairless fist. "I told her not to go there," he yelled, hitting the shattered screen after each word, "but she went anyway, and now she's...dead." Shivering, he went silent. Out loud, the word "dead" felt like a cold disfigured hand sliding down his spine.

"John?"

Sheriff Coleman pulled his hand away from the laptop, leaving an interweaving cluster of bloodied cracks. Embedded in the soft webbing between his knuckles, the jagged pieces of glass from the screen shot a fiery course of torment through his arm. Ignoring the pain, he looked out the windshield as a broken man, the closest to death he'd ever been.

"John, are you there? Hello? Sheriff Coleman, can you hear me?"

He grabbed the microphone from the dashboard and stated, "Yeah."

"What do you want the officers to do?"

Sheriff Coleman's mouth hung open, waiting on his inner hero to order a genius plan of action. "I don't know," he finally said. "Could you give me a moment?"

"Yeah, of course."

Lowering the microphone, he kept his hopeless gaze on the gray sky over the passing woods, his right foot punching the gas pedal. Creeping toward ninety-five miles per hour, he sped down the road, disregarding its subtle curves for the smoky screen ahead of him. His daughter's graffitied tombstone, standing next to his wife's, returned to view. Then, like a ghost superimposed onto a silent film, he appeared sitting in a folding chair with a can of Natural Ice in his hand. His ruffled, black hair turned gray as he took a sip of the warm monkey-spit-tasting beverage. After a second sip, he went bald. A third drink covered his head in liver spots.

After he finished the beer, another one magically appeared in his hand. He drank this second can of bum sweat in two gulps—the first causing the lean muscles in his legs and arms to deflate while the second transformed his olive skin into a sickly yellow. When another beer materialized, he chugged it down in one swig. Surging through his esophagus, the chalky liquid had an instant effect: his yellowish skin changed to a light brown, boiled into hundreds of moles and weird-shaped warts, then melted off in gooey layers like a marshmallow over a campfire.

"I'm not strong enough," Sheriff Coleman said, hypnotized by this hideous transformation. "If she's gone, I'll drink myself to death. I know it." A fresh wave of tears rolled down his cheeks as he lifted his hands from the wheel. "I'm sorry, Patricia. I-I just can't do it. I can't live alone."

The moment the cruiser made a life-threatening jerk to the right, Sheriff Coleman grabbed the steering wheel and regained control. "Shit," he said, then slapped himself hard across the face. Taking a deep breath, he eased out of the nightmarish daze and fixed his attention on the road. "She's your daughter, John. She's not gone until she's in a fucking coffin." Gradually he brought the speed down to sixty miles per hour, then took the hand microphone from the passenger seat. "Bill?"

"Yes, John."

"Tell the officers not to touch anything. I want you to—fuck!"

"What's going on?" Sergeant Bill asked with a note of panic.

"I think I passed the Rathburns' house," he said, catching the flashing lights of a cop car in the corner of his eye. "Hold on." He moved to the side of the road then made a quick U-turn and continued to the wooden gate. "All right, I'm here. Call the state police and tell them to get the FBI on the line. This is a lot bigger than we can handle."

"Will do," Sergeant Bill replied.

"Good. Get everybody on the road, too—our team, highway patrol, state troopers. We need to catch this goddamn monster before he strikes again. Okay, Bill?"

"Um, okay," he answered shakily.

"What?"

Sergeant Bill made an uneasy groan of protest. "Well, it's sinful to take the Lord's name in vain."

Sheriff Coleman heaved a deafening sigh. "I'm sorry," he said, pulling into the wooded driveway of the Rathburn residence. "I'll say an Our Father as soon as we nab our visiting psychopath. Over and—"

"Wait, John. I got one more thing."

"What is it?"

"Dr. Bonesteel had an accident."

"What kind of accident?" Sheriff Coleman asked, his focus drifting off to the cabin/Norwegian ski resort that was slowly coming to view.

"He shot himself in the foot."

"Jesus *fucking* Christ!" Sheriff Coleman's emerald-colored eyes flicked with instant guilt. "Shit. I'm sorry, Bill. I didn't mean to say that. Is he okay?"

"Yes," Bill said flatly. "A patrol car was there, so they took him to the hospital."

Crazy old kook, Sheriff Coleman thought, parking his car next to the police cruiser at the end of the driveway. "Make sure he's all right and get another car over there."

"Okay," Sergeant Bill said. "Over and out."

"Over and out," Sheriff Coleman echoed, then returned the hand microphone and opened the door. As he stepped out, Denny Hansen—a portly ginger, fresh from the academy—approached him.

"We've got, um…six bodies, Sheriff." His flushed cheeks matched his wavy red hair, indicating this was his first time seeing six dead bodies at once. Or his first time seeing a dead body—outside of *Grand Theft Auto*—altogether.

"Where are they, Denny?" Sheriff Coleman said, heading for the house. At the doorway, he stopped, seeing two lifeless bodies—a boy with dark auburn hair and a blond girl who wore an odd squash-shaped mask—lying in the living room, which was a mess of blood and pushed-over furniture. He didn't recognize the boy, but without a doubt, he knew the girl—by the cowgirl stripper outfit itself—wasn't Betsy. "Show me the others," he said, turning to Denny.

"Yes, sir," the squeaky officer responded, then led him to the bodies of four other teenagers scattered at the bottom of an old-looking staircase—none of whom were Betsy either.

"Oh, God, thank you," Sheriff Coleman said, bowing his head and folding his hands. "Thank you so, *so* much." He then looked up to see the nervous officer staring back with a curious "You're thanking God that these kids have been brutally murdered" eye. "Sorry. My daughter might've have been at this party." An awkward silence tried to wedge itself between boss and employee, but Sheriff Coleman avoided the moment by clearing his throat and adding, "Is anyone else in the house?"

Denny shook his head. "No, sir."

"You went through the entire house and yard and didn't find anyone else?"

"That's right."

Frowning, Sheriff Coleman brought his fingers to the stubble of his chin. *Where the hell is she?* "Did you find anything suspicious?"

"Yes, sir. Besides the living room and kitchen, we found a few things that might indicate some scuffles took place."

"Like what?"

Denny stared at the sheriff for a moment, his eyes squinting in search for the answer, then looked down as he scratched his smooth chin. "Sorry. I'll have to look at my notes." With an anxious chuckle, he took out a pencil—its tail chewed down to the lead—and a mini notebook from his belt. Sheriff Coleman's jaw clenched down on a puff of frustration as the short kid flipped through the first ten pages, each filled with drawings of Marvin the Martian and various-size boobs. "Okay, so there's a broken vase in the first hallway of the ground floor; there's a picture frame in the upstairs bedroom with blood on it, and the window was opened; and below the window outside, there's blood on a tree stump and some sort of card next to it."

"Like a birthday card?"

"No. It's like one of those cards...with a woman on it."

No, you don't have time to get angry, Sheriff Coleman thought, as an invisible screw tightened his jaw, saving the young officer from a "talk." "What does the woman look like?"

"Well, I know she's got something to do with God." Denny's pale cheeks turned beet red. "But I'm not certain. I haven't been to church since my grandfather's—" Suddenly his eyes gleamed with knowledge. "That's it! It's one of those cards you get at a funeral."

Sheriff Coleman cocked an eyebrow. "A prayer card?"

"Yeah!"

"Show me," he said with a frosty look. As Denny led him to the other side of the massive cabin, the cold expression swelled into a prickly nervousness. *Why's there a prayer card at a Halloween party? Was it part of a costume or are these fucking kids today using them to cut up their Adderall or whatever else they're sniffing?*

"I marked it, Sheriff," Denny said as they reached a block of grass covered with crisp leaves, "so I wouldn't lose it." He stopped at a freshly cut tree stump ten feet from the house and pointed to a yellow flag sticking out of the ground.

"Mm-hmm," Sheriff Coleman said, coming up from behind him. He immediately stopped, catching sight of the Virgin Mary, her familiar blue and white robe wrapped around her gentle shoulders, poised on the front of a small laminated card. *No,* he thought, as an uneasy breath escaped his mouth. *That isn't Patricia's, is it?*

63

Nick, 6:15 p.m.

Lying across the bare mattress, Nick kept his eyes on the ceiling while a sweltering heat, fanned by his poker wounds, cooked his insides. Remaining still, he let the flames slow-smoke his organs as he enjoyed the solitude of his compact room. *Finally*, he thought; he was home with his smothering family gone and his comic collection untouched—to read and enjoy and escape into, all over again.

The corners of his blistered lips lifted, pricking the nerves in his cheeks to form a healthy smile.

"*Home!*" the big, black-haired girl shouted from the hallway.

Without thinking, Nick snapped his head, delivering a stinging Bowie-knife swipe across his neck. "That fucking, loud-ass bitch," he sneered at the empty hallway. "I'm going to rip her in half, and then I'm going to throw her over—"

Swept into his growing rage, he punched his left leg, sending a prong of immense pain through the charred meat. His mouth opened, preparing to rock the entire house with a violent "Motherfucker!" but with a flash of second thought, he stopped himself. *Hold on*, he thought, relaxing his giant shish-kebab body. *She'll shut that fucking loud cunt mouth of hers.*

Nick stared at the hallway, waiting for another outburst. Hearing nothing but the low whispers of the moldy air, he turned back to the ceiling. *Take a nap, and then you can read* Kingdom Come *when you wake up.* He lay motionless for a minute, then took a cautious breath as the heat grilling his organs started to weaken. *And maybe the girl could do that thing to my penis again.*

With another cheek-cutting smile, he closed his eyes and drifted off to sleep.

64

David, 6:00 p.m.

Okay, you can do this, he told himself, pretending a relaxed lookout for Kathleen, as he cautiously drove through the lifeless neighborhood. *Keep the glob of whatever's on your wrist nice and steady while you think of an amazing plan to save Kathleen. From Betsy.* Hearing a low series of dog-like panting, he kept his sight off the blood-hungry beast sitting next to him and continued his mock watch of the quiet suburb. *C'mon, David. Think. You need to escape from the truck and find Kathleen...so Betsy doesn't kill her...or you...while also protecting yourself from the gigantic maniac who didn't like Kathleen's hand job.*

His mouth tightened as he filled his lanky body with a booming whine. *Fuck horror. I'm watching nothing but super-gay musicals after this.*

Just then the glob glided across his wrist as if it had formed tiny guppy legs. Shuddering, David narrowed his eyes into two determined laser beams. The neighborhood was completely empty. *What the flying fuckery? Where the hell are the po' folk like me, looking for full-size candy bars?*

Betsy's breathing became the soupy-sounding pants of a Rick Baker creature. *Shit, shit, shit, shit*, David squealed internally while scanning the streets for anyone who could help him. *You'd better think of something now or—*

"You have reached your destination," Ms. Google Maps proclaimed. At that moment, David busted out two Arnold Schwarzenegger in *Total Recall* eyes. *Fuuuuuuuuuck!*

"All right, we're here," Betsy said. "Kathleen's piece-of-shit car should be around here, so keep your fucking eyes open. Got it, Cookie Puss?"

"Mm-hmm," David said, his bug eyes zipping through the unlit windows and vacant yards. *C'mon, Cookie Puss. You're supposed to be smart. Think!*

"If you see anything sharp, tell me," Betsy then added. "I need something sharp to ram into a skull."

David's shoulders tensed up, as he imagined the something sharp cracking his head open and releasing a stew of brains and glittered blood.

"M'kay." *Good Lord, this is getting real. You need to do something, like...now.* Passing the forty-second shit-stone mansion, he saw a row of cars lined in the driveway and a group of people standing behind the curtains of the first-floor windows. *Oh, God, yes! People!* He glanced at Betsy—her head, a blood-splattered matte of blond tangles, was pressed against the passenger's window, probably in search of a good skull-ramming object. He turned back to the windshield and instantaneously smiled when he saw a stop sign at the next intersection. *Double yes!*

A plan quickly formed in his head, and then, as he approached the intersection, he repeated it to himself. *All right, so you'll pull up to the stop sign, jump out of the car, then run like hell to the house. Okay?* He gave a quick nod. *Yup. You can do this. You can definitely do this.* He reached the stop sign and stepped on the brakes. *You just need a distraction...*

"Oh, my God!" David shouted, pointing to the line of trees facing Betsy's window. "Is that Kathleen?"

"Where?" As she whipped her slimy, monster head, he grabbed the driver-side door handle and, with an anxious scream, attempted his plan of escape. However, he'd forgotten to unlock the door and, like a tragic cartoon character, remained in the driver's seat, lifting the handle to the locked door over and over.

"Fuck me," he muttered, then turned to Betsy. Her big brown eyes, charged with supernatural anger, penetrated his flesh and slowly worked its way to his heart. Staring back, David held on to a rippled face of terror as if it were about to be molded into a Halloween mask (Queer Boy about to Be Death Dropped™) until Betsy lunged at him.

With another high-pitched scream, he blindly unlocked the door, swung it open, and bolted out of the car. "Oh, God!" he yelled, sprinting toward the tacky house in front of him. "Help! Please! She's going to kill me!" He reached the house, then pounded his fists against the door. "Please! Help! She's going to—"

David turned around and watched as Betsy ran up the gentle hill in front of the truck. "*Kill me?*" He placed his hands on his hips and slanted his body in confusion. "Why the *hell* did I do all that final gay running?"

Hearing the door open, David turned back. A frightened O shaped his mouth when he saw the Devil himself standing in front of him. "Holy fuck," Mike Barrett said with a hard laugh. "Hey, guys, it's the fag!"

David groaned as though he'd read some farfetched coincidence in a poorly written comedy-horror novel. "Honey bunches of *fuck* me."

65

Betsy, 6:10 p.m.

Fueled by a ravenous hunger for teen-girl revenge, Betsy stormed the gentle hill of Wheeler Avenue as a seething, blood-and-dirt-encrusted monster ensconced in Abercrombie & Fitch. Stopping at the top of the street, she flashed a deranged smile at the sight of Kathleen's bone-colored beater parked in front of a large brick house. She then continued to the car and, with a quick look through the passenger-side window, spotted the fire poker she'd plunged into the fat lunatic's leg back at Ashley's house. After opening Kathleen's car door and grabbing the poker from the floor, she turned to the mansion, exchanging her wicked grin for a militant gaze. "You're dead, you dumb cunt," she said, then marched toward the front door.

66

"How the fuck did this thing get bigger?" Kathleen said, sliding her finger along the circumference of her cyst. "Was it eating Chicken McNuggets or something?"

Boom! A loud crash—like a door being ripped off its hinges and thrown to the floor by a tornado—came from downstairs. Startled, Kathleen pulled her hand out of her pants and jumped back with a short yelp. "What the fuck?" she shouted, stepping toward the banister and looking over the living room. She sniggered, seeing Betsy standing at the front door in the Girl in a Horror Movie Starter Pack: disheveled, greasy hair; blood and dirt stains on designer jeans; household item gripped like a weapon; and a sad, vindictive look that read, *Stop everything. White girl has been wronged.*

"Can you do me a solid," Kathleen asked, moving to her side and sticking out her ass, "and scratch my cyst with that fire poker? It itches like a bitch. Thanks."

"No," Betsy said, her eyes narrowing into a hateful scowl. "I'm going to shove it down your fat mouth."

Kathleen laughed again. "Yeah, okay. Get the fuck out of here. I'm trying to hang out with my friend."

"That guy's your *friend?*" Betsy's face crumpled as though she'd been force-fed a mouthful of her grandmother's soup. "Are you fucking serious?"

"I'm *like* totally serious," Kathleen said in a stereotypical cheerleader voice. "But it's none of your fucking business, so like I said, you can get the fuck out. *Byeeeee.*"

Betsy's cherubic face wrenched into the evil version of Little Girl Eats Cotton Candy gif. "It's none of my fucking business?" She took two large steps to the staircase then started a slow, predatory climb up the stairs. "Really? Then why did you care so much about Luke and me?"

"Are you fucking kidding me?" Kathleen snarled. "You sold me out for a blowjob—"

Squeezing her hands around the poker, Betsy screamed until a patch of squiggly veins pushed against her forehead. "For the last fucking time, I didn't give him a blowjob! I was about to give him a *hand job*, but then we heard my father coming so Luke hid underneath my bed. And then when he came in, I panicked and told him you were drinking." Flushed in a candy apple red from head to toe, she stopped at the top of the staircase, a few feet from Kathleen. "*There*! I said it! Are you happy now?"

Kathleen gave a careless titter. *Handjobs are pretty popular this month.* "Um, yeah, I really don't care anymore, *so*...for the last time...you can get the fuck out, slut." She gave a quick wave goodbye.

Betsy stood still, her eyes set as two white orbs of pure hate. "Oh, my God," she said quietly, "you're a terrible person."

"And you're a terrible friend," Kathleen said without hesitation. "After all these years, you stab me in the back for a fucking hand job and not once did you try to apologize." She shook her head. "All you needed to do was to say you were sorry, and I probably would've forgiven you—"

Betsy released a hard laugh without opening her mouth. "You *probably* would've forgiven me? Yeah, right. You would've made fun of me for the rest of the year because you're *always* making fun of me! Ever since my mother died, you've treated me like shit." The lines of revenge running through Betsy's forehead softened, freeing herself from the long-kept secret she held as the last string to their friendship. "It's true, isn't it? You've been mean to me ever since my mom died. Why?"

Kathleen opened her mouth. "Because everyone treated you better than me. I was jealous. I've always been jealous of your sweet, perfect life," she was about to say, but it didn't sound like good ol' Kathleen. "Because I'm a fat cunt," she stated instead. "Now could you *please* get the fuck out of here and never talk to me again!"

"No," Betsy said, cocking her head in authority. "I want to know why you've been so mean to me."

Kathleen laughed in disbelief, then shouted as she clapped her hands, "Oh. My. God. Get the fuck out of here!"

"No!" Betsy screamed back and then, raising the poker in the air, lunged for Kathleen.

Suddenly the door down the hall swung open, and the man-child, a wax figure of Fat Sweaty Elvis come to life, rushed out of the room.

"Get the fuck out of my house!" he shouted, racing toward the two girls. Betsy turned to swing the poker, but he was too fast. With a ferocious growl, he lifted his leg and kicked Betsy in the stomach. *Boom!* Betsy fell backward to the floor then rolled down the stairs until she hit the bottom with a heavy thud.

"That's fucking right," Kathleen said, moving to the banister. "You mess with my friend and—"

Without warning, the man grabbed her thick ankles and pushed her over the railing. She performed a graceful, drunk-frat-boy flip midair and then, miraculously, landed on the green armchair below in an upright sitting position. *Pop!* Kathleen's cyst burst open like a cheese-filled balloon.

Toppling to the floor, she screamed with every muscle in her angry-bitch body. "*My fucking ass!*" she shrieked, as she lay on her stomach, her arms and legs squirming from the dozen of demon-baby injections of pain to her buttocks. "You popped my cyst, you goddamn motherfucking—"

Her head smacked the hardwood floor as she passed out.

67

David, 6:10 p.m.

"I'm sorry," David said with a nervous laugh. "I should probably go." He turned to make an escape, but Mike grabbed his arm and pushed him into a headlock.

"Nope," he said sharply. "You're not going anywhere, queer."

"Stop it!" David shouted. "Let me go!" He tried to wiggle himself free, but he wasn't stronger than Mike's football-throwing/masturbating-six-times-a-day arm.

Mike laughed a deep, barbaric laugh as low as his IQ. "C'mon, you just got here," he said, then pulled David into the house. "Hey, guys. Look who showed up."

Craning his neck through Mike's slimy pepperoni arm, David let out a dry gasp of terror. Standing in an all-white pre-circle jerk, around an obtrusively bright white marble foyer that looked like it had been rented for that said circle jerk, was a nightmarish mix of Dullen's varsity boys' sports teams and their too-dumb-or-fat-to-play-sports jerk-off buddies. Highlights included: Oscar Romo, his best friend in elementary school, who had kicked him out of their lunch table in seventh grade for being a "pooper snooper"; Garrett Newton, your typical shit-and-tackle tub of lard, who had pushed him into his locker in the ninth grade for no apparent reason other than he was "the gay kid"; and Lexi Hackler, the only girl at the party—who was present and conscious at that moment.

David turned to the strawberry-blonde, bird-like cheerleader with a frightened expression that signaled for help. Holding a red Solo cup (filled with Smirnoff Ice Peaches and Date Rape), Lexi stared back with a pop-eyed gaze that read, *What's math?*

"So what are we going to do to this little fag for breaking my rearview mirror today?" Mike asked the eager crowd. The slightly buzzed teenagers responded with a collective cheer, scattered with "Kick his ass."

"What? I didn't break your mirror!" David screamed, still trying to break free from Mike's hold. "C'mon, let me go! Betsy Coleman's going to kill Kathleen Strife!"

Everyone laughed.

"It's true!" David barked, his eyes brimming with tears. "She's gone insane! Some guy tried to kill her. He killed Luke and Ashley at her party! They're dead! I saw their bodies!"

Again the rowdy group laughed, except for Lexi, who was probably thinking, *Oh, my God, I wasn't invited to Ashley's party?*

"Okay," Mike said, rubbing David's shaggy hair with his knuckles. "Someone's had a little bit too much Halloween for the night. Maybe we should tape him to the roof so he can get some rest."

The bloodthirsty pack of apes roared in agreement. *Jesus Christ*, David thought, squirming for a better look at the crowd. *Are they serious?*

"Go get the duct tape, Pat," Mike said.

"Where is it?" Pat asked, standing between Oscar and Garrett like a proud potbelly pig awarded "Dirtiest Eater" at the state fair.

"In the drawer by the refrigerator."

"Okay," Pat said, his piggish mouth bent into a mischievous smile, then headed out of the room.

They're fucking serious! David shouted in his head. A frosty grip of fear seized his kidneys, threatening to rewet the faint streak of piss on his jeans. He screamed, attempting to free himself with a genius, Harry Houdini pop-of-the-shoulder-joint slight. "Please," he sobbed, giving up on a physical escape from Mike's python hold. "Let me go. You're hurting me."

Mike yanked him from his bent-over position, bringing them eye to eye. With a bloodshot, wasted glare, Mike pouted and said, "*Oh*, I'm sorry." His breath smelled like wet dog and cheap piss beer. "I didn't know I was hurting you. Here, let me—"

"Where's the duct tape?" Pat yelled from the other room.

Mike heaved a pickle-brine-smelling sigh directly into David's face. "In the drawer to the left of the refrigerator."

There was a moment of silence. "Your left or my left?"

Mike squeezed David's neck, yelling, "It's the same fucking left!"

Pat chuckled. "Oh, right. Just a second."

"Fucking retard." Mike grabbed David arm's and wrenched it backward. The monkeys hooted their turd-throwing giggles as he winced in pain. "Is that better, guys, or should I try something else?"

The brainless apes shouted out suggestions. "Kick him in the balls!" Garrett grunted.

"Yeah," the Thompson twins, a pair of freckled gingers in Mario and Luigi costumes, said in unison.

"I feel dizzy," Lexi said. At the same time, Oscar cried out, "Break the fag's arm like he broke your mirror."

"Hmm, that's not a bad idea," Mike slurred in a cheerful tone, then leaned in and whispered into David's ear. "What do you say? Should I break your arm for messing up my car?"

I didn't touch your car, you nutjob, David wanted to answer, but instead, he bowed his head and continued to sob a dry fit of tears. *You're a fucking coward. Always will be.*

"Hey," Mike said, twisting David's arm harder, "answer me!"

David let out a high screech. "Oh, my God!" he shouted in a pained outburst of real tears. "What's wrong with you? Why do you hate me so much?"

"What?" Mike hissed, then shoved him into the wall behind them. "What's wrong with *me?*" He laughed as he pressed his left arm into David's chest. "You're a fucking fag!"

"I'm not gay!" David huffed.

Mike and his troupe of apes jeered in disagreement. "Are you fucking kidding me?" he said, pushing him harder into the wall. "You're the biggest fag in school!"

"No, I'm not!"

"Yes, you are. Now say it!"

"No," David said, turning away from Mike's drunken stare.

Immediately Mike grabbed David's fingers and pulled back his hand, stretching the cluster of tendons into a fiery ache. "Say it, or I'll break your fucking hand!"

As the group of subhuman bullies applauded the torturous act, David screamed two full lungs of fear and hurt. "Okay, *okay.* I'm the biggest fag in school!" Looking at the curved staircase on his left, he took a long, uneasy breath and—tired from the day's ever-increasing fucked-up-ness—mumbled louder than he wanted, "Why does it even matter?"

Mike doubled over in laughter. "Why does it matter? Uh, because I hate fags!"

Without thinking, David looked at Mike and asked in a pleading innocence, "Why?"

Mike moved back, his forehead contorted into a big question mark, then said without his usual bro confidence, "Because the Bible says it's wrong."

David snorted. "The Bible? When did you start reading books?"

An evil scribble of homophobia overtook Mike's fat befuddled face as he slammed David into the wall. "Shut the fuck up, *faggot!*" His fellow primates shrieked as if someone had announced that Eminem and a pair of lesbian porn stars would perform during Super Bowl halftime. "Or I'll beat the shit out of you!"

Time then played in slow motion as Mike balled his free hand into a fist. Right then, David's instincts commanded him to cower at the big, bad bully's violent threat, but something—a surge of adrenaline or stupidity or both—awoke his inner final gay. *Snap out of it,* a Cher-like voice ordered. *Is this how you want to be treated for the rest of your life?*

"No!" David yelled back and then, with the strength of ten drag queens fighting for the shopping carts of dollar store props on *RuPaul's Drag Race,* pushed himself out of Mike's wrestling hold. "I'm a fucking fag, and you're going to have to deal with it!" Just then he felt the slimy chunk of Luke roll down from his wrist into the palm of his hand. A smile stretched out his bony cheeks as his next move popped into his head. "And you want to know why?" He didn't wait for an answer. "Because we have to learn to be civil with each other or we'll just keep on fighting and trying to get back at each other in bigger ways. And you definitely don't want that. I'm a *lot* more creative than you are."

Mike squinted as though David were speaking Chemistry Regents. "What the fuck are you talking about?"

"This!" David lunged forward and shoved the purplish chunk of Luke into Mike's mouth. There was a synchronized grunt from the band of apes, followed by a woozy "I feel funny" squeak from Lexi.

"What the fuck?" Mike bawled, staggering back as he rubbed the slime off his lips. "What did you put on my face?" As he spat the salty specks from his mouth, disgust stirred the hatred in his boozy eyes. "*Answer me, faggot!*"

"Taste the Luke, you damn dirty ape!" David wailed victoriously, then ran to the staircase.

"I'm going to fucking kill you!" Mike screamed, following him up the stairs.

Ignited by his final gay, David reached the top and, inspired by his favorite scream queen (Sarah Michelle Gellar in *Scream 2*), grabbed a large potted aloe plant and hurled it at Mike. A natural athlete, Mike dove downward, dodging the plant. "I got the duct tape!" Pat exclaimed, waving a roll of the silver adhesive. The clay pot plummeted into his empty, cardboard box head. He was immediately knocked out cold and fell backward into the Thompson twins.

"Ha!" David said with a madman's delight. "It's like playing dumb jock bowling!"

"You're fucking dead," Mike said, starting for him once again.

"Oh, I'm *sooo* scared," David replied sarcastically, then headed into the first room he saw and closed and locked the door behind him. Flicking on the lights revealed the bedroom of your average who-gives-a-shit-about-decor teenage boy. Infused with the scent of gym sweat and jizz, the room looked like a hoarder of Taco Bell wrappers had wreaked havoc on a Dick's Sporting Goods. "Wow," David exclaimed, "this is a *whole* lot of straight."

Boom! There was a heavy thud against the door. "Get the fuck out my room!" Mike said, pounding on the white slab of wood, a Madden 16 poster taped to the center. "Or I'll break this door down and...*and...bash in your fucking faggot skull!*" A furious cry echoed through the wide hallway like approaching thunder, then a barrage of hail-sounding blows pelted the door. "*Now, goddamn it. Get the fuck out, you little faggot!*"

In the tense moment of silence that followed, David breathlessly watched the door until a shiver fitted his body with a suit of gooseflesh. *What the hell are you doing?* he asked this new, final gay persona of his. *You're not some punk who smears blood on people's faces. Just tell them again about Luke and Ashley and maybe—*

There were two thumps against the door. "Get the fuck out, little faggot!" Oscar sang like a lighthearted football taunt. A round of laughter followed.

"Shit," David croaked, imagining the apes were huddled by the door, waiting to rip him into a light snack.

Two more thumps. "Get the fuck out, little faggot!" Oscar repeated.

Again the apes laughed, then joined in on the homophobic chanting. "Get the fuck out, little faggot!" they cheered, clapping together.

"Get the fuck out, little faggot!" Oscar recited, banging on the door. The monkey chorus came again, louder than the first time.

"C'mon, Mike," Oscar said playfully. "Lead the chant."

Mike gave a small laugh. "Get the fuck out, little faggot," he rasped as though he'd been crying, then hit the door with two lighter knocks than Oscar's.

"There ya go, man!" Oscar shouted, then led the Gay Men's Bashing Choir into their third round. Mike then took over as conductor, hammering the door with his fists.

"Get the fuck out, little faggot!" he barked.

Clap, clap. "Get the fuck out, little faggot" went the refrain.

This is not *good*, David groaned, his teeth bared at the door. As the chanting grew into a screaming competition, his mind drifted into a pathetic-little-faggot thought hole.

Boom, boom. "Get the fuck out, little faggot!" David remembered the Skittles thrown at him like he was a flytrap for queer mosquitoes.

Boom, boom. "Get the fuck out, little faggot!" He remembered Luke threatening to beat him up before school and then, not even five minutes into first period, receiving a second death threat from Mike.

Boom, boom. "Get the fuck out, little faggot!" As David breathed a series of hard breaths to the rhythm of the chant, his fingers clawed angrily through an invisible piece of paper as every homophobic insult or physical assault ran through his head. Why him? After three and a half years at Dullen, keeping his faggot ways far from the monkey jocks, why was he always the target of their prejudice? Because he was a weak piece of shit, who let everyone walk all over him?

"Get the fuck out, little faggot!"

"No," he whispered. Because he was a kindhearted, strong individual. Like the final gay of his very own '80s slasher, *Dress-Down Day.* "I'm...I'm a final gay."

"Get the fuck out, little faggot!"

David cleared his throat and said louder, "I'm a final gay."

"Get the fuck out—"

"What did you say, fag boy?"

David bowed his head with a Jessie Walsh, the original final gay, stare down. *That's the last fucking time he calls me a fag*, he told himself, then screamed, "I'm the final gay, you fucking dumbass breeder!"

Fired up by a devil-may-care, destruction-hungry courage, David picked up the neon-orange baseball bat leaning against the unmade bed and swung it aimlessly at the nearby wall. The end of the bat crashed into a glass picture frame with a Mr. Big Foosball Player poster in it.

"What the fuck was that?" Mike yelled. The pieces fell onto the cum-stained mess of sheets on top of the bed.

"The sound of freedom!" David yelled back, aiming the bat at his imaginary killer as though he was in the final act of *Dress-Down Day.*

"What?" Mike said, dumbfounded. "You'd better not touch anything, or I'll kill you, queer."

"Oh, honey, you can't kill good taste." Flashing a mischievous, smirk, he raised the bat over his head and let out a mighty roar. As Mike slammed his fists against the door, David redecorated the room with his final gay fury. He slammed the bat down on Mike's flat-screen TV and PS4; swiped his tinfoil football trophies off his dresser; knocked over his collection of Vin Diesel DVDs; then pushed over his "bookshelf" of video games and *Sports Illustrated.*

As the magazines flew across the room, David halted his rampage. Among the wreckage was the fiftieth-anniversary issue of *Fetish Magazine.* Sprawled across the cover was a big-breasted, Latino woman with a ten-inch erection, the words "Chicks with Dicks Spread, Extra Thick" written underneath her in hot pink. "Well, *hellooooo*, nurse," David said, holding the bat over his head in a frozen shock. Chuckling, he lowered the bat then turned to the door. "Hey, Mike. I *love* your magazine collection. Looks like everyone gots them skeletons, no?"

The banging instantly stopped. As David watched the door and waited with a dark curiosity, the air congealed into a swampy after-football-practice silence. And then, stirring the air into a thicker tension, Mike said in an uneasy hush, "There's a screwdriver in my father's toolbox in the garage. Somebody go get it... And the blue tarp in the corner, too. After I beat the shit outta the little faggot, I'm gonna take a big dump on him then roll up the tarp and throw it into the woods."

"All right," David said, dropping the bat. "It's time to retire from sports." He turned around and headed directly to the window. Pulling up the cheap white blinds, he opened the window and looked out over the short, slanted roof. Twenty feet down lay a freshly raked lawn with a stainless-steel grill, a wicker patio table and chairs, and a trampoline with an enclosed net— perfect for a Sunday barbecue with the entire Klan family.

"*You're fucking dead, faggot!*" Mike screamed, returning his fists to his bedroom door. "*I'm going to come in there and beat the shit out of you until—*"

"Warning," David said, imitating the menacing voice of an '80s movie-trailer announcer. "The makers of this terrifying film strongly suggest you bring an extra pair of pants in case of accidents. Happy *Dress-Down Day.*" He smiled, looking out at the gloomy autumn scene, then stepped onto the roof and jumped feetfirst toward the trampoline.

68

The Sheriff, 6:00 p.m.
Reaching for the prayer card, Sheriff Coleman already had the answer to his question. He knew he would see his wife's name on the back, and then—*bang!*—the memory of her torturous death would be a bullet to his brain. *Bang* again. The tangible piece of evidence that his daughter was suffering a similar agonizing death would be a bullet to his heart. Would he take a real bullet to escape the lonely life of a sad drunk, he questioned, grabbing the card anyway.

He turned the card over and saw his wife's name. As he rubbed his thumb over the black text, his eyes floated down to the dry bed of leaves at his feet. *Maybe she's okay,* he thought, sheathed in a tepid calm that felt neither good nor bad.

"Sheriff?"

Seeing a stubby hand wave across his central vision, Sheriff Coleman looked up at Denny, his ripe face marked with its first crinkle of stress. "Yeah?"

"Is it a prayer card?"

"Yeah," Sheriff Coleman responded quietly.

"Do you think it means anything?"

Sheriff Coleman shook his head. "I don't know," he replied, as his mind struggled to find any answers in the strange calm.

"Hm. Well, I think I have a guess how it got there." Denny licked his lips, then turned the page in his notebook. After quickly skimming his notes, he continued, "If you look up at the part of the gutter that's underneath the second-floor window"—he turned around and pointed—"you can see there's a slight bend. The window was opened, and it looks like there was some sort of struggle in the room. I'm thinking, Nick attacked someone, but they escaped out the window. Unfortunately, I think that person slipped and fell from the roof. They hit their head and dropped the card."

Sheriff Coleman eased out of the purgatory of thought. "And then what happened?"

"Well, sir, I'm not sure. Either they were one of the kids at the front door, or someone else here ran off into the woods."

Suddenly, Sheriff Coleman bolted toward the edge of the dense forest that separated the modern opulence of the cabin and a wide unknown. "Stop, it's not safe!" Denny shouted behind him, but the sheriff continued his hurried dive into the dim thicket, risking exposure to a second teenage bloodbath or his own nasty demise.

Rushing past the first line of maple trees, he barreled through the treescape toward the pre-dusk sun, until—*bam!*—he tripped and crashed, hands first, into a patch of wet leaves and spiny twigs. "Betsy!" he screamed through the chilly wilderness. "Are you here?" he screamed louder, ignoring the sharp ache in his knees, as he crawled through the sludge covering the hard earth.

He moved about two feet forward, and then Denny flew in front of him and held up his hands like a human stop sign. "Sir," he said, his palms shaking in the sheriff's face, "you can't be here. Nick Roesch could be hiding somewhere."

"No! My daughter," Sheriff Coleman balled, making a break past the trembling officer on hand and foot. "I know she's out here!"

He crawled for the mass of older maples in the distance, their knotted trunks hosting a multitude of hiding dens or booby traps. Denny grabbed his arm and shouted, "Are you crazy? We gotta go back. It isn't safe here."

"But my—"

"Listen to me, Sheriff," Denny demanded. "It's about to get dark, and that lunatic could be waiting to attack us. Now c'mon!" He tried to pull the sheriff with him, but he stayed planted to the ground, as though his legs had burrowed into the soil like his woodland brethren. "C'mon," Denny said, tugging harder on the sheriff's arm. "Even if your daughter *is* here, there's a very small chance we'll find her. This place is huge!"

"The prayer card was f-from my wife's funeral," Sheriff Coleman stammered, shaking off Denny's hold with a forceful push. "The only one who could have it is my daughter, so she has to be out here—" Exploding into another fit of tears, he fell forward, bringing his forehead against the mat of wet leaves. "Goddamn it. I just want my daughter back!"

As the sheriff continued crying, Denny crouched in front of him and placed his hands on his back. "We'll find her," he said with surprising confidence. "Trust me, sir. But we gotta do it right. We have to wait for a forensics team so they can do a thorough search or we'll wind up lost or dead. And what good would that do your daughter?"

Sheriff Coleman remained bent over, breathing in the flooded-basement stench of the soil. He then closed his eyes, cutting off the last tears streaming from the tear ducts, and thought, *He's right. Be a good father for once. Trust your instincts. Betsy's safe... Yeah, she's safe.* "Okay," he said, opening his eyes on the prayer card in his hand. He looked at Mary Magdalene, her serene, rosy-cheeked smile similar to his wife's, and gave a small smile in return. Then, wiping the tears from his soiled cheeks, he reached up and said, "Can you help me, Denny? We need to call for a search team."

69

Nick, 6:25 p.m.

Nick's sweat-covered face remained perfectly flat as he looked upon the two human-size rats sprawled out on the living room floor. Leaning against the railing of the staircase, he waited for their round, pasty bodies to awake, but seeing no signs of movement, he turned to the hallway. "Finally," he said, starting for his bedroom. "I can get some *peeeeeace!*"

Releasing an ear-shattering scream, he backed into the railing and lowered himself to the dusty hardwood floor, his greasy paw clenching the spit-roast of pain that suddenly shot through his injured leg. "No!" he shouted, removing his hand from a squirt of fresh blood oozing through the sunflower tourniquet. "I just wanted to go to my fucking room!" As he turned to his bedroom door, his vision blurred as an internal fog weighed down his head. "I just...wanted...room..."

70

David, 6:25 p.m.

He hit the center of the trampoline, bounced up to the rim of the polyethylene netting, and struck a Vargas-girl-riding-a-hot-dog pose. "*Yas!*" he cried out, coming back down. "I *am* the Trampoline Queen!"

"Get that fucking flamer!"

"Shit," David said, as Mike and his Douche Squad—sans the Thompson twins and Lexi, for reasons unknown—poured through the McMansion's sliding glass doors. After slipping out of the netting's exit flap, David sprinted across the Olympic-size backyard toward the wooden fence that separated Mike's house and the neighbors'. With two quick movements, he climbed the fence and jumped into the adjacent yard.

"Holy fuck, that faggot can climb," Mike exclaimed from behind the fence.

David smirked. "Aw, that was nice," he said and then, realizing the statement wasn't the best compliment, tore away and followed the fence until he reached the street. There, he raced up the small hill to his left and stopped at the top spotting Kathleen's car.

"Holy fuck," he said, turning to Nick's house. "This dude's *definitely* not homeless." Continuing to the car, he looked inside for the keys but found only a driver's seat sprinkled with dark-red blotches resembling blood. *Shit,* he thought; he wanted to believe it was period blood, but he—and a third of the teachers at Dullen—knew Kathleen menstruated the third week of every month.

"That faggot's dead!"

David turned with a pair of frightened Carol Kane eyes, seeing the pack of wild apes reach the top of the street. "Fuck," he said, then ran to the front door of the McMansion and knocked lightly on the side panel of unnecessary windows. "Hello? Kathleen?"

"There he is!" Mike screamed.

Oscar followed with, "Let's cut his fucking dick off and shove it up his ass!"

"Oh, God," David cried, knocking harder on the door. "Open the door, Kathleen! They're going to cut my dick off and ram it up my ass!" He paused. "And don't say it'll be good practice! Kathleen! Are you there?" Receiving no response, he flapped his hands in an automatic demonstration of queer exasperation. "Fuck it!" He opened the door, dashed into the house, and locked the door behind him. "All right," he said through a round of searing breaths, "I think I'm...*dead.*"

He let out a weak scream as he turned to the living room. "Holy shit!" he squawked, his frazzled eyes on Kathleen's lifeless body. Then Betsy's. And then on Kathleen's again. "They killed each other!"

"Get out!"

Taken by surprise, David flew back into the door with a second scream. His eyes moved up the staircase, then stopped on the crazy homeless (or formerly homeless) man at the top, leaning against the wall with a clammy, dead-eyed glare. "Um, I'm *really* sorry," David uttered through an uneasy voice, "but there's these guys out there and—"

"*Get out!*" the sickly-looking man shouted again.

"Yeah okay," David said, as his hands searched for the doorknob behind him. "Sorry for disturbing you."

Bam! A pair of hands crashed against the door. "Hey!" Mike yelled. "Get the fuck out here so we can kick your faggot ass!"

Fuck, David thought, as he looked back at the enormous madman and the red-hot rage exuding from his eyes. *This is bad.* "Um, I'm really sorry for asking, but would it be possible for me to go out the back?"

Silently the greasy-faced lunatic stood up and started down the staircase with slow, uneven steps, as the Jocks for Jesus outside rammed their bodies into the door, shouting a string of homophobic insults. *Oh, Christ,* David thought, sinking into an invisible shell of terror. *I'm going to die. I am* definitely *going to—*

A sudden spark of hope illuminated his face as he caught sight of the fire poker by Betsy's hand. *Yes!* he exclaimed internally, imagining he could grab it and...stab the slow-moving psycho in the gut? Open the door and wield it at the angry monkeys like a gay-Jedi lightsaber? Or maybe save everyone the time and shove it up his own ass?

The floor creaked as the heavy-set beast reached the bottom of the stairs. David looked up, watched him limp forward with his next kill in his eyes, then turned back to the poker. *All right, you can do this. You can definitely, one-hundred-percent do this...*

Slowly he slid down to the floor, looking back and forth—poker to man, poker to man—until the creature quickened his frail murder shuffle. *Oh, God,* David thought, trying to peel his hand from the floor. *C'mon! You can do this! You're the fucking final gay!*

With a jolt of courage, he sprang for the poker. At the same time, the queasy-looking lunatic lunged at him, letting out a bone-rattling scream. Grabbing the poker and aiming the pointed end like a harpoon, David shouted, "Get away from me or I'll...fuck you." His eyes widened in faux-pas embarrassment. "Up!"

Then, without warning, the big, oily chunk of man dropped to the floor with a loud boom. As he lay on his stomach between Kathleen and Betsy, David ogled the immobile slab of meat, his mouth opened in confusion. "Um, okay..."

A burst of laughter came from behind the door. "Holy fuck," Mike said. "He said he was going to fuck us!"

"What a fucking fag!" Oscar replied.

David closed his mouth into a tight squeeze. *I was almost slaughtered by a fucking serial killer, and I'm still being gay bashed.*

Suddenly the siren of a cop car rang in the distance. "Oh, shit!" Mike shouted. "It's the cops!"

"Run!"

As the apes scrambled away from the door, David snorted with laughter. "What a bunch of bitches." He remained on the floor with his back against the door and the poker pointed at the man's still body. "Nope," he said in the middle of a subtle body-movement scan. "I've seen every post-*Scream* meta-horror film. I know you're going to pop up for one last—"

There was a heavy knock on the door. "*Scare!*" David threw his hand over his mouth, waiting for the final pop-up scare from the resting giant.

"Police! Open up!" came a booming male voice from behind the door.

Damn it, David thought, gripping the fire poker. *Should I open the door, or is this dirty mofo going to come for me when I turn around?*

His inner horror-movie fan screamed, *Are you fucking stupid? You know he's gonna flip your canoe like Little Deformed Jason.*

With the poker locked on the killer's chest, David bit down on his bottom lip. *Maybe he was knocked out—*

Another heavy rap on the door. "Open up!" the police officer said in a deeper, more intimidating voice.

This motherfucker, David thought, after a second charge of fright to his nerves, then said in a fretful hush, "Um, sir. I'm so, *so* sorry, but I can't open the door."

"What? Why not?" the policeman asked.

David hesitated, trying to think of the least crazy explanation for the serial killer-and-the best-friend-falling-out sandwich lying in front of him. "Well, there's a man in here who tried to kill me." He paused, carefully choosing how to go on. "He's lying on the floor, but I'm not sure if he's unconscious or waiting to jump up and grab me while my back is turned. You know, like Jason Vorhees or Freddy Krueger at the end of every slasher film." Before the officer had a chance to respond, he quickly added, "So I guess...could you like...see if there's a back door or something and go through there, please?"

"Sure," the cop replied. "Are you all right?"

"Um, yeah," David said with a questionable shrug. "For the most part. Could you please hurry up, sir? There are two girls in here who also may or may not be dead."

"Two girls?"

"Yes, they're..." He wanted to say the man on the floor had tried to kill them, but he wasn't sure if Kathleen and Betsy had beaten him to the punch. "My friends."

"All right, I'll find a back door. Sit tight."

"Oh, I will, Mr. Policeman," David said under his breath, as he transferred all his final gay energy into his fire-poker grip. "I will." While the policeman walked away, he stayed pinned to the door, aiming the end of the poker at the man's boxlike head. *All right, you,* he thought in a motherly tone, *I won't skewer your brains if you stay just like that, 'kay?*

No movement came from the resting Leatherface. *Good,* David said to himself, continuing to keep a careful watch on the man until his curiosity won out over his horror movie ethics and he slowly moved his gaze to Kathleen. She lay in a comatose plank, her head sucking face with the hardwood floor. "Hey," he whispered. "Kathleen? Are you...still alive?"

He received silence, a very bad answer to his question. "Betsy?" he said, turning to his equally dead-looking friend. "Betsy? Can you hear me?"

Eyes closed, tongue out, hands and legs contorted into a flabby pretzel like she was playing Drunk Sorority Twister meant a solid no.

David shook his head. "God, what the hell happened to you guys? You were best friends, and now you're...dead? Maybe." For a moment, he stared at Kathleen's and Betsy's inanimate bodies. "Hello? Kathleen? Betsy? ...Crazy serial killer?"

71

The Sheriff, 7:00 p.m.

As a team of investigators walked in and out of the Rathburns' house with professional cameras and heavy-duty plastic bags filled with the spray-tanned remains of Dullen's most popular students, Sheriff Coleman sat in his cruiser with his eyes closed and the prayer card in his hand. "Hail Mary, full of grace. Our Lord is with thee. Blessed art thou among women and blessed is the fruit of thy womb, Jesus. Holy Mary, Mother of God, pray for us sinners now, and at the hour of death." He took a deep breath, keeping his eyes closed, then started his fifty-sixth Hail Mary. "Hail Mary, full of grace. Our Lord is with thee. Blessed art though among—"

"Praise be to God," Sergeant Bill said cheerfully over the radio. "We got Betsy!"

Opening his eyes, Sheriff Coleman tossed the prayer card onto the dashboard and shot his hand out for the microphone. "Is she all right?"

"She's alive but unconscious at the moment."

Sheriff Coleman took in a quick, fearful breath. "Jesus Christ, Bill! What do you mean she's unconscious?"

"I don't have all the details, but Sergeant Bobowski said she took a nasty fall at Nick Roesch's house in Manlius. She's on her way to St. Joseph's—"

"Hold on. I'm heading straight there." Sheriff Coleman dropped the hand microphone onto the passenger seat and started the engine. Once he had backed out of the driveway and reached the road, he picked up the microphone and asked, "Any word on Nick Roesch?"

"Yes," Sergeant Bill answered. "He's in an ambulance, unconscious as well. Two officers are transferring him to Crouse for multiple stab wounds to his leg and back."

"Multiple stab wounds? Who stabbed him?"

There was a moment of silence. "Um, we believe it was your daughter."

Sheriff Coleman let out an involuntary laugh. "Betsy?"

"Yes, Sheriff. She told one of the kids who was also at Nick Roesch's house. His name's David Ecklund."

David Ecklund, Sheriff Coleman repeated in his head. Was that the fruity kid who was always hanging out with Betsy and Kathleen? *C'mon, John*, he thought, his memory failing him. *Why don't you know who hangs out with your own daughter?*

"He's been talking to Gary for the last ten minutes," Sergeant Bill continued. "His account of what happened is very...interesting."

"What do you mean?" Sheriff Coleman asked. Again there was silence. "Bill?"

"Yeah, I'm here. I was just...looking over my notes. The kid says your daughter was hit by a car—"

Sheriff Coleman let go of the hand microphone. He immediately caught it, but the cruiser swerved into the emergency lane for a second, almost crashing into a sign that read, REPENT. JESUS IS WATCHING! "She was hit by a car!" Sheriff Coleman cried as he got back on the country road. "Jesus Christ! Does she have a concussion or any serious injuries?"

"The doctor will check for a concussion once she gets to the hospital," Bill replied. "She has some scrapes and black and blue marks here and there, but David stated she got up about a minute later and then...forced him to steal a truck and follow Nick so she could kill him."

Sheriff Coleman snarled in disbelief. "For crying out loud, Bill. Have you been watching those religious videos that make people hallucinate again?"

"No, John. I blocked that channel. I swear on the Bible, that's what the kid said. She got hit by a car and then woke up as—and I quote—'an angry bitch monster.'"

"No," Sheriff Coleman quickly said. "Betsy isn't like that. She's never been angry..." He was going to finish his statement with "in her life," but remembering their fight that morning, he stopped himself. *There's no use in lying. She's probably been angry with you since Patricia died. You were just too selfish to notice.*

The candid thought lingered in his head until he shook himself out of his daze. "All right, I'll read the report later. I'll be at St. Joseph's for the rest of the night. Is Tom still there as assistant sheriff?"

"Yes."

"Okay, you can relieve him in an hour and replace him with Stan. Make sure the patrols check the local neighborhoods for any more casualties. Got it?"

"Yes, Sheriff."

"All right. Thanks again for all your hard work."

"No need to thank me. I'm just glad the Lord kept Betsy safe."

Did he? Sheriff Coleman wondered, then said, "Yeah, me too. Over and out."

"Over and out."

Returning the microphone to the radio, Sheriff Coleman continued to speed down the unlit road, a puzzled expression creeping across his face. *Why would Betsy force someone to steal a car and then...* "Nope." Spotting the reflection of Patricia's prayer card in the windshield, he shook his head. "It doesn't matter. She's alive, and Nick's been caught." His mustache wiggled with his frustration before he sarcastically added, "Praise be."

72

Kathleen lay on a yellow-and-black gurney in the back of a speeding ambulance, her eyes shut and her arms crisscrossed over her bosom. Swaying back and forth with the vibrations of the ambulance, she remained a lifeless stack of flesh until the back-left wheel hit a pothole and a loud fart escaped her bowels. "Motherfucker," she shouted, as a sharp pain shot up her right ass cheek. She opened her eyes on the the paramedic version of Aziz Ansari watching her through a pair of Buddy Holly spectacles. "Who the fuck are you?" she asked.

The short, brown-skinned paramedic chuckled, then tapped the name tag on his navy-blue uniform. "Hey there, senorita. The name's Todd. I'm a paramedic for St. Joseph's. You had a bad fall and popped your cyst, so—" Gagging from the stench, he took off his black-rimmed spectacles and lowered his impish head. "Sorry. I just need a second."

Kathleen rolled her eyes. *It's just a fart, you little—* She turned to see Betsy, laying soundlessly on the neon-orange gurney across from her, her body wrapped tightly in a gray blanket and her mouth covered with a breathing tube that snaked underneath the blanket and ended in—Kathleen imagined—her vagina. "Hey," she said, as she studied Betsy's bluish eyelids lay idly over her large eyes, "is she dead?"

"No, she's alive," Todd answered, writing something on the paper fixed to the clipboard in his hands. "She's just unconscious."

"Well, isn't that a shame?" Kathleen said dryly. "What about the man?"

Todd leaned forward, adjusting his glasses over his round nose. "What man?"

"There was a big, weird-looking man back at the house. He really likes comic books, and has a dick the size of Long Island."

Todd brought his hand to his mouth, muffling a giggle. "Uh, I don't know anyone with *that* description—present company excluded. Are you feeling okay, chica? Do you need a drink of water or something?"

Kathleen blew off the sexist pet name with a sigh. "Is there any chance I can have a cigarette when we get to the hospital?"

Todd shook his head. "No, sorry. We have to get you to a room so you can see a doctor."

"I'm fine though. My ass hurts a little, but it always hurts."

Todd chuckled for the second time. "I'm sorry to hear that, but unfortunately a doctor has to take a look at you, so we know you're one hundred percent all right. It's standard procedure." He gave a big-toothed grin. "Okey doke, little lady?"

Little lady? I'm going to stomp that pervy smile off your fucking troll face, you cab driver with CPR training...

No, Kathleen told herself. *Don't waste your "fucks" on this asshole.* "Mm-hm," she said with a mocking smile in return. With another sigh, she looked up at the white metal ceiling and muttered, "I really should've stayed home today."

73

Betsy, 7:30 p.m.

A black chasm-like space, void of the infinite sparkle of Big Bang dust, stretched out forever until a godlike force flicked a switch, and an intense white light illuminated the pitch-black world. Immediately Betsy turned her head to the side and squeezed her eyes shut from the tremendous pressure pushing against them.

As the sensation subsided, she slowly opened her eyes to a fuzzy bright room with something moving in front of her. Something white and big and—

"Jesus Christ, my ass hurts!"

Oh, my God, Betsy thought, straightening up. She felt a hard pinch on the back of her neck but ignored it as she squinted through her hazy vision. *Is that Kathleen? Where are we?*

"Hello! Nurse!" Kathleen screamed. "Where the fuck are you? I've been pushing this motherfucking button for the last goddamn minute!"

Betsy's sight focused on Kathleen, who sat on the hospital bed across from her, a pile of empty pudding cups and apple-juice boxes on her over-bed tray. Quickly looking down, Betsy saw she was lying underneath the white sheet of a hospital bed, an IV line taped to her right wrist. She let out a low whimper, wondering why they were in the hospital. Did something bad happen to them? "K-k-k-kathleen?" she said, turning back to her.

Kathleen said nothing, keeping her eyes fixed on the wall with a crooked grimace, as though an invisible TV were stuck on a *Suicide Squad* marathon. Betsy tried again, worried something was wrong with her voice. Or Kathleen's ears. "K-k-k-kathleen?"

Again nothing. She took a long breath then cleared her throat and spoke even louder. "*Kathleen?*"

"Oh, my God," Kathleen said, whipping an angry gaze at her. "*What?*"

Frightened, Betsy grabbed the metal rails of her bed. *Why's she so mad?*

"Um, hello? Are you gonna say something or just stare at me like a fucking retard?"

Betsy's eyes widened with a sad, innocent look. "I'm s-s-s-sorry. I'm scared. What are we doing here?"

Kathleen let out a high-pitched peel of laughter. "Please, you know what you did," she said, then raised the remote control that had been concealed in her hand. "Lick my dirty twat!" she shouted, as she frantically pressed the buttons on the remote. "Why isn't this thing fucking working? Did they take out the batteries and stick 'em in the euthanasia machine?"

As she attempted to dismantle the remote, Betsy watched while her face compressed into a perplexed tomato. *You know what you did*, she repeated in her head and then, scanning her memory of that day, told herself, *I can't...remember anything.* Looking at the tangled sheet over her lap, she tried to think of the last thing she could recall. And then, with a sudden gasp, it hit her: her birthday party. "Oh, no," she said, turning her alarmed gaze onto Kathleen, "I'm s-s-s-so s-s-s-s-sorry. I didn't mean to get you in trouble at my party, but I—"

Kathleen's mouth cut through her cheeks, forming a thin smirk. "Oh, honey. It's a little late for apologies."

"B-b-b-but I—"

"Damn it!" she cried out, releasing the remote. She inhaled a deep breath, then let out the angry command of a sea witch. "*Nurse!*"

A gray-haired, heavy-armed woman in teal scrubs marched into the room with a fastened set of "I'm too tired for this bullshit" lips. "Excuse me, young lady," she said in a strong Jamaican accent, "but you need to keep quiet. People are trying to sleep."

"Well, excuse me, *ma'am*," Kathleen responded, "but my ass is on fire. Can I get some morphine or something?"

The pear-shaped nurse placed her hands on her wide hips. "I already gave you two pain pills. I can't give you anything else."

"Oh, okay," Kathleen said. "I guess I'll just keep screaming because these pills aren't doing *shit.*"

The nurse's sagging eyelids flickered in surprise. "*A wah di bloodclaat dew yuh*," she said. "That is no way to speak to a—" She gasped as she turned to Betsy. "Oh, thank goodness. You're awake." She hurried over to the side of Betsy's bed. "Are you all right, m'dear?"

"Um, I'm okay," Betsy said timidly. The pinch had burrowed deeper into her neck muscles, but it didn't matter. "Where exactly am I?" and "Why am I here?" were more important questions. "What happened?"

"You don't remember?"

Betsy shook her head.

"*Oh*, my poor sweetheart. You had a nasty accident and…"

Nasty accident, Betsy thought with a flash of alarm in her eyes. *What the hell happened to me?*

"…hit your head. Don't worry. You have a few cuts and bruises, but I cleaned you up while you were unconscious. I also put an IV in you, just in case you were dehydrated. I'll get the doctor in here so he can take a closer look at you. Do you remember your name?"

"Yes."

"What is it, sweetie?"

"B-b-b-betsy Coleman."

"Mm-hmm. And how old are you?"

"Eighteen."

"Good girl," the nurse said with an encouraging smile. "I'm going to get the doctor. I'll be quick as a bunny—"

"Jesus fucking Christ," Kathleen said, laughing. "Is there somewhere I can smoke? Because I need a break from all this ass kissing."

The nurse's smile vanished. "You know," she said, turning to Kathleen, hands returning to her hips, "normally I wouldn't encourage minors to smoke, but for you, I'll make an exception. There's a smoking area on the sixth floor. Take the walker in the corner, just in case."

"Thank you," Kathleen said, then threw off the sheets and, with a slight wince, got out of bed. She started for the medical walker by the door but stopped midway and turned to the nurse. "Um, you wouldn't happen to have a cigarette, would you?"

The nurse smacked her lips. "Are you serious, child?"

Kathleen smacked back. "Yes, very, *adult.*"

The nurse stared, her bloodshot eyes pointed like two white-girl-cutting nail files, then let out a snicker. "God, you're a lot like my daughter. All right. Go to the nurses' station and tell them Zadie says you can have a cigarette of mine."

"Thanks, doll." Kathleen smiled, then grabbed the walker and glided out of the room. "Watch out, Miss Daisy!" she shouted from the hallway. "Fat bitch with a walker coming through!"

"My Lord, that girl's crazy," Zadie said with a heavy sigh, then turned back to Betsy's bed and checked the bag of clear liquid attached to the IV line. "All right, let me get the doctor. Is there anything I can get you? Some food? Juice?"

"Uh, no, thank you," Betsy said, "but thank you."

"You're welcome, m'dear." Zadie headed for the door. "Oh, wait a minute." She stopped and turned around. "I almost forgot. Your father called. He should be here soon. Okay?"

Betsy straightened up. "Oh, okay. Thanks." She gave a small smile.

"Of course." Smiling back, Zadie turned and started for the door a second time. As she disappeared down the dimly lit hallway, Betsy's pensive gaze drifted toward the window next to her. "Good," she said softly, looking past her bruised, apricot-colored face reflected in the spotted glass and through the endless, nightmare-black sky. "I'm finally going to get some answers."

74

The Sheriff, 7:50 p.m.
Through the depressing glow of the hospital lights, Sheriff Coleman raced down the hallway toward his daughter's room, his stomach twisting into a slimy knot of sourdough. *Quit it,* he told himself, adjusting his belt, fixing his hat, combing his mustache—anything to keep his mind from the guilt that had been spreading since the car ride. *The doctor said there wasn't any major damage. Some bruises. Partial amnesia. She'll be fine.* Stopping at the wooden doorframe of Betsy's room, he raised a fist for a gentle knock, but it stayed midair as a trembling ball of white knuckles and hair. *For the last time, stop it,* he chided himself, feeling the sourdough knot pulling by its gnarled ends. *It's just a little white lie.*

After a firm breath and another round of straightening his uniform, the sheriff took a cautious step into the room, rapping on the door on his way in. "Betsy?"

Sitting cross-legged on her hospital bed and staring at the wall-size window, Betsy turned to him with a thin smile pointing toward the purplish-yellow bruise on her right cheek. "Hi, D-d-d-daddy."

Slowly entering the room, Sheriff Coleman grinned back as his twisted stomach began to unravel. *At least she's smiling.* "Hi, sweetie. How are you feeling?"

"I'm okay."

"No aches or pains?" He moved closer to the bed.

Betsy's face squinched up in thought. "Well, my neck hurts a little bit."

Sheriff Coleman's smile faded into the lean flesh of his lower face. "I'll ask the nurse for pain medication." He stopped in front of her. "Okay?"

"Thanks, D-d-d-daddy."

"You're very welcome." A small smile returned to the sheriff's face as silence followed. While Betsy looked at him, he looked back, his green eyes on those big brown pools she had inherited from her mother.

Sheriff Coleman's silent gaze shifted to the bruise on her clear, porcelain cheek. He grimaced slightly; his sweet, little girl—the last living thing he truly loved—had been nicked like a priceless China bowl. Not by the sticky hands of a clumsy teenage boy, but because of her own foolishness. Why'd she sneak out of his parents' house? Was it simple hormones or a long-awaited act of rebellion?

She's eighteen. She wanted to have fun, his rational mind tried to tell him, but the building steam of his temper drowned out that thought. "How could you sneak out?" formed on his tongue, ready to guilt-trip her to a convent in the Swiss Alps. *You could have died tonight. Is that what you wanted?* The muscles in his arms tightened, tempting him to grab his daughter and shake her until she confessed her stupidity. *Huh? Did you want to die so you could be with your mother?*

Sheriff Coleman's arms suddenly relaxed as Betsy's enormous eyes swelled into the sad, freakish stare of a Margaret Keane painting—as though she were listening to his inner rage. *Go on*, he ordered himself. *Lie. It's for the best. For the both of you.* "Betsy?" he said, pulling up a hard plastic chair and sitting down.

"Yes, D-d-d-daddy?"

"Do you remembered what happened to you a few hours ago?"

Betsy's eyes shone with curiosity through her despairing look of innocence. "No."

He leaned forward and took her right hand. "Are you sure?"

She nodded. "Yes. Was I in a c-c-c-car accident or something?"

Sheriff Coleman shivered. *Can she read my mind?* he wondered, then looked down at the nickel-colored floor, coated with a shiny epoxy. He questioned his next response, worried it would kick him to the bottom of the horrible-father hole he'd been digging since Patricia's death. Or would it put everything back together, like the push of a magical reset button on their relationship? With a deep breath, he looked up and said, "Yes, you were in a car accident."

Betsy flinched. "Really?"

"Yes," Sheriff Coleman said, twisting his cheeks into a look of mock sadness, "you were on your way to a Halloween party."

"Oh, my God," Betsy said. "Was K-K-K-Kathleen with me?"

Puzzled, Sheriff Coleman shook his head.

"She wasn't? B-b-b-but—"

"But what?"

Slowly Betsy turned to the other bed, her bruised face folded in confusion. *What the hell's she looking at?* the sheriff thought, turning to the wild mix of cotton sheets and empty snack containers. "What is it, Betsy?" he asked, looking back at his daughter.

Her expression unfurled into a blank gaze. "Who was driving me?"

"Oh," Sheriff Coleman said, caught by surprise. "Well..." He frowned. "I have some very bad news."

"What?" Wet films of misery already had formed over her naïve eyes.

"Um..." Sheriff Coleman's mouth remained opened, preparing to deliver the silver-tongued blow to his little girl's heart, but then he quickly closed his lips and glanced back at the glossy floor. Was he doing the right thing by lying, he wondered for the second time, or would it cause some sort of mental damage? And what would happen if Betsy found out the truth? *Stop it,* he scolded himself. *You have to lie so this—whatever* this *was—doesn't happen again.* He paused, taking another deep breath. *You'll just have to make sure she never finds out.* He looked up at his daughter and stated in his mechanical "I'm sorry, ma'am" sheriff tone, "Luke Gerasi was driving you to the party. He wasn't hurt in the car accident, so he went to the party after he took you to the hospital. And then, unfortunately, he and his friends were...murdered there."

Betsy's mouth opened in a silent whimper. "They were murdered? By who?"

Sheriff Coleman stood, his hand still holding onto Betsy's. "I'm sorry, sweetie," he said, squeezing her soft, clammy palm, "but let's not get into that right now. You've been through too much already."

"No," Betsy cried out, as a bright red rash spread over her purplish bruise. "T-t-t-tell me who—oh, Daddy!" She threw her face into her father's chest, drowning his button-up shirt with hot tears.

"It's okay, baby." Sheriff Coleman wrapped his arms around her heaving shoulders. "Everything's going to be all right. Just let it out." He gently placed his head on Betsy's and rocked her back and forth. "Just let it all out."

While Betsy lay convulsing against his slack chest, Sheriff Coleman kept his head on hers. As he alternated between "It's going to be all right" and "Let it out, sweetie," his exhausted eyes stared at the bare white wall across from him. *Please forgive me, God, and I'll do everything I can to be a good father.*

IV.
I Survived a Mass Murder and All I Got Was This Lousy Stockholm Syndrome

75

One Month Later, David, 7:45 a.m.
There was a light knock on David's bedroom door. "Poojoo?" Mrs. Ecklund said from the hallway. "You up yet?"

Crouching in the corner of his futon bed with his back pressed against the wall, David had his heavy raccoon eyes locked on the door, a butcher knife in his right hand, and a vial of holy water he had bought at his seventh-grade religious retreat in his left. "Yeah, I'm up."

"Oh, good. Is it okay if I come in?"

"Um, yeah," David replied, remaining in his Kirk Cameron in *Left Behind* crouch. "Just a second. I have to put on a shirt."

"Okay, honey bunny."

Donning his getaway outfit (a pair of teal jogging pants, a gray hoodie with "NYC" written in white, and his five-striped Adidas knockoffs), he tucked the vial of holy water underneath his pillow. Gripping the plastic handle of the knife, he crept to the edge of the futon and waited for the meaty claw of a runaway lunatic from the local mental hospital to swipe for his legs. Or worse, the thick digits of Betsy "Final Girl Gone Bad" Coleman. After five seconds of careful study, no murderous hands appeared.

He quickly looked under the futon. In the haze of the morning light, he found three boxes of *MAD* magazines, his Atomic Purple Nintendo 64, and a scattering of jizz socks, but no psycho killers. "God," he said, sitting back up. "I'm eighteen, and I'm still checking for monsters under my bed." Heaving a deep sigh, he looked at the closet door on the other side of the room, struggling with his strange reality. "I know nobody's in there, but my word, if I don't check, *fucking* Pumpkinhead will be in there."

With the butcher knife in hand, he walked over to the closet door and then, turning to his side with one foot forward and one foot back (learned from the *Krav Maga for Gays* videos on YouTube), swung it open. *Stab, stab, stab!* his instincts ordered his arm, and then he raised the knife and brought it down on the blue storage container stacked on top of the other four.

"Honey bunny, is everything okay?" Mrs. Ecklund asked, after the quick popping sound of cracked plastic echoed through the room.

"Yeah," David said with a Lucille Ball clench of the teeth. "I'm just...trying to get a shirt from the back of my closet." After closing the closet door on the butcher knife sticking out of the container lid, he kicked off his shoes, unlocked his bedroom door, and opened it to his pocket-size mother, a doting smile etched into her face.

"Good morning, poojoo." She planted a wet kiss on his forehead. "Did you sleep okay?"

David shrugged. "Yeah."

"No bad dreams?"

He shook his head.

"That's good," Mrs. Ecklund said, still smiling. "I think you've made a lot of progress."

"Yup," David said, feigning a smile to cover his blatant lie. Ever since his real-life LARP of Halloween Horror Nights, he'd stayed awake every night, on guard with his knife and holy water, like an ex-priest-turned-nineties-action-star. His motto: "Sleep during the day. Kill anyone who tries to come for me at night."

There was a rare moment of silence from his mother, and then she said, "I'm leaving for work in a few minutes. Would you like me to drive you to school?"

David lowered his head and pretended to brush the bushy, unwashed strands of hair (showers were also a hazard area) over his forehead. He'd expected his mother to wait at least another month until she asked if he wanted to go back to school. "Um..."

"It's okay if you need more time," she interjected. "I know it's tough going back. I just don't want you to get too far behind. It's been a whole month, you know?"

David laughed in his head. *Wow. A whole month, you say?* "Yeah, I know. But um..." He wanted to tell her he didn't want to go back—ever—but looking up, he caught the "*Do you want to let me down?*" look brewing in his mom's teary eyes and finished with, "It's all right. I'll go."

"Are you sure?"

"Yeah," he said, then added in his head, *Maybe Mike will kill me so I won't have to worry about dying anymore.*

"Okay," Mrs. Ecklund said. "Why don't you—"

"Angela!" Mr. Ecklund barked from the kitchen. "I need my shirt ironed!"

"Okay, Peter!" David's mom shouted back as she turned to the hallway. "I'll do it in a minute!" With a deep exhalation, she turned back to her son. "All right, I'd better iron your father's shirt before he gets crazy. Can you start getting ready?"

"Sure," David said with a quick laugh.

"Good." Mrs. Ecklund headed for the hallway with her Mary Poppins smile. "Oh, wait," she said, suddenly stopping. "I forgot to tell you. I called Fordham, and they said applications aren't due until January, so you've got plenty of time."

A flicker of "Goddamn it" whirled through David's weary eyes. "Oh, okay," he said, then faked another smile. "Thanks, Mom."

"You're welcome, my little poo," Mrs. Ecklund said, then walked away.

As she disappeared around the corner, he pulled back his head and stretched out his hands to the gay gods. "Liza, *please*," he groaned. "Give me the strength to tell her that I don't want to go to college." He paused. "And that I'm gay." He gave a short, bitter laugh to the ceiling then returned his head and arms to scrawny white boy-mode. "Yup, that'll be the day."

He turned to his plastic dresser, grabbed his school uniform, and started for the hallway. As he passed through his bedroom door, a thought popped into his head: *Should you call Kathleen?* "No," he responded with a queer wave of his hand. "You've called her like a million times. She's probably in hibernation." He laughed again, then continued down the hallway. As he approached the living room, he stopped a second time, turned around, and walked back to his room. "Fuck, you should try calling her anyway, just so she doesn't bitch about it later...and, you know, to make sure she's all right."

In his room, he went straight for his cell phone, which was underneath his other pillow, next to the vial of holy water and a collection of Subway gift cards, in case he got hungry on his emergency flee. He then called Kathleen's cell phone. "Of course," he said after it went to voice-mail. "Why would she answer the phone? She's either sleeping or planning to kill Betsy. For the sequel."

76

Kathleen, 7:55 a.m.

Ring, ring. Ring, ring. Ring, ring.

Kathleen, lying on her stomach in a heap of sweat-stained sheets and graphic novels, looked up from her bed, moaned something resembling a bath-salt rant at her phone, then went back to sleep. Two hours later, she woke up with a wet, camel-like neigh. After pulling up her pajama pants over her buttocks, she stood up and stumbled to the bathroom. There, she turned around and pulled down her pants, checking the scar from her popped cyst in the cracked mirror.

"Motherfucker," she grunted, ogling the discolored patch on her ass cheek. "I need a tattoo to cover this fucking shit up." She paused, considering her options. Her first thought: *A portrait of Bettie Page? Nah. Too SuicideGirls.*

Scratching at the abrupt tic in her cyst scar, she made a long "hmm" sound. "What about...a tattoo of Nick holding a fire poker?" She grinned excitedly, remembering the first time she had seen him, standing in Ashley's driveway with his silly, soulless, serial-killer gaze, then switched to the last time she had seen him (*Dateline* had a two-night special: *Nick Roesch, Michael Myers in the Flesh*). "Oh, my God, that's perfect! No one would have him but me."

Her smile disappeared as she looked up at her Pillsbury Doughboy face in the mirror. "I'm fucking hungry," she said after a couple of seconds, then pulled up her pants and headed downstairs, where her father, a three-hundred-pound Slim Jim, sat in his chair watching *Maury*. "Hey," Kathleen said, stopping in front of the TV. "Did you buy any food?"

"No," Mr. Strife said in his slow Southern accent. "Go check the kitchen."

Kathleen sighed. "I checked yesterday. There's no fucking food in there."

"Hey! Watch your *goddamn* mouth," he said with a hint of a smile.

"No." Kathleen laughed then added, "Do you have any fucking money?"

"No, I don't have any *fucking* money."

She threw her hands against her thick legs, producing a hard smack. "C'mon, Dad. I'm starving."

With a dry, tobacco-smelling sigh, Mr. Strife gave her a red-eyed stare then licked his teeth. "All right, fine. There's a twenty in the coffee jar. Go get food and some cigarettes for me, all right?"

"Uh-huh," Kathleen said, then walked to the kitchen, grabbed the twenty, and headed back to her room. After changing into a pair of sweats and a black hoodie, she took her laptop and car keys, then returned to the living room. "All right," she said, continuing to the door, "I'm going to the store and then the library to check my e-mail."

"Okay," Mr. Strife replied, as Maury told sixteen-year-old Oleta that Decardo wasn't the father of her baby. "Hey, when are you going back to school?"

Kathleen snorted as she walked out of her house. "Fuck school," she said, then headed to her car.

On her fourth attempt, the engine started, and she zoomed out of the driveway with the radio on full blast. At the library, she found a table in the back, opened her laptop, and connected to the Wi-Fi. She searched for "Nick Roesch" on Google News and clicked on the first article. It read:

On Wednesday afternoon, Judge Pedro Benitez, Jr. sentenced Nick Roesch of Manlius, NY, to the maximum time in prison possible for committing the Baldwinsville murders, a spree of savage killings that occurred on Halloween night of this year. Roesch was ordered to serve seven consecutive life sentences in prison—one for each person he killed— followed by another 3,000 years for trying to kill three unidentified minors. There is no chance for parole.

The millennia-spanning sentence is one of the longest ever handed down in the United States, and Benitez delivered it without once mentioning Mr. Roesch's name or even speaking directly to him. When he was finished, shortly before noon on the tenth day Mr. Roesch spent in court, Judge Benitez looked toward the killer with a scowl uncharacteristic of the usually even-tempered judge—

"Jesus Christ, this isn't fucking *In Cold Blood*," Kathleen said, ignoring the seven-year-old reading *Diary of a Wimpy Kid* at the adjacent table, then scrolled through the article. She stopped four paragraphs down and continued reading.

Mr. Roesch will be handed over to the New York Department of Corrections, which will first assess him at a facility in the Syracuse area before assigning him to a prison. It is entirely up to corrections officials whether Mr. Roesch will be placed in solitary confinement or with the general prison population.

"Hmm," Kathleen said, arching her right eyebrow. She stared at the screen for a moment, thinking, then opened up a new search tab and typed "Syracuse prisons."

77

Betsy, 7:55 a.m.

Standing at the entrance of a long Castle Black–like hallway, Betsy stared through the muted light from the stone windows, examining the pitch-black hole at the other end. She squinted, hoping to make out a door leading to the outside world, but it was too dark. She then exhaled an irritated huff through the cold air, wondering whether it was safe to continue.

"Are we going to go?" a male voice asked.

She turned to the four-foot beige-colored penis floating in a horizontal line next to her. "Mm, I don't know," she replied nonchalantly as if the talking cock was a family friend. "It looks too dangerous."

"It's okay," the penis said. "Take my hand."

Uncertainty held her full lips in a tight embrace as she eyed the penis, wondering where exactly the hands of the floating organ were (along with its eyes and mouth). Nonetheless, she reached out and started down the dark hallway, somehow hand in hand with her chubby friend.

As they made it to the halfway mark, Betsy felt a soft squeeze to her hand. "I love you," the penis said between her cautious footsteps.

She turned with a warm smile. "I love you—" Suddenly a large kitchen knife popped out of the darkness and stabbed the shaft of the penis, releasing a cherry-colored geyser of blood from its hazelnut skin.

"Run, Betsy," the penis coughed from its urethra. "Now!"

Without a glance at the knife-wielding assailant, she hurried down the dingy hallway and straight into the black hole at the end. Tracing the icy walls with her fingertips, she blindly moved through the tunnel until a skylight window offered a beam of gray moonlight onto a spiral staircase. She raced down the curved staircase to the steel door at the bottom. After she pushed through the door, an ear-shattering wail escaped her mouth as she fell headfirst into a Dario Argento pit of broken glass. "*Luuuuuuke—*"

The slow creak of a wooden door disrupted Betsy's cry. She woke up, her eyes landing directly on her father, who was poking his head into her bedroom. "Sorry, honey. I didn't mean to wake you," he said softly, holding the neck of his maroon robe. "Just wanted to check on you." He paused for a welcoming smirk. "How're you feeling?"

She slowly scanned the room, easing herself into the slightly less dark world. "I'm okay," she said, then sat up. The corners of her mouth pinched in disgust as a cold sweat crossed her back.

"Good. I'm going to get ready for work. Grandma should be here any second." He paused again. "You'll probably stay in bed for the day, so don't worry about asking her for anything. Remember, she'll bring you..."

As he continued talking, Betsy nodded away, her focus losing its attention to the strange dream she'd had for the third time this week. Why a castle with a glass pit? Why a talking penis who loved her? And why'd she scream for Luke? Was it all a creepy coincidence or something more?

And then, like a strange case of bodily clockwork, she got the same trust-the-diarrhea-stomach feeling that the dream was somehow connected to the Halloween accident. "Daddy," she said, bringing her attention back to the room, "who killed L-l-l-luke?"

With two fingers, Sheriff Coleman squeezed his nose, capturing a frustrated sigh. "Did you have another bad dream?"

"Yes," Betsy said, attempting the innocent calm of a teenage girl who didn't have nightmares of murdered penises. "But it wasn't that b-b-b-bad this t-t-t-time. I swear."

Sheriff Coleman bowed his head, keeping an irritated hold of his nose. After a moment of tense silence, he looked up and said, "Honey, I love you, but I...I don't want to worry you—"

"No, it's okay," Betsy interrupted him. "Really, D-d-d-daddy. I just want to know who killed Luke...and everyone else."

Sheriff Coleman shook his head. "Why?"

"Because I...I..." She looked at her father, angst glossing over her watery eyes. She wanted to tell him how much she liked Luke, but then she remembered how her dad had almost caught her giving him a hand job—the one thing she *could* remember—and knew it would make him angry. *It doesn't matter*, she thought, tucking the ratty strands of her hair behind her ears. *Luke was probably nice to you just so he could get a hand job.* "I don't know," she said coolly.

"Betsy, look. I know you're—" There was a knock at the front door. "Hold on. That's probably your grandma. We'll talk about this later, all right?"

Betsy opened her mouth, but before she could answer, her dad rushed out of the room. Inhaling her frustration, she threw the satin bedsheet soaked in her nightmare sweat onto the floor. She wanted to scream for her dad to return, then stopped, catching sight of the tiny red scars that lined her milky knuckles. *Are they from the car accident?* she wondered, then blew out her frustrations and thought, *The only way you'll find out anything is if you call Kathleen.* "Oh, God, no," she said, the angst in her eyes replaced with fear. "She hates you. She *definitely* still hates you."

78

David, 8:40 a.m.

Stopping in the doorway of his religion class, David picked his head up from the floor and released a heavenly breath. *Yas, Gawd*, he thought, seeing the empty desk behind his. *Thank you. I definitely owe you...one cheeseburger.* He let out a small laugh through a relaxed smile, then started for his desk.

"Excuse me. Are you in this class?"

David turned to the Jamie-Dornan-with-hot-daddy-beard look-alike standing at Sister Babcock's podium. "Um, yes," he said with a puzzled look at the gentleman's baby-blue eyes, perfectly proportionate to his square, neatly shaven jaw. *Who the hell are you, and where do you want me to bend over, sir?*

"Okay," the hunky man replied, his dazzling eyes tilted in a confused gaze. "Why haven't I seen you before?"

David looked at the gorgeous stranger for a moment, then glanced at the classroom of students staring at him with their *Children of the Damned*, "Holy shit, it's him" glares. He turned back to Mr. Grey with a pressing beam that read, *Hello! Don't you know I'm the final gay of the Baldwinsville Murders, or have you been taking a dump in your gorgeous-me world where everything revolves around you?*

Fifty Shades continued to stare at him. *All right, you can dominate me later*, David thought, then said, "I've been out for the last month. I was...sick."

"What's your name?"

"David Ecklund." *But you can call me your little pig.*

As if the hot substitute teacher could sense David's semi chub, he cruelly licked his full lips, then took a set of stapled sheets from the podium and searched through them. "Yup, you're here," he said after a couple of seconds. "I'm Mr. Chapman, Sister Babcock's substitute for the week. You can take a seat."

"Okay, thanks," David said with a polite smile, then added internally, *Mr. Asschaps Man.* As he headed for his desk, he returned his stare to the floor, ignoring the twenty-four pairs of evil Caucasian eyes following him like a Massachusetts witch being brought to the stakes—exactly like the thirty-six eyes on the bus, twenty-two in homeroom, and the hundreds in the hallways that would hound him that day and the rest of his high school life. *That's him,* he imagined them thinking. *The token queer who was almost killed by Nick Roesch. How did he survive? Does he have nightmares about the lunatic? Does he worry the guy will break out of jail and come back to kill him?*

An icy shot of fear tingled his heart as he sat at his desk, feeling a different pair of eyes—a small beady set—watch him from the parking lot. *Stop,* David scolded himself, keeping his sight on the 1970s, faux-oak top of his desk. *Nick Roesch is in prison now, so you're good. Nothing's going to happen to you. Okay?*

The second bell rang. "Okay," Mr. Chapman said. "Take out your books and turn to page 102."

David took a deep "Don't be a trauma mama" breath, then grabbed his book bag and opened it. As he flipped through his religion textbook, his horror-movie mind took two seconds to press pause on his current task and imagine Nick walking toward the school from the parking lot, preparing his gory revenge with the help of good ol' fire poker. *Run,* David's caveman instincts commanded him. *He's going to break open your skull and—*

No! he shouted in his head, while his eyes, inflated with terror, remained on his book. *He's not out there.* Nick crept closer to the window as David flipped past page 100. *You're perfectly—* He snapped his neck, hearing a sudden squeak against the window, as though Nick wanted to give the glass a quick squeegee clean before he crashed through it.

David let out an instant sigh of relief. The parking lot, a frozen wasteland underneath the early December sky, was free of homicidal maniacs. *See? You're perfectly safe.*

"Hey, you're late," Mr. Chapman said.

"Sorry, I was taking a dump."

As the rest of the class laughed, David looked up and released a "Lady Gaga didn't make the Top 40" gasp. Mike Barrett—Satan and the Republican Party's lovechild in the flesh—was walking past the beautiful substitute with a devilish grin. "C'mon, Mike," Mr. Chapman said. "I don't want any trouble today."

"Okay," Mike said, walking to his desk, and then, with a fake cough, added, "Cocksucker." Another round of laughter ensued as he continued to his desk. He then stopped, replacing his mischievous grin with a look of excitement and hatred as soon as he spotted David. *Oh, God*, David thought, returning to his frightened, slasher-film-obsessed imagination. *Dress-Down Day 2: Casual Frightday. Here we—*

"Hey, fag," Mike said, sitting down behind David. "It's been a long time…"

Using his fearful silence as a shield, David placed his eyes on his religion book.

"…since you destroyed my room," Mike went on, leaning into the back of David's neck. "Now I'm going to destroy your fucking life."

David's body tightened, knowing some sort of dumb-jock shenanigans was imminent. Suddenly his chair tipped backward, the front legs lifting off the floor. Instinctively he grabbed the sides of his desk, preparing for a backward-chair smackdown. Laughing, Mike pulled the chair farther back. "How's that, fag?" he asked with a sinister rasp. "You scared?"

David kept quiet as his arms and legs burned with embarrassment. And then, without warning, Mike let the chair go. The front legs dropped to the floor, producing a loud metallic thud against the tiled floor.

"What the heck was that?" Mr. Chapman said, in the middle of reading from the textbook.

Remaining silent, along with the rest of the class, David stared at the Tang-orange top of his desk, attempting to hide his involvement in Mike's prank. "C'mon, guys," Mr. Chapman said. "What was that noise? Mike?"

"Why are you asking me?" Mike said. "I didn't do anything."

"Then what was that noise?"

"I don't know. I think it was the radiator. Sometimes it acts up." A handful of students chuckled.

"Uh-huh. Let's get back to the lesson." As Mr. Chapman went back to reading, David stared at his book, his hand by the edges of his desk as he waited for round two. A moment later, he grimaced, hearing the sound of paper ripping. It was followed by Mike sucking up a glob of snot through his nose. *Fucking nasty. He's making spitballs, isn't he?*

He received his answer in the form of a small, wet ball of paper that struck his neck. A second soggy spitball confirmed it. *Well, isn't this fun. It's like the Skittles incident all over again.*

He made a mental *blehhhhgggh* of doubt. *Nope*, he thought. *Kathleen isn't here to save me this time. Mike's going to keep throwing spitballs at me until the end of the period and then what?* As the image of Mike dumping a bucket of his Gatorade Frost and Spicy Cheetos–infused spit flooded his brain, David's neck clenched as he felt the tip of a soda straw enter his right ear. "This is a special one for rubbing guts in my face," Mike said, then inhaled the class's air supply into his bulldog nostrils. *Bam!* A pellet of warm goo shot into David's ear canal.

Without thinking, he bolted up and pushed his desk to the floor. "Would you leave me alone!" he shouted, turning to Mike. "I mean seriously! I'm sorry for rubbing guts in your face, but that was a crazy *fucking* night! I saw Luke's brain for God's sake!"

A moment of silence followed, filling the class with tension as thick as burnt gravy. "Okay, just calm down," Mr. Chapman said, as David stared at Mike with a searing "Go fuck yourself" gaze he'd dreamt of giving him for the last four years. Mike stared back with a brutish smirk soaking up the dramatic scene. "Would you two like to go outside and talk?"

David turned to Mr. Chapman, who was slowly stepping toward him, his muscular arms reaching out like a hunky fireman in an NBC emergency romance. "No," David said, a blast of fear and anger turning his veiny, white flesh into a poison-ivy-rash red. "I...um...um..." Embarrassed from the "This pipsqueak is a psycho" look in the beautiful teacher's eyes, he glanced away and saw his classmates staring, their excited glares hungry for Kardashian family humiliation. "I'm sorry," he finally said, his tear ducts burning from his attempt to hold back a deluge of tears. "Can I go to the guidance office?"

Mr. Chapman nodded. "Of course."

"Thanks," David said and then, trying to avoid eye contact with Mike, turned toward his desk and grabbed his backpack and book in one swoop.

As he raced toward the hallway for a Sally Field in *Steel Magnolias* meltdown, Mike laughed his piggish squeal-laugh and said, "See ya later, fag."

79

"Grandma?" Wearing her sweat-stained T-shirt and sour-milk-smelling pajama bottoms, Betsy tiptoed downstairs, following the sound of Dr. Phil's faux psychology blasting from the TV. "G-g-g-grandma, 1-1-1 need a glass of water…"

Her thin voice stretched into an inaudible trickle as she approached the living room and found her grandmother dozing on the suede couch, a low wheeze struggling through the nicotine-laced phlegm in her throat. Watching the elderly woman lie stiffly, an unpleasant scowl pinning down her slack cheeks, Betsy laughed softly. *Even when she's sleeping she still looks mean,* she thought, then surveyed the somber room, the gray winter seeping through the tan curtains casting a funeral-home shadow. *Wow. This place looks so sad.*

As she remained still, the drab air coaxed her into a fixated trance, as if she'd been injected with a shot of Ritalin. *Sad, dark, loud snoring smoke sweat sour milk nightmares penis knife glass Luke Kathleen.* Her thoughts switched quickly, like a child dialing the line of radio stations for her favorite song, then miraculously finding said song. *Kathleen knows who killed Luke. Why would she be at the hospital? And why didn't Daddy know she was there?* She paused, confusion slithering through her hypnotized expression. *That was really strange.*

"Jessica, you're not going to get anything in life with that attitude," Dr. Phil roared from the TV. "If you want to get out of your funk, you need to *command*, not *demand.*"

As the audience applauded wildly, Betsy shook herself out of her daze and turned to the TV. "S-s-s-s-something's going on," she muttered, her subconscious taking the mock psychologist's television therapy as a sign. "And I'm going to find out what it is."

She returned to the staircase and tiptoed to the top, then continued to her father's room. There, she headed to his nightstand and reached for the discolored landline phone her father refused to throw away or donate to a museum. The phone immediately slipped out of her hand, falling and hitting the nightstand with a cracking sound. Sucking in a breath of frustration, Betsy held it, waiting for her grandmother to scream, "Christmas with the Jews! What's that ruckus?"

Hearing nothing but Dr. Phil's deep echo, Betsy bent down to investigate the phone situation. She sighed, finding the cord caught on the knob on the nightstand's drawer. "If he'd bought me a d-d-d-damn cell phone," she said, opening the drawer, "then this what*ever*—" A breath of shock halted her rant as she caught sight of a silver-framed picture of her mother and father, their thinner twenty-something selves standing hand in hand in their nineties wedding attire, among the drawer of white and black dress socks. "Oh, wow. Mom looks *so* beautiful."

Grabbing the photograph for a closer look at her mother's white lace, A-line dress, she raised the crusty ends of her mouth and smiled for the first time in a month. Studying the picture from top to bottom, she held her smile until she caught the white curve of a cord in the corner of her eye. "What's this?" she asked out loud, placing the picture on the bed and grabbing the thick, rolled-up cord. "Oh," she mumbled, as the rectangular stick of outlets connected to the cord emerged from the mound of socks. "Why the hell does he have a power cord in his drawer?" Examining the three-prong plug of the cord, she loosened her arm, letting the power cord flop to her side. "Do I have to plug this into the stupid old phone?"

After placing the power cord next to the photo, she grabbed the phone and searched for any holes to stick the prongs in but received no such luck. "Ugh, get a cell phone, you geezer," she said, then picked up the receiver and put it up to her ear. She rolled her eyes when she heard the soft dial tone.

She started to dial Kathleen's number. "No," she said suddenly, then retracted her hand. "She's probably still upset about the Luke thing." As she gazed at the phone, her forehead pleated with tiny folds like a strainer sifting through the current of thought for a grand explanation. Her efforts, however, failed to produce a single flake of gold. "Damn it. What the hell happened on Halloween?" She gave a second attempt, trying to sieve her memory, but she could only recall a hazy slideshow of her birthday party. Irritated, she shook her head. "Just stop. You c-c-c-can't remember *anything*, and K-k-k-kathleen will never t-t-t-t..." She paused for a deep breath. "...tell you." Her eyes opened like two rhino mouths screaming, *David!*

Her intuition replied, *Yes. Call David when he gets home from school. Kathleen probably told him everything.* She stood still, reviewing the thought for assurance, and then her eyes sank in disappointment. "What if he doesn't tell you, out of loyalty or whatever?" She immediately let out a gruff cry, determining that he wouldn't. "Christ, I'll figure it out myself."

After returning the picture of her parents and the power cord, she left the room and headed downstairs. Again she tiptoed pass her grandmother, who was volleying mucous snores against a surprise appearance from the "Cash Me Ousside" girl. *Why am I being so careful?* she wondered. Was it out of courtesy for her grandmother or the instinct that she needed to keep this mission of hers secret, as if she were a spy entering no man's land? She wrestled with the question as she continued to the small den that housed her dad's collection of flea-market radios, the family computer, and the subtle smell of a black mold problem. "What?" she said, receiving a black screen after pressing the power button to the ancient Dell desktop (another future donation to the museum) in the corner. She tried it again, but still nothing. "Oh, my God," she yelled. "Are you s-s-s-s-serious?"

"Christ on a cracker!" Grandma Coleman roared from the living room. "What was that? Betsy? Is that you?"

Startled by the sudden noise, Betsy backed away from the computer and shouted, "Yes, Grandma."

"What's going on? What are you doing out of your room?"

"Uh, nothing," Betsy said, moving into the kitchen. *Even though it's my house.* "I just...needed a glass of water." Turning to the sink for a cup, she inhaled a deep breath, nervously waiting for a response. Would Grandma cough out an irritated "Okay" or would she storm the kitchen to investigate?

"You're nothing without me," the Cash Me Ousside girl barked at Dr. Phil. "I made you."

"Mother Francis, this girl should be ashamed of her... *Eckk-eckk-eckkkk.*" Breaking into a hacking fit, Grandma Coleman sounded as though every muscle in her frail body—including those still left in her nubbins—was struggling to keep her blackened lungs from escaping. "Oh, God. Betsy, could you get me a glass of water?"

Betsy rolled her eyes. *Aren't you supposed to be helping me?* "Yeah, just a second," she said, then grabbed the adult sippy cup—reserved specifically for Grandma's deformed fingers—from the cupboard above the sink. As she filled the glass with tap water, she looked into the adjacent den at the computer. *It can't be broken. I used it like a month ago... Must be a loose cable or something.*

80

The Next Day, David, 4:30 p.m.

Crouched in the corner of his bed, on crazed-mental-patient/ex-best-friend-security watch, David vacantly stared at the orange glow of the evening sun painted on his bedroom door. As the butcher knife in his hand dangled in his soft grip, his eyes glazed over the hardwood of the door while he ignored the creeping footsteps of a vengeful killer (or his mother) in the hallway.

I'm sorry, he thought, imagining he was back in religion class, a death stare on Mike. *Did you just call me a fag?*

Yeah, Mike answered in his über-masculine drawl.

Oh, really, David said, strutting over to Mike's desk with a knowing smile. *Well, if I'm a fag, you must be bisexual...since you like chicks with dicks!* The class burst into a thunderous collective of "Oh, shits" and laughter as he held up Mike's copy of *Fetish* magazine with the big-breasted Latino woman sporting Sequoia-size wood.

David laughed along, watching the pasty fat of Mike's bulldog face ripple into the flushed humiliation he'd felt during every "Hey, fag."

"That's right," David said with a proud grin. "I'm not a fag. I'm a *final* fag."

There was a knock on the door. "It's your mama, poojoo. Can I come in?"

Die! Die! Die! David commanded in his head, as he snapped out of his school-hero fantasy and swung the knife through the cold air. After five seconds of this freak-out, he realized he was swinging at nothing. And then, as his brain squeezed out of a tube of horror through his eyes like a Halloween-themed Play-Doh factory, a question struck him: *Did you just say you were a final fag out loud?*

There was another knock. "Poojoo? Are you sleeping?"

Frozen in his Star Wars pajamas squat, he looked at the golden-lit door while a silent stutter flapped out of his lips. *Keep your stupid, Goody-Two-*

Shoes mouth shut, he ordered as he struggled to answer his sweet mother. *She'll go away if you don't—*

Watching the doorknob turn, David melted into a frayed knot of rubber bands. *Shit,* he thought, guessing he'd forgotten to lock the door when he'd gone to the bathroom, then pounced out of his patrol hunch into a freefall position, head on the pillow, knife under it.

"David?" Mrs. Ecklund said in a low voice, walking into the room. "Are you awake?"

He turned to her, faking a grumpy expression of sleep. "Yeah," he said, his voice strained with exhaustion. "I was just taking a nap."

"*Oh,* my poojoo was taking a nappety nap?"

Releasing the knife, he sat up with a tired chuckle. "Yeah."

"Well, that's good," Mrs. Ecklund said, standing in the doorway. "You'll be well rested for dinner. It'll be ready in five minutes."

"Okay," David replied. "Thanks."

"You're welcome, sweetie." Standing in a knitted turtleneck and Pajama Jeans from Ellen DeGeneres' fashion line, Mrs. Ecklund remained in the doorway of her son's room, staring at him with a pleasant smile.

Fuck, David thought with a faint smile back. *She's going to ask—*

"Betsy Coleman called again."

David's scraggy chest heaved forward as if the news had given him a surprise kick in his bony ass. "She did?"

"Yup."

"What did you say?"

"I said you weren't feeling well, so perhaps she could call in a couple of days. Was that okay?"

"Uh, yeah, that's fine," David answered with a pensive flinch. *That's like the tenth time in two days. Why does the crazy bitch keep calling me?*

"Are you sure? I can bring you the phone—"

David's head shot up. "No, that's all right. I think I'm going to need another lifetime before I talk to her again. *Kathleen* on the other hand..."

Mrs. Ecklund gave a light laugh. "I'm sure she'll call you soon. She's probably just taking some time off too."

"Oh, yeah," David said, pinching his lips into a sarcastic bend, "she's going to be back at school *real* soon."

"Hey, you never know." His mom's warmhearted smile turned playful. As a natural pause entered the conversation, mother and son enjoyed a telepathic exchange of love, deepening their bond. And then she rammed a steel pike through it by adding, "What about you? When do you think you're going back to school?"

He responded with an aggressive shrug. "Eh, I don't know. I'm thinking...*never.*"

With a fiery huff, Mrs. Ecklund's long face transformed from a glowing bubble of love into a racetrack of angry creases. "David Hyde Ecklund! You need to go back to school ASAP."

He let out a low snicker, somewhere between cocky teenager and scared little bitch. "*Why?*"

"*Why?* Because I called the school this morning and they said you won't be able to graduate if you miss too many days."

"So?"

"Okay!" Mrs. Ecklund raised her hands in the universal mother's "I'm done" gesture. "So you won't graduate. That's terrific, David."

"Yeah, it is," he said, then released his frustration from their tense exchange with a dismissive smack of his lips. "At least everyone won't call me gay again."

Mrs. Ecklund sighed, crooking her head into a motherly look of worried disbelief. "David, it might seem like everyone calls you that, but it isn't true. It's only a couple of bad people, and you need to ignore them. They're just names."

"No! They're not just...*names.*" David went Whole Foods in Brooklyn–white as he caught a flash of shock from his mom's gentle eyes. *Shit. You probably shouldn't have said that.*

There was a second pause in the conversation—this time, though, it tore through the remaining shreds of their bond like a cannonball through paper and mounted David's shoulders, forcing him to say something. But what? Should he finally admit he was gay or try to pass it off as a joke? Then, in the midst of his internal panic, Mrs. Ecklund asked, "David, are you gay?"

As he kept a struggling gaze on his futon, his stomach tightened as though those words had wrapped around him like chain-link Spanx. He wanted to say yes—*Let's get this whole "It Gets Better" thing started*—but he was afraid. If he came out, he worried his life would change for the worse. Would his mother still love him? Would his father avoid him altogether?

Maybe, he thought, but there were also advantages: he could finally venture out of the world of gay porn and anonymous chat rooms. Perhaps he could even find the answers to his most burning questions. What kind of gay was he? A versatile otter or a sloppy bottom twink? Was anal as easy as it looked in the movies? What did ass taste like?

He sighed internally. *Fuck it. If you can survive a real-life slasher, you can survive being gay.* He took a deep breath then looked up at his mother and said, "Yes."

"Oh, poojoo." Mrs. Ecklund frowned. "Why didn't you tell me earlier?"

David's stomach relaxed as though his mother had clipped the chain-link Spanx with metal shears. "I...don't know." He laughed at the good fortune of his mother's response. "I guess I was afraid you'd be angry with me."

Mrs. Ecklund tsk-tsked as she sat down next to him. "David, I would *never* be angry with you about that. I love you with all my heart." She wrapped her arms around his waist and squeezed his fresh-out-of-the-closet self with a big hug. "Don't you know? You're my baby boy."

David chuckled again. "Yeah, I know."

"Good," his mom replied, coming out of the hug, then asked, "How long have you known?"

"Oh," David said, straightening up with a pleasant curiosity. "That's a good question. Um, I don't know. Since I was nine or ten."

Mrs. Ecklund's eyes bulged. "*That young?*"

He let out another quick laugh, shrugging. "Yeah, I guess."

"How do you know?"

"What?"

"How do you know you're gay?"

David made a humorous "You've got balls, lady" smirk. "*Um...*"

Mrs. Ecklund went to the next question—both of them knowing he was going to respond with "Because I like dick." "Have you ever been with a man?"

"All right!" David said, bending backward into a quarter-Linda Blair spider walk. "I think I've been through enough lately. Don't you think?"

Mrs. Ecklund took a brisk inhalation, then nodded with a cautious smile. "Yes, you have. There's no doubt about that." Remaining on the futon, she stared at her son until her round, slightly wrinkled face blossomed into its full cheer. "I'm very proud of you, David. You're such a remarkable young man who's going to accomplish many great things." She paused, taking another breath. "But remember: I'm your mama, and you can always tell your mama anything, all right?"

David had to laugh again. "Yeah."

"Great," Mrs. Ecklund said. "All right, I'm going to finish making dinner—unless there's anything else you like to tell me."

David opened to his mouth to say "No," but stopped himself as the thought that he didn't want to go to college hit him once more. As his mouth remained opened, he thought about telling her then imagined it was probably easier informing her that he—a gay teenager—was hiding a knife under his pillow. "Only that I love you."

"I love you too, poo," Mrs. Ecklund said then kissed him on his slightly sweaty forehead. "I'll be in the kitchen. See you in a minute."

"Okay," David said, then smiled again as she stood up. "And thanks, for everything."

"Of course," Mrs. Ecklund responded, looking down at him with an angelic glow. "Anything for my baby boy."

Still smiling, David watched his mother leave the room with silent admiration. *Holy shit,* he thought, falling back to his pillow and shaking his legs in uncontrollable excitement. *Why were you so scared? That was so freaking easy.* "Right?" he said with a ditzy giggle, then propped himself against the back of his futon. As he stared through the orange-Creamsicle-colored sunlight shining from his window, his body buzzed with joyous freedom he'd never thought he would feel, until he remembered it wasn't so easy for others.

His gay bliss blew away like rainbow balloons caught by the wind at a pride parade. "Christ in a pair of Crocs. Why can't you ever be happy?"

81

One Week Later, Betsy, 7:15 a.m.

"I'm going to fucking kill you!" Betsy screamed as Kathleen raced around the corner of a wide hospital corridor lit by the sterile white light of a dystopian sci-fi show. Wielding a chef's knife with a bone-tight grip, Betsy slunk to the end of the hallway then continued around the corner. She stopped and smiled viciously when she approached a second, shorter hallway, with three doors on each side, leading to a dead end. "Okay, bitch," she said in a menacing tone as she started down the hall. "I know you're in one of these rooms, so just come out now and—"

She swung open the first door. "Die!" The word struck her spine like a chainsaw against a xylophone, sending waves of electric chills through her muscles. There, lying on a hospital bed in a wrap of bandages and pulsating machines like a Dr. Jekyll experiment, was Luke—the top of his beautiful, bronzed face cracked like a coconut via jackhammer, creating a half Zac Efron, half Manwich hybrid. "Oh, God!" Betsy shouted, quickly backing out of the room.

"Stop!" David cried, appearing from an unseen vortex. "You can't kill Kathleen! Please!" He grabbed her arm and pulled her toward him. "Please!"

"Get the fuck off me, faggot," Betsy snarled, then rammed the knife into his stomach. Wiggling off the sharp blade, David placed his hand over the oozing wound and then, with a set of surprised eyes, crashed to the floor.

Stepping forward, Betsy looked down at David's shivering body with a disgusted sneer. "You risked your own life for that useless slut rag?" She let out a quick laugh. "You're so pathetic."

"Betsy!"

"Fuck," Betsy huffed, as she turned toward her father, who was racing toward her from the end of the hallway. She bolted into the next room and locked the door behind her. As she turned around, her testosterone-raging body dissolved into a puddle of salt water at the sight of her mother—a perfect portrait of how she had looked the last time she had seen her alive.

Buried up to her neck in white linen, Mrs. Coleman stared into space with dark, sunken eyes and a straight set of bluish lips, as though she were a severed head a couple of morning joggers had found on the beach. Noticing the sharp pair of yellow-tinted bones she had for cheeks, Betsy remembered the first thought that had come to her during her last visit: *Why does Mommy look like a skeleton?*

Over five years, she slowly had pieced together the puzzle: because the cancer was eating her away.

"My little angel," Mrs. Coleman said, turning to her daughter with a weak smile. "I'm so glad you came to see me."

Betsy stood by the door with the same cautious silence she had when she was twelve years old. Back then, she was scared she would break her mother's bones with any loud movement. This time it was a different worry. *This isn't real*, she thought, tightening her hold on the knife. *Mom's dead.*

Mrs. Coleman's smile slipped into the yellow sick of her gaunt face. "Don't be scared, Betsy," she said slowly. "I know this is very sad, but remember I'll always be with you." Betsy mouthed her mother's final words with her: "If you ever need me, just talk. I'll be listening."

Loosening her grip on the knife, Betsy stepped forward, tears stinging her eyes. "I know," she said, but it was drowned out by a series of loud, quick knocks on the door.

"Betsy!" Sheriff Coleman shouted. "Open up!"

Betsy spun to the door, clutching the knife. "No," Mrs. Coleman said in a hushed tone. "Don't."

Her pale skin taut with rage, she stopped and turned to her mother. "Why not?"

Mrs. Coleman's almond-colored eyes narrowed in a sad, motherly look. "Because that's your father, Betsy, and he loves you very, very much."

As she gazed upon her mother's miserable expression—the sorrow magnified by her rotting complexion—she lowered her head, ashamed. "Yeah, I know."

Another loud knock came. "Open this door, Betsy, before I break it down!"

Keeping her eyes fixed on the sterile tiles, she wondered what to do. She didn't want to open the door for her father, but she didn't want to see her mother's "Please, Betsy, I'm sick" look either. Listening to the eerie whooshing of the machines attached to her mom's toothpick arms, Betsy contemplated the two choices, and then like a firework blast on the Fourth of July, a third knock boomed at the door. "C'mon, Betsy. Open up!"

Startled, she looked up with a sudden exhalation. "Oh, God. Should I open it, Mom?"

Through a heavily medicated glare, Mrs. Coleman let out a short, wheezy sigh. "In a second," she said, "but I need to tell you something first. Something very important."

"What?" Betsy asked, moving toward the bed.

In a slow, restless tone, Mrs. Coleman replied, "Well, you're not going to like it, *but* I talked to the doctor, and he said...that you're a *dirty cock-sucking whore!*" She burst into a loud, obnoxious laugh and then, as if she were under an evil, Hans Christian spell, transformed into Kathleen. "Oh, my God, I can't believe you fell for that," she said, throwing her swinelike head back through a raucous fit of laughter. "You're such a dumb slut!"

A warm, prickly rash spread across Betsy's skin as she scanned Kathleen's solidly built body for stabbing targets. "I'm going to fucking kill you!" she shouted, then raised the chef's knife. Kathleen rolled to the side of the bed, trying to escape, but it was too late; Betsy swung the knife into her back, producing a water-balloon-splattering-against-asphalt sound. As Kathleen screamed a string of curse words, Betsy pulled the knife out of her then stabbed her over and over—in her side, her neck, and once more in the back.

"You're a fucking whore!" Kathleen shouted, rolling onto her back. "You'll *always* be a whore and a terrible friend." She looked into Betsy's eyes and gave a wide, mocking smile stained with her own blood.

Gritting her teeth, Betsy raised the knife again and, aiming for Kathleen's heart, brought the knife into her doughy flesh. The tip of knife rattled against something hard, and a sharp, metallic noise followed.

Betsy opened her eyes and gasped; standing in the early morning light, she found herself at the kitchen sink with a bread knife in hand, its tip against a stainless steel bowl. "Damn it," she murmured, dropping the knife into the dish rack (This was the fourth time in the last week that she had woken up in the kitchen, the second time with a knife in her hand.) "That's it," she said, as she turned around and headed for her bedroom. "I don't care if Kathleen's still angry with me. I *have* to call her."

As she climbed the staircase, her father's bedroom door creaked open. *Shit,* she thought, then stopped at the top of the stairs without a clue what to do. "Betsy?" he asked, wearing a wife beater and blue pajama pants that read "Concord Academy." "What are you doing up so early?"

"S-s-s-sorry, Daddy," Betsy replied. "I was just...getting a drink of water."

"Is everything all right?" Sheriff Coleman scratched the left pocket of the black-and-white beard he'd been growing for the last month.

"Oh, yeah, I was just thirsty. The...uh...pizza last night was a little salty."

"You're right," her father said. "Palermo's always puts too much salt in their food."

"Yeah," Betsy responded with a small smile. Her weary eyes drifted to the sandstone carpet as she held on to the smile and waited for him to end their conversation.

"Well," Sheriff Coleman finally said, "I'm about to get ready for work. You know the drill. Grandma will be here soon. She'll get you what you need, and I'll drop off your homework after work and pick up the new stuff. Okay?"

"Okay. Thanks, Daddy."

"Of course." As Betsy took a step upstairs, he continued. "I'm very proud of you, Betsy. You're doing a great job keeping up with your assignments." He cleared his throat. "I know it's a little early, but I was thinking, we could take a look at the online classes they have at OCC one of these days."

What? Betsy cried internally at the mention of Onondaga Community College (aka thirteenth grade at Bishop Dullen). Although she hadn't given much thought to anything other than her chronic nightmares of talking penises, a lifetime of said dreams sounded better than attending that joke of a school. "Oh, um, sure." She would've continued to her room, leaving an argument about college for another day, but a clever plan struck her right then. "I'll take a look on the computer today."

Sheriff Coleman sighed. "Well, I was looking up classes the other night—while you were sleeping—and the damn thing crashed. It *was* more than ten years old. Don't worry, though. I'll pick up a course catalog this weekend. All right?"

"Mm-hmm," Betsy said, nodding. She had a feeling he'd say something like that.

"Great." Her father smiled as though he had won a secret competition. "All right, I gotta get ready. I'll say goodbye to you when Grandma comes, okay?"

"Okay," Betsy said, quickly smiling back, then started for her bedroom. *Something's going on*, she said to herself. *He's definitely hiding something. And the only person who knows what it is is Kathleen...and maybe David.*

Two hours later, she stood at the bottom of the staircase, watching her grandmother snore out of every dusty pore while *The Doctors'* V8 Splash–sponsored Diet Tuesday blasted from the TV. *All right, she's out until she has to turn off* Ellen, she thought, then turned around and slowly crept to her father's room. There, she sat on the bed and grabbed the phone. "C'mon," she said with a low growl, as her pointer finger hovered over the first number. "Just *do* it. Kathleen's been mad at you plenty of times." She looked at the phone, her finger shaking midair, and then, with a mental nod, dialed.

Suddenly she stopped, thinking, *What if she's at school?* She immediately laughed a guttural "ha" then finished dialing Kathleen's house number. "Yeah, right. She's definitely home."

"Hello?" Mr. Strife answered in his country twang.

"Oh, hello, sir," Betsy said, her tongue running anxiously across her lips. "This is Betsy, K-k-k-kathleen's friend." She paused to take a breath. "Is she home?"

"*Caffeine?* No, I don't got any caffeine."

Betsy blew a silent sigh into the receiver. *He's probably drunk.* "No," she said louder and more slowly. "*Kathleen.* Is. She. Home?"

"Oh," Mr. Strife responded. "Naw. She went out on a job interview."

"Shit," Betsy spat out, as the phone slipped out of her hand and hit the bed. *Is this a joke?* she asked her startled reflection in the brass bed frame, then recovered the phone and said, "Sorry. I dropped the phone."

"It's okay, suga'. Do you wanna leave a message for her?"

"Oh, um, no, it's okay. I'll c-c-c-call her b-b-b-back."

"You sure?"

"Yes," Betsy said, without a moment to think it over. "Bye, sir."

"Bye."

With a heavy breath, she hung up the phone. "All right, that was a little...awkward, but it's fine. You'll just try again later." Sitting on the edge of the bed, she stared at the nightstand across from her, aimlessly tracing her fingers through the purple stripes lining her pajama pants, then snorted with laughter. "Job interview? Who would *ever* hire Kathleen?"

82

Mr. Arnold Clinton, 10:00 a.m.

Mr. Clinton massaged his thinning brown-and-gray goatee with his stubby fingers as he scanned the short résumé in his other hand. "Well," he said, "I see you've had work experience at Taco Bell and McDonald's, but I don't see any college education. Is that a future goal of yours?" Removing his hand from his chin, he looked up at the plump dark-haired girl sitting across from his L-shaped desk.

"Yes, sir," she said with a professional flat tone. "I'd love to go to college, but I'd have to get my GED first."

"You didn't graduate from high school?" With a cocky smirk, Mr. Clinton straightened the navy tie pressed against his dowdy gray suit jacket. He was a proud alum of the Polytechnic Institute in Utica.

"No. Unfortunately, my father was diagnosed with liver failure in July, so I dropped out of school to take care of him."

"Ah, I see. Well, that's very commendable." Mr. Clinton's flaky, sunburned forehead folded into a look of mild concern. "I hope he's doing well."

"Yes. Thank you. He's doing...better."

"Good," he said, then erased his concern with a bucktooth smile. "Besides, you don't need a Harvard degree to be a food service worker at a prison, do you?"

The girl chuckled meekly. "No."

"No," Mr. Clinton echoed. His dry fingers returned to his chin as he studied the girl in silence. A heavy breath whistled through his inflamed sinuses; he always felt he could filter the weaklings from the heavy hitters, but he couldn't tell with this one. The girl was a conundrum. She had a solid build (good for lifting big pots and pans), but her black skirt and frilly pink blouse gave a strong girly-girl impression.

Returning to the résumé, Mr. Clinton pretended to reread the black, Times New Roman lettering, struggling to decide. The state's toughest, most overcrowded prison was a lightning rod of sexual harassment for their female workers. Even some of the softer-looking lads had their trouble with unwanted romance. After a weak sigh, Mr. Clinton finally spoke. "I'll be honest: I'm apprehensive about hiring you. The Attica Correctional Facility is a maximum-security state prison. We house more than a thousand criminally insane convicts, a large percentage of them repeat sex offenders."

The girl nodded, her large seductive lips sealed together with a solemn glue.

Mr. Clinton continued, "Honestly, in my twenty-six years as warden, I've always been worried about hiring women. Now don't get me wrong—I've had a lot of females on my staff, and most of them have proved themselves to be more than competent workers. But then there were others: girls who got so scared on their first day that they never came back. Not even to pick up an hour's worth of pay." He paused. "But this has had happened to some of the men too, so in order to prepare applicants for what's in store, I always show them around the facility. Do you mind taking a brief tour of the grounds?"

"Oh, no," the girl answered, as she ripped apart her lips for an excited beam from her powdered face. "That sounds terrific. Thank you, sir."

"Great," Mr. Clinton said with a guarded smile back. *The girl's excited now*, he thought, *but wait until she meets Nick Roesch*. He stood up from his Victorian-style desk, a gift from his "good friend" Rudy Giuliani. "All right. Let's put on our jackets and start with the cells. We try not to burden the taxpayers with a big heating bill."

Ten minutes later, the stout middle-aged man led the girl down a concrete hallway, painted a mind-numbing white, when he spotted Dr. Bonesteel walking toward them with his slow limp. *Perfect. The old coot will be a nice appetizer.* "Good morning, Dr. Bonesteel," Mr. Clinton said, stopping in front of him. He then gave the nutty doctor a strong "I'm the boss here" handshake. "I forgot you were seeing Nick today. How's he feeling?"

"The Devil doesn't have feelings," Dr. Bonesteel said with a cutting pitch. His eyes were already wide with madness. "Just *intentions*. That thing in there is planning to escape and take the lives of innocent children once more. I know it!"

Mr. Clinton produced a hint of a smile. "Well, I'm sure he's *thinking* about escaping, Doctor, but this institution has the most advanced security in the country. No one can escape these walls."

Dr. Bonesteel's eyes grew into UFO saucers radiating a pre-lift-off hum. "Walls are nothing to the Devil. He *will* get past your so-called advanced security. Trust me!" He then turned to the girl, his right eye reduced to a suspicious squint. "Who's this?"

Erasing the small smile from his wan cheeks, Mr. Clinton felt like saying, "At least my officers never blew off their big toes, you loony hack," but he had a stern reputation to keep, especially in front of potential recruits. "This is Ms. Strife. She applied for our third-shift food-line associate position. Ms. Strife, this is Dr. Bonesteel, one of our consulting psychiatrists. He works exclusively with Nick Roesch. Are you familiar with Mr. Roesch?"

The girl nodded as a twinkle lit her heavy brown eyes. "Yes. He was the man who broke out of the psychiatric hospital on Halloween and murdered a group of teenagers. I pretty much saw the whole thing happen...*on TV*." She turned to the doctor, offering to shake his hand. "Nice to meet you, Dr. Bonesteel."

"Be careful, Ms. Strife." The doctor looked down, his piercing eyes aimed at the girl's hand like a double-barrel shotgun. "If you take your eyes off Nick Roesch for one second, he'll grab you by your womanhood with his grizzly fists and split you in half with no remorse." He paused, taking a quick breath. "Good day, Ms. Strife." He turned away and briskly limped toward the security door at the end of the corridor.

Watching the nutbag hobble away, Mr. Clinton laughed to himself. *The crazy hobbit needs a good lay*, he thought, then looked at the girl to gauge her reaction. His weedy eyebrows lifted up to his gray brow when he saw a full smile on her face. *Why's she so happy?* "Dr. Bonesteel is a bit theatrical," he said with a drop of curiosity in his throaty voice, "but he's partially right. If Nick Roesch ever escaped—which would never happen, but let's speak hypothetically for a moment—if he *did* escape, he'd kill you without thinking about it. Would you like to see him?"

"Of course," the girl said with a fresh glow of enthusiasm. "Thank you, Mr. Clinton."

"You're very welcome," he said, hiding his confusion with an exaggerated smile. *All right*, he thought, starting for Nick Roesch's cell. *She must be one of those women who likes silly true crime shows.* He gave a silent chuckle, remembering his second wife's obsession with those sensationalized shows. *Let's see how excited she is when she's face-to-face—*

Bam! A volcanic blast erupted from the steel door to Nick Roesch's cell, setting off the flee-from-danger instinct in Mr. Clinton's weasel DNA. The older man fell back to the white wall opposite the door, his navy tie—a clip-on bought at a flea market—falling off his white button-down shirt. "Fucking Jesus!" he shouted, then turned and watched as the young lunatic—his obese face covered in a nappy bush of black curls—beat his fists against the window of his cell door, unleashing an incoherent angry rant. While the pounding continued, Mr. Clinton grabbed his clip-on from the floor, shoved it into his pocket, then stood up and puffed out his frail chest. "My God," he said, "the fat kid *really* is psycho."

"I don't know," the girl said in reply. "He doesn't seem that bad."

Without notice, Nick Roesch stopped his wild tantrum and looked at the girl with a dumb, caveman expression. She giggled as she turned to Mr. Clinton. "See?"

With tightlipped awe, Mr. Clinton nodded slowly, looking at the dark haired-girl standing calmly in her frilly blouse and skirt. He then turned to Nick, the large, hairy Devil-teen of Manlius. "Yeah," he muttered, then turned back to the girl and thought, *Maybe she can handle this job after all.*

83

The Next Day, Betsy, 3:00 p.m.
As QVC blared from the living room (Grandma Coleman was sleeping through the final hour of Meredith Baxter's avocado feminine gel Christmas special), Betsy sat in front of the computer—the back of the tower facing her—its dusty, mildew-riddled manual in her lap. As she felt her eyelids start to close into a well-needed nap (from her two-hour search for the manual and one hour reading it), she shook her head back into focus and looked down at the PC Tower Diagram 2 for the hundredth time. "What the hell is wrong with this thing?" she said, scanning the page, then taking a glance at the tower like a child furiously searching a "Spot the Differences" in Highlights magazine. "All the cords are here, and they're all plugged in. There has to be s-s-s-something wrong *inside.*" The last syllable lingered on her tongue, as she looked back at the diagram, her eyes landing on the word "power." "Wait. Is it the, uh...power thingy... Goddamn it. What's the word? Power...plug? Power...*protector? The surge protector!*"

Snapping her fingers, she looked down and let out a short laugh. "Wow," she said, picking up the long yellow-tinted device that connected a tangled mess of faded cords and ancient bug dust. "This thing is dirtier than Grandma's— What the heck?" Confusion scrambled the fatigue on her now slightly skinnier face as she clicked the power button on and off. "It doesn't even light up." Returning the surge protector to the floor, she looked around the tightly packed den, searching for something to test it with. After choosing her dad's strange-looking radio (an eighties cassette player), she turned it on using its batteries (the medieval tool actually worked), and then, after taking them out, she plugged the player into the surge protector. It didn't work.

"Oh, my God," she growled, "it was the surge protector this whole time." Smacking her lips, she ripped the cassette player's plug from the surge protector then stood up, letting the useless device fall to the floor. "I'll have to t-t-t-tell D-d-d-daddy to—"

"What on God's green earth are you doing?" Grandma Coleman wheezed from the doorway of the compact room.

Immediately Betsy's broad shoulders twitched, as if she'd felt the monstrous tickle of a daddy longlegs crawling up her back. "I'm just trying to fix the computer," she blurted out.

"What?" Grandma Coleman responded, her drawn-on eyebrows somehow raised in surprise. "Your father told you not to use the computer."

Betsy snapped into "teen girl with attitude." "*No, he didn't.*"

Grandma Coleman brought her nubbins to her wilted neck. "*Young lady*, I know your father didn't teach you to talk back to your elders like that. Apologize this instant!"

Betsy went still as a burst of anger heated her flesh like a slice of turkey on a rocket engine. *No, he didn't teach me that! He was too drunk!* she wanted to shout but stopped herself. A strange, low voice from her mind reminded her that something weird was going on—*Why would he tell Grandma I couldn't use the computer when it was broken?*—and if she continued to be rude, she knew her father would lock her in her room, barring her from finding out what that "something weird" was. "I'm sorry, Grandma," she said in a soft, shameful voice. "I just...wanted to see some pictures of my mom. Daddy scanned all our photos onto the computer last year."

"He did?"

"Yeah," Betsy said with a mental smirk (she was getting good at lying on the spot), "but I can look at the real ones. They're upstairs in the closet. Is that okay?"

Placing her swollen nubbins on her hips, Grandma Coleman stared at Betsy with her cheerless green eyes. "Yeah," she finally answered, "but don't mess everything up. Your dad's coming home at four, and I need to start dinner."

Betsy's stomach howled like a frightened cat. "He's coming home at *four?*" She looked at the walk clock. She had about fifty minutes to fix the old computer.

"Yeah. He said he was going to take a little time off so you two can look over a book or something."

"Oh, okay." Betsy feigned a bubbly smile. She was talking about the course catalog for OCC. "So it's all right if I look at the photos for a couple minutes?"

"Yeah, go ahead," Grandma Coleman responded with a dismissive wave. "'The Lord gave, and the Lord has taken away; blessed be the name of the Lord.'"

Betsy held on to her genial smile, unsure if her grandmother was quoting the Bible or one of her ceramic ducks. "Thanks," she said, walking away from the mean-spirited woman with her usual pace, then sped up until she was racing a make-believe friend to the top of the stairs. There, she moved directly to the hallway closet, slid opened the door, and moved down to her knees for the weathered Lowe's moving box in the bottom compartment. After removing a plastic bag of candles and a stack of unused hand towels, she took out the box, the words "Family Photos" written in her mother's bouncy cursive on the brown lid.

A familiar warmth—as though she were being hugged—moved through her as she traced her finger across her mother's handwriting. Then, after a brisk check that Grandma Coleman wasn't at the bottom of the stairs spying on her, she pushed the box to the side and reached into the unknown darkness of Disney VHS tapes and outdated animal calendars. She hoped she'd find the surge protector she'd used in her preteen days when she wanted to listen to her Barbie boom box and make gingersnaps in her Easy Bake Oven and not blow the house up.

"Yes!" she said through a soft breath of relief, finding the surge protector in the back corner, wrapped in a tumbleweed of hair and dust. She stood up with the surge protector and headed for her room, constructing her plan for tomorrow. *Hide it underneath your pillow. Then try it tomorrow as soon as Dad goes to work and Grandma...* She suddenly stopped, her hand on the knob of her bedroom door. What if the surge protector didn't work? Could she take one of her dad's? What if Grandma told him she was trying to fix the computer?

Releasing the doorknob, she slouched into a depressed stump. "Jesus Christ, it's like you're a prisoner here." She shook her head and laughed. "Go get Dad's power cord, just in case, and if Grandma can remember and tells him, then lie, and s-s-s-say you-you-you wanted to look at online courses." After a second peak at the bottom of the staircase, she snuck into her father's bedroom and opened the top drawer of the nightstand. Both the power cord and picture of her parents were missing.

"What the fuck?" she barked, slapping the bed with the surge protector in her hand. "This is...this is so...*ridiculous.*" The muscles in her ample body tightened as she held back an outpour of oppressed anger. After a slow set of long breaths, she relaxed her rigid body. "It's okay. I have my surge protector, and if it doesn't work, then I'll...I'll...just call K-k-k-kathleen."

As she turned to the prehistoric phone, a new set of questions punched the back of the skull. What if Kathleen was still angry with her? What if she hung up and never spoke to her again? Pondering these questions, Betsy continued to stare at the primitive device until she threw out her hands. "You've gotta call her, or the nightmares will never stop, and you'll be stuck here. For the rest of your life."

Shuddering, she grabbed the landline and, without a second guess of fear, dialed Kathleen's home number. It rang ten times until Kathleen answered. "Hello?" she said, sounding slightly annoyed.

Betsy opened her mouth, but nothing came out. *Should I apologize*, she wondered in a frozen state of indecision, *or just start asking questions?*

"Jesus," Kathleen said. "If you're going to prank me, at least have the decency to call me a cunt or something. I'm hanging up, you—"

"No," Betsy spat out. "It's me, K-k-k-kathleen. I want to know what happened on Halloween."

Kathleen let out a snide chuckle. "You know what happened."

"No, I don't!" Betsy snapped. "I can't remember anything." She let out a desperate huff, worried this was her last chance to find out the truth. "Please, Kathleen. Tell me, and I'll...I'll...leave you alone...for good."

"Are you serious?"

Betsy looked down as her tongue started its anxious wiggle. *Was* she serious? Would she never see or talk to Kathleen again? For a second, she eyed the roll-on wood floor, bent at the seams from years of neglect, and then, seizing her tongue with her lips, thought, *Just say yes. You need to know.* "Yes."

"All right. You went fucking crazy and tried to kill my boyfriend and me. Now don't ever bother me again." She hung up.

"Kathleen, I..." Betsy squeezed the phone in her hand, imagining it was Kathleen's black soul. "*Jesus*, why does she always have to joke around?" Suddenly the phone rolled from her hands as a jolt of shock zapped her insides. "She has a *boyfriend*?"

"Betsy?" Grandma Coleman called from downstairs. "I need help opening these cans!"

She stomped her foot. "That's because you don't have any fingers, you fucking witch," she muttered, then cheerily shouted back, "Okay, Grandma. I'll be right down." She stood still, holding the discolored cord of the landline by her fingers like the tail of a dead rat. Her mind buzzed with a wild party of thoughts. Boyfriend? Job interview? When did Kathleen become normal? "I gotta try David again," she told herself. "He'll tell me the truth. Sooner or later."

Her round cheeks contoured with determination as she dialed the number to David's house. "Hello, Betsy," Mrs. Ecklund answered politely. "How are you doing?"

"I'm good," Betsy replied. "I was wondering if I could speak to D-d-d-david."

"Um, I think he's taking a nap, but let me check. Hold on." Mrs. Ecklund placed the phone down. After a minute, she returned. "I'm sorry, sweetie, but he's sleeping. Maybe you can try another time."

"Okay," Betsy said. "Thanks, Mrs. Ecklund."

"Of course. Have a good night."

"You too. Bye."

"Great," Betsy said, hanging up. "Why won't David take my calls?" Brushing her hair away from her face, she looked down at the power cord, which looked more busted than the surge protector that had been connected to the computer, and studied it with a hesitant glower. "Guess this crummy thing is my last chance."

84

She stood at the middle point of the staircase, the power cord pressed against her chest and a calculating gaze on the bathroom door, while she listened to her grandmother's awkward grunting from behind it. *You've got thirty minutes until Dad gets home*, she told herself, then turned to the TV (Gordon Ramsay was screaming at a cold lasagna). *Grandma should be in there for at least ten minutes.* Her pensive eyes moved to the coffee table, a half-empty glass of prune juice standing between a finished bowl of smoke-flavored chowder and an ashtray packed with cigarette butts and Grandma's lungs. *Maybe twenty.*

"Yup," Betsy said, clutching the power cord. "It's now or never." Nodding, she hurried across the living room, into the kitchen, then entered the dank den. There, she sat on the floor, removed the broken surge protector, and after a short prayer to her mother, replaced it with the one in her hands. After pressing the power button on the tower, she exclaimed a hushed "Yes!" as the monitor flickered to life.

Betsy immediately went to the metal orange stool serving as their computer chair and waited for the desktop to load. As soon as the home screen appeared, she clicked on Safari and typed "Halloween + Syracuse" into Google News. An arrow of ice shot straight through her feeble heart; on the new page, there were nearly 500,000 related articles, the same picture of a large pale-faced man accompanying the first pair. "Oh, my God," she said, leaning in. "I know him."

She narrowed her eyes as she moved even closer. *Did* she know him? She wasn't positive, but he certainly looked like someone she'd seen before. Like someone she'd met recently, at the grocery store or something. She clicked on the first article. It read:

Less than a month after his trial, Nick Roesch, the eighteen-year-old Manlius, NY, resident convicted of the Baldwinsville murders, has begun serving his first of seven life sentences—plus an additional 3,000 years—in New York's highest-security prison, Attica Correctional Facility (ACF).

The supermax houses some of the system's most dangerous inmates in isolation, but sources inside ACF say Roesch is getting special treatment.

According to a letter to The Herald-Journal *from another ACF inmate, "Roesch is in a sixteen-man pod all by himself. He gets to leave his cell two hours in the morning and two hours at night. His meals are served to him in his cell. The dude is definitely being coddled."*

ACF warden Arnold Clinton remarked that…

Betsy opened a new tab and typed "Baldwinsville murders" into the search box. She clicked on the first link, a Wikipedia entry titled, "The Baldwinsville Halloween Serial Murders." It began, "The Baldwinsville Halloween serial murders were seven murders committed by eighteen-year-old Nick Roesch…"

She continued reading until she stopped at the sight of her father's name. "What. The. Fuck?" she said, then reread the passage: "Nick Roesch murdered the first victim, seventy-two-year-old Carl Blume, four miles from Summer Hill House, a mental hospital in Hannibal, New York, by running him over after stealing his car. Six other victims died at a luxury log cabin in Baldwinsville. The victims' names have not been released because they were minors. Various media outlets have reported that three minors survived the incident in Baldwinsville. However, Sheriff John Coleman of Onondaga County, who was at the scene of the crime, declined to comment on those reports."

Betsy closed her eyes and huffed in amazement. *Finally*, she thought. Her teachers had told her not to trust Wikipedia, but a surge of confidence rising from the bottom of her stomach made her believe she was one of the three survivors. She had to be. It seemed like too much of a coincidence.

Grimacing, she opened her eyes. There was one problem left. Did she really try to kill Kathleen on the same day she was attacked by Nick Roesch? Maybe that was just Kathleen's twisted take on the event. Or maybe it wasn't. Perhaps they were two separate incidents that had happened on the same day. Or perhaps there was a connection.

Betsy stared at the white glow of the computer screen, considering what to do next. She couldn't ask David (she had a feeling he didn't want to talk to her), and she definitely couldn't call Kathleen. Her only option was to ask her dad. "Yeah, right. He's never going to—" She straightened up, a stern expression washing over her dismal expression. "No, you *have* to ask him, and you *have* to do it tonight." Her tongue swept across her teeth as her eyes narrowed on her father's name on the screen. "You have to."

85

A carefree smirk peeking through his gray beard, Sheriff Coleman walked into the living room with a Party Pack from Taco Bell in one hand and a bag of Nacho Cheese Doritos in the other. "All right," he said, placing the bags on the coffee table in front of Grandma Coleman and Betsy, who were sitting on the couch, watching *Wheel of Fortune.* "Eat it before it gets cold."

"Dinner?" Grandma Goleman asked, eyeing the box of tacos and bag of chips with a beady glare. "I made a whole pot of chowder."

Shit, Sheriff Coleman thought, his smirk fading into his rough chin, then dropped his sight to the food as she looked up at him. "Uh, yeah, I know. But some of the guys at the station tried it today, so I am bringing them more tomorrow."

"Oh." As Grandma Coleman looked back down at the fast food with suspicion still carved into her wrinkled face, Sheriff Coleman turned to Betsy with a "Thank God we got out of eating the chowder" wink. Betsy tucked her head into the rest of her whey-colored body as though she were a frightened bird. "What is it?"

She had another nightmare, didn't she? Sheriff Coleman thought, his faded smile eroding into an anxious frown.

"John?"

"It's six soft tacos and six crunchy," he replied, turning to his mother. "Do you want some?"

Grandma Coleman's scaly cheeks squirmed as though her sinuses had magically cleared and she'd gotten a sudden sniff of her soup. "No. I don't like that *Mexican* stuff. *Eckkkkkkk-eckkk-eck.*"

"Are you okay, Mom?" the sheriff asked, moving over to her with a helping hand.

"Yeah, yeah, I'm fine," she answered through the last pair of wet coughs, her right hand on her misshaped bosom and the other reaching out as a sign to let her be. "I gotta go home and fix your father supper or he'll have a fit."

With a succession of quick, bone-cracking snaps, she stood up and started for her pickled-colored coat by the front door. "See you tomorrow."

"Yeah, you too," Sheriff Coleman said, opening the door as she put on her jacket. "Thanks, Mom. Have a safe drive." As Grandma Coleman walked to her station wagon through the bitter gray of another hellish winter, Sheriff Coleman closed the door quickly and locked it, keeping the organ-numbing cold outside. *Should you ask if she's okay*, he wondered, his hand still on the doorknob, *or will that stir up trouble?*

As he gripped the knob, he blew a heavy sigh. *You've already lied to her, John. You can at least try to be a decent father and—*

"What happened on Halloween, D-d-d-dad?"

Sheriff Coleman turned around and hopped off his heels, the sweaty skin underneath his nylon jacket shocked with the sudden blow of a jump scare. Standing in front of him, with the ominous scowl of a Manson family follower, was Betsy. "What happened on Halloween?" she repeated slowly, a menacing sneer fixed on her bloodless face.

He stared at her, his eyes glazed with a sad innocence that he had to lie again. He then opened his mouth, preparing the car accident story. *Tell her the truth*, his conscience commanded him, *or she'll find out one day and really—*

"I switched out the surge protector in the computer room," Betsy stated coldly. "I know Nick Roesch tried to kill me. But I want to know why I tried to kill Kathleen."

A sharp chill rushed through his extremities. *Tell her*, his conscience roared, but he merely continued to stare, his lips sewn with the fear that Betsy would use the lie as an excuse to sneak out again and never return.

"You owe me, Dad," she blurted, her threatening stare swelling with tears. "I was all by myself after Mom died, so *please*"—her voice rose to a shaky squall—"do this one thing for me and tell me why I attacked Kathleen." Throwing her hands over her face, she burst into a powerful sob.

"Oh, God, Betsy." Sheriff Coleman moved to her, his eyes blurred by a stinging mist. "You attacked Kathleen," he said, placing his hands on Betsy's trembling shoulders, "because she hit you with her car."

Betsy immediately looked up. "What?"

"She ran into you. Kathleen and a friend of hers—"

"David?"

Sheriff Coleman nodded. "He said Kathleen was trying to drive away from Nick Roesch when she accidentally hit you with her car. You were out for a couple of minutes, and then you"—he hesitated, worried the following statement would destroy her psyche, then took a breath, thinking, *She deserves to know*—"got up and tried to kill them."

"Who?"

"Kathleen and Nick Roesch."

"I did?"

"Yes."

Betsy's eyes expanded as though she had witnessed a powder keg of multicolored feathers and shit explode in front of her. "Oh, my God. That's...so crazy..."

Damn straight, Sheriff Coleman thought with a second nod then said, "Yes, it is, but the important thing is that it's over. You're safe, and Nick Roesch's in prison, all right?"

"Mm-hmm," Betsy replied.

Sheriff Coleman frowned through his beard as he took in the sad, pensive expression on his daughter's graceful face. He imagined she was trying to make sense of what he had told her, but after a short moment of silence, without a hint of a smile or a flash of understanding in her eyes, the situation seemed hopeless. This was too much for his daughter—or anyone—to understand. "Everything's going to be okay, Betsy," he said, taking her hands. "I know it doesn't make any sense now, but...we'll figure it out. Okay?"

Betsy remained silent as the innocent sheen on her face darkened with the miserable truth. Sheriff Coleman scowled, thinking, *C'mon, John. She's your daughter.* "Please, Betsy," he said, squeezing her hands. "You can trust me. I promise I'll help you figure everything out. We'll find a good therapist for you. Maybe take some nice, relaxing vacations, anything. We just need to take things one day at a time. Okay?"

Betsy's brooding gaze passed her father's inviting smile to the wild story in her head, strung together by her distant father, a former friend, and the ever-trusting Internet. It didn't quite add up: her dad had said she'd tried to kill Kathleen and Nick Roesch, but Kathleen had said she'd tried to kill her and her mystery boyfriend. Who the hell was telling the truth?

Betsy gave a long, mental groan. It seemed like every time she learned something new about what had happened, she had a fresh list of questions.

"Betsy?" her father said, squeezing her hand.

She was silent while her focus remained on the chaos stirred by her confusion. *Just forget it*, she thought, as she finally felt the fatigue of the mental marathon she'd been running take the last of her strength. *You'll never find out the whole truth because he'll—*

"*Squee, squee, squeeeee.*" Hearing her father squeal like a baby pig, Betsy looked up, her brow knitted with surprise. Sheriff Coleman stared at his daughter with a soft, pleading look, then performed an encore of the funny animal noises. "*Squeeee, squeeee, squeeeeee.*"

Betsy smirked. "What are you doing, Daddy?"

"Making little-piggy noises to cheer you up. Just like I did when you were a little girl. Or do you prefer an older pig now that you've grown up?" Her father lifted his nose into a pig snout and grunted like an eight-hundred-pound swine. "*Oink, oink, oink, oink, oink.*"

Betsy let out a light laugh. *How sweet,* she thought, but the charm of the goofy sentiment lasted as long as the sugary taste of cheap gum. Frowning, she lowered her head. "Daddy, I'm sorry, but—"

"Please, Betsy," her father said, firmly grasping her wrists. "I know I've been an asshole for a long, *long* time, but I want to help you get through this."

Betsy looked up, a cautious curiosity issuing from her eyes. "You do?"

"Yes. *Starting now,* I'm going to do everything I can because you're my daughter and I love you."

Betsy's lips quivered. This wasn't something she'd expected her father to say, but at that moment, it was exactly what she wanted to hear. "I love you too, Daddy," she said with a small explosion of joy, then let go of his hands and hugged him.

As she rested her head against his stiff chest, he replied, "I love you so much, Betsy. More than you can ever imagine."

86

Four Months Later, Kathleen, 4:55 p.m.

Squeezing her hands into a pair of extra-large plastic gloves, Kathleen completed her work uniform (hairnet, black pants, and a white polo with Attica Correctional Facility's logo on the breast—a fancy coat of arms with two elks fighting over a skeleton key) then grabbed a food cart and pushed it toward the stack of maroon trays in the corner of the sterile, stainless-steel kitchen. She put a tray on the cart and continued to the food line, placing a carton of milk, a handful of baby carrots, and an oatmeal cookie in the top compartments. She then scooped a serving of green beans and mashed potatoes into the bottom compartments. "All right," she said, turning to the massive cooking pot behind her. "Now it's time for the shitloaf."

After grabbing the ladle next to the pot, she poured two scoops of brown goo into the remaining compartment. Her face crinkled in disgust as the sour beef smell hit her nose. "Eck, this shit smells worse than my yeast infections," she said, watching the slimy substance fill the square space. As soon as it landed, it started to congeal into a lumpy sponge that looked like it was used to wipe down the inmates' toilets.

Kathleen glanced up at the clock: 4:58 p.m. "Fuck," she said, then moved to the five-foot-tall box of plastic utensils. As she reached in, she stopped, her bright eyes locking on the faded sign above the box: THE FOLLOWING INMATES DO NOT RECEIVE FORKS OR SPOONS. At the bottom of the list, penciled in, was NICK ROESCH.

"Good suggestion," Kathleen said with a sarcastic frown at the sign. "But you forgot to mention sporks." Dropping a spork behind the cardboard box, she bent down (into the blind spot of the security camera in the corner), grabbed it from the recently mopped floor, broke off the top, and tucked it into her pants pocket. She then trashed the handle of the spork and returned to the cart.

A minute later, Joe Sampson, a white corrections officer with a beer gut and permanent garlic breath, stepped into the kitchen. "Hey, little darlin'," he said in his fake country twang, as he headed toward her.

Ignoring the chubby hillbilly's sexism, Kathleen put on a mask of cool cheer. "Hey. What's up?"

"The sky." The oversize redneck gave a deep laugh at his lame joke. "Is Nick Roesch's food ready?"

"Yup," Kathleen said, taking a step back.

"All right," Officer Joe said, moving to the cart. "Lemme check it." He grabbed a metal spatula from the counter and poked at the food in the top compartments. And then, as he flipped over the mystery meat, his pathetic attempt at a mustache made a nauseated curl. "Woo-boy," he declared with a big puff of garlic, "this stuff smells so bad it could gag a maggot."

Ignoring the man's vile breath, Kathleen pretended to laugh. "Yeah," she said and then, with a big smile, thought, *I hope he rips off your balls, Cowboy Garlic Bread.*

"All right, it's good," Officer Joe said, dropping the greasy spatula on the counter, which Kathleen had wiped down an hour ago. "I'll get the door."

"Thanks," Kathleen said, stepping back to the cart. As he headed for the door, she slipped the head of the spork out of her pocket and hid it underneath the shitloaf. Walking over to the door, she ignored the toxic-smelling tray in her hands and enjoyed a mental clip of the cowboy's torturous death.

Ten minutes later, they arrived at Nick Roesch's cell. While Kathleen stopped at the opposite wall, Officer Joe knocked on the steel door. "Dinnertime, Roesch. Turn around and place your hands behind your back."

Kathleen remained by the wall, waiting for a glance of her strong, troubled man, then smiled as he appeared at the window, his squash-shaped face void of emotion. Locking eyes with the empty black marbles, she gave a quick nod at the food. Nick's slimmer face—complete with werewolf-in-midlife-crisis beard—remained a pasty strudel of nothing as he turned around and placed his arms behind his back.

"All right, partner. Put your wrists together and bring them to me," Officer Joe said, sliding open the rectangular port by the small window. After Nick put his wrists through the opening, the mock cowboy handcuffed them with a pair of nylon strands. "Good. Stay right there." He opened the second port on the other side of the door then turned to Kathleen. "Can I get the food, sugar?"

"Sure thing, boss," Kathleen answered sweetly. *He's going to spork your fucking eyes out, and I'm going to watch.*

As she handed him the tray, Officer Joe smiled his pencil-dick grin. "Thanks," he said, then added with a wink, "Don't worry about getting the tray back, sweetie. Officer Joe will take care of *everything.*"

The instinct to punch the man in his slimy smile rushed through her thick knuckles, but then, knowing Nick would soon make sure the fat hick would never lay his perverted eyes on another innocent girl, she held on to her good-lil'-worker front while keeping her clenched fists at her sides. "Okay," she said, smiling the last smile he would see, then started down the hallway. While Officer Joe slid the tray through the second port, she stopped and turned to Nick's cell with a quick smoker's cough. Turning slightly, with his hands still cuffed, Nick stared at her with his beady, blank eyes.

Kathleen then lifted her shirt, exposing her hefty oval-shaped breasts underneath her dingy white bra. Watching the shock warp Nick's chalky slab of a face into Boy Scout chaos, she let out a quiet laugh. *God, he is* such *a twelve-year-old boy,* she thought, then turned around and headed back to the kitchen. *It's gonna be a hell of a time turning him into a man.*

87

Two Months Later, David, 10:00 a.m.

Dressed in the green graduation robe and mortarboard his mother had ordered without his knowledge, David stood on the steps that led to the gym stage; he was fourth in line to receive his high school diploma from Mr. Miehan. *All righty,* he thought, as the weight of a thousand eyes from his class and their families pressed against his grape-size bladder. *Nothing to be anxious about. Mom basically put a gun to your head to get you to walk, but…you're here now, so you should just go with the flow and be proud of yourself for once. I mean, holy hell. You got all your work done and passed your regents, at home, with Mom hovering over you like a fucking drill instructor.*

As Mr. Miehan called another name, David moved up to the next step with a soft sigh. *Whatever. It's done. He'll call your name; you'll get your diploma, and you can say "Fuck off" to Bishop Dullen forever…* Another name was called, another step up and a quiet exhalation. *Everything's going to be fine. Fordham will probably be tough, but hey, if you can survive a serial killer attack and come out to your mom in the same year, you can manage it.* He let out a low laugh. *Actually, that sounds like a good idea for a horror movie. Maybe you can work on it with Kathleen over the summer. If she ever—*

"David Ecklund."

At the sound of his name, an instant good-boy-for-Mama smile formed on his clean-shaven face. He stepped onto the stage and made his way to Mr. Miehan. "Congratulations," the gristly pork chop of a principal said, offering his hand to David. "You did an excellent job."

David maintained his smile, keeping a bitter sneer from ripping through his cheeks. *I was almost murdered, and that's all—* The thought was drowned out by the overzealous blows of his mother's party horn. *Screw him. Just take the damn paper.* David reached out and shook Mr. Miehan's hand. "Thank—"

"*Fag*!" someone shouted from the audience.

The following took less than three seconds, but to David, time moved in Carrie-White-covered-with-pig's-blood slow motion. *They're all going to laugh at you*, he heard in his head as he turned to the audience, a saltine-colored sea of conjecturing eyes. *They're all going to laugh at you.* Among them, Mike and his gang of apes were attempting to hide their giggles. *They're all going to laugh at you.* He looked at his mother, standing on the top row of the bleachers, mouthing the words, "What'd they say?" to his disinterested father. His sister was practicing her nautical-themed nail art. *They're all going to laugh—*

A faint anxiety-and-apple-fritter-fueled-fart popped out of David. The rush of sugary dough and shit smell brought time to its normal pace. *Oh, no,* he thought, receiving a whiff of the bad wind. *Please tell me Mr. Miehan lost his sense of smell in a smelting accident.* Grimacing, he turned to the principal. Mr. Miehan's meaty cheeks were quivering rolls of purple tissue as he struggled to keep one last class-of-2018-fart from entering his nose or mouth. *Nope. Sorry.*

Removing his hand from David's, the principal responded with a tight-lipped nod.

Grabbing his diploma, David marched to the opposite side of the stage. *All right, all right,* all right, *it's fine*, he thought, as his heart pounded against his chest, attempting to burst out and crawl into someone who hadn't almost shit his pants in front of his graduating class and their families. *Just find your seat and sit down.*

Leaving the stage, he kept his head down and continued to the rows of folding chairs where his classmates were sitting. As he passed the second row, he heard a sinister, goatlike laugh and then, without thinking, looked toward the grating sound. It was Mike, watching him with his proud, feral smile. Immediately David looked back down, mentally groaning. *Fucking Satan. If I had the balls, I'd…I'd take one of these chairs and bash it over his head.*

With a muted laugh, he entered his row and shuffled down to his seat. *Yeah, right, you'd get in so much trouble.* He stopped and sat down, chucking to himself once more. *But then again, you'd get to hit Mike with a chair.*

As David stared vacantly at the backs of his classmates/future struggling subway artists, a drop of villainy trickled through the network of gears spinning behind his wholesome pink-cheeked face. Slowly he transformed from a calculating, Sheev Palpatine spectator to Darth "Let's Build a Death Star" Sidious. *Yeah, I think you should hit Mike with your chair.* He then stood up with a fiendish smile and picked up his chair. *Sorry, brah, but you don't fuck with a final gay gone bad!*

He quickly folded the chair, walked over to Mike, and slammed the back of the chair against his head. With a sharp, metallic crack, Mike fell over and hit the floor like an overfilled sack of brick-size Pop-Tarts. "That's right, bitch!" David shouted over the excessive white-people gasps and "Dear Gods." "This fag knocked you out cold with a motherfuckin' chair! *Peace*!" He then tossed the chair aside and raced for the doors at the back of the gym with the same, sweet surge of adrenaline he had felt on Halloween night.

Epilogue

One Month Later; Amie Shrode; Wapakoneta, Ohio; 2 p.m.
"Amie...? Hello, Amie Shrode? Earth to Amie?" Crossing her short, saggy arms over her lopsided chest, Norma Reed fluttered her eyelashes over her deep-set eyes, thinking, *Cheese and crackers, this girl's a real space case.* She entered the cramp, nickel soap-smelling break room and continued to the table in the corner. Sitting there, staring out the one mildew-stained window, was Amie, a toothpick brunette in black pants and a King's Inn apron. "Amie?"

As Norma reached for the girl's soft, swanlike shoulder, the tiled floor creaked beneath the insole-less tennis shoes she'd bought at Payless in 1986. As soon as the young girl heard the squeak, she jumped out of her chair and grabbed a metal fork from the Formica counter. "Oh, my God," Amie said, biting the pointer finger on her right hand, while the left held the fork prongs about an inch from the old woman's turkey neck. "I'm *so*, so sorry... But you know you can't sneak up on me like that."

Norma's gray eyes focused on the sharp tool aimed at her throat, delivering an overdramatic flare. "Christ, honey," she said, as a tight squeeze in her chest attempted to turn her heart into strawberry jam. "I'm sixty-two. Sometimes I forget. What's your excuse for forgetting your name?"

"I'm sorry," Amie repeated, returning the fork to the counter. "I was just...thinking."

Norma huffed a stifled breath as the slight tightness in her chest started to relax. "*Well*, don't think too hard. I called you three times, and you still didn't answer. Your name's still Amie Shrode, right?"

Amie's Invisalign braces pinched the back of her gums as she made a crooked smile. "Yes." *For now.*

"Good," Norma said, her bugged-out eyes retreating to their cavernous depths. "Now that we've got that straightened out, we can start our shift. You wanna start on the third floor this time?"

"Sure."

"Okay. Then I'll start on the first floor, and we can meet in the middle."

"Yup." Amie brought her hand up to brush the blond curls from her forehead, but then, remembering she had cut and dyed her hair brown about two months ago, she gave a nervous titter and speed walked away. In the outdated oat-colored hallway—infused with the same generic soap smell as the break room and the rest of the small-town motel—she picked up her cleaning cart from the maid's closet and then, five minutes later, parked it in the hall farthest from the front entrance. "Housekeeping," she said with a light tap on the first door of her shift. She waited a few seconds then knocked again. Receiving no response, she unlocked the door.

"Crap," Amie said, flicking on the light. The room, bathed in the motel's signature "royal red" decor, was a truck-stop-bathroom disaster. A trail of chewed-up chicken wings, pizza remnants, and crushed beer cans led up to the king-size mattress, which was flipped onto its side with a display of red and brown streaks she hoped was the result of too much makeup rather than a snuff film. Among the pillows and crumpled sheets—which also were defiled by the mysterious red and brown marks—was a line of mayonnaise jars filled with various colored liquids. Any hint of what those liquids were and what they were used for was suppressed into a well-hidden bank of Amie's horrendous memories. "*You know*, some people are just...they're just..." A flash of surprise swirled through the middle of her purple contacts as she caught her reflection in the mirror by the coat closet. Who was this worn-out maid with the bad DIY dye job and heavy goth makeup, she wondered in the moment of surprise. Wasn't there a bubbly young lady behind the dime-store disguise, a girl who had planned to go to vet school then marry her high school sweetheart? She released a long restless sigh. "You already attract enough attention with your mini freak-outs. Just shut up and do your job, *Amie Shrode*."

She went to her cart, put on a pair of plastic gloves, and returned to the gruesome display with a heavy-duty trash bag and mindless gape, hoping she could ignore the godless speculation creeping into her head as well as the potent musk of semen and Vicks VapoRub.

She turned on the television to numb her senses. "He said you believed alien lizards were trying to kill you," Dr. Phil said.

"No, I didn't say that," a curly-haired, beaver-like woman replied, turning to her husband, Humpty Dumpty with a Goatee, sitting next to her. "That was his attempt to discredit me."

"Okay," Dr. Phil continued. "What about the government? You've made numerous Facebook posts saying there was a conspiracy to brainwash you so they could take away your son."

"Yes, that's true," the woman answered. "I've got proof."

Amie let out a light chuckle as she picked up the scattered pizza boxes. "What's your proof?"

"Well, there was a Papa John's van—" A sudden burst of music came from the TV, followed by the baritone voice of an older Latino man. "WHEC's George Valez here. We're interrupting our regularly scheduled programming due to this morning's prison break in Attica, New York—"

Amie dropped the trash bag and whipped her head toward the TV. As a row of overweight Mr. Magoo–looking policemen stood next to an empty podium, the male announcer continued, "Governor Andrew Lawler will arrive shortly to make a statement. The inmate who escaped has been identified as Nick Roesch—"

Amie's knees buckled as the image of thirteen-year-old Nick, standing in front of her first love, a splash of blood across his ghostly face, ejected from her hidden bank of dreadful memories. "Oh, God, Steve!" she screamed, then caught the wooden headboard of the bed, saving herself from a fall into unknown grime. "No, no, no. This isn't happening—"

"The prisoner escaped this morning at around nine o'clock. There have been reports that he received help from an unidentified accomplice. We now go live..."

Amie shook her wild gaze at the TV. "I-I-I gotta get outta here!" She raced out of the room, flew through the soap- and bleach-scented air of the dated hallway, and continued down the concrete staircase to the first floor.

"Amie?"

She stopped, puffing through a cold sweat, and turned to Norma, who was staring at her from one of the doorways. "I'm so sorry, but I gotta go. I gotta leave right now."

Norma's embedded eyes fired two white-hot flares. "Why?"

Amie's lips, coated with a dark red lipstick made by a family of Austrian, business-savvy vampires, trembled to answer. "Because...he's going to kill me."

"What?" Norma stumbled back into the battered beige door. "Who's going to kill you?"

"Nick Roesch!"

"Who's that?"

Amie held her uneasy gaze on her older coworker as she squeezed her lips together to keep the truth from erupting into a tearful meltdown. She took a long breath and replied, "He was this boy I was babysitting several years back, and he...he...killed my boyfriend Steve!" Her delicate eyes finally burst into tears. "Oh, God, I'm *so*, so sorry, but I gotta—" Hearing the sudden sound of footsteps, she grabbed the broom from Norma's cart then spun around and swung it through the air. "Get away from me, you sick bastard!" Amie shouted as she swatted thirteen-year-old Nick, a bloody piece of lamp in his hand, over and over with her hardest strikes. In reality, it was Sherman T. Williams, a Presbyterian organist on vacation, returning from the motel's disappointing complimentary breakfast of Sara Lee doughnuts.

"Amie, stop it!" Norma shrieked. "You're hurting him!"

She froze, holding the broom midair. "Oh, God." She watched in horror as a gray-haired man lay across the floor, his gauzy hands covering his face for protection. She dropped the broom and reached for him. "I'm sorry, mister. I didn't mean to—" She stopped, bringing her right hand to her mouth and biting the skin of her quivering knuckles. "No, I gotta go. He's going to come and kill me!" she said, then dashed for the break room.

"Amie?" Norma cried. "Where are you going?"

Propelled by a silent fear, Amie sprinted to the break room, grabbed her purse and denim jacket, and made a fast break for the front entrance. A light summer rain was a gift from God, cooling the sweltering wrap of sweat around her tiny body as she raced across the parking lot and into her inconspicuous maroon Ford Focus. After firing up the engine, she backed out of her spot and slowly drove out of the parking lot. "You're going to be all right," she said, pulling away from the motel. "Just drive home, pack your things, and go somewhere faraway."

Following her own orders, she drove down the long industrial road through the mild drizzle at thirty miles per hour (her usual speed ever since last year's brake malfunction she swore was the work of Nick). Then, approaching the first traffic light, she sped up to thirty-two. As the light turned yellow, she punched the speedometer up to a frightening forty, trying to catch it, then stomped on the brakes just as the light switched to red. With a life-threatening screech, the car came to a sliding halt, throwing her chest into the steering wheel. "What the fuck, Jamie!" she yelled, as she tried to rub off the throbbing sting in her breasts. "Do you want to get yourself killed?"

Exhaling a warm breath, she checked the intersection, making sure she hadn't driven past the streetlight or accidentally run over a jogger caught in the rain. She lucked out; about a foot past the lights, she was free of any visible crushed bodies. And then, at that moment, a disturbing thought popped into her head: *Kill him before he kills again.* "Stop it!" she cried, looking up at the red light. "*Just. Drive. Home.*" Squeezing the wheel, she sat up as she waited for the signal to go.

Finally, the light turned green. "Okay," she said, then lifted her foot off the brake. As the car moved forward, she quickly returned her foot to the brake pedal. "No! You need to get help. Call the police!" Her right purple eye and left brown one (now missing its contact) fluttered in fear. "Are you stupid? He escaped a maximum-security prison, for Christ's sake. You need...you need...that doctor!" She paused, trying to remember the name of the bald, agitated man who had spoken with her after Steve's murder. *I think I can help the poor boy*, she recalled him saying. *But let's keep in touch, just in case the Devil made him do it.* The odd statement—a joke to break the tension, she guessed—accompanied by a wide rupture of his brilliant blue eyes refreshed her memory. "Dr. Bonesteel! His name was Dr. Bonesteel. He'll help you!"

NOTE FROM THE AUTHOR

Word-of-mouth is crucial for any author to succeed. If you enjoyed the book, please leave a review online—anywhere you are able. Even if it's just a sentence or two. It would make all the difference and would be very much appreciated.

Thanks!
David

ABOUT THE AUTHOR

Born in Syracuse, NY, David Nora was a normal child until he saw *The Exorcist* at the age of seven. Sleeping with an actual vile of holy water, he finally recovered with his first viewing of the meta-slasher comedy, *Scream*. Since then he has been devouring everything horror related—except the Chuckie movies. He wants nothing to do with that devil doll. Currently, he lives in NYC with his beloved stuffed polar bear, Po Po.

Thank you so much for reading one of our **Horror** novels.

If you enjoyed our book, please check out our recommended title for your next great read!

Doll House by John Hunt

"Scary, disturbing, creepy, suspenseful. It might be too intense for some people."

-Amazon Review

View other Black Rose Writing titles at www.blackrosewriting.com/books and use promo code **PRINT** to receive a **20% discount** when purchasing.